BARN POLITICS

Philip Marshall

BLACK WALNUT
PUBLISHING
Seattle, Washington

Copyright © 2009 Philip Marshall

All rights reserved.

Published in the United States by
Black Walnut Publishing

PUBLISHER'S CATALOGING-IN-PUBLICATION DATA
(PREPARED BY THE DONOHUE GROUP, INC.)

Marshall, Philip, 1966-
  Barn politics / Philip Marshall.
     p. ; cm.

  ISBN: 978-0-615-28039-4

  1. Veterinarians--Fiction. 2. Insurance adjusters--Fiction. 3. Horse industry--Blue Ridge Mountains--Fiction. 4. Upper class--Blue Ridge Mountains--Fiction. 5. Mystery fiction. I. Title.

PS3613.A7743 B37 2009
813/.6   2009924231

www.blackwalnutpublishing.com

author photo by Jennie Tucker

cover design by Cathi Stevenson

*For Lynne,
who wanted to find out
how it ended*

PROLOGUE

Tum tadda-dum, tum tadda-dum, tum tadda-dum. This is the gallop. Four beats. Less regimented than the two-beat trot, more earnest than the three of a canter. A primal rhythm, it massages the earth and soothes the soul surely as a mother's heartbeat, and every creature on the grounds went about their business embraced in its familiar cadence. All knew when it faltered.

Virginia summer-air is still and stifling, and a sharp crack bounces off the rusty clay hardpan and ricochets among dense hardwood like a sour note in a concert hall. The ubiquitous pack of Corgis and Jack Russells terrorizing the stabling area noticed first, halted their frenetic game of tag and cocked harried ears. Thoroughbreds skittered, bowling over handlers and displacing riders. Warmbloods, continental in blood and attitude, turned away from the sound and pretended disinterest. Riders, engaged in a battle between sweaty legs and cotton breeches, paused and balanced one-legged, like flamingos. Grooms stopped brushing, bathing, and braiding. Spectators, many of whom came hoping secretly for a dramatic fall, drifted toward the commotion.

Jordan Pascoe was parked in an ideal spot, shaded by a gargantuan oak that even a century ago must have so impressed a farmer that he chose to plow around the behemoth rather than topple it. The shade was nice, but more importantly, it provided the necessary solitude to scribble notes in the margins of *The Daily Racing Form*, where some nice odds were emerging from the eighth at Belmont. From his vantage point, a small rise in the geographic center of the lima bean shaped course, the noise sounded like a little leaguer putting good wood on a hanging curve. Most people would, by force of habit, search the sky for the high, arcing flight of a home run. Pascoe had no such inclination. No one was playing baseball on this grassy field, and the crack, now fading to echo, came not from ash on rawhide but the femur of Hunter Stuart's most promising three-day horse, Bathsheba.

The big, Irish-born mare was normally spectacular: nimble and forward minded, and gifted with a knack for spotting jumps. She had won three Preliminary events so far this season, been in the ribbons in two others, and was expected to graduate to the Intermediate Division shortly. Today however, Sheba spooked at an inviting bench jump and been penalized for a refusal before catching her right hind over the second obstacle in a combination and going down, hard.

Pascoe set aside the paper and threw the truck into gear well before the public address system screeched out a call for the vet. It had not rained for weeks and the pickup navigated the rolling hayfields quickly, cut stems crunching like insect husks under the tires. Ahead, flashing red lights signaled that the county EMT unit attended to Hunter.

Pascoe grabbed the stethoscope hanging from the rearview mirror and considered drugs he might need: Rompun for sedation, Torbugesic and Bute for pain, Solu-Delta Cortef for shock. As the truck rolled to a stop it became obvious only one bottle was going to be necessary.

Bathsheba, driven by a fervent flight instinct, had thrashed upright. The effort had inflicted tremendous suffering. Sweat ran in torrents along the curves of her body and poured off her muzzle and belly, forming a muddy shadow on the ground. Every muscle quivered. Knees buckled and straightened, buckled and straightened, threatening to cast her to earth again. Yet Bathsheba would not yield. She planted her left hind leg under the center of her body like a tent pole and extended her neck to transfer weight to her undamaged front end. In this fashion she was able to keep her right hind, the source of pain, raised a couple of inches off the ground. The femur, thick as a man's arm and white as chalk, thrust upward through the mass of muscle covering the hip and burst through the skin. Its jagged end, speckled with bits of grass and mud and already gathering flies, oscillated like a metronome as the leg swung uselessly below.

Christ, Pascoe thought, *eleven months to create, seconds to destroy.*

It was hard to comprehend how much force was needed to generate a break this severe, harder still to acknowledge that nothing man-made was strong enough to repair it. There was only one solution: end the suffering, and do it soon.

"Sheba!"

Hunter, conscious now, shrugged off paramedics. Plugs of sod were planted in the ventilation holes of her helmet, forearms were scraped bloody to the elbow, and her britches had a ragged hole at the thigh. One boot was missing a heel. She hobbled to Sheba, threw an arm around the horse's great neck and, pressed her face tightly to sweat-soaked skin.

"It's all right baby, all right. Calm down now, shhhhhh," she whispered, voice hitching between words. "Relax, I know it hurts. Shhhhh."

For a wonder, the mare relaxed. Sheba's wide eyes softened and she nuzzled her rider as if apologizing for the fall. Pascoe was drawing up a second sixty cc syringe of euthanasia solution. The bright blue color was familiar to horse people and Hunter's face blanched at the sight of it.

"There's nothing that can be done," she said, eyes as lost and frightened as Sheba's. Pascoe hated this.

"No," he said. "If it was below the stifle she might be salvaged as a broodmare. But a broken femur...putting her down is the only option." It was cold, discussing the taking of life as easy as popping the head off a dandelion, but distance allowed him to maintain composure and continue to drive to work every morning.

Hunter buried her face in her hands, and her helmet, chinstrap detached from the fall, tumbled to the ground. "Do it. Don't let her suffer while I come to grips with this."

Pascoe nodded and moved to the mare. Though in shock, Sheba's blood pressure was strong enough to fill the jugular when compressed at the base of the neck. Once the vein was pierced and blood ran freely from the needle's hub, both syringes of the thick blue barbiturate were injected. At first, as is often the case, there was no recognizable change. After a short time her head drooped and eyelids closed to slits. Then suddenly, as if yanked to earth by invisible hands, she pitched forward, drove her head into the dirt, toppled, and was still. Twelve hundred pounds of dead weight does not go to the ground gently. Pascoe placed stethoscope to the mare's chest and listened to her heart fade away like spent thunder.

CHAPTER ONE

The eventing season ended as summer turned to fall. Northern Virginia shone this time of year. Ozone haze trapped by sultry summer air lifted as cooler weather moved in and exposed the gold and rust patchwork of the Blue Ridge. Hundreds of cider presses began filling the clarified air with the scent of cinnamon and nutmeg.

Suburban sprawl infiltrated much of the surrounding area to the east as the Metro extended its tentacles, and hundreds of family farms had been pushed out to make room for townhouses and strip malls. But in a swath of land straddling route 50, miles of stone and black board supplanted the chain link and cedar privacy fences. Instead of developments crowded with "plantation homes"—four thousand square-foot cookie-cutters with faux marble pillars on quarter acre lots—great hunks of land supported one authentic mansion, a handful of barns, and pastures of alfalfa. This barrier to progress, in a strange reversal of fortune, was not poverty but prosperity.

Names rarely change in Hunt Country. Occasionally a Cinderella slips in or a black sheep is culled, but mostly mergers create a new, hyphenated empire—a kind of societal Austria-Hungary. Names like Firestone, Dupont and Cooke grace the quaint, thin phone books of towns like Middleburg and Upperville. Moneyed families able to spurn developer's offers make the gated communities of Los Angeles or restricted buildings of Manhattan unnecessary. Covenants restrict how land is bought, sold, or built upon, thwarting those who might be tempted to let the rabble gain purchase.

It is a world not much different from that of their eighteenth century counterparts. Cheap Mexican labor replaces slavery, in its way, but the manors, and the lords presiding over them, persist. They stand at big bay windows, as did their predecessors, admire the sugar maples' garish color and watch as the help rakes fallen leaves.

Routine had been the order of things for Pascoe. The quick jab of vaccination or long ordeal of dentistry was occasionally spiced up with a laceration or some other minor emergency. Here and there, the onset of cooler, wetter weather brewed up a case or two of colic, but nights were quiet overall. Deep down he knew, as all veterinarians do, this was a sure sign of karmic hoarding by the universe and eventually, in the middle of the night, the pager would settle the balance.

Pascoe had a knack for sleeping through phone calls, fire alarms, and most noises below twenty decibels. To avoid missing emergency calls, he devised a system where he set his pager to vibrate and placed it in an empty soup can by the bed. When it went off it made a racket like a mechanical insect trapped in a guitar-string spider web.

Tin can, pager, and table lamp hit the ground simultaneously. The bulb of the lamp broke, forcing him to get out of bed and turn on an overhead light. It took a few moments for his foggy brain to sort out the jumble of numbers that appeared on the pager's display clearly enough to dial.

"Yeah," said the voice on the other end, sounding less insistent than the pager.

Pascoe rubbed his face. If this was a middle-of-the-night call for deworming advice, the caller was about to get an earful. "This is Doctor Pascoe. You paged?"

"Doctor, Vaughn Dowry. My sister's horse is having problems. We expect to see you ASAP."

Pascoe started to reply that it would take about twenty minutes for him to dress and drive over, but Vaughn had already disconnected. The clock, sole-survivor on the nightstand, showed two in the morning. Most emergency calls came earlier in the evening, as people were arriving home from work. Past eleven, the pager was usually silent until feeding time the following morning. Pascoe had no idea why someone would be in a barn this time of night.

"Hey bud, want to come along?" Pascoe asked as he slipped into a pair of jeans.

Barclay, a border collie mix who had wandered into his life a year before, lifted his head from the bed, but the prospects of being able to stretch across the entire mattress and steal a pillow far outweighed a ride in a cold truck. He placed his head back on his front paws and huffed.

"Suit yourself," Pascoe said.

Like his dog, Pascoe was a bit of a mutt. His mother, a mix of Creole and Chickasaw, had given him coppery skin and sharp cheekbones. His father's French heritage was expressed in deep-set eyes and a thin, blade-like nose, which threw sinister shadows across the middle of his face in low light. The angles continued in the rest of his frame—square shoulders, bony hips and knobby knees were tied together with wiry muscles that lent him grace and strength and made working with horses six times his weight come easy.

Anybody glimpsing the driver of the Dodge as it barreled east might have steered a bit closer to the shoulder. When deep in thought, as he was now, contemplating what he might be walking into, furry black eyebrows knitted and lips pursed, and he appeared on the verge of violence. His father said it looked like someone had pissed in his Corn Flakes and called it The Scowl. It had kept him out of more fights as a teenager than he would have believed, classmates erring on the side of caution rather than find out if he could back up the message in his face. He had learned to soften the expression in the presence of clients, but the bearing fell naturally into place when he was alone. If Vaughn Dowry had seen him now, he would have cancelled the call on the off chance Pascoe was thinking about him, which, in truth, he was.

Vaughn was the eldest child of Oliver Dowry, founder of Marketplace, the trendiest supermarket in the mid-Atlantic. Dowry Senior started inauspiciously, sweeping floors in a neighborhood convenience store as a young man, and worked his way up from stock boy, to cashier, to manager. He later bought the store and developed a niche by catering to upscale consumers and carrying hard to find gourmet products. Eventually, he had stores in every major suburban enclave and became one of the wealthiest men in the area. More recently, he had purchased a two hundred acre estate near Upperville, much to the chagrin of the locals, who disdained the *nouveau riche*.

Dowry didn't know much about country living and even less about running a working horse farm, but reveled in his role as lord of the manor. Vaughn, on the other hand, was as comfortable with country life as a hemorrhoidic pagan in a church pew. Irrationally afraid of horses and unable to ride, he nevertheless chose to wear britches and boots about town. Too important by birth to be ignored, he was reluctantly added to guest lists and laughed at behind his back. In contrast, his younger sister Devon flourished and became one of the top young riders on the hunter-jumper circuit, earning both attention and respect. The resulting damage to Vaughn's ego made her a target, and he berated her constantly. This vitriol spilled over onto anyone friendly with his sister and below him in the social hierarchy, which was most.

This made visits to Stonemason trying. For starters, Vaughn made a point of calling Jordan "Pass-cow" regardless of how many times he was corrected. One time, Vaughn had observed—from a safe distance—a fractious mare get the best of Pascoe and for months afterward clients who had heard Vaughn deride the horse-handling skills of their young vet teased him mercilessly. Fortunately, Vaughn's opinion was no real threat to his reputation, but it always took a great deal of restraint to keep from smacking the overweening prick in the forehead.

Devon made the trips bearable. Barely five feet tall with a thin, boy-like figure dwarfed by her mounts, Devon had a poise that made her seem older than fifteen, though she still tended to glitter her horses' manes and tails. Fine, straw colored hair framed a freckled face set with large, dark eyes.

Horses filled those eyes with joy, and Pascoe was certain Dowry had purchased the farm so the expression would never leave his daughter's face.

Although oversight of the farm was handled by a number of hired hands, Devon could always be found picking a stone from a hoof, untangling a tail, or handing out carrots and apples. She had a voracious appetite for veterinary knowledge and peppered him with questions, armed with information from university web sites. To her, he was always Doctor Jordan, or simply Jordan, and she often confided to him feelings that she couldn't, or wouldn't, discuss with her own family. He, in return, liked to bring an easy blush to her cheeks by teasing about rumored boyfriends. It was like having a little sister without sharing a bathroom. That Vaughn had answered the telephone, and been civil, could only spell trouble.

From the state road he spied the main house perched dark and sleepy on the highest ridge of the property. Below, as the land flattened to pastures, barns blazed with light. Shadow figures scurried like mice out of the barn door and transformed into flashlight blobs dancing back and forth to the house. It looked like a damn circus.

Devon met the truck first, jogging alongside the driver's window, face pale and words flying.

"It's Goldrush. He was fine at dinner time, ate all of his grain and hay. At bedtime, he seemed a bit colicky, just looking at his side a bit, but never tried to roll. I've checked him every hour, and he's been fine, but he's gone downhill fast."

"Slow down," Pascoe said as he gathered supplies. "Have you changed his feed at all? I mean anything, even vitamins, supplements." Stethoscope.

"No."

"Started a fresh bale or new bag of grain?" Thermometer.

"It's all the same. Besides, all the others, even Dad's mares, eat the same stuff as Goldie."

"Tell me about this last hour." Pascoe shoved a palpation sleeve into the front pocket of his Levis and grabbed a bottle of lube.

"Like I said, he started off looking at his side, but not a lot…then farted and pooped and seemed to feel fine. Right before we called he began kicking at his belly and now he looks," she hesitated, frowning, "well, he looks like he wants to fall down."

Devon was rarely confused. Pascoe was drawing up a mixture of xylazine and butorphanol for pain when he paused with a needle cap between teeth and asked, "Are you saying he wants to lie down?"

Devon shook her head. "No, no, he's not buckling or anything. It's like he's drunk, you know, wobbly. If he tries to move, his back legs interfere and he'll almost go down."

The description was disconcerting. He had everything he needed for the moment and continued the conversation as they walked. He asked if any new horses had come into the barn. She answered no, adding Goldrush had not left the property in over a month. He had passed more manure in the last hour, and although a bit softer than usual, it wasn't what she would call diarrhea. Pascoe knew Goldrush was up to date on his vaccinations, he had administered them himself less than three months ago, and though he couldn't completely rule out infectious disease, it certainly made it less likely.

Thank God for Devon. Half the adults he dealt with didn't have even rudimentary knowledge of equine health and left gaping holes in a case's history, and here was a teenager who rattled off concise, accurate answers to all his questions.

Stonemason's two barns ran perpendicular to each other, forming an ell with a small space between. They headed to the barn that formed the bottom line, where Devon kept a string of riding horses. Her father housed a small collection of thoroughbred brood mares in the other.

Both barns were designed by Kentucky architects to mimic the style of Lexington, but made grander with cathedral ceilings and huge fourteen by fourteen stalls. Interlocking rubber bricks cushioned feet and hooves and gave the aisles the look of cobblestone without the slickness. Larger, rectangular versions covered the stall floors, which were piled high with pine shavings. Every wall was constructed from tongue-in-groove oak, stained and varnished to a gleaming amber finish. Dutch doors at both front and rear stalls gave the horses a choice of view and, in case of fire, allowed for speedy evacuation. A small army of Hispanic men kept the place so spotless it was ready to pass a white glove inspection even at this hour.

Oliver and his newest wife, Taylor, stood near Goldrush's stall, nauseated. Devon never discussed her stepmother's youth (she was only slightly older than Vaughn), but made no secret about her lack of respect for the woman, who couldn't ride, couldn't cook, and to hear Devon talk, couldn't read. Oliver, eyes rheumy above spidery cheeks, wrapped a proprietary arm around her waist.

Next to them was Devon's trainer Gerald, explaining dramatically, and unnecessarily, that whatever was wrong couldn't possibly be blamed on the jumping lesson he had given earlier. Tall and thin—too thin really—Gerald had a pronounced stoop that made him stork-like, an image enhanced by a rhythmic head bob acquired from years of watching students on horseback. Gerald had found a style and stuck with it. Unfortunately, the style was preppy, and the trainer shivered in the cold autumn air wearing a sea foam green polo shirt, a yellow sweater with the sleeves tied around his neck, and penny loafers—with actual pennies in them—on sockless feet.

No one moved to comfort Devon, and nattering speculation about the horse's condition was starting to unnerve her. Pascoe suggested they wait in the house; Goldrush required a quiet environment and all the commotion would make it difficult to assess his condition. Dowry looked only slightly less grateful for the opportunity than his wife, and Gerald looked as if he might kiss him. Once the small crowd was gone Devon and Pascoe made for the stall.

Goldrush had fallen to his side with his head facing the aisle, swollen, purple tongue lolling out of his mouth. His ribcage heaved, and the groan that accompanied each exhalation ended sharply as he struggled to inhale. A green, watery discharge flecked with scarlet trickled from flared nostrils, clumping the shavings into bloody pine-balls.

Devon rushed to open the door and Goldrush thrashed wildly in an attempt to rise. He succeeded in lifting his torso a foot off the ground, but his back end remained glued to the floor, and after a moments straining crashed violently back to his side. The big bay's eyes never left the face of his young owner.

Vaughn, shoulders hunched against the cold, clumped into the barn and squatted on his heels across from the stall. He took a drag off the cigarette held loosely in his hand, blew a few passable smoke rings and said, "What happened Sis, your precious pony fall down?"

Devon shot him a threatening glance. She turned to Pascoe. "The stuff from his nose is new." To her brother she said, "Listen asshole, nobody, not even Dad, smokes in this barn. I don't want you in here. I don't need you in here. I want you the hell out of here."

Vaughn wisely checked his tongue. Shrugging like he could care less about her wishes, he nevertheless turned to leave. He flicked the remainder of his cigarette at the stall next to Goldrush's and hit its occupant on the bridge of the nose. The horse scrambled to the rear of the stall.

Devon clenched her hands into fists and ran from Goldrush. For a second Pascoe thought she was going to throw herself at Vaughn, but she went instead to the smoldering butt and extinguished it under her heel.

"Sorry," she said, returning. "Tell me what to do."

"Stay near his head," Pascoe said, "and try to calm him. If he thrashes, lie across his neck. It won't keep him down, but you should have enough leverage to slow him. Remember, if I get squished, you'll waste a lot of time getting another vet out here."

Devon punched him lightly in the shoulder and sat down while Pascoe started his exam. A thermometer went into the anus first, it would be ready to read once the other vitals had been checked. With a stethoscope, he heard the heart pound out an erratic one hundred twenty beats a minute, four times its normal rate. The lungs, despite their effort, were clear. Pascoe moved to the abdomen. Silence.

Normally, intestines rumble loudly as hay and grain move through the digestive system. Increased noise can mean diarrhea or gas spasms. Silence, and the entire system has shut down. He draped the stethoscope over his neck, took off his jacket, and pushed up his sleeves.

"I need to do a rectal," he said to Devon. "It's going to be a bit dicey, I'll have to lie on the floor, and I don't want to tranq him given the state he's in.

Can you distract him? Devon?"

She startled out of her reverie. After Pascoe repeated his instructions, she started talking and stroking the horse's face. "Relax babe. If you break Jordan's leg I'll have to shoot him, and then where will we be?"

Pascoe removed the thermometer. It read 94.2, which is what it had read before insertion. Goldrush was certainly critical, but should have been able to maintain his core temperature. Puzzled, Pascoe slipped on an arm-length plastic sleeve and applied a liberal amount of lube.

The answer became clear as he lay behind the horse. Goldrush's anus was flaccid and sagging, and air had been sucked into the rectum, cooling it below body temperature.

Pascoe chided himself for missing this sign earlier and slid his arm gently into the big gelding. Intense pressure surrounded his forearm and Pascoe's first thought was that the colon had twisted, cutting off its blood supply like a tourniquet. It wouldn't take long for the oxygen-starved tissue to swell and fill the abdomen. However, he was unable to feel anatomical clues called bands, which distinguish the colon from other structures. He groped blindly with numb fingers for a minute and realized the organ he was palpating was the bladder, filled to the size of a beach ball. He applied light pressure. Goldrush cramped and kicked ineffectually as urine gushed onto the floor. Pooling urine soaked his pants, but Pascoe was too engaged to care. Devon looked up quizzically when she heard the splashing, but he motioned with his free hand for her to wait.

Once the bladder was emptied, the remainder of the abdomen could be explored with relative ease. Intestines were in their normal position. Spleen and left kidney also felt normal. Everything else was too forward to reach.

Goldrush lurched. His hind leg jerked convulsively and grazed Pascoe's knee. To her credit, Devon leapt onto the horse's head and delayed the struggle long enough to prevent Pascoe from leaving with a separated shoulder. Goldrush fought the restraint and rolled to his chest, flinging her against the wall. She managed to slip out of the stall before the horse pushed onto his front legs and sat with one hip rolled to the side like a puppy. He paused, panting, before surging with his back legs. For a second it appeared he would stand, but quickly overbalanced and crashed into the wall where Devon had been moments before. He lay stunned; blood ran from a split in the white star on his forehead. It was too much.

"What the hell is happening?" Devon screamed.

"He may be starting to seize. Things are progressing so fast it's hard to tell." Pascoe hugged the wall and made his way from the back of the stall to join her. He kept his voice even, hoping to calm her and prevent startling the horse. "I'm sure of one thing: the bladder is paralyzed, which means something is attacking his nervous system. My guess is that his diaphragm and stomach are also affected, which is why he's refluxing from his nose and having trouble breathing."

"What can we do?" Devon asked. "He was my thirteenth birthday present. Daddy will spend anything to fix him."

"Honestly, I don't think there's a whole lot to do. Whatever's happening already has a strong foothold. I can pump him full of fluids, DMSO, cortisone, but that's supportive care. We may be too late for anything else."

"We've got to try."

"We will."

Pascoe rushed back to the truck to grab a nasogastric tube, medications and supplies for starting an IV. When he returned, Goldrush paddled weakly and uncontrollably with his front legs. His breathing sounded wet. The hind legs had stopped moving altogether.

The stall became a makeshift ICU. Bags of Lactated Ringers laced with DMSO were hung from the ceiling and allowed to run freely into a catheter. Anti-inflammatories and anti-toxins were bolused by syringe and stomach tube. Devon sat by her horse's head, braiding and unbraiding his forelock, and told stories about their time together.

In the end nothing—not the medicine, not the love, not his will to live—was enough. The paralysis spread and Goldrush was unable to breathe on his own. Pascoe ended it and left Devon to grieve alone.

When he came back she sat cross-legged in the stall cradling Goldrush's muzzle in her lap. The stroking stopped. "You're not going to cut him up."

"I have to," Pascoe said, kneeling down beside the girl. She wouldn't look at him. "If this is something contagious, we have to know so we can protect the others. Besides, without a post the insurance company won't accept the claim."

Devon turned on him in a fury. "I don't care! You can't hack him up like he's a piece of meat."

"That's all he is now," Pascoe said. He put an arm around her. "Goldrush is gone."

Tears ran to the tip of Devon's nose and dripped onto the stall floor. "If you do this, will it prevent it from happening again?"

"Maybe. How do you think I'll feel if another horse dies and missed the chance to stop it? How will you feel?"

"Can I stay with him a little longer?"

"As long as you want. I'm going to clean up and gather the stuff I need. If you're not done by then, I'll wait."

She leaned over and kissed his cheek. "Thanks."

Traces of morning light bled into the eastern horizon as Pascoe bundled up trash and cleaned up equipment he had used in treating Goldrush. Devon was still in the stall when he returned, so he busied himself collecting samples of the hay, grain, and vitamins that had been fed to the horse. By the time he was finished, Devon had slipped away, and her horse's steaming corpse was alone in the stall.

Earlier in the night, as Goldrush languished on the floor, a sample of blood had been collected, but an additional specimen was required for any chance of a diagnosis: spinal fluid. Pascoe clipped and scrubbed a patch of skin near the base of the skull. He pulled on surgical gloves and slid a four-inch needle into the atlanto-occipital junction, a half dollar sized gap in the spine that allowed access to the cord. Such precaution might seem oxymoronic in a dead animal, but a contaminated sample would cloud any results. Pascoe was rewarded with five milliliters of clear fluid the color of chardonnay. He divided the sample in half: one for microscopic evaluation and the other for cultures and titers.

Grunt work lay ahead. Pascoe kept a butcher's knife in the glove compartment of his truck. It was sharpened to a keen edge and used specifically for this purpose. He began at the abdomen.

Putting a horse on it's back and expecting it to stay without support is wishful thinking—even the most mutton-withered Arab will tip over—so post-mortems are performed with a horse lying on its side. In this position, the up-side front and rear legs block access to the organs; the first cuts are designed to clear this problem.

The initial incision cuts deep into the groin until the hip joint stops the blade. The leg can then, with little effort, be pushed back until the hip dislocates and the leg flops to the ground. Because a horse has no collarbone, the shoulder can likewise be separated from the trunk until all four legs are on the ground in a grisly spread eagle posture. The skin and muscle are parted from sternum to pelvis along the curve of the rib cage and up the flank, creating a flap that can be lifted to expose the abdomen in its entirety.

Goldrush's organs appeared to be normal. The bowel was in place and of a size and color that it should be. The bladder, at its base, still held a small puddle of urine and Pascoe aspirated it with a syringe and needle before continuing. The gastrointestinal tract was severed at esophagus and anus, allowing the entire system to be removed intact. Stomach contents went into a sterile jar for later analysis. He ran the entire length of intestine, looking and feeling for abnormalities, but found only a solitary botfly larva in the stomach. Even so, pieces of stomach, small intestine, and colon splashed into jars of formalin to wait for a pathologist's assessment. Liver, kidney, and spleen followed, each sinking to the bottom of their own tiny container.

After finishing the abdomen, he went back to the truck for another tool. Long handled loppers, the kind for pruning trees, were needed to crack through the thick, flat ribs of Goldrush's chest. Sweat plastered shirt to chest by the time the eighteenth rib cracked between the lopper's blades. The tissues of the chest cavity appeared to be normal as well, but pieces of heart and lung were added to Pascoe's collection.

Finished now, every question unanswered, he woke Emilio, the farm manager, to help with the body. A was chain wrapped around his neck and Goldrush unceremoniously dragged behind a tractor from the barn. Later, a backhoe would dig a deep grave at the far end of a pasture Goldrush had galloped in the day before.

Pascoe shielded his eyes as he drove between Stonemason's wrought iron gates. The sun peeked above the horizon, bathing the mottled colors of Appalachia in a rosy glow. It depressed Pascoe. He had hoped to finish the necropsy and catch a catnap before work, but sun's appearance was sure sign he had just enough time to race home, shower, load up the dog, and head to the office.

Less than an hour later, better disposed and working on a second cup of coffee, Pascoe pulled into the parking lot of Harkin Veterinary Associates. Barclay, feeling chipper after a full night's rest, trotted ahead to greet clinic's namesake, King Harkin.

At seventy-five, Harkin had vetted horses for three generations of pony-clubbers and it showed. He had a sailor's rolling gait, having had the kneecap of one leg shattered by the hoof of an unruly stallion and hip of the other dislocated twice in separate incidences. His left shoulder blade was crushed when a filly had bolted from a stall and pinned him against a six-by-six post. Now the arm hung a couple of inches lower than the right, and he looked as if he always carried an invisible suitcase. As a boy, a blow to the head had detached both retinas. It was rumored his father, as famously temperamental as Harkin was affable, had delivered the blow. The resulting damage forced him to wear thick, tinted glasses and a battered straw hat to protect his eyes from sunlight. Though broken in body, Harkin's hands remained agile enough to suture skin as easily as zippering a jacket and sensitive enough to outperform ultrasound. Those hands cast him into legend.

Of course, the name didn't hurt. Harkin would tell anyone who would listen (which, given his standing, was everyone) he came by it honestly, being the sole child of five to survive birth. His mother, either in honor of the infant or as a talisman for his protection (Pascoe had heard it both ways), bestowed upon her baby a name of power. "I was the first," Harkin would say. "Before Elvis, before the reverend Martin Luther, a Harkin was King." Years ago, in his prime, a debutante from one of the established lines had been so suitably convinced by this pronouncement that she curtsied during her own coming out party. Harkin took the girl's hand, kissed it, raised his eyebrows to the giggling onlookers and chided, "I hope y'all were paying attention. Here's a young lady who knows how to show respect."

Harkin had been a part of his life since the old veterinarian had come to work at the stable where Pascoe's father was resident trainer. Harkin encouraged the boy to aspire to be more than a backstretch rat, gave him copies of Herriot's *All Creatures* series, and taught him to see lameness in a trot. Pascoe's father, busy scratching out enough wins to keep employed and supplied with Pabst Blue Ribbon, never begrudged Harkin for assuming the responsibility of raising his son. In summer, Pascoe escaped and rode shotgun with King, helping when permitted and absorbing as much as possible. Pascoe would tell clients, only half-joking, that once the admissions department saw Harkin's name on a letter of recommendation there was no chance he'd have to apply to vet school a second time. It had been understood, though never said outright, that Pascoe would become Harkin's first and only associate upon graduating.

Pascoe joined the practice two years ago, right out of vet school. The practice's name had included "Associates" long before his arrival. "Well," Harkin explained, "it sounds one hell of a lot better than 'overworked, ornery old shit that might call you back' in the yellow pages." Pascoe agreed with him on that point. With Harkin's stamp of approval, Pascoe slipped into daily practice with more ease than most new graduates. Of course, if he made an unusual or unexpected diagnosis, Harkin was called for a second opinion. Pascoe took no offense, he was new to the job after all, and Harkin saved his ass a couple of times. Two years passed quickly, and Pascoe's reputation grew to the extent that some clients, like Devon Dowry, preferred him to Harkin.

The practice ran out of a clinic on property that had been in Harkin's family for years. A four-bay barn had been turned into stalls for patients needing more intensive care than could be provided in the field. Simple dirt floors and wood walls scarred from decades of gnawing horses made for plain housing, but were bedded deeply and kept clean and served well. Because Harkin and Pascoe were almost always away, the attached office was a simple, flat-roofed brick rectangle stocked with three desks and as many phones.

When Pascoe walked in the door, Barclay lay by his desk, finished with his hellos. Maggie Wright, the office manager, gazed with rapt attention at Harkin, who sat on the desk's corner and gestured wildly.

Maggie started working for Harkin right out of high school in the early seventies, answering phones and gradually assuming responsibilities until it the phones would hardly remember how to ring if she left. It was said Maggie and Harkin engaged in a passionate affair in those early days, a scandalous rumor that would have not surprised Pascoe in the least. Maggie was striking in her late forties; few lines creased her face and she kept her body taut. The only thing that marked her age was an unwillingness to change her hairstyle from the shag she wore as a girl and the tabby-cat orange it was dyed. It was difficult to tell if she pined to be Harkin's lover, was still his lover, or just plain worshipped the man. Pascoe had to be content with guessing, the fount of gossip ran dry on that one.

"Jordie!" Harkin roared, spinning to face him. "You look exhausted." He looked at his watch and tapped its face. "Coming in a late too. Only thing I know that puts bags like that under your eyes is a horsewoman. Fill us in boy, we're all family here." He winked at Pascoe. Maggie shuffled papers.

A perennial bachelor, Harkin never tired of fishing for tales from Pascoe's social life. Harkin had squired many a socialite in his time, leaving broken hearts, and sometimes more, in his wake. It was whispered that some of the wealthiest families in the area had a bit of Harkin blood pass through their nurseries. Pascoe wondered if irate husbands and fathers, rather than horses, had meted out some of his employer's injuries. Regardless, His skill with the ladies only added a dash of the rogue to his mythic status and social worth. Pascoe's nonexistent dating life fell far short of expectations.

"Hate to disappoint you, but it was a horse-man that had me up all night," Pascoe said, and smiled at Harkin's raised eyebrows. "Big. Muscular. Bay. Definitely your type."

"I'm a chestnut man born and bred. Always have been a sucker for a red-head," he replied. Maggie dropped her stack of papers.

Harkin's playful grin changed as Pascoe related the events at Stonemason. "Took every sample I could think of," Pascoe said, "but I'll be damned if I know what killed that horse."

"That's what labs are for my friend, to see the stuff we can't. What are you planning to test for?"

"EPM, Rhino, West Nile, encephalitis. Shit! I should have taken the head for rabies."

"I wouldn't be too worried about that, it sounds like the symptoms came on too fast. Botulism?"

"Think so?"

"Haven't seen a case in years, but it was similar, and if you're wondering, I had as much success as you. Turned out nobody cleaned the water trough in a while and a squirrel had fallen in and drowned. That water was certain death for any horse drinking it, but by the time I figured it out three horses had been lost."

"I'll put it on my list."

"How's the girl?"

"Shook up. Stuck with me right to the end though. My guess is she'll have nightmares for a bit and check on the others in the middle of the night for a while after that."

"Tough kid that one, and smart." Harkin spat into the trash can next to the desk. "I guess she'd have to be to put up with a father who can't find his own ass and a brother who is one. Knew the mother before she split, that's who the child takes after." An awkward pause ensued as Harkin attempted to redirect the conversation. "Breeder's Cup this weekend."

"Is it?"

"I can hold your check 'til Monday."

"Cupboard's getting bare, I've got to eat."

"You gonna?"

"Sure."

"Your money has a way of making its way into other hands."

"It'll find its way to Safeway, that's it."

Harkin searched for the lie in his face. "I'll have it for you Friday."

Maggie, who was answering incoming calls, disrupted the tête-à-tête. "Doctor P, line one for you, Virginia Bloodstock Insurance. Are you available?"

Pascoe answered the call at his desk.

A woman's voice, husky and infused with the genteel South, answered. "Doctor, this is Ruth Wallace. We insured a horse named Goldrush for Oliver Dowry. You called early this morning to let us know the horse had been put down, correct?"

Odd, insurance companies usually sent claim forms by mail. Phone calls didn't start until he had forgotten, or put off, filling them out for more than a week. He wondered if Dowry was raising hell about something.

"Afraid I don't have records written up yet. Lab tests will take a few days, and then I might have an answer. If you're concerned about the necessity of the euthanasia I can assure you—"

"No, no, that won't be necessary. It's just that there are some, um, sensitive issues regarding the case. Things I'd rather not discuss over the phone. Can we meet for lunch?"

It was futile to argue with insurance companies, all it would accomplish was a delay in Dowry's check. Pascoe flipped through his schedule. "Today is impossible. I can fit you in tomorrow, one o'clock,"

"Fine. The Iron Jockey is close by your office, how does that sound?"

"That works for me, but—"

"Great, one o'clock tomorrow then. I'm sure there's no need to remind you that this is a confidential matter?"

And with that, she was gone. Pascoe stared at the receiver. Lawyers handled questionable claims, and even they waited on lab findings and conclusions. He penciled in the appointment. Harkin and Maggie looked quizzically in his direction.

"You should be proud of me King, I have a date tomorrow," Pascoe said.

Harkin, heading to his first appointment, shrugged on his jacket. "Hope you've got the right species this time."

CHAPTER TWO

True fall weather hit the following day. It is not unusual for Indian summer to last into late October or early November, requiring short sleeves at noon and down comforters at night. Too many days sweating through clothes perfect for frosty mornings and unbearable by midday had made Pascoe wish for fall to hurry up and arrive. Now he had second thoughts about meteorological preferences and wishes.

Storm clouds with jade skin and coal hearts commanded the sky and dumped relentless and unforgiving sheets of rain on his windshield. The defroster whirred and squeaked at its highest setting, barely dispersing the fogged glass. He concentrated on the red blur of taillights ahead of him and tried not to let the mesmerizing *thwack-thwack* of the wipers lead him into a ditch. Random whip-cracks of thunder and flashes of lightning kept him alert and intact.

Pascoe was as much of a disaster as the weather. His hair was feebly drying after his last call, and water continued to trickle under the collar of his storm shell. He had just come from Old Mrs. Simmons' place. Everyone, including Harkin, called her Old Mrs. Simmons because anyone who had ever known her first name was dead. Simmons was prolonging, with little success, the family legacy as horse people, though even in their glory days 'horse traders' would have been a more accurate designation. In any case, Simmons had neither know-how nor revenue to do a proper job, and both Harkin and he regularly repaired rank animals with neglected problems as inexpensively as possible.

This day, he had the good fortune to have Kit, a sway-backed, bench-kneed stallion, as a patient. Kit cut his hock two weeks ago and since then Simmons had applied a cut medicine concocted from an old family recipe. Turpentine was the main ingredient, judging by the salve's smell and Kit's intense reaction. With the horse tied to a rotten fencepost, Pascoe cut away proud flesh and bandaged the hock. While he worked, Kit's squirming legs painted his pants with wide strokes of mud, but the most difficult part of the procedure was convincing Simmons to replace her mixture with an antibiotic cream.

When he climbed back into the truck, Barclay eyed him with a mixture of mirth and pity. The prospect of a hot lunch, for whatever reason, cheered Pascoe.

The Iron Jockey was a community oasis, providing hearty food and respite from the baking heat, frigid snow, or, as was the case today, drenching rain. The restaurant had been a Civil War Era plantation house, converted to its present use in the nineties by the owner and head chef, Lars Altman. Altman had left a choice position at a chichi eatery in D.C. for the slower pace of the country, much to the benefit of the latter. Altman's metropolitan clients made the westward trek on weekends and, along with local fans, created a reservation backlog weeks long.

The main floor was open only for dinner, but lunch could be had downstairs. The basement served as a bar for the main restaurant and grill for casual dining and compensated for its lack of view with atmosphere and comfort food. On Friday and Saturday nights, owners of racers, hunters, jumpers, and dressage stars dined alongside politicos with quiet elegance while jockeys and trainers raised hell downstairs. The bar, or tavern, as those in the area called it, was named Grant's Tomb, and Pascoe knew from experience that the heavy-handed bartender could bury unwary patrons.

Pascoe squinted through the windshield, focused on the driveway, and barely navigated the turn without harming the restaurants namesake statuette. Once parked, Pascoe bolted across the twenty yards separating his truck from the entrance, dodging water-filled potholes along the way. Still, he entered the tavern only a tad drier than when he had left Kit.

The cool climate of the basement drew gooseflesh to his skin. He was relieved to see the fireplace at the far end of the bar roaring. The lighting was dim, but rough timbers and a brass mirror reflecting the fire's flame suggested frontier hominess rather than dungeon dreariness. Mason jar candles on the tables and small, wavy windows set high in the stone foundation provided additional light. Mingling with fresh scents of soup, crab cake, and barbeque were hints of earth and onion: memories of a root cellar. The lunch crowd must have left recently; silverware clattered and glass tinkled behind swinging doors leading to the kitchen.

One section of the tavern remained occupied: two tables near the bar hosted fresh pitchers of beer and a rowdy crowd of men and women clothed in mud-splattered riding attire recounted a wild ride with animated hand gestures and raucous laughter. Talking about a gallop through a lighting storm was a hell of a lot more fun than actually doing it.

He chose a spot by the fire, hoping to dry off, and glanced at his watch.

The rain must have delayed Wallace. One of the riders in the group noticed him, spoke to the others, and came over. Subdued laughter followed the figure, who, coming closer, he recognized as Hunter Stuart.

Straight, swallow-brown hair was pulled back into a ponytail jutting out the back of an Orioles cap. She wore chaps over blue jeans and paddock boots. A sweatshirt with an advertisement for a mail order tack shop covered a dark blue turtleneck. The entire ensemble was splattered in the red, brown and green hues of the countryside. Her face had been wiped, not washed, and streaks of clay highlighted high cheekbones like rouge. Mischievousness shone in mismatched eyes of green and gray. Here was one person who would find a wild ride through the rain preferable to discussing it over drinks. Her smile was contagious.

"Nice outfit," Pascoe said. "Maybe a little too couture for the Tomb though."

Hunter flicked her ponytail, showering him with water. "Continue to be a smart ass and I may decide not to invite you to join me. You will lose out on the pleasure of my company and miss the chance to be accosted for free vet advice. So, are you going to shape up?"

"Gotta pass. I'm waiting for someone and expect her to walk in any minute."

"Her?"

"Business meeting."

"Ah, business," Hunter said. "Listen, I wanted to thank you. The driver of rendering truck told me you paid to deliver Sheba's body to the farm instead of the plant."

"You were at the hospital. I figured it was what you would have wanted." It was illegal to bury horses in the county, something about the water table, but it was done anyway. Neighbors were more likely to bring a backhoe and help than call the authorities—even horseless landowners were fed up with regulations intruding upon country life.

"Even so, it was a nice thing to do." Hunter said. "Why don't you stop by my place tomorrow? I've found a replacement for Sheba and he needs a going over. I'll make sandwiches," she offered in a singsong voice.

"Sure. No problem." Pascoe had no idea what was scheduled for the next day, but he was sure as hell not going to turn down an offer twice.

"Great, see you tomorrow." She nodded to the door. "Looks like your meeting is here."

A slim figure wrapped in an overcoat entered the room, shaking out an umbrella before folding it into a flashlight-sized package. Pascoe turned to say goodbye, but Hunter had rejoined her friends and changed to a seat with an unobstructed view of his table. The woman, who she had rightly assumed to be Wallace, waved and headed over.

"A fire!" she exclaimed. "Thank the gods, I'm soaked to the bone!"

Pascoe had a hard time believing it. Few raindrops beaded on the coat and her graying blonde hair was undisturbed blunt symmetry. She removed the coat and slung it over the back of an empty chair.

Wallace looked to be in her late thirties and had the figure of either a smoker or an anorexic. A trendy, olive business suit, absent any watermarks, was expertly tailored to this frame and gave her an aura of constrained sexuality. A bracelet of heavy gold links hung on her wrist and was her only jewelry. The hand offered to him was calloused and the fingers thick and muscular, sure trademarks of a rider. Her makeup was sparse and precise, rich tones that complimented her fair skin and hazel eyes. With an air of familiarity, she sat in the chair next to him.

"Sorry about being late," she said. "Nobody around here seems to know how to drive when the roads get wet."

"Miss Wallace, can we get to the point of this meeting? My schedule is unforgiving, and honestly, I can't figure out why we need to meet in person."

"Doctor, please call me Ruth."

"Fine, call me Jordan, everyone else does."

"Wonderful. As you'll see, this is too important to discuss—oh, here's our waiter. I'm sooo hungry. Let's order."

Pascoe waited patiently as Wallace asked about the specials, the soups, the salads, and the selection of diet sodas and finally decided on having a cup of tomato soup and seltzer. Pascoe began to wonder what she would eat if she weren't hungry. *Two leaves of lettuce and warm tap water, please.* He ordered a crab cake sandwich with fries on the side and a cup of hot tea. When the waiter left, Pascoe continued.

"Too important? Look, I've come here at your request, to be polite, and would appreciate a little more directness."

"Oh Jordan," she said loudly, finishing with a giggle that raised Hunter's eyebrows. "I hope you don't think that Virginia Bloodstock has any misgivings about you. In truth, the thoroughness of your reports is the reason I contacted you." Pascoe must have looked entirely lost, so she added, "I'd like you to help with some investigative work."

"I don't understand any of this."

"Of course not, that's why we're meeting." She patted his hand. "I'll sum it up for you. We normally process ten, fifteen claims a year in this area. Most are mortality claims: colic, broken legs," she raised her eyes to the ceiling as a large boom of thunder echoed outside, "lightning strikes. A loss-of-use claim from time to time, but what the company is really concerned with is mortality. Lately, claims of a certain nature have jumped by fifty percent. An increase like that and we take a second look."

"What kind of claims?"

"What did Oliver Dowry's horse die of?"

"I have no idea."

"*That* kind of claim. Educated guesses about what killed a horse, but nobody willing to go out on a limb and say they know for sure. It raises suspicions."

"You're talking about fraud. Around here? Guys like Dowry buy horses with pocket change."

Wallace shrugged. "It's not always about money. A few years ago a there was a trainer who bought some horses for clients and they didn't work out. Poor little Heather and Tiffany and Britney had trouble steering their push-button horses around the ring and lost out on the blue ribbons. This made the trainer look very bad. Next thing, one of those horses was found dead. Month later, same thing. Post mortem exams normal, cause of death unknown.

"But this guy got greedy. No one was asking questions, so he started buying investment horses. He'd get cheap horses, put some training on them, jack up their insurance and put on a show of trying to sell them—lots of advertising, et cetera. Some sold to some suckers who overpaid for mediocre horseflesh. Others wound up dead. The paperwork reported 'heart attack' or 'stroke' as the cause of death, but you and I both know that's code for 'I don't know what happened'. When one of our clerks noticed an awful lot of cash going to one guy, we checked into it."

"What did you find?" Pascoe asked.

"The horses were dying of strokes and heart attacks! That fucker, pardon my French, was electrocuting his own stock. He had split an extension cord and used alligator clips to attach one end to a lip and the other to the ass. Plug it in and—wham! Cash a check."

The tale had drawn him in. "How did you catch him?"

"With a veterinarian who paid attention. One of his reports mentioned tiny zigzag burn marks on the lip. After that, we hired a detective to do some surveillance. Caught the bastard frying a pregnant mare, trying for a two-for-one deal."

The waiter arrived and distributed the food with the practiced inattention of an eavesdropper. Both Pascoe and Wallace remained silent until he left unsatisfied. Wallace sipped her seltzer and had a few spoonfuls of soup. Pascoe watched his sandwich cool.

"Sounds like this detective did a good job," Pascoe said. "Why don't you hire him?"

"If we knew who to scrutinize, if we knew for sure that something was being done, we would. But we don't. What we have are isolated cases with nothing in common except some similarity surrounding their deaths."

"What's so special about me?"

"From everything I've gathered, you're very particular about working up a case and the claims you've submitted support that reputation. If you could look over my files, you might flag something we missed. We would pay you of course."

Pascoe took a bite of his sandwich and chewed thoughtfully. Wallace was pandering. There were a number of vets in the area with more experience.

"Don't think I can help you," he said. "Try my boss, King Harkin. If you'd like I could ask—"

"No!" Wallace clutched his hand, releasing it just as quickly. "What I mean is, I would prefer you. You haven't been out of school long, but it's an advantage, really. No ties, no loyalties to the big players. Harkin has connections to everyone. Do you think he could be objective? This county is like a goddamn high school clique. Harkin's too much of an insider and our detectives are outsiders, they can't wrangle a job mucking stalls. It's got to be you Jordan, and it has to be kept secret."

"What if someone were to find out? How's that going to look? I'm just now gaining the trust of some clients, I don't want to lose that."

"They're my clients too," Wallace said. "They'll be just as angry at Virginia Bloodstock if someone thinks we suspect them of killing a horse. I'm not asking you to dig up dirt, just look at some files. If you don't see anything, keep your ears open, or ask a question or two. What's the harm in that?"

Pascoe dipped a fry into in a paper cup filled with ketchup. He had worked all his life to get to this point; wasn't about to screw it up helping a stranger. "I've got a lot of lab work still running. When I get some results, whatever they are, I'll report them, but you'll have to find someone else to take it from there."

"I see," Wallace said. Deliberately, she spooned some more soup into her mouth and then dabbed her lips with a napkin. "Jordan, is it true that you had a run in with the Board of Veterinary Medicine?"

"The Board? I don't know what you're talking about."

"Gambling wasn't it? Something about moral standards, insider information, integrity of the sport. Do I have that right? Aren't you still on probation?"

Pascoe was furious. His case was supposed to have been sealed.

"Bitch," he hissed. "That's my private business. You're right. I'm on probation, for something that's over and done with. Another year and the whole thing goes away, clean slate."

Wallace stirred her soup, making a red whirlpool. "Is that so? It's my understanding your probation is contingent upon an agreement to stop gambling. I met a funny little man the other day named Bimbo Carlyle. Know him?" Pascoe paled. "Hmmm, thought you might. He's a bookie, just the kind of guy you're supposed to stay clear of. And you two have had some recent transactions." Wallace took her spoon out of the bowl and laid it across the rim. "What do you suppose would happen if the Board got wind of this?"

"You know damn well my license will get pulled. I'd be out of a job. You're not giving me any choice."

"Of course I am. Haven't I explained it well enough?"

"You have at that." Pascoe massaged his forehead. "What about the police?"

Wallace shook her head. "The police are clumsy. The company wants to keep this quiet. No egos get bent out of shape this way, and VBI won't look like it mistrusts its clients."

"What about me?"

"Sugar, not even Harkin will hear a whisper of it if you just try."

Pascoe slumped in his chair and pushed his plate away. He was no longer hungry. "How do I start?"

"That's the right attitude. We start with case files. Don't make any plans for tomorrow evening, I'll bring them over to your place and bring you up to date." She tossed a business card onto his plate. "Call me with directions. We'll improvise from there. Here, let me get the check."

Wallace stood and threw a twenty on the table. Most of her soup remained uneaten.

Pascoe watched as she bundled back into her overcoat and swept out the door without another word. The waiter approached timidly and asked if he had finished. Pascoe waved at him to take the plate.

Hunter and her friends were still at their table as he made for the door. He smiled cheerfully and waved, hoping he looked more convincing than he felt. Hunter winked and blew him a kiss and the others at the table laughed. He continued the charade all the way to his truck, in case he ran into any clients. He let go once he was back on the road, pounding the steering wheel and yelling, "Shitshitshit!" at the top of his lungs. Barclay tilted his head, wondering why Pascoe had forgotten to bring him leftovers.

Pascoe learned the basics of racing at an early age. If a horse that his father was training came in first, second or third, Dad got paid and the family bought groceries. George Pascoe won more than he lost, or at least he had until his wife left and then he won less and drank more. Vivian Pascoe left when her son was six. She grew tired of living in trailers and following winter meets like a migratory animal, and decided men who could afford to race horses held more promise than men who trained them. Pascoe hadn't seen her since, and, though a psychologist might say he repressed feelings of abandonment, never thought he missed much.

He loved getting up in the early morning and watching his father time furlongs on the stopwatch hung around his neck. Horses flew by, barely visible in the darkness, pounding the ground and vibrating the body of the little boy whose heart pounded in his chest. His first dreams were of being a jockey.

By twelve, those dreams fell away when he shot up four inches and was taller than any jock at the track. George started drinking beer with breakfast, and the joy was gone from the morning workout. They had not yet moved to Virginia, where he would meet Harkin, and the boy spent his afternoons wandering the track, watching horses run, jockeys curse trainers, and trainers curse owners. It was during this time he met his first professional gambler.

As far as Pascoe knew, his father had never bet on a race. "Jordie," he would say, gesturing with the beer that was now always at hand, "I thought your mother was a safe bet, and look what happened. Nope, I take money home from the track when my horse shows or better. If he don't, I get nothin' above my monthly fee, but it beats leaving money at the window."

Decker, the gambler, had a more convincing argument. He never drank, at least not at the track, wore nice suits, and smelled of musk and cigars instead of horses. One day, he treated Pascoe to a steak dinner in the clubhouse, peeling off cash from a thick roll of bills carried in a brown paper lunch sack.

"Listen Jordan," he said, mouth crammed with food, "no disrespect to your father, but he's working the wrong end of the horse, so to speak. He trains for a fifty thousand dollar purse, puts in lots of time, and, God-willing, the nag wins. Dad gets what, five?" Pascoe nodded, having no idea. "Okay. Come race day, I, having put in zero hours," Decker put an eye to a thumb-and-forefinger circle for effect, "can invest five hundred dollars on the same nag at ten-to-one, no disrespect to your father, and leave with the same amount in my pocket." He leaned back in his chair, satisfied smile on his face, hands resting on ample belly, thumbs twiddling. Pascoe was sold.

Decker continued to mentor his young student, showing Pascoe how to spread bets among the whole field, lessening the risk to his wallet. "I don't care if you overhear Don Corleone say so-and-so is a sure thing," Decker was fond of saying, "stick with a system and you won't get bit in the ass." In time, Pascoe convinced Decker to front a bet. Two dollars returned ten, and the boy was hooked. It wouldn't have mattered if he lost; the rush was worth the price of admission. He paid attention to the rumors circulating in the stables, to the shady characters that seemed to always be near when a long shot came in. After a while he experimented with exactas, trifectas and daily doubles. He came to look at horses as abstracts, as shares in his portfolio.

Isolation curbed his habit. Pascoe hardly noticed when his father strung together a half dozen wins, so it came as a shock when he was told they were moving to Virginia, where George was to be the trainer for Fieldstone Stables. Pascoe was crushed. The farm had its own training track and the nearest betting window was hours away. *The Daily Racing Form* was like methadone, and allowed him to continue handicapping. He began a game of recording the bets he would have made and their outcome in a spiral bound notebook that was supposed to be used for math homework.

By the time Harkin came into his life, the pari-mutuel fever had cooled and Pascoe was receptive to a new teacher. Before long even the *Form* went by the wayside and the notebook was used once again for Algebra, and by the time George's liver failed vet school was half over the only bets laid were with classmates during the Triple Crown. There was always plenty of beer money in May.

Graduated and working for Harkin, the problem resurfaced. Ostentatious amounts of money surrounded him, lavished on homes, clothes, cars, trailers, and especially horses, and Pascoe felt he had climbed no higher than his father, shackled to the rich who deigned to hire him. The thought terrified him. He bought a truck he couldn't afford, had trouble making the payments and needed a way to supplement his paycheck.

He bet money on steeplechase races and lost fabulously. His system, developed for flat racing, fell apart applied to horses running hell bent over timber and brush. Bloodlines meant nothing. Beyer scores meant nothing. As far as he could see, a horse and jockey with no fear was all that meant anything, and those combinations fell prey to luck as often as not.

Carlyle smelled blood in the water. He sidled up to Pascoe after a race and introduced himself, claiming to have been a jockey at one time. He was certainly short enough, but judging by the spare tire around his midsection, those days were long gone. Now he trained steeplechasers and managed a book on the side. Because Pascoe was new to the area, Carlyle was willing to give him some tips, if he was interested. Pascoe was.

Things went well at first. He bet within his means and was rewarded with a small, but regular income. Carlyle grumbled that Pascoe's luck was too good. The fire was rekindled and it burned hot.

Soon, it devoured ever-larger hunks of Pascoe's wages, losses pushing the next bet upward until he was playing with money he hadn't earned, certain the next race would bring him even. Carlyle offered action on other sporting events, and now Pascoe had more choices than he knew what to do with. A devastating string of near misses during the NCAA tournament signaled the end of Carlyle's charity. He wanted the money he was owed, and Pascoe needed four months salary to make good. A compromise was offered.

The bookie had two horses in his possession: one was a creaky, high mileage ten-year old, the other a fresh-legged full brother seven years younger with identical markings. The older horse was scheduled to race at Pimlico the following Saturday, and having raced poorly the last two years, was likely to go off at forty-to-one or better. All Carlyle needed was Pascoe to fudge some paperwork, duplicate a lip tattoo, and the three-year old could take his brother's place. Regardless of the outcome, the entire debt would be wiped clean. Pascoe took the chance. The ruse would have gone unnoticed if the youngster hadn't spat out a baby tooth in the winner's circle.

The Veterinary Board was apoplectic. They were prepared to revoke Pacoe's license until Harkin stepped in. He called old friends on the Board, as well as those on the outside who held power in the state, and secured enough votes to ensure his protégé was only wrist-slapped with a small fine and probation. During probation he was banned from the track and betting of all kinds. Attendance at weekly Gamblers Anonymous meetings was mandatory. Pascoe kept part of the bargain. He signed into the meetings and stayed a bit at first, but after a few months started laying bets with Carlyle again, budgeting bets as he would any other household expense. If Harkin found out, he was finished, so he pored over the *Form* in private and only met Carlyle to pay off a loss or collect a win. He was positive no one else knew about the relationship. But Wallace knew, and if she wanted to talk, the Board would listen, a player like Virginia Bloodstock wouldn't be ignored. The rain outside was lifting, but a new storm gathered.

CHAPTER THREE

Maggie was not pleased to learn an appointment had been made without consulting her. "Come on," she said, "I've booked a castration in Lovettesville. What do you expect me to do?"

"Explain that the mud left over from the storm creates too much risk for infection."

"Do this to me again, and you'll be the one having his balls cut off."

Timberbrook Farm hugged the border between Virginia and West Virginia, its name taken from a stream that meandered through the forest on the north side of the property. The stream had been dug out where it skirted the pastures and made into a water-complex used for training and swimming the horses. Black board fence enclosed fields dotted with tables, coffins, hogbacks, and other obstacles such that when all gates were opened an entire cross-country course was at Hunter's disposal.

Unlike Stonemason, Timberbrook's barn was built solely of efficiency and economy. A steel skeleton and sheet metal roof covered both riding arena and the twenty stalls that ran along one side. High ceilings ensured good ventilation and only the faintest odor of urine could be detected even with doors closed against the bite of winter. Aisles and stall floors were dirt, but cleaned well and often, so the barn always smelled of fresh sawdust. Horses spent days in the fields and were brought to comfortably bedded stalls in the evenings, ample pile of hay in one corner. All the horses were fit from regular work; Hunter was a kind rider, but a demanding one.

A small apartment was built at one end of the barn. A single, square room on the ground floor had kitchen and living room defined by a change from linoleum to carpet. Steep stairs led to a loft, truly named, for hay was stored on the other side of the room's far wall. Hunter slept here, and its nearness to the stalls allowed her to sleep without worry. Any irregularity to the normal rhythms of snoring, chewing and rustling, and she could be downstairs in a moment to investigate.

A high-pressure system had pushed out the clouds and moderate temperature with them. Pastures were hoary with frost and Pascoe's truck cracked thin panes of ice covering potholes in the gravel driveway.

When he opened the door of the truck, Barclay shouldered his way past, impatient to fraternize with Timberbrook's motley pack. Bear, a shaggy Shepherd/Rottweiler mix was already poking his nose under Barclay's tail before Pascoe put a foot to the ground. Candy, a beagle, licked at his face between howls while Chinook, a stoic, blue-eyed husky, waited to the side until all the embarrassing displays were over. David, Hunter's older brother, bundled in a hooded parka and clumsy ski gloves, exited the barn pushing a wheelbarrow obscenely overloaded with stall mucking.

"Hey Doc, what time is it?" David asked.

Pascoe knew what was coming, but feigned otherwise. "I don't know. What time is it?"

"Time to work!" David continued off toward the manure pile, shaking his head, chuckling and snorting. The dogs finished their hellos and bounded off to join him.

David had been the top three-day rider in the country. He led the nation in points with his horse, Gallipoli, and was a shoe-in for the next Olympic team. Then the unthinkable happened. Harkin, who had stopped by to examine a different horse, found David unconscious in Gallipoli's stall, hand clutched tightly around a grooming brush. The gelding munched hay alongside as if nothing had happened. Dried sweat crusted the horse's neck and back. Gallipoli had always been even-tempered; it was thought something, a horse fly perhaps, had spooked him, and a kick at the pest inadvertently struck his rider. Fortunately, Hunter had come home at about the same time and she and Harkin kept her brother alive until an ambulance arrived.

David's scalp had been peeled back like the skin of an orange and his skull shattered. Surgery removed a great deal of bone, leaving the right side of his face dented deep as a china saucer. A scalloped scar, livid against skin lighter than his sister's, ran from hairline to cheekbone. No one knew how much memory, if any, of life before the accident remained. David could be prompted with stories, visitors, or photographs and responded to all with the same vague, drooping smile. He remembered some people, like Hunter, who had been around his entire life, but could not give the specifics of their relationship. He performed rudimentary duties around the farm, mucking and feeding if he was reminded to do it. It was only recently that Pascoe didn't have to be reintroduced when visiting.

The sounds of a working horse came from the arena. They became clearer as he walked down the aisle: transitions from trot to canter and back again, footing rattling off the wall, horse and rider breathing as one. Hunter was on her new horse.

At the arena gate, he stopped and watched. The horse was black with stockings that reached to the hock in the hind end and mid-cannon in the front. Its head, which has a star and thin stripe, was the blocky, full-cheeked face of a stallion. He had the long back and lean profile of a thoroughbred, the breed of choice with event riders because of their courage and stamina. Hunter, unaware of her audience, continued to work. Sure, light hands and tight calves guided the horse through serpentines and lead changes. When she noticed Pascoe, a slight change in the tension of her abdomen slowed the horse to a trot, a walk, and finally to a halt by the gate. She patted his neck and hopped off.

"What do you think?" she asked.

"Looks sound, but I need to see a bit more."

"But what do you *think* of him?"

Pascoe felt like he was back before the admissions committee at vet school. "Oh, ah...well, he's flashy, the dressage judges will love the symmetry of the chrome on his legs. From the aisle I could hear the power of his canter, if he can use it to jump he'll have no problems there. He seems to have a good mind for a stud, didn't miss a step when I walked up. Overall, I'd say a solid prospect."

Hunter put a finger to her lip and studied Pascoe. "Yeah, that's pretty much what I thought, let's grab some lunch."

"Don't you want me to go over him a little more thoroughly?"

"King did the prepurchase exam last week. Like I told you, I just wanted you to take a look."

Pascoe stood dumbly while Hunter hooked the horse into the crossties in the aisle and removed the tack. David returned with an empty wheelbarrow and Hunter asked him to finish cooling out the horse. She turned to Pascoe.

"I did say there'd be sandwiches. Coming?"

Lunch was as promised: sandwiches of thickly sliced turkey on rye bread and a steaming bowl of lentil soup.

"Where did you find the stud?" he asked between mouthfuls.

"Pennsylvania. Had a short and unsuccessful career at the track. Seems he doesn't care much for running in circles. Bit the tip off his owner's middle finger and I was able to get him for a smidge over meat price. His registered name is Wallstreet, but I'm calling him Banker. I wanted a horse that didn't remind me of Sheba, and he's nothing like her. Got the talent and fire I like in my horses, but not her moodiness. I think he'll do well once he knows his job."

"How long before you began looking?"

"Not as long as you might think," she said. "Sheba and I had been on that course three, maybe four times before, and she always flew around it without blinking an eye. On the day I lost her, it was like she had never seen a jump, much less that course, before." She wiped away a stray tear. "This may sound harsh, but something was brewing inside that mare, something really wrong, and I'd rather she go the way she did than have it happen here and have David see the whole thing. He had a hard enough time with the aftermath of the fall as it was. He insisted on helping to bury her like it was his responsibility, and continued to put food in her stall for a week afterward."

Pascoe looked out the window. Banker must have cooled off and been taken back to a stall, because David had resumed hauling another load of manure out of the barn. He reminded Pascoe of a wayward broom conjured by Mickey in *The Sorcerer's Apprentice*, single-minded and indefatigable.

"How are things with David?" he asked. "Any progress?"

"Sometimes I think so. He's been asking about riding lately and the other day he came in and told me one of the horses looked off, sounding just as lucid as he used to. But when we went to the barn, he couldn't remember which horse it was. His doctors say a short circuit in his brain might dredge up a memory, or it may be signs of repair, they can't say for sure. On a brighter note, he has moved into a place of his own."

"Really," Pascoe said. "I wouldn't have thought he was able. Sorry, that's rude."

Hunter waved him off. "No, it's not. I'm surprised too. Anyway, it sounds like a bigger step than it is. The Donaldson's have an outbuilding they renovated into an apartment, and they're only three miles down the road. David used to train horses for their daughter, Megan, and though he doesn't remember, they do, and wanted to help. He cleans a few stalls, feeds, and turns out the horses for them in exchange for rent. He rides his bike here and earns spending money. He's almost never unsupervised, but you should see how proud he is."

"Well then, here's to David," said Pascoe, raising his glass. Hunter grinned and clinked her glass to his.

"You know Doc, with David in his own place I have some time of my own now."

"Have you ever, ever, been accused of being subtle?"

"No. Have you ever been accused of being thick? I've made puppy eyes at you since you started working for King. In case you haven't noticed, you've been getting called out to do most of my work, and King's been the vet for my family since we had our first pony. My horses, my dogs, and my brother all like you, and they're exceptional judges of character. You're not bad to look at and you're straight, a combination hard to come by in this business. As far as I've been able to find out, you have no local love and you're not pining over a long distance romance. Unless, of course, there was more to your lunch date than it appeared?"

"Just business I'm afraid."

Hunter waited for further explanation, but when Pascoe remained silent, continued. "Good, I would find you much less attractive if she was your type. All I'm saying is, if you're looking for someone to spend some time with, I'm available. If you're not, say so, but goddamn it, say something."

"Are you done?" Pascoe said. Hunter nodded. Pascoe rubbed his chin and pretended to weigh his options.

"Hum the 'Jeopardy' theme and I kick your ass," Hunter said.

"Okay, okay, I'm thick. But I'm not a fool."

Hunter, pleased, said nothing for some time. She leaned back in her chair, crossed her legs, and bounced her foot up and down. "Well?"

"Well what?"

"Well, aren't you going to ask me out?"

Pascoe laughed. "You mean you haven't already made reservations somewhere?"

"Doc, don't you think I've worked hard enough?"

They settled for Saturday evening. Pascoe rounded up a muddy and reluctant Barclay and drove back to the clinic. Maggie shoved a sheaf of papers in his face as soon as he walked in the door. "These were faxed over."

Pascoe scanned the top sheet; Goldrush's results were back. "Thanks," he said. Maggie, still angry about the schedule change, hadn't met his eye yet. "Is King around?"

"Stonemason. Oliver's worried about his mares. Wanted King to check them over in case that horse you worked on had something contagious."

Pascoe sat down at his desk and sifted through the fax. The blood showed no abnormalities, either in serum chemistry or blood counts. The West Nile Virus titer was also normal, but the results did rule out overwhelming bacterial infection, organ failure and one disease as the cause of death. He flipped to the report on the spinal fluid.

Again, the tests yielded little, but in doing so shortened the list of possibilities. Titers for both rhinopneumonitis and encephalitis were negative, as was the PCR—a test for the genetic fingerprints of *Sarcocystis neurona*, the agent of Equine Protozoal Myelitis. No growth from bacterial cultures. Pascoe tried histopathology. Nothing. Every tissue was normal under the microscope. The last page stated that tests for botulism were still pending. Frustrated, he called the lab.

"Histopath." Lee Bridges, head of the Pathology Department at Eastern Labs, answered the phone.

"Lee, it's Jordan Pascoe."

"Looks like you've been busy slicing and dicing lately."

"Unfortunately. Any gut feelings? I've got nothing to work with here."

"I sends what I sees. As far as I can tell, the Lord God Almighty smote your horse."

"The insurance company would prefer a better explanation."

"Pagans."

"What about botulism?"

"Just waiting for the mice to die."

"What?"

Bridges sighed. "What did you do, sleep through Bacteriology?"

"Er..."

"Never mind, that's what I'm here for. The botulinum toxin is notoriously difficult to detect because even miniscule quantities can kill. So we distill the stomach contents of potential victims and inject it into a group of mice. If they develop botulism, bingo. But it's a primitive method, so even if the mice live, it doesn't mean conclusively that botulism wasn't the cause of death. Considering the case history, if the other tests rule out everything else botulism poisoning is as good a diagnosis as any."

"Yeah, King sure thinks so."

"But you're not sure. Ah, the recent graduate. I remember those days, when I thought there was an answer to everything. Look, plenty of freezer space here; I'll hang on to the samples. Let me know if you think of another test."

"Thanks. I promise to let it go before the holidays."

Harkin entered the office as Pascoe was hanging up. "Let me tell you something," he said, blowing on his hands, "it is too cold out there for a man my age to be working. Every joint in my body is seizing up."

"Everyone all right at Stonemason?" Pascoe asked.

"Healthy as a horse," Harkin said, laughing. "Oliver can't take his eyes off his mares, I think he expects them all to abort or drop over dead any second. Hell, I could tell they were fine by their expressions, but I had to go through the whole group, one by one, to make him happy."

"Devon's?"

Harkin rolled his eyes. "Yours is the only opinion she cares about."

"I'll run over later. The first reports were faxed over today, I'm sure she'll want to know."

"Do they help any?"

Pascoe shook his head. "Not a bit. Bridges has narrowed it down to providence and botulism."

"Well, you've done what you could. Might want to get those forms sent in so Oliver can get his check, he wants to get the girl another horse."

"I suppose I should. The horse is dead, whichever way the tests go. I'll get on it."

"Good man. One thing I've learned, people who want their money soonest are the ones who need it least."

Pascoe made it to Stonemason at dusk. Devon was in the arena on Camden, the hunter on which she won last year's High Point award. Gerald had her cantering through a gymnastics course, six one-stride rail fences running the long side of the arena. Devon and Camden negotiated the line flawlessly twice, but on the third try bumped the top rail of the fifth fence, faltered, and plowed through the last.

"You lost contact," Gerald said. "Pay attention. Run through it again."

Devon waved at Pascoe. "She's tired Gerald," she said. "The sun will be gone in a few minutes anyway, why don't we stop?"

"Because Goldrush is gone, you leave for Florida in two months, and Camden is the only horse talented enough to change disciplines and still be competitive. Your father expects better this year."

"We'll be ready," Devon said, turning her horse. "See you tomorrow."

Pascoe waited at the end of the arena. He held Camden's reins while Devon hopped off. "What was all that about?" he asked. Behind them, Gerald fumed.

"Dad. Thought Goldrush should have won everything last year, considering what he paid." She took the reins back and walked away from the barn. "I need to cool her out, want to come?"

"Sure. You're not cold?" Devon was covered only in britches and a cotton sweater.

"Warm from the lesson."

"So what about you?" Pascoe asked.

"What?"

"How do you feel about last year?"

"With Goldrush? I got beat, what can I say? There were better horses. Goldie was a blast to ride, but he was cautious, and we had time faults more often than not. Dad cares more about that stuff than I do, and he doesn't understand that some horses take a little longer to get it than others. And Gerald understands, but worries Dad will fire him if we don't clean up this season."

"Will he?"

"No. I like Gerald. He might get a little whiny sometimes, but my riding has really improved from his lessons. Dad will listen to me." The wind picked up and Devon shivered. Pascoe gave his coat to her. The sleeves hung past her hands, so he took hold of Camden again. "Thanks. Wasn't expecting you today, what's up?"

"Labs came in. Nothing yet, but not all the tests are done. There's a chance Goldrush died of botulism, which might mean contaminated feed or water. The others should be watched carefully, just in case. King told me he was by today, to look over your father's horses. Has the impression you didn't want him to look at yours."

Devon stared at the ground. "I know what you're going to say, 'King's a great vet'. Dad says that all the time too, he can't understand why I use you—thinks you're too young—but I keep telling him how good you are with the horses and how you keep up with the latest treatments. It's not that I don't like King. I just like you better." Devon turned back toward the stables, which was fine, Pascoe felt the loss of his coat. "How old are you anyway?"

"Twenty-seven."

"See, we're only twelve years apart, not all that much, really." Devon glanced sideways at Pascoe. "I bet your girlfriend is a couple of years younger than you are."

Pascoe didn't like this direction. Not knowing how to answer the question, he avoided it. "We should pick up the pace, it's getting colder and Camden should get into a blanket."

"Do you think I'm pretty, Jordan?"

Pascoe stopped the horse and turned to face Devon. The oversized coat made her look tiny and helpless, and she wore expectancy on her face as if bracing for a blow. He squatted and clasped her hands through the coatsleeves. "You are beautiful. Beautiful in the way you look, beautiful in the way you act."

Devon pulled her hands from Pascoe's grip and turned her back on him. "But?"

"But I'm too old for you, and you know it."

"Says who?"

"The law, for one. And I'm sure Oliver would have a few thoughts on it. And, of course, there's me."

"It's not fair."

"Sure it is, it keeps you from skipping the fun part of your life and hooking up with an old, decidedly un-fun guy like me. Come on, lets get Camden in her stall, I'm freezing."

Devon sulked. She still wasn't speaking to him when they got back to the barn, so Pascoe slipped away and checked the other horses. No signs of illness, only annoyance at having dinner interrupted. When he finished with the last horse, he went back to check Camden. She stood alone in the crossties; his coat hung nearby on a bit-hook. Pascoe examined the horse, and, finding her healthy, put on a winter blanket and led her into a stall.

Pascoe rented a guesthouse on property outside of Delaplane. Close friends of Harkin owned the main house. The Lowells traveled extensively, which meant Pascoe ran into them about twice a year. Because his presence provided security to the estate, rent was only three hundred a month. Some days, especially in winter, he thought he was overpaying.

Visitors told him the house had 'character', which translated to mean he needed an awfully strong one to live in it. The cabin was nothing more than log rectangle with an inside corner awkwardly framed out to form a bathroom that jutted into the living room, marring its symmetry. Exposed beams on the ceiling were scarred from past termite infections and fires. Breezes wove around window casings and fluttered heavy curtains that were always closed in winter as a makeshift barrier to the wind. This time of year he wore a coat inside until he could light a fire in the woodstove that sat in the corner opposite the bathroom. A pine floor, aged to the color of clover honey, was gouged and gapped but gave the home sturdiness and beauty, especially on still nights when flames from the stove danced on its surface.

At the east end of the cabin, a plastic deep sink, tilting factory cabinets,

Barn Politics

a humming refrigerator, and an electric stove with two functioning burners masqueraded as a kitchen. Pascoe had added a microwave and a toaster, as well as a vinyl topped card table with four folding chairs.

He also contributed a sleeper-sofa to the living room, and folded it up if guests were expected. His stereo from college, with its overly large speakers, was set on milk-crate-and-board shelving against the wall next to the sofa. At its other end was a night table that was dragged around when the bed was folded away and pulled duty as a coffee table. Against the opposite wall was a large screen TV, a purchase made when he first started betting with Carlyle and was flush with cash. There was a great deal of open space around this sparse collection of furniture, but Pascoe enjoyed the quiet it provided at the end of the day, and its small size allowed him to straighten up before Wallace's arrival.

Pascoe called her office earlier and left directions on voice mail. "Left at the general store, it's the only building at the intersection and says 'post office' in the window. As you near the top of the hill, take a left, if you come to a mailbox with a picture of a rooster on it, you've gone to far. My place is the first right after a big pond, the driveway makes a 'y', stay to the right, it's the small log cabin next to the dock at the pond." After considering how dark it might be when she showed up, Pascoe also left the street address, Mapquest could fill in the street names.

Pascoe was folding a pizza box into fourths when Barclay ambled into the kitchen and sat in front of the door, head cocked expectantly. Before long, Tires crunched in the driveway, followed by the thunk of a car door. Barclay went up on all fours, wagging his tail in anticipation. When the knock came, Pascoe looked back at the dog. "No jumping. Easy." The admonishment intensified Barclay's excitement, now his entire hind end was wagging. Pascoe held the dog's collar when he opened the door, but to his surprise Barclay gave a cursory sniff to Wallace's shoes and headed back to lie in his bed by the woodstove.

Wallace was dressed casually. Under a fleece-lined leather jacket she was wearing jeans topped with a William and Mary sweatshirt and had applied only traces of eye shadow and lip-gloss to her face. One hand held a bulging accordion file, the other a bottle of wine.

"I brought the closest thing to an apology you're likely to get. Hope you like red," she said, handing him the bottle. She surveyed the cabin. "Perhaps beer would have been more appropriate."

"It screams Budweiser, but has box-wine sensibilities." Pascoe took the bottle. "That's the closest thing to accepting the apology you're likely to get."

"Smart man. Where should we set up?"

Pascoe motioned to the living room. With the couch folded, a great expanse of floor opened up. "That will give us the most room to spread out. I'll get some glasses and open the wine while you get organized."

When he returned, Wallace was on the floor with her legs splayed open, four manila folders placed between them. Her coat hung over the couch's armrest. The accordion file lay outside of her legs, half full. He poured the wine while she dealt sheets of photocopied papers onto the folders.

"The company has no idea you're doing this," Pascoe said.

A sheet fluttered in her hand for a moment before she dropped it onto one of the piles, then snatched it away to move it one pile to the left. "What makes you say that?"

Pascoe handed her a glass of wine and pointed to the folders. "You've got copies instead of originals, are building the case files from scratch, and the papers are all mixed up instead of being grouped by case. Looks to me like you've been copying sheets from the master file one at a time, which means sneaking around."

"So?" Wallace gulped down half of her wine.

"You told me the company doesn't want to involve the police for public relations reasons, but that can't be true. They don't know about this. Start being straight with me Ruth, or you can find somebody else to blackmail. I'll take my chances with the Board."

Wallace downed the rest of her wine and held up her glass for a refill. While Pascoe poured, she asked, "Do you know how insurance companies work?"

Pascoe put down the bottle, sat on the couch, and picked up the glass he had poured for himself. "Sure, people pay a premium and if something goes wrong, you guys pay. You bet most owners will pay more in premiums before their horse dies or rings up huge vet bills."

"Right, we play the odds, and try to stack them in our favor. We insure horses all over the country, and most of our clients are upper income horse owners. They might insure ten, twelve horses with us at a time, all for six figure payouts. You know how news travels in the horse business. If we start making a fuss over claims, delaying payments, we get the reputation of being difficult and people move on. Our policy is to make as few waves as possible, prevent horse owners from getting pissed off, and keep premiums flowing. Sure, if a horse gets its throat slit, or a vet tips us to something shady, we look into it, but it's win-win for the company."

"And this is good business?" Pascoe asked.

"If you knew wine, you'd know the answer. '99 was a great year for Cab, and they don't come easy or cheap, and this particular bottle, as you can see, retains its complex palate in Wal-Mart glasses."

"I upgraded to Target last year," Pascoe said. To him, the wine tasted like every other red he had tried. "I understand the company keeping quiet, but it still doesn't explain your secrecy."

"Call it calculation. I know these cases by heart. Every one of them doubled their insurance shortly before the horse died. My gut tells me something ties them together. If I'm wrong, nobody—not the owners, not the company—knows, and we go our separate ways. If I'm right, and we expose a fraud which has cost the company close to a million dollars, my initiative puts me on the fast track for management."

"Making me what? A key to a bigger office?"

"Call it what you want. I need your help and I've got it, the how and whys don't matter." She went back to sorting papers. After a few minutes the accordion file was empty and she got up and sat next to him. She handed him her glass for another refill. "There you are. Clockwise from the top left: Dearborne, Sinclair, Rasmussen, Dowry. Dearborne was the first horse, Dowry the last. Take a look and tell me what you think."

He took her place on the floor and picked up the first file. It was the thinnest of the four, containing only the standard two-sided mortality claim form provided by Virginia Bloodstock. No post mortem report had been attached, and in the short space under the heading Cause of Death, the veterinarian had written *seizures, possible stroke or tumor*. The horse had been eight years old at the time of death. Pascoe glanced at the signature at the bottom of the form. Steve Randolph, DVM. *Thanks a lot Steve, you've given me a lot to work with*. He grabbed the next folder.

Harkin attended the Sinclair horse, and this file was more complete. The horse, Systematic, had been a three year-old racehorse on sabbatical when found dead in the pasture. Grooves in the ground by his feet indicated a drawn out struggle had taken place. A full post on the horse turned up nothing. A diagnosis of botulism was based on a dead rat discovered in the bale of hay the Sinclairs had recently started feeding.

The claim on the third horse read like it had been plagiarized from Pascoe's folder, though it was submitted six months before. The vet, Morgan Stokes, arrived shortly after the horse was found dead. Her necropsy report was slick and professional. Stokes snapped pictures of the procedure with a digital camera and included them along with the written report but her conclusion, ambiguous as Randolph's, was that the horse died of heart failure. Pascoe flipped through the file and cursed; because the tissues were normal in appearance no samples had been sent to a lab.

He dropped the paperwork to the floor. Four cases, and even the most in depth exam could claim no more of a diagnosis than the most cursory. He was being asked to make connections when there was no evidence the horses had even died of the same cause. He felt Wallace's hand drop onto his shoulder.

"What do you think?" she asked.

Pascoe shrugged her off and stood to face her. "You've got to be kidding. There's nothing here, Ruth. Nothing. Similarities, but nothing suspicious. I don't understand why you think I can do better."

She patted the couch cushion next to her and pursed her lips when Pascoe remained standing. "I've studied these files Jordan. I didn't expect you to divine a conspiracy after a quick scan, but you need to be familiar with the cases before we move on to the next step."

"And what's that?"

"Interviews." Wallace talked over his protest. "Obviously I can't do them myself, everybody knows I work for VBI." Wallace's wine glass squeaked like a squeegee as she ran her finger around its rim. She regarded it disapprovingly. "You just lost a patient and you don't know what it died from. You've heard about these other cases through the grapevine and are concerned that a new disease might be circulating in the area. You want to find out if these owners have information that can lead to a diagnosis. All of which is true, so you won't really be lying. More like research."

"Have you thought about how the other veterinarians are going to feel? One of them is my boss, in case you forgot, and won't be thrilled if he thinks I'm second-guessing him. Our competitors will be even more put out."

"Then don't tell them. If the owner's ask, tell them you don't want their vet to prejudice your opinion."

"You've thought this through."

"Yes."

Pascoe walked over to the couch and sat down. He stared at the four piles in front of him. "Okay, you're plan makes sense, but there are a few things you need to deal with. Do you know Randolph?" Wallace nodded. "Good. Get him to talk to you about this Dearborne case. His report is for shit. Go to the Jockey Club's website and find out what you can about Systematic's record. Wins, losses, whatever you can find, because if that horse was winning it makes no sense for his owners to kill him for the insurance. And I'm going to have to talk to King about that one."

"Jordan—"

Pascoe held up a finger. "Can't be avoided. If the Sinclairs tell King I stopped by, he'll be furious I went behind his back. He thinks Goldrush died of botulism, and knows I need convincing, so it makes sense to compare the two cases."

Wallace chewed the inside of her cheek. "Fine. Anything else?"

"Tell me about the policies. All the horses had increased coverage?"

"Doubled. Dearborne went from one-twenty-five to two-hundred-fifty thousand. So did Sinclair. Rasmussen went from seventy-five to one hundred even, and Dowry went from two hundred to half a million."

"How soon after this did the horses die?"

"Dearborne and Sinclair changed their policies a month before. Red flags went up, but when the vet reports came in, there was no suspicion of fraud and—"

"The company didn't want to make waves."

"Exactly. The Rasmussen horse had been insured for seventy-five by its previous owner and she upped it to an even hundred shortly after she got it. I think the horse died a few months later. Dowry changed his policy almost a year before the horse died. I remember seeing the date on the policy when

the claim came in. It was going to expire in a couple of weeks."
"And if it had?"
"The horse wouldn't have been insured. But I'm sure Dowry would have renewed the policy; he always has in the past. All that's needed is a vet exam stating the horse isn't about to drop dead, enclose a check for part of the premium, and the horse would be completely covered."
"How do you know if the horses are as valuable as the owners say they are? Everybody thinks their new jumper is going to be the next superstar."
"Honestly, it's pretty arbitrary. Partially depends on what someone paid for an animal, and we keep close watch on the market of course, but a horses value comes down to what someone is willing to pay for it."
"And when the value of their horse doubles?"
"I've told you the way the business works. As the value of the horse increases, so does the premium. We ask the reason for the increase: show or race records, the demand for a certain type of horse, that sort of thing. It's just a formality, really. Somebody like Dowry isn't going to be questioned."
"Think he realized that?"
"I don't know, why?"
"Just curious."
Wallace leaned back into the couch and picked invisible lint off Pascoe's shoulder. "Has a way of drawing you in, doesn't it?"
"What?"
"The hunt. I see it in your eyes. When I showed up tonight, all you did was glower and pout. But the wheels are turning now." Her fingers moved up to play with Pascoe's hair, twirling it in circles above his ear. "You might even start to enjoy our meetings."
He turned his head and disentangled her fingers. "Don't bet on it."
A smile flitted across Wallace's face. "I should get back home. Keep the files here; they might help you prepare for the interviews. When should we get together next?" She stood up and pulled on her coat.
"I'll talk to Dearborne, Sinclair, and Rasmussen this week and set something up for the weekend. Monday?"
"Fine, but let me return the hospitality. Do you have e-mail?" Pascoe gave her the address. "I'll send directions." As she was walking to the kitchen, Wallace spied the folded pizza box crammed into the kitchen trashcan. "Don't worry about dinner, I'll fix something."
Barclay didn't bother to move as Wallace left. Pascoe managed a polite wave from the threshold. He tried to appear disinterested, but Wallace was right. There was something wrong about the files, like a faint whiff of rot. Something was buried nearby.

CHAPTER FOUR

Harkin was not at the office in the morning.

"Boss under the weather?" Despite his age, Harkin was always at the office earlier and seeing patients later than any other vet in the county.

"Give him a break," Maggie said. Her eyes were red and brimmed with tears. "He's getting older you know, and he was on call last night. It might do you good to work as hard."

"Didn't mean anything by it. I just need to talk." Pascoe walked around the desk and put a hand to Maggie's shoulder. "Are you all right?"

Maggie sniffed. "Sorry. Protective, that's all." She wiped her eyes and nodded at the door. "Speak of the devil."

The devil was a little worn out. Harkin shuffled in without glancing at either Pascoe or Maggie. Rumpled coveralls were stained with blood and manure. He fell into his chair with a groan.

"King, got a second?"

The old man shot Pascoe a tired smile and motioned to Maggie. "My nanny already lectured me over the phone. Am I about to get one from my physician as well?"

Pascoe sat on the edge of Harkin's desk. "Nothing like that. I need to ask you about a case."

"Shoot." Harkin leaned back and put his feet up on the desk. The soles of his boots were caked with mud.

"Systematic. Owned by people named Sinclair."

Harkin wrinkled his nose. "Not ringing a bell."

"You did a post on it. Word is you thought it was botulism. Is this a different case than the one you told me about the other day? The one with the squirrel in the water trough?"

Harkin closed his eyes. Pascoe began to think the old man had drifted off. Then his eyes snapped open. "I had forgotten about that one. Where did you hear about it?"

Pascoe fumbled for a few seconds. "Ah, from Hunter. I was telling her about Goldrush and how you thought it was botulism and she brought it up. You must have mentioned it to her."

"Hmmm. Not much to tell. Those folks aren't even our clients. Couldn't get hold of their regular vet and called me out to do the exam. Last time I ever saw them."

"What do you remember?"

Harkin closed his eyes again. "The horse had been dead a while before I got there, twelve hours at least, and it was warm. Buzzards had already been at the carcass. I remember the stink more than anything, took days to get out of my skin. The samples I sent to the lab were half rotted and useless for culture, but even so, I hoped there might be enough cells left to look at under the microscope. Botulism was the last thing I was thinking of and if I hadn't gone to the barn to clean up, I doubt it would have entered my mind.

"There was a deep sink directly under the hay loft, and while I was washing I realized something in the barn smelled worse than me. I climbed up and found a bale with maybe a flake or two missing and smelling like a knacker truck. Tore it apart and found a rat baled up right in the middle of it. Somehow, the Sinclairs never noticed the smell and had started feeding the bale the day before. Why are you interested?"

"I thought I might talk to them, see if there are any similarities with Goldrush."

"You can try, but I don't think you'll get anywhere. They told me the horse was fine one day, dead the next."

"I'm having a tough time not knowing about Goldrush."

"Stay at this job as long as I have," King said, settling into his chair and yawning, "and you'll get over that."

Pascoe spent the next couple of evenings trying to set up appointments with Dearborne, Sinclair, and Rasmussen. Nobody was keen to open the door for a stranger. He found if he dropped Harkin's name, or mentioned it was Oliver Dowry's horse that had died, doors opened wider and more quickly. By the end of the week, meetings were scheduled with all three for Saturday.

Matthew Dearborne was first in line. His farm, Three Sisters, had been named after three fillies from the first crop sired by Dearborne's stud, Montpelier. Their success in a couple of Grade I Stakes skyrocketed Montpelier's stud fee to six figures a pop. Breed ninety mares a season and it starts to add up.

New money meant saplings along the driveway and unwarped boards on the fences. Cultured fieldstone hid masonry foundations and vinyl siding wrapped buildings; Three Sisters was an attractive, if soulless, facsimile of its neighbors, absent the stain of slave blood and musket fire pockmarks.

A somber, balding attendant met Pascoe at the door, led him through a high-ceilinged foyer to a small office and instructed him to wait. Cheaply framed photos of the sort handed to winning owners at the track hung on the walls. These pictures were divided into tiers: the top held a photo of the finish; the middle, printed information about the horse, trainer, jockey, owner, and the race's length and purse; and on the bottom, the winners circle: horse, jockey, and owner center stage surrounded by various officials and hangers-on. Pascoe had been in more than a few as a boy.

A lean, hard man, possessive hand on each winner, appeared in all. Sandy hair divided severely down the center of the skull was touched with gray at the temples. A sharply hooked, narrow nose further divided the face between deep and shadowed eye sockets. Thin lips hovered above an equally steadfast jaw. Behind Pascoe, the hard man from the photos entered. He was a full half-foot taller than Pascoe's six, and crossed the small room in two purposeful strides. He stuck out a hand attached to a corded forearm.

"Matthew Dearborne."

"Jordan Pascoe." The offered hand felt as unbending as the man looked.

Dearborne motioned to a leather bench against the wall with the pictures before folding into a chair behind a mission-style desk. Pascoe pulled a small spiral-bound notebook and pen from his back pocket. Dearborne studied with pale gray eyes.

"Not sure why you want to talk to me Doctor Pascoe," Dearborne said. "I know an awful lot about the outside of horses, but little about the inside. You might have better luck talking to Doctor Randolph." He pulled a pack of cigarettes from his desk drawer and showed them to Pascoe. "Mind?"

Pascoe waved away his concern. "Exactly why I do want to talk to you, Mr. Dearborne. As veterinarians we observe, we quantify, we label. If I need temperatures, heart rates, blood values, I'll call a vet. But you see these horses daily and might pick up on something subtle. A behavioral or personality change for example. Sometimes small details turn out to be the most important."

"This horse, Gizmo, was truly my wife's, but I can tell you what I saw."

"I could talk to your wife as well."

Dearborne shifted uncomfortably in his chair and lit the cigarette. "You're welcome to, if you can find her," he said. "Shortly after Gizmo died, Linda took off. I suspect she was screwing someone on the side and used the death as a convenient excuse. I came back from a weekend in Lexington and she had cleared out. No note, no forwarding addresses. If you find her, I've got a Visa bill you can give her."

"I'm sorry."

Dearborne ran his hand through his hair. Bits of ash fell onto his scalp and were quickly brushed away. "Don't mind my bitching, you came here about Giz. One of our better prospects, black type a mile long. Built like a brick shithouse, but couldn't run a lick. So slow I never entered him in a race; instead I had his balls cut off and gave him to Linda."

"I hope the other stallions took notice," Pascoe said.

Dearborne coughed a laugh. "Maybe I should have hung those nuts from a tree as a warning. Anyway, Linda found Gizmo's true calling. Put a jump in front of him and he was a different horse. Excited to work, good form, effortless, even over big stuff. People offered more for that horse than he could have ever earned at the track, but Linda claimed him for her own, and they won everything."

Dearborne took a long drag, pulled the ash to the filter and ground it into the ashtray on his desk. He turned to the side and blew out a long column of smoke. "Never had any problems with Giz, no lameness, no colic. Hell, I don't remember him having a snotty nose. I would swear on my father's soul not a hair was out of place. Around midnight there was a commotion in the barn. Banging so loud you could feel it in your chest, know what I mean?"

Pascoe nodded. When a horse put its weight into a kick, it could knock down a wall at one end of the barn and rattle teeth at the other.

"When I got there, Giz was thrashing and flopping on the ground and tearing the stall to pieces. He had broken through the wall in two places. Linda screamed at me to do something." He tapped another cigarette into his hand and lit it, cupping his hand around the match even though they were indoors. "I called Doc Randolph and waited. By the time he showed up, the worst was over. Giz stood quietly, though he wobbled like a newborn foal. When I went in to put a halter on him for the Doc, I swear he didn't recognize me. His eyes darted back and forth and he spooked at the softest noises. Randolph called it a seizure. Gave him some tranquilizers, I think, and maybe some steroids. By the time the doc left, Giz seemed a lot better, though he was never really all there in the eye.

"Linda and I stayed for another hour or so. Gizmo was the same as when Randolph left, so we figured it was safe to try and get some sleep. In the morning we found him in the stall, stone cold dead. Randolph said another seizure had killed him and there wasn't anything we could have done. Linda didn't want the body lying around, so I had the renderer come right away."

Pascoe scribbled notes for a few moments after Dearborne stopped. "Up until the time you found Gizmo thrashing, everything was normal?"

"Perfectly. Giz took a dump in the same spot every day and even that didn't change. He ate breakfast, he ate lunch, he ate dinner, and he played in the pasture just like he did every other day. My horses are valuable enough that I call the vet if they look at me sideways."

"Randolph didn't want to see the body?"

"Said it was unnecessary. That there was only a slim change we'd find out the cause."

"None of your other horses were affected?"

Dearborne wrapped his knuckles on the desk. "Thank God, no."

Pascoe closed the notebook and put it back into his pocket. "Thanks Mr. Dearborne. You're right, none of this looks like it will help, but I appreciate the time."

Dearborne, halfway through his cigarette, stubbed it out and walked to the door to open it. "Don't mention it. I hope you find the answers you're looking for. Can you find your way out?"

If Dearborne was little help, the Sinclairs were less so. An identical egg-shaped couple that raced horses and kept cattle for tax purposes, the Sinclairs allowed gangly thoroughbreds and stocky, horned Herefords to graze side-by-side. Pascoe cringed, imagining the horrific disemboweling accidents possible with such a coupling. Then he met Persephone and Bryce Sinclair, and realized their husbandry skills ended at feeding, watering, and sheltering their charges.

He spent an hour attempting to get the couple to agree to the simplest questions. Bryce would no sooner say Systematic had been acting normally when Percy, as she insisted on being called, would interrupt to say the horse had rolled on the ground the previous day, she had seen it herself. At one point they argued for ten minutes over who had fed the horse on the night of its death. It turned out they both had, but not told the other. They were able to agree on two points: Systematic had been alive when they went to bed, and dead when they woke up. All of the back and forth chatter was giving him a headache. He concluded the interview as quickly and politely as possible and left to meet with Rasmussen.

Pascoe passed the driveway twice before noticing the weathered plank with the name "Samfield" he had been told to look for. It hung crookedly on unequal lengths of chain from a dented mailbox and blended in with the dead brambles behind it. He would have driven by a third time if a gust of wind had not caused it to swing and catch his eye.

Samfield's driveway divided weedy pastures barely contained by mismatched fences: fragments of wood, varying from two to four boards, all in need of paint, alternated with strands of drooping hot wire. Where horse-size gaps occurred, lengths of barbed wire were strung across, loose ends wrapped around posts. There weren't any horses, but a large, spotted goat enjoyed a patch of buttercup on Pascoe's near side.

The house was worn, but better kept than the fields. Old yellow paint, faded almost to white, peeled from clapboard siding. A covered porch sagged and forced Pascoe to duck, but was swept clean. Two pairs of muddy boots, one slightly smaller than the other, stood in a neat line next to the door. The screen door, frayed and punched with holes larger than a the bodies of small game birds, surprised him by not squeaking open.

Thunderous barking announced and was followed by jamb-rattling impact that blew hair back from his forehead. Nails scrambled on the other side at shoulder-height. Pascoe cautiously stepped back.

"Down! Down!" a woman's voice shouted. "Calm down Deadbolt!"

The porch trembled when the dog thumped to all fours. The door opened and revealed a slight woman gripping the collar of a dog that outweighed her by fifty pounds. It stood higher than her hip and its head was larger than a watermelon. Floppy ears and a long, wide nose hinted at Bloodhound lineage, but its powerful neck was ruffed with folds of skin and its mass was more reminiscent of Mastiff. Pascoe wondered, while remaining immobile, if he was about to be eaten by a purebred or a mutt.

"Can I help you?" the handler said. She made no effort to remove the dog.

"Doctor Pascoe. I called a few days ago?"

"Right. About the horse. Hold on," she said turning to the dog. "Deadbolt! Sit!" The dog obeyed immediately. The woman reached out and touched Pascoe's shoulder. "Friend!" she exclaimed with a wide smile. Turning back to Pascoe she said, "Squat down to his level." Pascoe obeyed as quickly as the dog. "I didn't catch your first name."

"Jordan."

"Deadbolt! Jordan!" Then, with less enthusiasm, "Jordan, this is Deadbolt."

"Nice to meet you." He hoped he sounded sincere.

Introductions over, Deadbolt, hackles flat but no less intimidating, collected Pascoe's inventory of smells, starting with his boots.

"I'm Gail, by the way," the woman said, "Rasmussen. Sorry about all that, but until introductions are made, it's unlikely he would have let you past the door."

"Then he comes by his name honestly." Pascoe, still on his haunches, looked up at Rasmussen. "Am I allowed to stand up now?"

Rasmussen's laugh was easy and sincere. "It might make it easier to get around. Deadbolt! Kennel!"

Pascoe was treated to a final snuffle behind the ear before Deadbolt ambled off in a rolling walk to lie in a nest of blankets in the adjacent room. "Impressive dog," Pascoe said. "I don't suppose you need a 'No Soliciting' sign. Where did you find him?"

"He was a gift," Rasmussen said, "from someone who thought he might come in handy. Have you seen one before?"

"Never."

"He's a Fila. Think of him as a Brazilian mastiff. You won't come across them too often in this country. Wonderful dogs, but very suspicious of strangers. He actually took to you pretty quickly. When it comes to people, I trust his judgment more than my own."

"I'll take it as a compliment."

"You should. If he had read you differently you'd be out on your ass. Have a seat in the kitchen. I just made some coffee, care for a cup?"

"Absolutely. Black." Pascoe followed her into the kitchen and sat down.

The room was small, but well used. Jars of spices and vinegars lined the counters. Braids of garlic hung from a curtain rod above a large window, filling the room with their pungent aroma. A circular rack suspended from the ceiling was hung with saucepans, frying pans, and pots of various sizes. He sat at a table made of straight-grained maple that, if the grooves at one corner were any indication, had served as a cutting board for multiple generations. The chairs were less substantial; aluminum framed with water-stained psychedelic green vinyl seats and backs. Short legs met the floor unevenly and forced him to steady against the table.

"Sorry," Rasmussen said, toeing the floor. "Got a bit of a foundation problem."

She came to the table holding two mismatched cups of steaming coffee and handed him the larger. Pascoe found it hard to affix an age to Rasmussen. She was of average height and had an unlined face. She wore a baggy, cable-knit sweater that hung to her knees and heavy, oversized rag-wool socks pooled at her ankles—she looked like an adolescent wearing her jock boyfriend's clothes.

Her eyes however, were aged. They were the color of sun-bleached cedar flecked with moss and regarded Pascoe over her coffee cup, searching for something Deadbolt might have missed. Seeing nothing, or perhaps everything, she closed her eyes and pressed the heel of her hand to the bridge of her nose. After a few moments of silence, she rearranged her hands around her cup and looked at Pascoe again. Her gaze was less probing, but still focused.

"Doctor Pascoe, am I right in understanding you work for King Harkin?"

"That's correct. Do you know him?"

Rasmussen snorted. "Is there anyone in the county that doesn't? When my daughter was still riding, Doctor Harkin gave her pony club some lectures on horse care. He was very kind. I assume he wouldn't hire just anyone to work for him. How long have you been a vet?"

"Just over two years. Does that matter?"

"I doubt it," she said. "Does your boss know you're here?"

"Not exactly. He knows I'm frustrated by the case I told you about, and that I'm trying to round up some similar cases to see if I can make sense out of it all. I realize I may have implied that King has more to do with this than he does, but his reputation helps get my foot in the door."

"I understand," Rasmussen said.

Pascoe couldn't tell if the smile on her lips came from his unexpected truthfulness or the brashness of his white lie. Either way, it was an inroad, so he pressed on.

"Great," Pascoe said. "Your horse, um..."

"Lexus."

"Lexus. Only six when she died?"

Rasmussen nodded. "Quite a shock. You know in your heart anything can happen, but you're never prepared when it does. It might have been easier if it was something you expect, like a twisted gut."

"What did happen?"

"We went out to feed one morning and found her dead in the stall."

"That's it?"

"Fraid so. No signs of struggle, no wounds, nothing."

"Any ideas, suspicions?"

"None. Lexus had been kicking her heels up in the pasture the day before and whinnied for hay when I did night check. In the morning I called the insurance company and they said to get a vet to look her over. We did, and the best she could come up with was a heart attack."

"And the insurance company was okay with that?"

"We had a check within the week."

"A lot of good it's done us. Look at this dump," came a voice from the doorway.

Pascoe jumped, Deadbolt hadn't warned of anyone's approach. A teenage girl stood in the doorway. Despite the coolness of the house, she wore a pair of tight gym shorts and a half-shirt that exposed a tight belly with a stud piercing. She had similar features as Rasmussen, but while the older woman wore no makeup, the girl had large brushstrokes of rouge on her cheeks, glistening cherry lips and thick, clumping lashes. She was heavy with the scent of honeysuckle.

Rasmussen sighed. "Doctor Pascoe, my daughter Samantha. Sam, honey, why don't you go back upstairs?"

"Why? Lexus was my horse." Sam walked over and sat on the table facing Pascoe. He dared not look anywhere but the girl's face. "Don't you think Doc, if it was my horse, I should decide what to do with the money?"

"Sam!" Rasmussen said in the same tone used with Deadbolt. "Lexus was a gift, and if the money is going to be used for anything, it will be to buy a new horse. If you don't feel like riding right now, fine, but you may change your mind yet."

Sam, back to her mother, rolled her eyes at Pascoe. "Whatever," she said and hopped down. Pascoe couldn't help watching her walk away. The rattle of Rasmussen's coffee cup on the table spun him back.

"Sorry about that," she said, holding steepled hands in front of a flushed face. "The teenage years have been tough."

Pascoe sipped his coffee. "Lexus was a gift?"

"From an old boyfriend. Sam grew out of her pony and he wanted her to have a competitive mount. I never could have afforded one." Rasmussen frowned at the room. "You can see the farm needs fixing up. I know Sam is embarrassed by the place; she never brings her Foxfield friends over anymore and since Lexus died, she's shown no interest in getting another horse. I keep hoping she'll change her mind, and if she does, I want the money handy. When Lexus was around, Sam kept herself better...occupied."

Pascoe choked on his coffee. "You're daughter attends Foxfield?" It was hard to believe, tuition for the girls-only private school was more than he made in a year.

Rasmussen shrugged. "I'm willing to sacrifice certain comforts for my daughter."

"I'm sure she'll appreciate it when she's older." Pascoe emptied his cup and pushed away from the table. "Thanks for the time, and the coffee. If I come up with a better explanation for Lexus' death I'll let you know, maybe it would help Sam deal with things better. And if she does become interested again, give me a call, I know plenty of people you could trust to give you a fair price on a good horse."

"That's sweet, thanks. Wait a minute." She patted her leg for Deadbolt to come over. "He might not like it if you leave without saying goodbye."

Pascoe wiped Fila spittle off the side of his face as he reached the end of the driveway. He could go either left or right to get back home, such was the nature of country roads. Right was the more direct route, but he turned left. He had been too busy hunting for the Samfield sign to fully realize where he was. As it turned out, three left turns away was a piece of land recently depreciated by Bimbo Carlyle's presence, and Pascoe had a debt to settle. A heretofore-unproductive day was turning around.

After the horse-swapping incident landed Pascoe on probation, Carlyle, banned from flat races, turned his attention to point-to point. Point-to-point racing requires horses to run for longer distances than flat racing, as much as three-and-a-half miles, and jump timber and brush obstacles along the course. A trainer needs plenty of space to condition a horse properly for competition, and Carlyle built a course of his own on land he rented for this purpose.

Pascoe had to admit, whatever else Carlyle was, he knew how to train for timber. The rented pastures were a mix of gradually rising slopes and steep hillocks interspersed with flat stretches, which helped train for strength as well as speed. In colonial times the land had been worked vigorously, and every spring, buckets of stones, heaved to the surface in winter, were hauled away as plows turned the soil. Now a stone wall meandered along the property line and twenty-four inches of clean topsoil was covered with a cushioning mat of fescue. Bruised hooves and bowed tendons, common to the sport, were rare on Carlyle's field.

The bookie stood on a rise near a row of dual-wheeled pickup trucks with gooseneck trailers hooked to their beds. Half a dozen men watched along with him as horses galloped and jumped in the field. All the men had their backs to Pascoe, but Carlyle's silhouette gave him away, he was a butternut squash in a field of corn.

The cornstalks wore identical calf-length oilskin coats to protect against the mizzle that had drifted in. Gray fringe poked from under wool fedoras. *Owners.* They would be friendly with Harkin and likely recognize Pascoe. He certainly didn't want any of these men overhearing his conversation. He slowed the Dodge to a crawl, turned around, and put the truck in park about fifty yards from the group. At this distance, with the diesel idling, it would be impossible for anyone to hear even the most heated argument.

None of the men turned when Pascoe arrived, but Carlyle glanced over his shoulder. Pascoe rolled down the window and motioned enthusiastically for Carlyle to come over. In doing so, a toolbox lying on the floorboards behind the seat grabbed his attention. The box contained all of the instruments he used to diagnose and treat hoof problems. An idea took shape.

Carlyle appeared confused, he didn't do much business with Pascoe other than taking bets, and that was done over the phone. Nevertheless, he exchanged a few words with the men and trotted over. At the open window, he did exactly what Pascoe planned on—he leaned on the door and rested his forearms in the opening.

Pascoe, squeezing as hard as he could, pinched the meaty part of Carlyle's hand between the jaws of his hoof testers. Basically oversized pliers, a hoof tester opens wide enough to allow placement of the bottom jaw on the sole of the hoof and the upper on the wall. Long handles provide enough leverage to compress the horny capsule of the hoof and probe for soft or tender spots, which help to locate bruises and abscesses. The human hand is much more sensitive to pressure than a horse's hoof, and the testers were crushing Carlyle's median nerve. If he applied a little more pressure, the two jaws just might be able to meet.

"Hi Bimbo," he said.

Carlyle's mouth gaped. Blood drained from his face and was replaced by sweat. A high-pitched wail rose from his throat. Pascoe clamped a bit harder and the wail either stopped or climbed above the register of the human ear. Pascoe didn't care which, a quick glance in the rearview mirror told him the cornstalks hadn't noticed.

"Listen to me," Pascoe continued. "I'm not going to let go, but I will let up, provided you agree to a nice, quiet, *frank* discussion. Understand?"

Carlyle bounced up and down on his toes. Pascoe took this for a yes and released his grip until the jaws held, but no longer crushed, the metacarpals. Carlyle pinked up and inhaled deeply.

"What the fuck?"

"Remember talking to a lady named Ruth Wallace?"

"What's this abou—" Pascoe clamped. Carlyle levitated. "I ain't shittin' you man! I don't know no Wallace! What does she look like?"

Pascoe eased up. "That should have been your first question. Blonde. Tall. Skinny. Looks like she stepped out of a Lands End Catalog. If you dined with her, you probably ate more in one mouthful than she did the entire meal."

Carlyle's mouth worked silently as he searched his memory. "Rose," he said after a few seconds. "Said her name was Rose, if it's the same gal. I met her across the river in a pub a few months ago. I thought she was some Potomac society bitch trolling for white trash. Thought if I talked her up I might get lucky." Bimbo went white again. "You ain't screwin' her or anything?"

"No. But she knows a great deal about us. I want to know how. Any ideas?"

"Look, I had a few drinks in me and was trying to get laid. Maybe I was bragging a bit, saying I know so-and-so and did such-and-such. Your name could have come up. If I had known who she was I wouldn't have said nuthin'. Who is she anyway?"

"Doesn't matter."

Pascoe released the handles. Carlyle snatched his hand back and rubbed fretfully at the welt left by the hoof testers. "That's going to leave a nasty bruise."

"Lucky it's not broken. You should know better than to go shooting off at the mouth."

Carlyle smiled, showing yellow teeth. "Poontang is my kryptonite. Tell you what, the next bet you lay down I'll double the odds. I've got the Lakers giving ten if you want it."

Pascoe bit his lip. The offer was tempting. "I'm done with everything but the ponies."

"You come all the way out here just to ask me about the chick?"

"I was in the neighborhood." Pascoe inclined his head toward the road. "Samfield."

"You get a look at the piece of ass that lives there?"

"Rasmussen? She's all right, I suppose. Tired looking, or sick, or something. Maybe if she fixed herself up—. What?"

Carlyle bent double with laughter. When he straightened he was pinching the bridge of his nose to stop his eyes from tearing. "I'm not talking about the mother, I'm talking about that sweet little Sam."

"Jailbait."

"Even so, might be worth it. You should see her walking down the road in the summer. Tits like that...yummy." Carlyle squeezed imaginary breasts in the air in front of him.

"I know a big, hairy dude who might have something to say about that."

"Boyfriend?"

"Kinda." Pascoe put the truck in gear and drove off. Carlyle attempted a wave, dropped his hand, and rubbed it some more. Pascoe watched in the mirror as Carlyle returned to the owners and brushed off their questions.

That's right Bimbo. No big deal.

Satisfied, he pulled onto the main road. He hadn't realized how much time the side trip had taken; the dashboard clock read quarter past six, which meant he was supposed to be at Hunter's in forty-five minutes and he still had to get home, feed and walk Barclay, and drive twenty miles of winding back roads. Gravel sprayed from rear wheels as Pasco headed for home.

CHAPTER FIVE

By quirk of physics or intervention of a benevolent God, Pascoe arrived at Timberbrook at quarter past the hour. Fortunately, he had worn his only sport coat and embarrassingly out of fashion tie to the interviews and was relatively creased, pressed, and free of body odor, so he didn't take the time to change during his brief stop home.

The aisle of the barn was dark and quiet; horses had finished dinner and were in the throes of a postprandial nap. A first knock at the door went unanswered, but a hair dryer whined from inside, so he let himself in.

"Hello? Hunter?" he called, shutting the door.

The dryer stopped, followed by the long pause of someone trying to determine if they actually heard the noise they thought they heard.

"Jordan?"

"Yeah, I'm a bit late."

Hunter, wrapped in a white terrycloth robe, peeked over the railing of the loft. "Are you?" she asked. "I've been running around like a madwoman and have no idea what time it is. David left early, so I had to finish barn chores. Banker threw a shoe today and I spent an hour tracking Tony down so he can nail it back on." She blew a wisp of hair from her face. "Anyway, there's beer in the fridge."

Pascoe helped himself to a Fat Tire and wandered around examining pictures scattered on the walls of the apartment. Many featured David in his prime: sailing over fences at Rolex and Badminton; covers of *Practical Horseman*; smiling and clear-eyed with an arm around his baby sister. Hunter was the subject of others, including one of her on Bathsheba barreling through the water hazard at a course he didn't recognize.

"Had potential, didn't she?" Hunter asked, startling him.

Here was a woman he hardly recognized. Hunter lived her life in britches and boots, an outfit her shape complimented, but she might as well have been dressed in a burlap sack. Her hair, normally hidden under a ball cap or helmet, fell past her shoulders and gleamed like polished wood. She wore a thin, vertically ribbed, cream turtleneck emphasizing the muscular lines of her arms and abdomen. A knee-length leather skirt exposed toned legs and calves propped on stiletto heels.

Few horsewomen wore makeup in the barn; sweat made it run, it collected dust and attracted bugs. Hunter was no exception, and Pascoe couldn't remember ever having seen her with any. It was unclear what had been done, but tonight he found the curve of her mouth wanting tasting and the smokiness above her eyes boldly declaring their, and her, singularity. The subtle scent of lavender and cloves teased, an invitation to hunt for the fragrance in her hair, her neck, her body. Belatedly, her question penetrated the spell. Answering took little effort, as his mouth was already hanging open.

"Potential. Yes. Yes she did."

Hunter, pleased by his reaction, smiled crookedly. "Are we actually going somewhere, or were you planning to stare at me all evening?"

"Both, if that's alright with you," Pascoe said.

Hunter laughed as she maneuvered into a leather overcoat. "Oh, goooood boy," she said, patting his head.

Pascoe thought hard about where to go on this first date. Hunter would be unimpressed by any attempt at opulence. He toyed briefly with going back to the Iron Jockey and eating upstairs, but impossibilities of wrangling a reservation aside, wanted something less familiar. He decided to cross the border into West Virginia and bring her to the Appalachian Inn.

Several years ago, after his acceptance to vet school, Harkin had taken him to the Inn for a celebratory dinner. The hostel/restaurant was nestled in a mountain valley far from anywhere but an offshoot of the Appalachian Trail. Hikers in the Blue Ridge, weary of tents and freeze-dried meals, often stayed in the hostel to recharge before continuing south to Georgia or north to Maine.

The inn was run by a gruff, stocky couple from Eastern Europe who acted inconvenienced if anyone showed up to eat, which many did, despite the vibe of the hosts. The food was too good to pass up. This was not a restaurant concerned with calories, saturated fat, or carbs. Fresh greens were an afterthought, the house salad consisted of a mound of limp lettuce sprinkled with carrot rounds and mushy half-moons of cucumber. Topped with a dollop of Thousand Island and a single, overripe cherry tomato it became a perversion of ice cream sundae architecture. Professional eaters appreciated the attempt, but pushed shallow wooden bowls aside and waited for the main course. Provincial proteins of venison, pheasant and salmon anchored the menu, and came surrounded by sides of potatoes and cabbage and beets bobbing in earthy gravies. This was food to comfort the soul and expand the waistline.

Hunter glanced curiously at Pascoe as they crossed over the Potomac, but asked no questions. Instead, she filled the long drive past farmland and forest with small talk. Her restraint broke a half hour later.

"Don't mean to sound unappreciative, but I'm starting to wonder if you're taking me to dinner, banjo recital, or a shallow grave."

"We're here." The Appalachian Inn was before them, in all her kitchy glory. In the dark of night, it looked two dimensional, like the false front of a movie set. The Inn was built to look like an Old Country chalet: dark wood crisscrossed a white stucco façade. Carved cornices hung from the eaves like curlicue icicles.

"Oh, no banjos. The Von Trapps perhaps?"

"It's a long walk back to the farm, smart ass," Pascoe said.

A thick, bosomy woman promptly informed him they were twenty minutes late. "I vill sitz you anyway," she said, swiping a pair of menus from a cubbyhole and marching to the dining room. Pascoe and Hunter hurried to catch up and were led to a cozy corner table. The hostess threw the menus at them and buzzed off without a word. A short time later a harried waitress sporting a bang-curtain and blue eye-shadow came for their order. Pascoe begged for more time, but ordered wine. The waitress sighed and turned away.

"Zo, you vant more time?" Hunter said, raising one eyebrow and wagging a finger at Pascoe. "It is not permitted! Charming Pascoe, very charming."

"Wait for the food before writing the review," Pascoe said. "Artists can be eccentric."

Hunter flipped open her menu, which was printed in large Bavarian script. "If they treat dinner like their customers it'll be quite tender from the beating."

The wine arrived and their server asked again if they were ready. Pascoe assured her they needed just a few more minutes, and she hovered nearby for an egg-timer's span before returning. When Hunter was offered the choice of salad, Pascoe made a noise in his throat. She chose the house soup instead, a hot borsht poured over mashed potatoes. For their entrees, she ordered a salmon fillet baked in a mustard crust and he had the venison steak smothered in cherry marmalade. Both entrees came with a pile of baked squash spiced with onions and rosemary. They spent the first moments after the food arrived with their eyes shut, enjoying the meal's fragrance.

Conversation initially centered on dinner; forkfuls were exchanged and guesses made about the pleasant tang in the crust of the fish. Hunter insisted it was horseradish, Pascoe sure it was mustard seed. Eventually, as the food shrunk, the pace of eating slowed, more time was spent sipping wine, and talk moved into personal territory.

"King tells me you grew up around the track," Hunter said.

"Yeah."

"Exciting?"

Pascoe shrugged. "Occasionally. I always liked to watch the horses run, but Dad never had enough to keep busy. By the time the training day was done he was either drunk or halfway there, so I spent a lot of time wandering the stables."

"Must have learned a lot."

"The other trainers knew whose kid I was and were paranoid I would steal their secrets, like I was some kind of savant spy. I could cuss better than any kid in second grade though."

"Prove it." A string of expletives followed that would have made a major league manager blush. Hunter clapped a hand over her mouth. "Second grade? Your mother must have run out of soap and wooden spoons."

"She wasn't around to care."

"I'm sorry. Did she die?"

"It might have been better for my dad if she had. No, she found a thicker wallet to latch onto and took off."

"And you haven't seen her since?"

"Nope. Look, don't feel bad. I used to be really angry that she wasn't around, fighting at school, giving teachers a hard time, that kind of thing. When I was twelve, thirteen, I got so angry I took the only picture we had of her—it was the two of them on their wedding day—pulled it out to the frame and ripped it in half. I threw Vivian's half in the garbage and put the half with Dad back on the wall. He took down the frame and never said anything about it to me, but must have rummaged through the trash for the other half. When he was dying, he gave it back to me in one piece, taped together. Said, 'Be mad all you want, but don't pretend she doesn't exist.' It's in a box somewhere."

"And are you still angry?"

"A little, but not so much for my sake. I wonder sometimes, if she hadn't left, if Dad might have made it as a big-time trainer. Maybe he would have drank himself to death anyway. King is the most responsible adult I ever had in my life. Disappointing him? That's something that matters." Pascoe stabbed his steak and started sawing off a piece with his knife, with perhaps a little more vigor than necessary. "What about you? Parents still together?"

"Retired and living the good life in Scottsdale. They offered to take David after the accident, but I couldn't bear the thought." Hunter flinched as a shadow fell across the table. They hadn't noticed the glares directed at them from the hostess as the restaurant emptied. Now here she was, tapping a foot, impossible to ignore.

"Vill you be haffing dessert?" Cheesecake sounded like an invitation for thumbscrews.

Pascoe shielded his face with one hand and appealed to Hunter with a look of terror. Hunter bit her lower lip and shook her head.

Pascoe smiled charmingly at the hostess. "No thank you, the check will be fine."

Their young waitress, absent through the meal and uneasy at seeing her boss tableside, jogged over. The hostess cut her off.

"No dessert. Check."

The waitress rummaged in the pocket of the small apron she wore and found the bill. The hostess snatched it and shoved it at Pascoe, managing a curt nod before storming back to her post.

"Sorry about that, y'all," the waitress said in a thick hillbilly accent, "she likes to close on time."

"Apparently," Hunter said. "It's okay, artists can be eccentric."

The waitress furrowed her brow. "Yeah," she said uncertainly.

The drive back to Timberbrook took longer than the drive out. Thick fog hugged the road and black ice had formed, making the tires slip unpredictably. Hunter, unconcerned, unbuckled and scooted closer. They talked little as the mist parted and billowed past the windows.

Watchful eyes and low nickers greeted the pair as they walked, arms around each other, down the aisle of the barn. Standing behind Hunter as she unlocked the door, Pascoe found himself overpowered once again by her essence. No thought of reproach entered his mind when he turned her around and pressed his eager mouth to hers. Hunter met the advance enthusiastically, lifting onto her toes and pressing her tongue into his mouth. When they parted, she led him by the wrist up the stairs to the loft.

Pascoe woke first. Not wanting to wake Hunter with his restlessness, he stepped into boxers and crept downstairs. The air on the main level was much cooler. He paced and rubbed at his arms, passing the wall of photographs. He paid little attention, moving to stay warm more than anything. Something clicked in a small corner of his mind as he passed by one of the frames. He stopped, arms hugging his chest, and leaned closer. It was a picture of Hunter and Bathsheba, posing, blue ribbon fluttering from the mare's bridle. A pre-accident David stood to the side, clapping and grinning from ear to ear. A petite woman stood next to him with an arm around his waist. She carried an ungainly puppy under her other arm, its head a wriggling blur. Pascoe rubbed his eyes and squinted, but nothing changed: the woman next to David was Gail Rasmussen.

CHAPTER SIX

Hunter climbed from the loft. She had thrown on a long shirt barely covering her rear and when she stretched it produced a bare ass and wicked grin.

"Hey champ, hungry?" she said, standing tiptoe to nibble Pascoe's neck. "Don't know about you, but I worked up one hell of an appetite last night."

"May be too weak to eat, but I'll give it a shot," Pascoe said, wrapping his arms around her. "Want some help?"

"Sit, sit," she said, patting his chest. "I'll put coffee on, you'll need to wash down my home cooking with something." She noticed the photo in front of Pascoe. "I love that picture, it captures who David was. A novice course, Sheba's first, and he carried on like I just won the World Championship." She smiled wistfully. "I see traces of that happiness now and then, but don't know if the capacity to love in quite the same way is still there."

"The woman, was she his girlfriend?"

"More of an unofficial fiancé. Tried to give her a ring once, but she had a kid and seemed pretty down on the whole concept of marriage, so he gave her the pup. Said, 'If she won't take a ring I'll find something else to scare away the men.' He searched all over for the biggest, baddest breed out there. It's a—"

"Fila," Pascoe finished. "I've seen one before. He chose well."

Hunter mussed his hair. "Guess you learned something in school after all. Hope you like broken yolks and rubbery whites."

"You know," Pascoe started. The peek-a-boo shirt was irresistible. "I do feel my strength returning. May not need coffee just yet."

"There are things I do in the morning much better than cook."

"What, you want me to help with the laundry?"

Hunter ran back and jumped into his arms, wrapping her legs around his waist. She gave his ribs a healthy squeeze and hopped back to the floor. "Race you upstairs." He caught her at the landing.

Barclay's greeting was stiff when Pascoe arrived home shortly before noon, punishment for being abandoned. Pascoe's unpredictable schedule made long stretches alone a common occurrence, but that didn't mean a dog had to like it, and besides, he *really* had to pee. Once business was done, Barclay went to the empty food bowl and waited, making it clear the surest way to good graces was a full belly.

As the dog munched through a generous pile of kibble, Pascoe bounced around the cabin—flipping on the television, searching the refrigerator, washing the stack of dishes that had been put off—but found it hard to concentrate on any one thing. He was tired, but when he tried to take a nap, Wallace's files nipped him awake. The Rasmussen-Stuart connection was a surprise, but there was more, an underlying cohesive structure. Frustrated, he grabbed a red ballpoint pen, sat cross-legged on the bed, which had not been folded or made for two days, and spread the *Form* in front of him.

Handicapping was meditation for Pascoe. Statistics on horses, trainers and jockeys, pole position and track condition, blended into a larger pattern from which winners and losers emerged. The *Form* contained data on tracks from across the country, but by now the Atlantic coast was familiar enough to be routine. Wanting more distraction, Pascoe turned to the offerings at Santa Anita. The second race was a six-furlong sprint for three year-old maiden fillies, exactly the challenge he needed—inexperienced, winless horses made picking a favorite more difficult.

Like every handicapper, he had a system, and like every gambler, he believed it was a sure way to win money over the long haul, current results notwithstanding. Each statistic was given a letter grade, a quirk adopted in school where GPAs separated Cum Lauds from come-latelys. The horse in the position closest to the rail was assigned an 'A', simply because it would run the shortest distance. The second and third positions were given a 'B+' and 'B' respectively. Likewise, horses in the middle of the pack, with no clear advantage over one another were given 'C's, and so on until the outside horse was given a 'D'.

Now came the real work. Jockeys and trainers were given grades based on earnings for the year, the only real objective measure of performance. Strength of bloodline was graded separately, as were most recent performances, in which speed, competition, and placing were combined into a single mark. If a horse had an 'M' next to its name, indicating it was running on medication, it received an extra 'B' grade. When every horse had a report card, Pacoe punched grades into a calculator like a crusty English Lit professor, averaged them, and uncovered his star pupils.

As it turned out, the number eight horse, Miss Muffett, overcame a poor draw and led the class with a 3.4 GPA. Pascoe wrote a large red '25' next to her name, which meant that twenty-five percent of his total wager would be placed on Miss Muffett to win. The two and the three horses graduated with a 3.15, and garnered fifteen percent each. The filly at the pole was next with a solid 3.0 and would get ten. The remaining thirty-five percent was split among the remaining five horses in proportion to their ranking.

The morning line on Miss Muffett had her going off at five to one, not bad in a field where Pascoe's lowest score, a respectable 2.1, went to an over-raced horse with the unfortunate name of Fillybuster. A long shot at thirty five-to-one, the five percent she rated would still put him ahead if she came in, and Carlyle had offered to double the odds on his next bet. Pascoe capped the pen. No epiphany, but he may have found a way to pay for last night's date. He reached for the phone to call Carlyle—certain the bookie would overcome hurt feelings and fingers for the chance to make a buck—and it rang.

"I've been trying to reach you since yesterday. Don't you check e-mail?" It was Wallace.

"I'm off. I was going to check it when I got in on Monday." He didn't tell her his computer had been hocked eight months ago.

"I need you to come over. Something's come up and I can't get out of it."

"There's no rush, I've got nothing. You might have to admit these claims are legitimate."

"You don't know that!" Wallace snapped, before softening. "Maybe you're right, but until we compare notes we don't know for sure. I have the information on Systematic and talked to Randolph, both might shed some light on things."

"And get you off my back a day earlier? Give me directions, I've got a pen handy."

Wallace's place was neat and attractive, though dwarfed by the expansive estates surrounding it. Originally built to serve as guest lodgings for a larger estate, it had been short-plotted and sold off during the market crash of '29. A foursquare farmhouse with tiny windows and steep roofline perched on a fieldstone foundation. Painted a conservative sky blue with white trim, it was unnaturally cheery under a sky of gun-metal clouds. A wide porch with a wooden swing hung near the front entrance encircled the house. Flower-beds of dormant lavender and groomed mulch lined a brick walkway angling to the door. A stream heavy with rain and the scent of fallen leaves rushed by on the far side of the house and a red, plank-sided barn stood on the near. Two horses, liver chestnuts dressed in matching hunter green blankets, nibbled strands of grass behind electric braid fence. A brindle greyhound, wearing a smart navy blanket of its own, trotted up to the truck. Wallace had invited Barclay as well, and after wary greetings he and the sighthound romped away, body checking each other as they went. Pascoe walked with less exuberance to the house.

Wallace met him at the door, took his arm, and led him over gleaming pine floors to a room he had been in many times before. He called it The Hunt Room, and it was a fixture of Appalachian interior design. Inevitably, the rooms were painted or wallpapered in similar shades of deep green and maroon and abounded with brass accents: lamps, switch plates, heater vents, fireplace grates, and naked coat hooks scattered round it all. And, because no self-respecting Hunt Room would be without them, icons of the hunt somewhere, often everywhere.

This version was no exception: a wallpaper border with a repeating merlot diamonds ran along the top of walls the color of her horses' blankets. Nineteenth century prints hung in brass frames, horses rendered with excessively long necks and backs, implausibly joyful, heads pulled back by a portly rider. A rascally fox evaded a pack of hounds in the distance. A pair of overstuffed leather couches set at right angles dominated the room, each draped with a cotton blanket folded such that their fox-head pattern ran along the back.

A coffee table sat between the two couches and on its glass top, arranged in a fan shape seen only in catalogs, were copies of *The Chronicle of the Horse, Equus, Practical Horseman,* and *The Blood Horse.* God help him, it was the seventh circle of Pottery Barn Hell.

"Wine?" Wallace offered.

"Hot tea, if you've got it."

"It'll take a minute to boil the water. Make yourself comfortable."

Pascoe thumbed through *The Blood Horse* while she bustled. There was a blurb about a young jockey who had impressed at some low-rent tracks in the Midwest and was now riding stakes. The first time or two the jock rode in the big leagues he was likely to go off at favorable odds.

The high-pitched whistle of a teapot interrupted his thoughts. Shortly afterwards, Wallace returned, bearing a tray containing an entire china tea set and a small plate with baby carrots, celery, and cherry tomatoes. She set the tray on the table then disappeared briefly to retrieve a half-empty glass of red wine and sat down next to him.

"Okay," she said, "tell me about the interviews."

Pascoe ripped open a packet of English Breakfast Tea from the selection on the tray and placed the bag in his cup. He filled the cup and dunked the bag a few times.

"There's nothing."

"You're sure."

"All you've got are similar signs in three of the four, but no indication any of a common cause and no motive tying the group together."

"What about money?"

"Dowry doesn't need money, neither does Dearborn. The Sinclairs are doing all right. Rasmussen could use the money, but it's being kept in an account for her daughter, so it's not doing her any good."

"What if I were to tell you Dowry might not be in such great shape? Marketplace has closed fifteen stores. With the economy slumping, even the yuppies are willing to forego artisan bread and slap some tuna salad on a slice of Wonder. Nobody knows for certain how Dowry's personal finances are faring, but he must be feeling the squeeze."

"Dowry would kill his daughter's horse, when he could sell a stable full of mares?"

Wallace shrugged. "He's a businessman, right? Maybe he sees more value in an animal that can reproduce than one that hasn't lived up to expectations."

"You've heard Goldrush wasn't exactly lighting the world on fire."

"I keep my ears open. Gerald crowed to everyone how Dowry paid him to fly to Germany and find the perfect horse. He got a lot quieter after the season started."

Pascoe digested this. "Even if this is true," he said, munching on celery and wishing there was something with actual calories on the plate, "and Dowry gets rid of Goldrush even though it will destroy his daughter, because he needs the money or maybe he just hates a loser, you can't make the same case for Gizmo. I don't think Dearborne cared much for his wife even before the claim, and that horse was winning everything."

Wallace tapped a lacquered nail to bleached teeth. "The Sinclair horse, Systematic, was doing well also. Won some, placed in a couple of others. Made fifty grand his first year, reason enough to be optimistic and increase his coverage. Any help from Harkin?"

"Convinced the horse was fed some bad hay," Pascoe replied. "And doesn't know what kind of people the Sinclairs are, he had never been to the farm before."

"What?"

"They called our practice when their regular vet was unavailable. Harkin was on call."

"Did you bring the files with you?"

"Sure, they're in the truck."

"Get them."

Wallace refilled her wineglass in his absence. She waved him over impatiently, taking a long pull from her drink. Finding the Sinclair case, she opened it on top of the others, and scanned the pages. Stopping at a form near the back, she stabbed at the signature in triumph.

"Here's our connection."

"I don't understand," Pascoe said.

Wallace stabbed repeatedly at the line. "Randolph. Randolph. Randolph. Randolph did the exam for the increase to two hundred grand. Same with Dearborne."

"But not with Dowry or Rasmussen," Pascoe said.

"It doesn't really matter," she said excitedly. "They were the first. You said his report for Dearborn was shit. And then he's 'unavailable' to look at Systematic? After, that kill a couple of horses he had *no* connection to, so no one gets suspicious."

"Being unavailable doesn't mean Randolph had anything to do with Systematic's death, and neither does filing a crappy report. You're stretching."

Wallace stared straight ahead, a zealous gleam in her eye, wine forgotten. "Perhaps. But I haven't told you about my lunch date with Randolph."

"I suppose he confessed."

"As a matter of fact he did, in a way."

Wallace had danced with Randolph last Christmas at Virginia Bloodstock's charity auction, so it was easy to call out of the blue and invite him to lunch.

"Between you and me," she said, "the old boy likes to tip 'em back. I figured a few over lunch and he might open up. We make small talk, he's trying to get in my pants, and pretty soon he's on his third drink. At this point I grab his hand. I'm so concerned for him, and we're practically best friends you know, and I tell him to watch his back, there's a rumor that VBI might be reopening an old claim. 'Which one?' he asks, kissing my hand like I'm frigging royalty. When I told him it was Dearborne, I swear he almost passed out. Dropped my hand, even. 'Ruth, you've got to stop it,' he says. When I ask why, he leans in so I could taste the salt from his margarita and whispers, 'I killed that horse.'

"He was drunk the night he went to Three Sisters. He's sure he gave Bute instead of steroids and shut down that horse's kidneys. So he didn't do a post. Dearborne is his biggest client—sounds like one of the few he has left—and if Dearborne's claim was denied, Randolph is sure he'd have one less client and be defending a malpractice suit. I left feeling sorry for him, well, a little anyway, but now I wonder if he wasn't as tipsy as he seemed."

"You're thinking he wanted sympathy."

"If he killed the horse on purpose, why not see if I can make an investigation go away?" Wallace waved her hands above her head in frustration. "But it still comes down to money, and if anybody is sitting pretty, it's Dearborne."

"Nobody had a decent motive. This is a wild goose chase."

Wallace held a folder to Pascoe's face in desperation. "You said Rasmussen could use the money. Wasn't there anything unusual?"

Like lying about David? "Nothing."

Wallace slumped and grabbed for her wine. "You're not trying hard enough."

"Screw you, I did everything you asked. I'm done."

When Pascoe stood and turned to leave, Wallace threw the folder as his retreating back and screamed, "I can still go to the Board! You better not mention this to anyone!"

Barclay slept in the passenger seat, ragged from running with Wallace's dog. In the silence, doubt crept under the sanctimonious fence he had built against Wallace. Admittedly, a sense of connection was still there, but he couldn't pass on the opportunity to be free of her manipulation. His thumb beat a simple rhythm on the steering wheel, a child's song perhaps, or symphonic melody. Turning his back on Wallace felt wrong. He hated being wrong; no, it was more personal than that. Being wrong made him feel small and common. His mother was wrong to leave, his father wrong to choose booze over a son. The last thing Pascoe wanted was to be like either.

His cell phone beeped shrilly, startling him and indicating a voice message. He must have climbed into a pocket of coverage. Though in the shadow of the nation's capital, rural reception was spotty. Rolling hills blocked signal, and few locals wanted a tower in their pastures. Already, as Pascoe coasted into the next valley, strength diminished to a single, short bar. A few attempts to retrieve the message resulted in moments of clarity too brief to access anything but garbled computer-voiced prompts. Messages would have to wait.

Clouds moved on to trouble the Atlantic and a pink sky spoke to the crisp night to come. Pascoe carried in enough wood from the two cords stacked outside the front door to feed the stove through the night. Then he tackled the phone. Few people had his cell number; more and he'd spend more time scheduling appointments than practicing medicine, so he expected a message from Maggie or Harkin, not Devon Dowry.

"Jordan," it began, scratchy and garbled. "Don't be mad at Maggie. I whined for at least ten minutes before she gave me this number. So I called to say, to ask you, well, I was wondering, you know, if any more tests on Goldrush were back yet."

There was a lot of rustling and mumbling, as if she was switching the phone to her other hand, as well as a string of unintelligible words. "That's not the real reason I called. Listen, I want to apologize. Call it peer pressure or whatever. A friend at school goes on about how hot she is and her older boyfriend and how in love they are and—ugh! Anyway, you don't need to hear about that. Sorry, and I hope you'll still be my vet...and my friend. So, uh, call. Bye."

The message cheered him. It was not unusual for girls to get crushes on vets in the same way they would other authority figures, like teachers, but Devon had always behaved more like a sister than a seductress. Her sudden change was disheartening, and dangerous. Awkward for her, but the apology and the conversation it allowed him to dodge were a relief. The sooner things were resolved the better.

A return call went unanswered. That was something; a teenage girl and her cell phone were not easily parted. A call to Stonemason went directly to voicemail. Pascoe lit a fire in the stove and tried both numbers again with the same result. A third try a half hour later and a fourth a half hour after that and still no answer. Something was wrong. It was that vague sense of unease coming from Wallace's cases. This time though, Pascoe wanted to be wrong.

The barns were quiet, so he continued to the main house. Staying at the cabin wasn't an option; he needed to see that Devon was alright. A cluster of vehicles faced the woods at the edge of a field; exhaust billowed, obscuring all but silhouettes. Arranged in a semicircle, their headlights focused on specific area, but no people could be discerned. His unease grew.

Stonemason's house always made Pascoe feel like he should use a servant's entrance. Wide stamped-concrete stairs flanked by topiary stags climbed from parking area to the pillared entry. Curtains were shut against the night and there was no sign of activity. For a moment, he considered turning around. Instead, he zipped up his jacket, pulled on a knit hat, and stepped out into the cold.

A knock against the mahogany door echoed from the tree line. Purposeful footsteps approached and a slender black man flung the door open. He wore the green and brown of the Sheriff's Department "May I help you?"

Dowry sat on a couch in a room at the end of the hall, head buried in his hands, weeping. The officer reached behind him and closed the door, blocking the view. "May I help you, sir?" he repeated forcefully.

"I'm looking for Devon Dowry."

The officer put right hand to his holster. It was a casual movement, in the way a cat will yawn and stretch as if the bird in front of him is of no particular interest. The nametag pinned above his left shirt pocket identified him as Elias Ridgeway. He was serving his second term as Sheriff. Five years ago he had been the first African-American elected to the position in the history of the county. According to Harkin, when Ridgeway was a deputy he had nurtured the money-men of the area by doing favors. Charges dropped, evidence misplaced, witnesses forgot. When he decided to run for the head job, their support allowed Ridgeway to out-spend his opponent five times over. Most voters didn't even hear of the other guy on the ballot.

"Sir, I think you better tell me your name," Ridgeway said.

"Jordan Pascoe. I do vet work for the Dowry's."

"What brings you here tonight, sir?"

"I stopped by to talk to Devon. One of her horses died recently. Look, is everything okay?"

"I'm afraid not, Miss Dowry is dead."

CHAPTER SEVEN

Darkness bled into the edge of Pascoe's vision. Bile shot into his mouth and filled it with a sour, metallic taste. After a few deep breaths the blackness retreated, the icy fist in his belly loosened, and he was able to stand.

Ridgeway studied Pascoe through narrowed eyes. "Mr. Pascoe, do you need to call a lawyer?"

"Doctor. It's Doctor," Pascoe corrected, though he didn't know why. Ridgeway watched disapprovingly as he spat the sourness from his mouth. "I'm not under arrest am I?"

"No sir. But anyone who has had recent contact with the victim might have some important information. You will be interviewed and it will be your right to have a lawyer present." He nodded back toward he house. "Mr. Dowry has two in there."

Pascoe's blood rose. He would have jammed his forefinger into the sheriff's chest, but indignation wasn't worth a forty-five hollowpoint in the forehead. "I don't need a lawyer," he said. "If you want to question me, I'll follow you anywhere right now."

Ridgeway held up a well-manicured hand. "Not necessary." The sheriff's hand brushed by his gun again, but he reached past it for his wallet. He rummaged around and handed Pascoe a business card.

"This is the detective in charge of the case. Give him a call and set something up." The card read: *Detective Monroe Ridgeway*. Pascoe looked up questioningly. "My son."

"Is there anything I can do?"

"Just get on home Doctor Pascoe," Ridgeway said, opening the door. "We'll take care of everything." Inside, Dowry had not moved, but now Vaughn sat next to him, cigarette flagging wildly as he talked. Noticing the door, he sprang from sight. Ridgeway frowned. "Drive safe," he said, closing the door, insulating Stonemason from the outside once again.

Coals glowed in the stove when Pascoe arrived, a few pieces of firewood got it blazing. He had not eaten since his meeting with Wallace, and a dull, hypoglycemic ache resided behind his eyes. A sniff of some deli turkey in the refrigerator assured him there was minimal risk in throwing it between two slices of stale-ish bread for a quick snack. In penance to Barclay, Pascoe made a second and gave it to the dog, who grudgingly carried it over to his bed.

An image of Devon, dead at the edge of the forest, illuminated by a cordon of squad car headlights, crept into his head and lay next to the pain. She would be probed and cut up by a coroner in the same fashion, and with the same detachment, as Goldrush had been a few days before. He put the sandwich aside and grabbed the phone.

Hunter answered after the fourth ring. "Hello," she said sleepily. "David?"
"No. Jordan."
"Jordan? What's wrong?"
"Devon Dowry is dead."
"Oh my God. What happened? Did she have a fall?"
"I think she might have been murdered. The sheriff was there. He wants me to give a statement."
"You can't be a suspect?"
"Hard to tell. The sheriff made it sound routine. Honestly, I haven't thought things through. I needed to talk, and you were the first person that came to mind."
"I'm glad. Were you and Devon close?"
"More so than most clients. She was a good kid, you know? Nobody else in her family knows beans about horses, so I dealt with her. With all those horses in competition, I was over there every week for one thing or another."
"I'll bet she made up a problem more than once to get you over."
"What's that supposed to mean?"
"I mean, who else did she have? She was as much a trophy to her father as that young wife and her brother is about the biggest ass I've ever met." There was no hiding the venom in her voice.
"You sound as if you know the Dowrys." This was puzzling. Hunter did not travel in the upper levels of the equestrian social strata and, as an event rider, she wouldn't spend much time, if any, on the jumper circuit. It seemed unlikely she would have had opportunity to mingle with Oliver, Vaughn, or Devon.
"Unfortunately, I've had the pleasure. When David got the okay to go back to work, Oliver offered him a job cleaning stalls on the days their regular guy had off. I'm pretty sure Devon was behind it all. Oscar is not exactly Mr. Compassion. He's all about the bottom line, and I doubt he considers disabled people the most efficient workers. I figure Devon knew David from articles about the accident and felt sorry for him. She was the only one of them who treated him like a human being. Shook his hand when he came to

work, laughed at his silly jokes...." Hunter's voice caught and a sob escaped her throat. She put the phone down and Pascoe heard her hop out of bed. He waited. She blew her nose. "Still there?"

"Got nowhere else to go."

"Jesus, if you could see me now, I'd never get you over here again." Hunter laughed nervously and blew her nose again, loudly.

"Don't bet on it. So what happened?"

"Oliver scurried away after one look at David's face and that idiot Vaughn laughed. David can't tell the difference between someone laughing with him and someone laughing at him. I wanted nothing more than to rip Vaughn to shreds, but the job was his first real taste of responsibility, and I wasn't going to take it away. So I gritted my teeth and drove him to work. Usually I would just hang out, watch Devon ride, read a book, or whatever until David was finished. After a while, Vaughn started stopping by.

"The first time, he apologized for laughing. Said it was nerves, like laughing at a funeral. He sounded sincere, and that was all he did. Apologize and leave. Then sometimes he would come by and watch his sister, or pretend to. Eventually, he started chatting me up and after a while, asked me out."

Pascoe groaned. "You didn't."

"No one else was knocking at my door. I figured it might be fun, get out of the house, go dancing or something—are you laughing?"

"No m'am," Pascoe said, stifling a chuckle. "But Vaughn? Really?"

"Desperate times, smart ass, desperate times. Besides, one date was enough. He droned on and on about the fabulous wealth of the family over dinner at some ridiculously overpriced, stuffy restaurant. And I swear he was on speed or something, his eyes were all goofy and his movements were all jerky and awkward."

"Maybe it was love."

"Shut up. He drove me home, I said I had to be up early to ride and sprinted to the door."

"Ouch," Pascoe said. "Not even a polite peck on the cheek."

"Hey, you spend an hour cooped up in a car with Vaughn. I had enough of his fabulous BO and wasn't getting an inch closer."

"Bet he was none too happy about that."

"Let me tell you what a big man Vaughn Dowry is," Hunter said. "Next day, David was scheduled to clean stalls. Vaughn catches up with me, tells me what a great time he had and asks me out again. I told him the truth, or at least the part I thought he could handle. Said he was a great guy, but there was no spark and I needed a spark if I was going to keep seeing someone.

"He seemed to take it all right, thanked me for a wonderful time the night before, and walked off. The next time David and I show up, the whole family is down at the barn. Oliver, Devon, and Vaughn all lined up in a row. Oliver won't look at me, Devon is red-eyed, and Vaughn has got this smug, punk-ass grin on his face.

"Oliver walks up, still won't meet my eye, ignores David, and says, 'I'm afraid we have to let your brother go, there's been an incident.' When I ask what he's talking about he says, 'One of the horses was injured. Apparently your brother got a little rough with a pitchfork and punctured one of Devon's jumpers. The vet says everything will be fine, but these are expensive horses and can't be treated this way.'"

"I remember," Pascoe said. "It was Goldrush, he had arrived from Germany the week before. Four little holes at the base of his neck."

"Well David didn't do it. When Oliver finished, David started shaking his head back and forth wailing, 'No, no, no, no,' which is what he does when he's stressed. I screamed about how David would never hurt a horse, how I trust him with my own, there must be a nail in the stall. Then Vaughn pipes up, 'See Dad, even the retard's sister has a temper, how can we trust him?' I went ballistic. Maybe I could have talked Oliver into giving David a second chance, but I called Vaughn a smelly dickless psycho taking it out on David because I wouldn't spread my legs for him. That ended any second chance."

"I would have given anything to have seen the look on Oliver's face," Pascoe said. "I don't think he's used to anyone, especially women, talking to him that way."

"You see the same expression every time you catch a deer in your high beams." Hunter sighed. "Poor David, he bawled the whole way home. I couldn't convince him it wasn't his fault."

"Do you really think it was Vaughn? I know he's an asshole, but would he really harm his sister's horse?"

"Vaughn doesn't care about anything but himself." Hunter yawned, and Pascoe was painfully aware of the late hour.

"Get some sleep," He said. Hunter yawned again. "Yeah, got a ton of horses to work tomorrow, uh, today. Call when things settle down."

Pascoe assured her he would, and, after engaging in the niceties of a new, undefined relationship, hung up. The sudden emptiness of the house was overwhelming. Devon was dead. The bile that had surged upward earlier returned. He needed to wash it down.

Watching a father yellow and die from alcohol poising will make you a cautious drinker. However, Pascoe had a cabinet filled with scotches of various ages and mixtures given by appreciative clients. On occasion, a few fingers of warmth and smoke and peat on a cold night were better than just about anything in the world.

Tonight was not about indulgence; it was about dulling the edges of his mind. A spotty water glass filled halfway with Glenfiddich and topped off with Pepsi was chugged as if he were at a frat party. Once his stomach stopped threatening to rebel, he refilled the glass. Sipping now, he drifted off before it was a third gone. For the time being, he had exorcised the ghost of a young girl, but the problem with ghosts was their immortality, and she would haunt his dreams another night.

Pascoe woke late, right hand numb from head resting against forearm all night. His skull throbbed like the inside of a rave, and his eyelids were glued shut by an otherworldly crust. A double measure of beans went into the coffee. While it brewed, Pascoe stumbled into the shower, where water felt like pebbles thrown against the skin. It took two brushings with large dollops of toothpaste before saliva made a tentative return to his mouth.

Dressed, he filled a stainless steel thermos and poured the rest of the coffee into a travel mug. Any thought of food threatened to undo the gains he had made, so before getting behind the wheel he pinched a cc of Banamine from his truck. A professor at school who tended to party with the students too much had introduced Pascoe to the wonders of Banamine. Its bitterness could be hidden in coffee, and was superior to both aspirin and ibuprofen.

One look at the dour faces of Harkin and Maggie was enough to know they had heard about Devon. Harkin eyed Pascoe's condition.

"You okay?"

"How do I look?"

"Like you've been drinking." Harkin sniffed. "Smell like it too. Take the day off Jordie."

"Work will keep my mind off things."

"No it won't. You'll pretend it will, but you'll be thinking about the girl all day, and make mistakes. I don't need you getting hurt. Your appointments have been called, so go on home."

Pascoe turned to Maggie. "Don't look at me," she said. "I agree with King. Wouldn't want you working on my horse the way you look. Take the day. Your clients understand, not a one complained about rescheduling. They all knew her too."

Pascoe rubbed his face in frustration and realized he still had a full days growth of beard. His eyes were probably bloodshot as well. Harkin was right. He was simply going through the motions—and doing a poor job.

"You win," he said. "I'll make it up to you."

"I know you will. Once fishing season starts I might feel a cold coming on. Then you pay me back." Harkin winked and clapped him on the back. "I know this is tough Jordie, it's tough for everyone. The whole community is scared shitless DC and all its problems have finally made it out this far."

"You think some kind of...transient killed Devon?"

"That's what I'm hearing. Who else could it be? Anyway, the cops will figure it out."

Pascoe cursed. "The cops want to talk to me today."

"About the girl?"

"Yeah. I stopped by the Dowry's last night. The sheriff wants a statement." Pascoe touched his face again. "I'm gonna look like a complete psycho."

"Run up to the house. There's an electric razor in the upstairs bathroom. You also might want to re-button your shirt."

He used the Visene in the medicine cabinet as well. He phoned the Sheriff's Department and was told to come in after noon, which gave him the rest of the morning. He needed to see Wallace.

Pascoe had filled out enough forms from Virginia Bloodstock to have its location memorized. The Potomac Valley Office Complex was an infamous boondoggle. In the early eighties Japanese corporations bought large tracts of land in the then undeveloped northeastern edge of the county. Soon, sprawling steel and glass cities sprang from the pastures that had recently fattened sheep and white-faced cattle. Then recession hit, and Loudon overflowed with thousands of square feet of cheap office space. Lawyers, lenders, and insurance companies accustomed to doing business in cramped but historic homes found the lure of high speed internet and central air irresistible.

The Complex was the most recognized monument to financial recklessness in the area, not for its daring architecture or thoughtful landscaping, but because it was tall. In an area where few buildings topped five stories, the Complex jutted high above the forest canopy and could be seen from any hilltop in the county, like a beacon of civilization to the great unwashed.

Pascoe's truck, crusted with bluestone dust, was decidedly out of place in the seamless asphalt parking lot. The spaces were narrow, so he parked at the far end where there was room to straddle two. On the way in he walked through an automobile caste system: cars ten years and older furthest out, then past spaces occupied by newer Toyotas and Chevys which became Volvos and Saabs closer in. Mercedes, Infinities, and BMWs guarded the entry in spots closer to the door than handicapped spaces.

A black board with interchangeable plastic letters directed him to the second floor, where Virginia Bloodstock leased a suite. Pascoe stepped out of the elevator in the middle of a hallway with a string of identical glass doors running its length. On a hunch, he went left and found VBI at the end of the hall.

A stunning receptionist guarded the grid of cubicles behind her like an advanced pawn. Behind her, the office hummed with conversation and hard drives. He asked for Wallace and she spat out a series of lefts and rights accentuated with spastic and unhelpful hand motions.

"Left, right, second right, second left, then fifth on the right," Pascoe repeated as he skirted cubicle walls.

Peripherally, he was aware of nameless, sexless business suits hunched over the desks he passed. One passageway took him along the back edge of the hive, where management lived. These offices had walls reaching all the way to the ceiling, and, judging by their location, had a view to the outside. Emblazoned glass doors proclaimed the names and titles of the occupants— Mr. Boatwright, President; Mr. Miles, Vice President; Ms. Hazelton; Senior Associate.

From this vantage point, with the mass of cubicles to his right, it struck Pascoe that it was the dream of these private rooms that drove Wallace and he wondered if any, or all, of the other cubicle-dwellers had similar ambition. The thought broke his concentration and he stopped and tried to recall whether it was the fourth or fifth right. A loud, familiar, sycophantic laugh came from the path directly to his right. Three spaces down he found Wallace on the phone, feet propped on her desk. She was dressed much more richly than her co-workers. How far did she have to stretch her paycheck for the clothes and farm? His presence brought her up short.

"Listen sugar, I have an unexpected visitor. No, no, just a friend dropping by. Yeah. Talk to you soon." Neighbors poked heads out of their cubicles.

"Doctor Pascoe, what a pleasant surprise. Have a seat," she said through a forced smile. She grabbed his arm and leaned close. "What the fuck are you doing here?"

He lowered his voice to a whisper. "I'm here for the files. You must have heard about the murder. I'm meeting with a detective later and I want to give him the information, see if he can make sense out of it."

"Hold on a second," Wallace said. "Yesterday you didn't believe those cases meant anything and now you want to take them to the police? Fat chance. Giving you access was a huge risk, and if you take them to the cops I might as well resign."

"You're giving me those files," Pascoe said, voice rising. "Quietly if you want. Shouting. Your choice. I'm not dicking around. A friend of mine is dead, and I'll risk both our careers if it might help find out who did this. If you won't give me the files they can subpoena your boss."

Wallace cocked her head like a robin listening for worms.

"Threats. You're threatening me? Don't you think I read the papers? I know Dowry was murdered sometime yesterday afternoon. Where were you? Personally, I can't remember, but then again, the cops have no reason to talk to me. My memory can be fleeting. Sometimes it's downright flawed.

"Take my advice. Have your meeting. If they want to know where you were, give them my name but forget about those files. Hell, if you want I'll tell them you fucked me twice with the biggest cock I've ever seen. But mention my pet project and I'll find it difficult to remember any guests at all."

"So that's the way it is. You'd rather a murderer go free than risk your precious job."

Wallace didn't blink. "That's the way it is."

Pascoe, defeated and haggard, pushed into the lobby of the Loudon County Sheriff's Department. "Detective Ridgeway please," Pascoe muttered to the duty officer. "It's about the Dowry murder."

The deputy lifted the telephone receiver and punched a button, keeping his eyes fixed on Pascoe. He covered his mouth as he talked; apparently convinced his visitor had the lip-reading ability of a master criminal. Pascoe could have cared less. Devon was dead and Wallace had him by the balls. Scrutinization by a low-level police drone was the least of concerns.

Barn Politics

Monroe Ridgeway pushed through a door behind the duty desk. While his father was slight and the color of desert sand, Monroe was dark and imposing as an Angus bull. The collar of his uniform accommodated a neck so thick his head sank into it like a stone thrown onto wet ground. Arms and legs projected from a refrigerator-sized torso at forty-five degrees. His hands were smooth and fat like those of an infant, with stubby fingers of equal length. It was the perfect body for tossing hay bales, lugging water buckets, or carrying a newborn calf under each arm. He nodded and scouted the lobby.

"No lawyer?" he asked.

"Don't need one," Pascoe said.

"Glad to hear it." The detective motioned for him to follow. "Come on back to the office."

Pascoe was led to a tiny, windowless room with a single desk at its center. A metal folding chair sat on either side. The room was otherwise unadorned.

"No phone, file cabinet, family pictures—doesn't look much like an office," Pascoe said.

Monroe sighed. "Look Doc, my office is a squad car. I share a desk with two other deputies. I'm giving you the courtesy of the only private space inside the building other a bathroom stall so you can give a statement without half the county knowing. If I wanted to grill you there'd be a tape recorder on this desk and before I said a word I'd be reminding you of your rights. Coffee?"

"No thanks, stomach's a little iffy." Pascoe sat down into one of the chairs. It made a hollow *plink* when it unfolded completely. Monroe sat on the corner of the desk and removed a spiral notepad and pen from a breast pocket with a large ink-stain in one corner.

"Any ink left in the pen?" Pascoe asked.

"If I need more I'll wring it out of the shirt," Monroe replied. "I hear you knew the girl."

"I was her vet."

"Were you close?"

"We were friends."

"And how is it you showed up at her house on Sunday night?"

"She left a voicemail. One of her horses died and she was asking about lab results. I tried repeatedly to reach her by phone, and when I couldn't, I decided to drop by."

"The results were that important?"

"The results aren't back yet."

"Uh-huh. So why was it so important to see Miss Dowry?"

"I was concerned when I couldn't reach her or the family."

"This message from the girl, when did it come in?"

"Don't know exactly. I got the message late afternoon, but I suppose it could have come in anytime."

"And where were you during the day?"

"Visiting a friend."

"Uh-huh. You got a name for me?" Monroe jotted down Wallace's name and number. "How long were you there?"

"From around one thirty to four."

"Before that?"

"I was at a friend's house until around noon, home alone until I left again." Pascoe volunteered Hunter's name and address.

"You get around Doc," Monroe tapped the end of the pen against his front teeth. "This Stuart gal, she got a brother named David?"

"Yeah, why?"

"The name has come up." Monroe went back to his notes. "This horse of Dowry's, anything strange about the way it died?"

"What do you mean?"

"I mean, it seems strange to me. A girl's horse dies, and soon after the girl is murdered. Curious."

"Guess so." Pascoe cursed Wallace in his mind. "So far, the best I've come up with is botulism poisoning, but if the lab comes up with anything suspicious I'll let you know."

"Is there any way someone could have deliberately poisoned the horse with botulism?"

"I suppose. You'd have to get hold of the toxin of course, maybe from a dead animal or a bad batch of preserves, and it would have to be fed to the horse, but it could be done."

"Do you know the Dowry's well?"

"I knew Devon best, but I know the whole family."

"How was her relationship with the family?"

"She was close to her father, but ambivalent towards her stepmother."

"And the brother?"

"Why don't you ask him?"

"I'm asking you."

"Devon and Vaughn had a...strained relationship. Probably not much different than the way a lot of brothers and sisters are."

"How would he react to his sister's death?"

"No idea. Ask your father, he had a front row seat."

Monroe stopped writing. "Sheriff Ridgeway told me Vaughn Dowry was nowhere to be found last night. The family's lawyer set up a time for his statement."

"Vaughn was at Stonemason last night. I saw him talking to Oliver."

Monroe rubbed the back of his head, flipped the notebook closed and stood. "We're done. Your story sounds solid. I'll call if I need anything."

Pascoe bundled himself against the biting wind shooting across the Sheriff's Department parking lot. He considered retuning to the station once his alibi had been substantiated, but Monroe Ridgeway didn't strike him as the type to respond favorably to being misled. Besides, if he did go back, Wallace would undoubtedly retract her statement and say she was covering for a friend. He could quickly become a suspect with no alibi.

Better to return with evidence. If there was a connection between Devon's murder and Goldrush's death, then there had to be a connection, somewhere, among the other horses. All he had to do was find it.

The turmoil of the last twenty-four hours gave way. Similar transformations happened at the track. Horses head to the starting gate and spin and kick. Men dodge aluminum-shod hooves as the horse flails against the confines of the gate, and then, a sudden and unexpected stillness. A realization that in seconds there was going to be an opening, a direction to run. Pascoe had the same clarity. All the guilt, frustration, and anger were replaced with the desire, the need, to go forward. The race was on, and Pascoe was going to be first out of the gate.

CHAPTER EIGHT

Martin Kutulas was a professional muckraker, though he preferred the term newsman. He had no formal training in journalism or publishing, but had the good fortune of being born into a family who, until his arrival, had a long-standing tradition of hard work and financial success. As such, he had the luxury of trying and failing at law school, art school, and film school before deciding on politics.

Kutulas was one of the few beings alive with anti-charisma. He ran for city council, state senator, congressman, and governor, and write-in candidates like Yoda and Elvis garnered more votes. When time and again these self-financed campaigns failed, Kutulas proclaimed the system broken and decided to be a force for change at the 'grass-roots' level. Thus *The Freedom Monitor* was born.

The *Monitor* published weekly and ran six pages front to back. It was found in wobbly stainless steel racks just inside the automatic doors of most supermarkets. The word FREE! was printed in the upper right corner, but most readers would gladly pay for this guilty pleasure.

A small litter of yellow-dog journalists worked for the paper, all veterans of Kutulas' varied campaigns; individuals of petty meanness drawn to his black hole of a personality. No one at the paper was familiar with the term "reporting". "Agenda", on the other hand, was an old friend. The *Monitor* brimmed with opinion pieces masquerading as articles. Anonymous letters to the editor, crammed with gossip and innuendo, were similar in content and tone to Kutulas' campaign speeches. It was glorious, until you became front-page news.

Pascoe stopped at a 7-11 on the way to work for coffee and *The Daily Racing Form*. Fillybuster had won at Santa Anita by a neck. Irritated for not placing the bet, he tossed the paper on the counter. Digging in his front pocket for change, he noticed the picture on the *Monitor*'s front page. Someone had captured him hunched against the wind, scowling in thought as he walked to his truck. "Police Question 'Friend' of Murdered Girl" blazed across the top of the paper while the caption beneath the photo asked, "What's He Hiding?"

"Fuck me," he muttered and shoved a copy under an arm.

The chair behind Maggie's desk was empty. Harkin perched on his own chair, waiting like a father at three in the morning who had expected his son home at midnight. A copy of the *Monitor* lay on his lap.

"Any publicity is better than none, right?" Pascoe offered.

Pascoe had seen Harkin furious, exultant, despondent, and smug. He had seen him contentious and contemplative. Today, behind heavy spectacles, he was an expressionless mannequin.

"I don't believe that turn of phrase applies here," Harkin said evenly.

"King I—"

"Jordan Pascoe, a veterinarian at Harkin Veterinary Associates, spent almost two hours being grilled about his connection to Devon Dowry," Harkin read.

"Two hours? No way. And I wasn't grilled, I—"

"Sources close to the family admit Doctor Pascoe and Miss Dowry had an unusual fondness for each other. Shortly before her grisly murder, Miss Dowry was seen walking side by side with Doctor Pascoe and wearing his coat. Should I continue?"

"I've read it."

"And?"

"And, it's the *Monitor* for Christ's sake. A few paragraphs later Kutulas implies Oliver has ties to the Russian mob. Who's going to believe it?"

Harkin's face became animated. Pascoe took it as a positive sign.

"Doesn't matter. You've noticed Maggie's absence? I sent her home. For the first time since I hung a shingle, the phones are quiet. It's like walking into a party with dog shit on your shoe. Nobody believes you smell like shit all the time, but you smell God-awful right then and they're not going to come within thirty feet."

"The police are just doing their job. They seem satisfied, why aren't you?"

Harkin erupted. "It's not me you should be worried about! Look at this picture." He waved the paper under Pascoe's nose. "You look sneaky. This is just the thing to get the Board to revisit your probation. I don't know if I have enough pull to get you through another hearing. You better walk a straight line from here on out, boy."

"Understood," Pascoe said. "What do you want me to do?"

"Might as well go home. Even if the phones start ringing, it won't be to get on your schedule. Keep your pager on though, if I need you I'll call."

The *Monitor* article and the accompanying photograph bothered him all day. Harkin was right; it did make him look sneaky, which was obviously the point. The existence of such a photo bothered him. How on earth did Kutulas know he was going to show up? Was some stooge sent to snap pictures of anyone going into and out of the building? The text suggested otherwise. Maybe Wallace tipped off the paper as a warning shot. Maybe it was Monroe, or the sheriff.

Somebody was manipulating Kutulas, surely as a crooked jockey checking a fast horse. Fortunately, there was someone who could help figure out who was pulling on the reins, and he owed Pascoe a favor.

"You know, I still can't make a fist with this damn hand," Carlyle said. "I'm thinking of suing your ass."

"There's big money for loss of marital relations," Pascoe said.

There was silence on the other end of the line as Carlyle worked it out.

"Funny. But I'm serious man, that hurt."

"Okay, sorry. You still owe me a favor though."

More silence as Carlyle consulted his Code of Ethics.

"Ain't nobody running today."

"I know. I want to trade. You service everyone from stall pickers to stockbrokers and hear things. I just want to know if you've heard something useful."

"I don't owe you nearly enough to risk losing my business. If people think I'm running off at the mouth, no one's gonna send me a horse, and for damn sure no one's gonna lay a bet. There's a certain amount of trust required in my line of work."

"You'd rather give me double odds?" Pascoe asked.

"Damn straight."

"Tell you what, I'll hold off on placing that bet until another Bloody Rule comes along and then make a really, really big bet. Will that help business?"

"You got lucky."

"Want to take that chance?"

Silence again. Two years ago Bloody Rule was the favorite in the Arlington Mile and set to go off at three-to-two. A few days before the race the *Form* reported a cracked hoof had been patched with acrylic. It was unlikely he would run. When it became evident the owner was not going to scratch the horse, his line went to twenty-to-one. Most were scared away from laying any money at all on the rangy colt, so Carlyle tripled the odds to make the bet irresistible to a few suckers. Pascoe knew Bloody Rule was too valuable to risk running with patched hoof; when the horse remained in the field, he smelled misdirection. The stewards would test for medication, but were unlikely to dremel away the hoof of a horse owned by a cable network owner in order to check if it had actually suffered a crack. Bloody Rule won going away and Pascoe did very well.

"All right," Carlyle said finally. "But nowhere local."

"Have a place in mind?"

"Dulles. A bar called The Sporting Booze. They know me well enough, but won't know you, and the chances of running into clients are slim and none. I can get there by ten."

"Fine."

"Leave the hoof testers at home."

The Sporting Booze was like every other bar in every airport around the country. Clusters of round Formica tables big enough to seat two spilled into the corridor where travelers could keep an eye on the length of the security line. Flickering televisions and the glow from hundreds of neon beer signs augmented dim lighting. The bar was twice as deep as it was wide, and Pascoe found Carlyle at a table crammed against the back wall, bathed in the silvery blue glow of a Coors Light sign.

Carlyle was drinking tonic, vodka if Pascoe's memory served, which he raised in greeting. "Whatcha drinking?"

"You buying? Must have been a good weekend."

"Not for most, that's why I'm buying," Carlyle snorted.

"Old Dominion," Pascoe said to the waiter who had swooped in when he saw Pascoe sit.

When the beer arrived, Carlyle lifted his glass again. "To luck."

"To luck," Pascoe said.

"Saw your picture in the paper," Carlyle said. "Is that what this is about?"

"Pretty much. Harkin's not too happy, and I want to find who let Kutulas loose."

Carlyle laughed, expelling more phlegm than air. "Don't think you're so special, everyone is fair game to Kutulas. He'll say anything about anybody, and if you don't like it, too bad. He's got enough money to keep lawyers going round and round with each other until people give up. I think the only person he regrets going after is your boss."

"Harkin?"

"Yeah." Carlyle drained his glass and motioned to the waiter to bring another. "Happened years ago. Kutulas printed a story about Harkin and a senator's wife. I think the guy's name was Wasserman. Anyway, the story had been circulating at parties for a while before Kutulas printed it, but Harkin went ballistic once it was in the paper."

"He sued?"

"Harkin? From what I hear, he paid a personal visit. Don't know what Harkin said, or did, but the *Monitor* printed a retraction the following week. Only time I've seen that happen. You may not realize it, but that old man has a helluva mean streak. Not many around here want to be on his bad side. Kutulas has got to know who you work for. Maybe it's payback."

"What about Kutulas and Dowry?"

"You don't get it. Kutulas is the wealthiest guy in the area. Throw any name in the county at me and that person and Kutulas would have some connection." Carlyle's drink came. The bookie plucked a wedge of lime out of the glass with grubby fingers and ate it before twisting the rind into the glass and taking a drink.

"I mean," Pascoe said, exasperated. "Is there any sort of feud between Dowry and Kutulas, like with Harkin?"

Carlyle sucked on an ice cube, and then spat it back into his glass. "Are you kidding? Dowry is a pussy. So concerned with being accepted by the natives he'll put up with anything to look like a good sport, and Kutulas knows it."

"Word is, Dowry might be hurting for cash."

"I've heard it too. Common enough. Lot of shrinking bank accounts behind fresh paint. If Kutulas printed *that*, maybe he'd get a rise out of Dowry."

"Do you know the son?"

"Vin?"

"Vaughn."

"Don't think so, maybe ran into him at a bar sometime." Carlyle reached for his shirt pocket, pulled out a can of Copenhagen and proceeded to pack a huge pinch of snuff under his lower lip. "Finished?"

Pascoe slid the empty beer bottle across the table. Carlyle nodded thanks and spit down the neck.

"Matthew Dearborne? Heard of him?" Pascoe asked.

"Sure. Three Sisters. Stands that fancy stud."

"You've got to know more than that."

"Wife went missing a couple of years ago."

"That's it?"

"That's it."

"Bryce and Percy Sinclair?"

Carlyle looked at him blankly.

"Bimbo, you're killing me. I thought you kept your ear to the ground."

"Can't help if I don't know the folks you're talking about." Carlyle emptied his mouth into the bottle. "Why make such a fuss anyway? Kutulas will move on soon enough."

"He's implying I had something to do with a murder."

"Done worse. Want my advice? Stop asking questions. That's the bigger sin. Remember, you're the hired help, a horse mechanic. You don't come from shit, so you don't count for shit. Hell, when I was a jock, a winning jock, and putting money in pockets, I was still one step below you and one step above the Mexicans and the niggers. They don't really need me to train their horses. Hell, you can't swing a dead cat without hitting a trainer in these parts. But, if they have a betting jones, they need me. They may not like me, but they need me. You, they don't need."

CHAPTER NINE

For the first time in memory, Harkin Veterinary Associates closed its doors. Normally, even on holidays, either Harkin or Pascoe wore a pager, but Harkin would have none of it on the day of Devon's funeral.

"Anyone gonna hold our paying respects against us, I don't want them as a client," Harkin said. And that was that.

Service and reception were held at Stonemason Farm. Devon, after viewing a Discovery Channel program on morticians, had in typically precocious fashion, made clear her distaste for traditional burial and desire for cremation. Pascoe felt differently, it was hard enough visiting the grave of his father, having him in an urn on a shelf would be impossible.

Clear skies brought bitter cold. An autumn sun sat low to the south, tracing skeletal shadows of leafless trees across the land. Against the brown decay, a sober white canvas pavilion had been erected to the side of the barns. The veterinarians arrived together in Harkin's Volvo station wagon. It was easier for the old man to get in and out of and less obtrusive than a rattling diesel.

A large crowd milled under the pavilion. Mourners clustered in familiar groups. Shiny Italian double-breasted jackets consoled tailored British suits, all swathed in identical charcoal overcoats. Women decades younger orbited the men erratically, like tiny moonlets. Jewelry, too garish to be faux, glittered on ears and necks and hands like attendant stars. Nearby, a collection of riders and trainers gathered, layered in earth-toned corduroy and wool. Gerald stood in the center, accepting the condolences of his peers.

The farmhands of Stonemason waited far to the back, near one of the supports. Pascoe spotted Emilio praying silently to the side. The farm manager had doted on Devon most of her life. Immigration policy was such that his wife and daughter were forced to remain in Mexico, and Devon became a surrogate for his fatherly attention. His face was pinched and sallow, and his hair poorly combed. Pascoe excused himself from Harkin and headed over.

Emilio started when Pascoe rested a hand on his shoulder.

"Emilio, I'm so sorry."

"Ey, Doctor, *gracias*. It's not going to be the same around here without the little one. She knew the horses very good."

"Are you getting enough sleep? I can find someone to help with the stalls for a few days."

Emilio waved him off. "No, no. I'll be okay. The work helps to clear the head. I'm still having some *pesadilla*, bad dreams, after finding Devon. I worry now some monster might get my Annalisa." Emilio's face convulsed.

"I hadn't realized you were the one," Pascoe said. "There hasn't been much detail coming out."

Emilio nodded, blowing his nose into a cloth handkerchief. He shoved it into a front pants pocket. "Mr. Dowry knows a lot of people at the paper. I've heard him arguing about this. He doesn't want his daughter used to sell papers, but I think he's wrong. If it were my Annalisa, I would want everyone to know what happened. That way, when the police catch him, no one will show him mercy. But Mr. Dowry won't listen."

The police had questioned him roughly and accusingly, and Emilio was grateful for a friendly ear. He had been with Dowry all day at the house building something—Pascoe had a hard time deciphering exactly what it was, either an entertainment center or a kitchen cabinet—but whatever it was, Dowry kept checking in on the project to make sure it was done to his specifications. It wasn't until dark that Dowry mentioned he hadn't seen or heard Devon for some time. Fearful she had fallen from her horse, he sent Emilio to search the estate's trails.

It took him over an hour to find her. Devon's body lay only fifty yards or so into the stretch of trees curving around the east side of the house, but the muted colors of her riding gear blended into the forest litter. Emilio spat out a string of Spanish curses at this, brightly colored clothes would have been spotted sooner and maybe, maybe, an extra few minutes could have made a difference. The lack of conviction in his voice argued against it.

He found Devon in a small clearing off one of the trails. Face up with her mouth slightly open, for a moment she seemed to be alive and calling for help. Only at her side did he notice the blood. It pooled around the lower half of her body like a crimson skirt, unabsorbed by the frozen ground. Four inches of smooth, blunted wood protruded from between her legs. Emilio turned and rushed back to inform Dowry, who called the police.

The police initially focused on Emilio because of the murder weapon. She had been stabbed, through her britches, with the jagged end of a broken pitchfork handle. The fork was found a short distance away, blood and clumps of hair stuck to the tines. Both, suspended in plastic evidence bags, had been shoved in his face as a detective badgered him. The pitchfork had come from the barn—Emilio had burned 'SF' into the handle with a soldering iron—but he swore again and again he would never harm Devon. Emilio was sure he was about to be jailed, confession or not, but Dowry intervened and vouched for him.

"Ey," Emilio sighed. "I never even got to say goodbye to my *ninā*. Now I have to say goodbye to a jar." He inclined his head over Pascoe's shoulder.

Previously, attendants had obscured the front of the pavilion. Now they cleared and left a long, linen covered table in their wake. At its center, surrounded by towering arrangements of daylilies and orchids, was an elegant silver canister that in different circumstances could have been mistaken for a martini shaker. It didn't seem right a girl could be reduced to elements so small.

An easel holding a black and white photograph of Devon and an unadorned wooden podium flanked the table. It was elegant and subdued, and emphasized the complexity of the girl. This arrangement forced contemplation of Devon's life, rather than her death, and maybe that was better.

An organ started playing Ave Maria. Emilio, lighter from sharing his burden, squeezed Pascoe's arm and found his seat. Pascoe hunted for Harkin and spotted him talking closely with a squat, swarthy man near the viewing table. Pascoe was on his way to join him when a clergyman stepped to the podium. "If you could all be seated, I think we're ready," he said.

Harkin broke off and headed for the second row of seats. Pascoe caught up with him there. "I didn't recognize the man you were talking with," he said.

"That's Kutulas."

"What the hell are you talking to him about?"

"Just giving him my thoughts on his writing," Harkin said. His face was flushed from the exchange.

The service was the standard Protestant model. A few Psalms read, a few Psalms sung. The pastor expounded on God's Plan and how Devon was in a better place with the Father, a comforting thought for those not yet passed on, inadequate for those with ones who had. Another song, the preacher sat, and Dowry came to the podium.

His skin was the color of dishwater, his eyes red and swollen. A streak of dried mucous marred his coat sleeve and fresh snot bubbled from one nostril. Shaking hands gripped the podium, causing it to rattle.

"My friends," Dowry began. "Not all of you knew my daughter. Many of you came to support me. I thank you, but it is an unnecessary kindness. The purpose of this gathering is not to support me, or Taylor, or Vaughn. Rather, we are here to remember, and celebrate, the life of my daughter, and my job is to make sure everyone leaves understanding the type of person we have lost. If I can do this, then perhaps I have made up, in some small part, for my failures."

Dowry straightened, ready to do right by his daughter. The podium stopped rattling.

"I'm going to tell you a story. It happened some time ago, but it doesn't matter, the girl Devon was became the teenager Devon was and, if she had not been taken from us, would have grown, unchanged in spirit, to womanhood.

"Devon's mother and I split up when she was tiny, and when she was old enough to realize our home was missing a mother, she became very angry. Wouldn't talk to me for days. One Christmas, she wouldn't even bring me a list for Santa, and gave it to Vaughn instead, hoping an older brother might have connections with the North Pole. I did everything wrong to try to win her affection. I married twice, badly, just to bring a woman into the house. I tried gifts, but she was too principled to be bought off. She was disciplining me, and wasn't about to back down.

"Her first day of kindergarten came around. I've had to rely on nannies for a lot of things, but never to take my kids to their first day of school. I went on and on about what a big day it was: don't be scared, I'm sure the teacher is nice; you'll make lots of new friends. The car seat might as well have been empty. When we arrived, she unbuckled herself, hopped out, and walked to the door without looking back. It was an arrow in the heart. It was at that moment, watching my little girl leave, that in my soul, truly, sincerely, I asked her to forgive me. Maybe I even whispered it, I don't know, but Devon knew. She stopped halfway to the door, came back, and gave me the first hug and kiss I'd received in forever and whispered, 'Time Out is over Daddy, don't cry, I'll be back soon and tell you about my day.' That's the kind of girl I lost. Smart. Strong. Forgiving. Better than me. All of you here, for my sake, need to know that. She was better than me."

Dowry finished and walked over to the table, cradled the urn in his hands and walked out. The pastor took his place at the podium. "If you will all follow Oliver, we will now disperse the ashes," he said.

A low murmur ran through the crowd. Pascoe glanced at Harkin, who shrugged, but stood and left along with everyone else. Dowry stopped in the middle of the huge outdoor arena and waited. Once the mourners were huddled in a semi-circle around him, Dowry took the lid off the urn and poured what amounted to a large handful of Devon's remains onto the footing.

"Support every footfall of your beloved mounts," he said.

Another portion of ashes were poured into his cupped hand and flung it into the air.

"Be carried to the pastures and nourish the grass."

Dowry walked over to far end of the arena where a thin birch sapling was newly planted, its peeling bark stark and white as a tombstone. He scooped soft dirt away from the base of the tree, making a hole, and turned the rest of Devon's ashes into it. "Be bound to the earth. Goodbye sweet one."

Vaughn, quietly absent from the ceremony, was conspicuously present at the reception. He was energetic and neat in a pressed black crepe suit, greeting guests loudly and slapping a few on the back. He flitted hyperactively from group to group, but Kutulas was the only one willing to engage for any length of time.

Pascoe scanned the room, hoping Hunter might show up, though he knew there was little chance. Harkin left to commiserate with the Mayor, an heiress, and a collection of non-elected sovereigns of the realm. Wallace, hanging on the arm of an unfamiliar gentleman, waved politely but made no effort at conversation. Monroe Ridgeway observed from a corner in an ill-fitting sport coat poorly hiding a shoulder holster. Pascoe looked at his watch. He had been standing by himself for the last fifteen minutes. The *Monitor* piece had made him sufficiently undesirable.

"Well if it isn't Doctor Pass-cow!" Vaughn unbalanced Pascoe with a vigorous thump between the shoulder blades.

Pascoe straightened and turned. Vaughn waited for a response with a fresh drink and a smirk. His pupils were wide and danced in their sockets.

"Vaughn, I'm so sorry—"

"Sorry?" Vaughn asked. "For my losing a sister or you losing a pet?"

People turned to the commotion. Monroe left his corner.

"No more fan club at Stonemason." Vaughn raised his voice to a falsetto. "Oh Jordan, you're soooo good with the horse. Oh Jordan, you can figure it out."

Pascoe's ears were burning. Vaughn made an awkward attempt at snapping his fingers.

"I've got it," he said. "You missed an opportunity. A couple more years and you could have started humping your way into the family fortune." Vaughn leered at Pascoe. "Come on, just between you and me, *did* you wait?"

Pascoe had never had any training in throwing a punch, but bracing against horses all his life had taught him to root his feet to the ground. When Pascoe's fist slammed into Vaughn's face, his head snapped back so forcefully that, had he remained conscious, he would have been able to see the people standing behind him. Vaughn didn't feel his nose crumple, his lips part, or his incisors loosen as they bit into the knuckles of Pascoe's right hand. Blood pooled on the parquet floor under his head. Before the beating could continue, Pascoe was wrapped up from behind and dragged away, arms pinned uselessly against his body.

"Bastard!" Pascoe screamed as he struggled. "You were nothing but an asshole while she was alive. She needed someone to look up to because she sure as hell couldn't look up to you."

"Listen to me Pascoe," Monroe whispered in his ear. "I'm going to let you go, but I want you out of here. If you're not around when I explain what happened, maybe you can avoid a battery charge."

Pascoe slumped in Monroe's grip. The detective released him and nodded in the direction of the exit. A few people knelt next to Vaughn and staunched the blood gushing from his nose. Harkin broke through the crowd and shook his head when he saw the body on the floor. He glared at Pascoe, seized his arm, and pulled him toward the exit. The crowd gave them plenty of room. The women looked horrified by the incident, but Pascoe got a few winks from a cluster of grinning men. One older gentleman with a walrus mustache gave him a thumb's up. Kutulas stood to the side, scribbling madly into a notebook.

Harkin fumed on the trip back to the clinic. He slammed the transmission into park, and the station wagon rocked to a stop next to the Dodge. "Damn it Jordie."

Pascoe rubbed a thumb over sore knuckles, something avoided during the ride back so as not to draw Harkin's attention. "He baited me."

"And you took it, though I doubt he expected such a strong strike." Harkin chuckled. "In a way, this might work in your favor, the South still likes a man who will defend his honor. But," he said, wagging a knobby finger, "I expect you to apologize to Oliver."

"I will," Pascoe said, stepping out of the car. "Still taking call?"

Harkin sighed. "Don't know if I'm up to it. Funerals put me in a mood. At my age and they're a little too prophetic."

"I'll take tonight," Pascoe said. "See you in the morning. We can take bets on the *Monitor*'s next headline."

"I've got ten says 'Punching Pascoe' is at least part of it," Harkin said, pulling away toward the main house.

Pascoe used the office phone to call the answering service and let them know he was available for emergencies and worked through a stack of patient records. At the bottom was a curled fax from Eastern Labs. Goldrush's botulinum test. Negative. Bridges scrawled a handwritten note across the bottom: *Take comfort, the mice are throwing a party.*

After a half hour of paperwork, there was nothing more to do and Pascoe went home. He half expected to see a squad car waiting, but the only black and white in residence was Barclay. He picked up on Pascoe's mood and was uncharacteristically subdued, and when they went for a long walk at dusk, the dog, usually a wanderer, stayed close at heel. Pascoe was in bed and asleep before eight.

The rattle of the pager/soup can combination woke him in the middle of the night. Forgetting he was on duty, he stared curiously at Barclay for a few moments, wondering why such an odd noise was coming from his dog. The confusion cleared, and Pascoe rolled over and grabbed the phone.

"Doctor Pascoe, you've got to help me. Something's wrong with Deadbolt and he's too big for me to get into the car and I don't know who else to call. He seemed to like you and he really doesn't take to Doctor Stokes and oh my God this can't be happing again!"

"Gail?"

"Can you come?"

Pascoe rubbed his face. "I specialize in horses. I don't even work on my own dog; I won't be much help."

"What can I do? He's stumbling into furniture and growling like he doesn't recognize me. It's like Lexus all over again."

"I thought you found Lexus dead in her stall."

"Please come," Rasmussen pleaded. She started crying. "Please."

Pascoe relented. "I've got a textbook around here somewhere, but I'm not promising anything."

"You know the way, just come in when you get here."

Moonlight hid Samfield's flaws by bathing chipped paint in a uniform glow, blending sagging roof into black horizon, and mending fence lines with shadow. This lovely mirage lasted only until he was close enough to see the large holes in the screen door.

Rasmussen sat on the floor in a long flannel nightgown, cradling Deadbolt's head in her lap. His neck arched and all four legs extended so that topside paws floated above the floor. His chest rose and fell regularly, but the dog was stiff as a corpse.

"How long has he been this way?" Pascoe asked.

"A couple of minutes."

Pascoe knelt beside the dog. Deadbolt's eyes were wide and unblinking. His tongue, meaty and pink, hung flaccidly and dripped saliva, soaking a large section of Rasmussen's nightgown. Pascoe placed stethoscope to the dog's chest. A strong, regular heart thudded beneath the ribs. Pascoe moved the stethoscope around. Dry, rustling air moved smoothly in and out of the lungs. He plucked a thermometer from his shirt pocket and stuffed it into Deadbolt's rectum, which, he noted, had normal tone. While the thermometer was registering, Pascoe shined a penlight into the dog's eyes. No response from the pupils. Pascoe tapped the corner of each eye, eliciting a reflexive blink. He grabbed a foreleg and tried to bend it at the elbow. It moved reluctantly, like a rusty pump handle. Pascoe tapped his forefinger just below Deadbolt's kneecap. The leg kicked sharply.

"Has he had seizures before?" Pascoe asked.

"Is that what this is?"

"I'm not sure." Deadbolt's temperature was normal. "Be right back."

At his truck, Pascoe grabbed a sixty cc syringe, a four-inch wide roll of Elastikon tape, activated charcoal, and a foal-sized stomach tube—the three-quarter inch diameter tube used for adult horses would never fit a dog, even one as large as Deadbolt. He also took the copy of *The Handbook of Small Animal Emergency Medicine* found buried in a cardboard box at the house, a three cc syringe topped with a twenty-two-gauge needle and a bottle of Valium. It was cumbersome, but he managed it in one trip.

"Do you have a bowl this deep?" Pascoe held his hands about eight inches apart.

"In the kitchen, first cabinet to the right of the sink," Rasmussen said.

Pascoe cringed. All she had was white porcelain. *Easier to replace than the dog*, he thought, grabbed two and filled both half full with tap water.

Back at Deadbolt's side, he dumped charcoal into a bowl and mixed it with the large syringe until it became slurry. Then, with difficulty, he pried open Deadbolt's jaws and set the roll of tape lengthwise in his mouth as a speculum. His slid the foal tube through the cardboard tube at the center of the tape, down the esophagus to the stomach. Foul smelling, digested kibble refluxed onto the floor. When the flow stopped, he primed the tube with clean water and sucked with his mouth to get the contents moving again. He repeated this procedure five times until the stomach disgorged only brown tinged water, sent the charcoal mixture down, and pulled tube and tape from the dog's mouth.

"What's this?" Pascoe pointed to chunks of black material scattered among the refluxed kibble.

"Looks like black plastic."

"Do you keep any pesticides, like snail bait, in the house? Something that comes in a black plastic container?"

Rasmussen raised an eyebrow. "Does it look like I'm overly concerned with snails in my petunias?" She wiped an errant glob of charcoal from Deadbolt's muzzle. "You think he was poisoned? I thought you said he had a seizure."

"I asked if he had ever had a seizure." Pascoe flipped through the textbook's formulary, found the dose for Valium, guessed Deadbolt's weight at one fifty, and pulled a cc and a half into the small syringe. "I don't know exactly what to make of this, but it looks like he got into something other than his normal dinner, and it's altered his brain function. His pupils aren't responding normally, reflexes are hyperactive, and his extensor muscles are rigid. The Valium will relax him and give his body time to process whatever is in his system."

Pascoe showed Rasmussen how to grip Deadbolt at the elbow in order to raise the cephalic vein. After popping the needle into the vein, he asked her to lift her thumb, and he injected the tranquilizer. In seconds, Deadbolt's eyelids closed and his body melted to the floor, sleeping comfortably.

Rasmussen pushed Deadbolt's tongue back into his mouth and slid gently from underneath his head. "Will he be all right?"

"I'm not sure." Pascoe wiped blackened fingers on his pant legs. "Have you talked to Sam, asked her if she brought anything home from school?"

"What, like drugs you mean?" Rasmussen snapped. "You think Sam did this?"

"Whoa. I'm not saying she did it on purpose, I'm just saying it might be a good idea to ask. You wouldn't be the first mother unaware of her daughter's extracurricular activities, and Deadbolt wouldn't be the first dog to fall victim to an accidental overdose.

"When I was in school, an undergrad brought in a puppy because it had eaten an entire batch of marijuana brownies, including the foil they were wrapped in. He was afraid of expulsion, and kept quiet. The internist was about to empty the kid's bank account running lab tests and ordering an MRI. That's when he explained what had happened."

Rasmussen's manic laugh collapsed into sobs. "I can't, I can't, I can't," she whispered, hugging her knees. Pascoe observed silently, unsure what to make of the outburst. She cried for a minute or two before pressing the heels of her hands against her eyes and regaining composure. "She's gone. We got into argument earlier today about her grades and I grounded her for a week. When Deadbolt started acting strangely I went to her room to ask for help, but she was gone. She wouldn't hurt Deadbolt," she said flatly.

"Have you called the cops?"

"Plenty of times, but not tonight. This isn't the first time Sam has taken off. They won't do anything about a runaway unless she's gone for more than forty eight hours, and she's always back before then."

"There you go," Pascoe said. "She'll crash at a friend's house and be back tomorrow."

"Sam doesn't have a lot of friends. Her only real friend was killed the other day and I wouldn't let her skip class for the funeral. She was furious."

"Not Devon's funeral?"

"Did you know her?"

"You don't read the *Monitor*?"

"I wouldn't let Deadbolt take a dump on that rag."

"Why not let her go?"

"It's complicated. Let's go into the kitchen and clean up," Rasmussen said, grabbing the bowls and stomach tube.

Despite Rasmussen's scrubbing, the bowl that held the charcoal remained a smoky gray.

"Sorry," Pascoe said. "You could try bleach."

"Don't worry about it," Rasmussen said, "it'll do as long as it doesn't leak." She placed the bowl onto a drying rack and reached under the sink to grab a handful of rags and a bottle of 409. After the floor was clean and Deadbolt re-examined and found to be stable, Rasmussen asked if Pascoe wanted coffee.

Pascoe checked his watch. "What the hell, too late to try to get back to sleep."

While Rasmussen made coffee, Pascoe stayed by Deadbolt and absentmindedly stroked the dog's long ears. His tail thumped heavily against the floor.

"He's coming around," Pascoe said.

Rasmussen hurried into the room holding two cups. She handed Pascoe his and put hers on the floor so she could pet the dog. More thumping rattled the cup in its saucer.

"He's going to be okay?"

"We'll see, but it's a good sign."

Rasmussen smiled radiantly. "You don't know how much this means to me. The man who gave Deadbolt to me..."

"I know David." When she looked at him curiously, he explained. "I saw a picture of the two of you at Hunter's."

"How is he?"

"Good as can be expected. He's living on his own now, at a farm down the road."

"How wonderful." Rasmussen hung her head. "God I miss him, but can't bear to visit. Imagine what it's like for a man who was your lover, and practically a father to your child, to barely remember your name."

"He and Sam were close?"

"Adored each other. David had been her riding instructor even before we started dating. She was furious when I refused David's proposal."

"Why did you?"

"Ever been married?"

"No."

"I'm ten years older than David. I got married for the first time when I was very young, and it was a mistake. It lasted two years. David was still very young when we started seeing each other, and it would have killed me if he decided I had been a mistake." Rasmussen smiled wearily and sipped her coffee.

"Do you think he would have asked you again?"

"I like to think so. In a few years I would have said yes."

"I was told Deadbolt was given to you to deter other men."

"Deadbolt was supposed to scare men away, but not from me, from Sam."

"I don't follow you."

Rasmussen eyed Pascoe skeptically. "Right. It was your evil twin checking out her ass the other day. No, no, no, don't apologize. The way she dresses invites attention. She wasn't always so provocative, and the change really bothered David. He tried to talk to her about it, but then she stopped riding Lexus. David believed it was her way of avoiding him and his questions, so he stopped asking."

"Did you figure out what brought on the change?"

"It would be easy to blame it on hormones and boys. Hell, I stopped riding when I was fifteen so I could go to parties on the weekend instead of horse shows. David figured a puppy might distract her, and a really big one might distract the boys. But it was more than that. David got hurt, Lexus died, and Sam withdrew. She would scream at me over the littlest thing and take off for a day or two. Sometimes, she'd spend the entire day in her room. I have to admit, I did worry about drugs. The only difference between Foxfield and any other school is that the drugs are more expensive, and though Sam couldn't afford any, someone could have given her some. I even ordered one of those home test kits, the kind where you swipe a cloth around your kid's room and send it back for the company to test, but it came back with nothing."

Deadbolt curled his body toward the ceiling and flailed so he was lying upright. His head swung back and forth like a pendulum. Pascoe grabbed his muzzle and shined the penlight into the dog's eyes. The pupils were responding normally, but the eyes were nystagmic, darting involuntarily from side to side.

"I'm going," he said. "The worst appears over. He'll be his old self by sunup. Offer him water in another hour, but no food until he's back to normal."

Pascoe started to stand, but Rasmussen grabbed his wrist and kept him on the floor. "Doctor Pascoe, when you came by asking questions about Lexus I was sure you were working for the insurance company, and it scared me to death. Do you understand why?"

"I suppose you're afraid the money might be the only thing keeping Sam around."

"Do you believe I had nothing to do with the Lexus' death?"

"Yes."

"What you said, about having a similar case, and trying to find out why it died—true?"

"It was Devon's horse."

"And more information might help you?"

"In many ways."

Rasmussen kneaded the ruff of skin at Deadbolt's neck. Pascoe started to get up again.

"Things started a few weeks before," Rasmussen said. "Deadbolt woke me, barking furiously and clawing at the front door. I didn't think anything of it at first, figured he had to go and was miffed he hadn't done his business earlier. When I opened the door he bolted towards the barn. That's completely unlike him, so I threw on my old field-jacket and a pair of muck boots and headed out. When I caught up, he was trapped in a stall, howling like mad, and when I let him out he flew past me to the woods. He came back after a few minutes, sniffed around the barn for a bit, and went back to the house.

"In the morning I had a closer look and noticed the padlock securing the tack and feed room had been pried off, but nothing was missing. I figured he had foiled a robbery, every weekend you hear of a saddle stolen. Sam was sure someone had come to the barn specifically to hurt Lexus, but couldn't explain why. For more than a week afterward she and Deadbolt camped out in the tack room.

"Two days after I convinced her to sleep in her bed, Deadbolt woke me up again, but this time I knew why: an awful racket was coming from the barn. It was Lexus, flopping against the walls. It was horrible, her eyes were bloodied and swollen shut and she would circle, run face first into a wall, collapse, get up, and do it again. By the time Doctor Stokes arrived, Lexus was dead and Sam was inconsolable. The next night was the first time Sam went missing."

"What happened with the insurance report? Why did Stokes say there was no sign of struggle?"

"Did me a favor, I guess. I told her everything, even about the break-in. She didn't know what killed Lexus, but knew if Virginia Bloodstock caught a whiff of anything suspicious they would try to deny the claim, so she sanitized the report and called it a heart attack. She's been our vet for some time, and knows no amount of money could persuade me or Sam to harm Lexus."

Pascoe understood what Stokes had done. Somr insurance companies were more than happy to settle claims quickly with the big accounts, but hunt for any excuse to stiff a backyard owner without means or influence.

"Would you mind if I talk to Doctor Stokes about the case?"

"Not anymore. I'll call her and let her know she can talk freely. It's the least I can do after tonight."

"Then I'm glad I came. Are you going to be all right if I leave? Is there someone you can call? Your ex maybe? He might want to know about Sam."

Rasmussen laughed, the first light-hearted sound she had made all night. "You have no idea how terrible that suggestion is. My ex-husband doesn't want to have anything to do with us."

"That's a shame."

Rasmussen shrugged. "The way it goes. Like I said, the marriage was a mistake. Sam gripes about missing out on all the Montpelier money, but I think her bitterness comes from not having a father around."

"Montpelier? Dearborne's stud?"

"The very same. Matthew is my ex-husband."

CHAPTER TEN

Over the next few days, Pascoe was bit, bumped, and kicked by more patients since graduation. Horses had little tolerance for inattention, especially when it resulted in bent needles and sore muscles, and they took advantage.

Devon's death weighed heavy on his mind—he found it difficult to sleep without scotch—and Rasmussen's marriage to Dearborne and Sam's friendship with Devon further convinced him of a common thread that just needed plucking to free up a loose end.

He left multiple messages for Stokes. If she was anything like him, he was in for more of the same. Veterinarians have an annoying habit of classifying messages from colleagues as low priority—they were, after all, the competition and did nothing to generate income. He was therefore not unhappy to arrive home one evening and find Wallace sitting on his front step.

"Didn't think you wanted to know me anymore," Pascoe said.

Wallace reached to ruffle Barclay's fur, but the dog stepped aside. She frowned at the dog, and turned back to Pascoe. "You're a celebrity. Who could resist the man who floored Vaughn Dowry?"

"So you drove over here to congratulate me. 'Fraid you won't have much company."

"You'd be surprised. Just because nobody's patting you on the back doesn't mean they don't want to. Why do you think you're not sitting in a cell right now? After Harkin dragged you away, Dowry screamed for your head. Only calmed down after the old timers convinced him it would be better for him, and Devon, if he let it go."

"And how do you know this?" Pascoe asked.

"Because I was with one of the old timers." Wallace stamped her feet and pulled a briefcase from behind her. "I came to buy some forgiveness. Fix a drink and I'll give you a present."

Intrigued, Pascoe let Wallace in and poured them both a scotch on the rocks. The recent bouts of insomnia made for a well kept home, and after making a fire he joined Wallace on a fully folded and cushioned couch.

"You have better taste in scotch than you do in wine," she said, holding her glass to the light. She patted the case. "You haven't asked what I have in here yet. It's going to make you very happy."

"One-way tickets for you and Kutulas to Argentina?"

"You're going to die a bitter old man." The briefcase locks popped open. "When things heated up, I shredded my copies, but had a change of heart after the funeral and convinced the my office clerk to let me take the originals."

"How did you manage that?"

"Promised to blow him."

Wallace punched Pascoe in the bicep when she saw his expression. "I'm kidding, you moron."

Wallace sipped from her scotch. She removed her shoes while Pascoe argued, and sat languidly on one hip. The position halved the distance between them.

"No, Jordan, I mean it," she said when he finished. "Same deal. No cops. I brought these files because I feel bad I got you into this in the first place. These are originals, and someone knows who has them, so I'm dead if this gets out. If I go, you know I'll take you with me. Besides, what makes you think cops can make any more sense out of these cases?"

"Nothing," Pascoe admitted. "Thought I was onto something with Goldrush, but the botulism test came back negative."

"So it wasn't botulism?"

"I should make a presumptive diagnosis of botulism even with these results, but it doesn't feel right. That's the problem. If I don't know why those horses died, I can't string them together, and if I can't do that, I can't connect them to Devon." Pascoe slumped into the couch and tossed the folders on the coffee table.

"This isn't going to make you feel better," Wallace said. "I checked up on Randolph. At a lameness conference in Kentucky for four days before the Sinclair horse died."

Pascoe took a long pull from his glass. The ice was melted, taking the bite, and subtlety, from the liquor. Wallace leaned across Pascoe to place her empty glass on the table. When she sat back, there was no longer any distance between them.

"So, what's next?" she asked.

"I'm trying to get hold of Morgan Stokes to ask her about the Rasmussen case."

"Anything I should know about?"

Pascoe deflected the question. He didn't want to cause trouble for Stokes. "Did you know Rasmussen was married to Dearborne?"

"She was the first wife? No kidding."
"You knew?"
"Hmmm? Not specifically that it was her. I mean, I knew about the divorce, who doesn't? You think the *Monitor* is a pain in *your* ass? They crucified her."

Pascoe stared blankly.

"The divorce? Paternity case? I guess it's true what they say: gossip is like a tornado, it can blow through and hit every house but one.

"Long before Dearborne hit big with Montpelier, he was a small time guy with a good eye for young stock. Made a decent living pinhooking and running claimers, so people in the area knew of him. The divorce shocked everyone, not the split, but because he demanded a paternity test. The story goes it was a shot in the dark, Dearborne trying to avoid parting with his cash, but the lab came back saying the kid wasn't his. The wife, Rasmussen I guess, denied everything and accused Dearborne of paying somebody off."

"Did he?"

"Nobody knows, which is why the story still circulates. Anyway, Dearborne got a sympathetic judge, this is the South after all, and all she got was the house. No alimony, no support. Spent what little money she had on appeals, but he had more time, more money, and more lawyers. Guess who came out on top?"

"Dearborne thinks his current wife left him for another man," Pascoe said.

"Ain't karma beautiful?"

"Better hope not."

"Feelings still hurt? I apologized—even brought you a present."

"I don't recall an apology."

"Let me make it up to you."

She moved in slowly, expertly, striking with lips and tongue first, mouthing Pascoe's earlobe, and then running her tongue down his neck. He didn't push away when she slid to his mouth, which was open in surprise, and if he was forced to admit, desire. Encouraged, Wallace swung around to straddle his leg and brought her hand to his crotch. His response made her smile. His hands found her breasts, stiff nipples straining against silk.

The shrill ring of the phone sent Wallace tumbling from her perch, flabbergasted. "You're not actually going to answer it?"

He hadn't planned to, but dislodging Wallace gave him an opportunity. "It might be important," he said sheepishly. Given his state, the walk to the phone was both awkward and uncomfortable. He could feel her grin bore into his back. Pascoe lifted the receiver.

"Miracle of miracles, you're actually home."

"Hunter...hi!" Pascoe said, much to cheerfully.

Wallace snorted from the couch. Organized rustling followed.

"Thought I'd check up on you," Hunter said. "Heard what happened between you and Vaughn and figured you might need to talk."

"Orders to lay low from Harkin."

Another snort.

"Is that Barclay?"

Pascoe glared. Wallace responded with quizzical innocence. "Uh-huh. He was digging around in the yard and must have gotten into something."

"Try giving him some ginger."

"I'll do that."

Wallace had put her jacket on and grabbed her briefcase. She tapped Pascoe on the shoulder, indicated she was leaving the files, and bit him gently on the base of the neck. She dropped her free hand around his waist and gave him a firm, lingering squeeze. Satisfied, she bounced to the door and let herself out.

"You there, Jordan?" Hunter asked.

"Huh?"

"Do you want to come to dinner tomorrow? I'm making pot roast and there's going to be too much for just the two of us."

"Sorry, spaced out for a second. Sure, sounds great."

"Come over after work."

"I'll be there."

"Oh—and Jordan?"

"Yes?"

"Barclay's welcome, but really, teach him not to slam the door."

Pascoe needed to figure out how to handle Hunter. His first instinct was to ignore the entire incident and hope it wouldn't come up. As he moved the coffee table to unfold the couch, photographs from the Rasmussen report slid from the pile. The originals were glossy, color prints much more detailed than the photocopies Wallace initially brought. One of the liver was quite beautiful really, with its muddy color and stippling. Enlarged and cropped so nobody would know what it was, it might look like any other modern abstract work. If only its symmetry wasn't marred by the sample taken from the left lobe.

Sample? He opened the Rasmussen file to the autopsy report. Just as he thought; no mention of any pathology. He looked at the other photos. In the close-up of the chest, there were small pieces missing from the heart and lungs. Both kidneys had also been sampled. Pascoe carefully put the file back together.

Doctor Stokes was going to have to reorder her priorities.

Pascoe brought a purposely vague, early-relationship bouquet of wildflowers and a bottle of Cabernet to Timberbrook. He didn't know if the wine was any good, but it was from California and there had been a tag taped to the shelf where the bottle sat touting its boldness and hints of cherry, and it was only nine dollars, all of which sounded good.

"How...appropriate," Hunter said, taking the flowers and giving Pascoe a deep, possessive kiss. "David is watching TV. Dinner's almost ready, I just need to pop some rolls in the oven."

David brightened. "What time is it?"

"Time for work?"

"Time for dinner!" David said, collapsing in a fit of laughter.

"Got some new material." Pascoe sat down next to a sniggering David. "How are things at the Donaldson's?"

"They have a tractor and a truck, and Mr. Donaldson lets me drive."

"Only on the grass, David," Hunter said from the kitchen.

David leaned in and whispered conspiratorially. "If I practice, they might let me go to the feed store and pick up hay," he said, putting a finger to his lips.

"Well, well, well," Hunter said, leaning over the couch, handing Pascoe a glass of wine. "Isn't it just like men to keep secrets."

"David was just telling me what he was getting you for Christmas," Pascoe said. David sighed with relief.

"Just have to torture you to find out," she said, much too pleased with the idea.

The smell of baking bread ripened as the three of them sat. David went back to watching Jimmy Neutron. Pascoe sipped his wine. Hunter's eyes roamed over the photographs of David on the walls and back to the scarred, rapt face of her brother, and she chewed at the inside of her cheek. The kitchen timer broke the silence.

Hunter proved to be an excellent cook. She begged off praise, but was pleased all the same. Pushed for details, she admitted making the rolls from scratch and using carrots and potatoes from a small garden behind the barn. Pascoe, used to Pillsbury and Green Giant, wolfed down one plateful and was filling another before realizing he hadn't spoken since asking about the meal. Belatedly, and to the amusement of his hostess, he washed down his current mouthful and put down the fork.

"How's the new horse, uh, Banker, coming along?"

"I think he might be the one," Hunter said.

"The one?"

"The Olympic mount I've been looking for. I don't know if I'll have him up to speed in time for the next Games, if they even keep three-day, but definitely for the ones after that, or for the World Championships."

"Hunter's going to win me a medal!" David chimed in. "She showed me pictures. It's so big, they don't pin it on your clothes, they hang it around your neck!"

Hunter squeezed her brother's hand. "I'm not giving you anything David, it's been yours for years. They've just been holding on to it until I'm good enough to pick it up."

After dinner, Pascoe offered to drive back to the Donaldson's, but David would have none of it. He bundled into a parka, zipping the hood until only his nose and smile were visible within a deep, fur-trimmed tunnel. Clumsy mittens protected his hands from freezing to the bike's handlebars. Before long, he was halfway down the driveway, wobbling as he waved back toward the farm. Pascoe and Hunter, shivering without their coats, waited until David had made the shaky turn onto the main road before heading back inside and clearing plates.

"I could have tied the bike to my truck," Pascoe said, squirting soap into the sink.

"He doesn't want to be babied," Hunter said. "He needs to do what he can on his own."

"You didn't sound so excited about his driving."

"I have no problem with David careening around a pasture, where the most damage he can do is knock down a post, but I'll kill Donaldson if he lets David go to the feed store." Hunter snapped the top on a Tupperware container holding the leftover pot roast.

"You heard."

"Good ears," she replied, tapping one for emphasis. "But even my ninety year-old grandma could have picked up on your visitor."

"Barclay? He promised to behave, and we haven't heard a peep from him all night." Hunter didn't crack a smile. "Look, she's not even a friend. More like a business acquaintance."

"Then why lie?"

"I don't know—you caught me off guard." Pascoe turned back to the sink and scrubbed at a plate.

"So what kind of business is she in? Strange time of night to be making house calls."

"Hmmm?"

"You said she was a business acquaintance. What kind?"

Pascoe turned off the water and rubbed his hands on a towel. "I can't tell you."

"Ah."

"I know it sounds evasive—"

"Ya think?"

"Kind of a confidentiality agreement."

"I could tell by her stealth that confidentiality is a priority. Mares make less noise when they're in heat."

"Maybe she has a thing for me, is it my fault? Besides, what do you care? We just started going out, it's not like we're a couple or anything." *Uh-oh.*

"You're right Jordan, we're not a couple or anything. Thanks for the help with the dishes. Need help rounding up Barclay?" Hunter smiled, teeth like a snow-bank. Pascoe had a lot of shoveling to do.

"No, I'll be fine."

The outside air painted ice across his corneas. Downright balmy compared to the apartment.

    Morgan Stokes tested his patience. Pascoe left message after message and paged her to no avail. When she did call back, he was at his desk, and avoided beginning a perpetual game of phone tag.

"Christ Morgan, I was getting ready to camp out at your front door," Pascoe said.

"I had to confirm with Rasmussen first, you know that. The horse isn't going anywhere."

"Ever hear of professional courtesy?"

"I'm not going to get into it with you Pascoe. You'd ignore the bang-up job I did suturing a wound and criticize the wrap if it would gain your clinic a client—and you know I'd do the same."

    If you wrapped to the inside like everyone else I wouldn't have to cover your ass for the bandage bow, Pascoe wanted to say. "A truce then? The info you have on the Rasmussen horse could really help on another case I'm working."

"Rasmussen told you the story. The horse was dead when I arrived. It had scrapes on its head, so it must have thrashed some. What more do you want?"

"What about the tissue samples?"

"I didn't take any samples."

"Stop shitting me Morgan. I've seen your entire report, including the pictures. You should have taken those first, because I can see the wedges you cut out of pretty much every organ in the body." Pascoe pushed. "The insurance company doesn't know about this, Rasmussen just gave permission for me to see your report. Be straight with me, or I'll let them know, and maybe they'll come after you for the hundred grand."

"You're a dickhead Pascoe."

"Been hearing that a lot lately."

"You've been to Samfield?" Pascoe admitted he had. "Lexus was slumming. It's obvious Gail needs money, who's to say she wouldn't take out the horse and get some new windows or something, right?"

"So you turn the other way because someone needs money? My, what a big heart you have."

"Let me finish. I did exactly what you would have done; I went into CYA mode. I grabbed samples and took pictures. I had all my little bottles of formalin lined up on the hood of my truck and there's Sam looking like a grenade just went off in her head. Rasmussen knows I'm not buying her story, and she knows if I'm not on board the chances of her getting a check are slim. I've got two kids I'm raising by myself because their father couldn't handle the fact that I had to be on call and couldn't be counted on to have dinner on the table by six. It's not easy, and Rasmussen is trying to get by slicing meat behind a deli counter."

"I don't know what you would have done, but I said fuck it. I don't know what happened to Lexus. Dropped dead or maybe she killed her. Don't care. Rasmussen needed a break. I never sent the samples to the lab, just reported what I saw: no abnormalities, probable heart attack."

"And the samples?" Pascoe asked. "Do you still have them?"

"Never said I went out of CYA mode, did I?"

"I'll never speak of your inability to hit a jugular vein again."

"Won't hold my breath," Stokes said. "Want me to send them over?"

"I'll run by and pick them up."

"Better. I don't need my pager going off because the mail is to slow for your liking."

"You want me to do what?" Maggie asked incredulously.

"Reschedule the rest of my calls, I have an errand to run," Pascoe said.

"Jordan, listen. You may not believe this, but your little scuffle has actually helped repair the damage caused by the *Monitor*. King's schedule is full again, and you're catching up, but if I start changing appointments around at the last minute, people are going to use it as an excuse to stay away."

"This is more important."

"King's not going to be happy."

"He'll understand, trust me."

Picking up the tissue samples and driving to the lab took more than two hours. There was a state-run lab a mere twenty miles from the practice, but Pascoe had lost confidence in that facility more than a year ago when the resident pathologist diagnosed an insect bite as an aggressive lymphosarcoma and recommended radical surgery. Pascoe's gut told him the horse didn't fit the cancer profile and he resubmitted the sample to Eastern Labs, a private facility. Lee Bridges, the head pathologist, concluded spider venom the most likely culprit. Pascoe followed her recommendation of steroid injection and the horse recovered within the week. He hadn't used anyone else since.

He had met Bridges in person before, when he dropped off time-sensitive samples, and cultivated the kind of friendly relationship men develop with women they don't want to sleep with. Short to the point of dwarfishness, Bridges had the soft, wide, shape that comes from the pursuit of knowledge and avoidance of exercise. Lustrous black hair hung in a tight braid to the back of her knees, and when she moved, even slightly, the end would bob like a jig at the end of a fishing line. Pascoe suspected the hair hadn't been cut in over a decade, but if it ever were, wigmakers would fight over every strand. Though Bridges' face had the same doughy inexpressiveness of her body, discriminating intelligence enlivened her eyes.

To her credit, Bridges had worn away the prejudices Pascoe harbored for lab veterinarians. Certainly, she never could have made it in private practice: too messy and imprecise for her liking. He imagined patients dying while she waited for test results. And, in fairness, she likely considered him a kind of rogue, administering medications *en masse*, not entirely certain which ones were appropriate, and instead, like an anti-aircraft gunner, relied on volume rather than precision. Still, they recognized each other's competence and love for the job, which led to mutual respect and a friendship of sorts.

Eastern Labs leased a small space in a nondescript brick building next door to a Kentucky Fried Chicken. Pascoe wondered if other tenants realized more meat passed through their own building.

Bridges was in a typical pose—face pushed harshly into the eyepieces of a microscope. She sat on a vinyl covered stool that looked like it had been lifted from a diner, and had piled the seven hundred dollar, company provided ergonomic chair with textbooks so it could serve as a portable library. The height of the stool raised her hips level with the countertop and forced her to lean into the scope with enough force to blanch the skin at her brow.

"A chiropractor's dream," Pascoe said.

Bridges didn't look up. "Okay Zhivago, tell me what you think of this," she said, sliding off the stool. Pascoe chose to stand, he was a foot taller than Bridges and sitting would have folded him in half.

"Pop quizzes aren't a fair assessment of overall knowledge, haven't you heard?" Pascoe twirled the knob on the side of the scope to bring the slide into focus; the jumble of blue-stained, star shaped cells gave him no more information than the organ they came from. "It's a brain. My diagnosis, based on the small sample size, is that it must be from a relative of yours."

"At least you got the organ right this time," Bridges said. "It is in fact the cerebellum of *Procyon lotor*, a raccoon. It bit some kid and they needed a rabies check. Negative, fortunately, but it did survive a distemper infection at some point in its life." Bridges hopped back on the stool. "What brings you by?"

"I brought you a present."

Pascoe handed her the bag of samples he had picked up from Stokes. Bridges clucked with displeasure as each jar was removed. "How slow did you drive? These samples are falling apart. This hunk of kidney is all cortex, this heart sample is too thick, the liver looks like its been chewed on...what do you expect me to do with this?"

"Dazzle me. Sorry about the tissue. It's an older case; the samples have been sitting around. Think you can get a good read?"

Bridges held one of the bottles to the light and squinted. "I'm not promising anything. Why wait so long?"

"Not my case. These samples were misplaced, kind of, but they come from a horse that died of similar symptoms to Goldrush."

"Ah, my puzzle." Bridges looked at the samples with new appreciation.

"Yeah, mine too."

"Patience, patience. The oracle has not given her final word."

"I thought you said botulism was as good a diagnosis as any."

"As good as any for you, but I have this thing about not knowing."

"A thing?"

"Gets my panties in a knot. But now you've brought this sample and I can get back on the zebra trail."

"What?"

"Grandma's expression. It's like the needle-in-the haystack analogy. Say you've got a zebra running with a herd of mustangs, and you really want to get your hands on that zebra. He's real obvious if you spot him running with the herd, what with the stripes and all, but what if all you've got are a bunch of hoof prints? You follow every trail you can find, eventually one leads to the zebra. I kept running into dead ends with Goldrush, but now you've given me something new."

"Another zebra."

"And a new set of prints. With any luck, these samples will point me in a direction I haven't thought of." Her eyes gleamed with excitement. Pascoe knew she would prepare the slides as soon as he left.

He arrived home in darkness. Thick fog covered the cabin like a shroud. Cold seeped through the walls on nights like this and Pascoe stopped to gather an armload of logs from the woodpile. He was balancing the pile in one arm and digging for his keys with the other when he realized Barclay had already run inside. He was not likely to have forgotten to lock the door when he left and it was even more unlikely that Barclay could have pushed it open if he had: in damp weather the oak stiles swelled and Pascoe had to brace his full weight against he door to get it open. He dropped the firewood, reconsidered, and grabbed a stout log.

Matthew Dearborne sat on a chair in the kitchen. Barclay, in an embarrassing failure of loyalty, lay belly-up on the floor received a vigorous rubbing.

"I do like dogs," Dearborne said. "Easy to understand. Feed me. Love me. They know when somebody gets it."

"I would have hoped he'd be less accommodating."

"Door was unlocked."

"I don't believe that."

Dearborne shrugged. "Suit yourself. But unless you're going to play fetch, you won't be needing the stick."

Pascoe dropped it with the rest of the wood and closed the door. "What exactly do I need?"

"A little common sense. I was kind enough to let you into my home, and now I understand it might have been under false pretenses."

"You're wrong."

"I don't believe *that*. Now we're even, so stop the bullshit. I'll tell you some things I know for certain. Your father was a decent trainer, but had he stayed away from the booze still never would have had high rollers beating a path to his door. I imagine you know enough about horses to best your old man, but you've got a different monkey riding your back, don't you?"

Dearborne pulled a pack of Winstons from his shirt pocket, shook it and pulled a cigarette from the opening with his lips. He looked to Pascoe for permission.

"Go ahead," Pascoe said. He found a short glass in the sink and placed it on the table. Dearborne nodded thanks, dropped in the match he had used to light the Winston, and aimed cloud of smoke toward the ceiling.

"So," he continued, "you wind up in a tight place only Bimbo Carlyle can extricate you from. Now, I know you're not in deep with Carlyle again, but you show up at my door with an earnest face and noble intent and then scamper over to my ex-wife's place. I'm not real big on coincidence, and past history indicates you might be doing a favor for someone who has your sack in a vise. I want to know who's doing the squeezing."

Pascoe ground his teeth. "Carlyle. Does he also pick up your dry cleaning?"

"Sources should be kept secret," Dearborne said, taping ash into the glass. "Keeping a secret can be beneficial, or it can be dangerous. Depends on the secret. I don't like feeling threatened. I'm offering you a choice, even though you have not, to this point, shown a predilection for choosing wisely.

"You know, I started out much like you—my father was also involved in the industry, a farrier of great talent. He shod horses at fancy barns all over the country, when air travel wasn't as cheap as taking a bus. Could charge whatever he wanted, but didn't. He charged what he thought was 'fair', pocket change to his clients, and made it so he had to work twelve, fourteen hours a day to pay the mortgage. He used up his body to make horses run faster, jump higher, and move better until he walked humped over like a troll. Took pills to keep working and those ate a hole in his stomach, and when *that* pain bested him, blew his head off with a shotgun. His clients took no more notice of his passing then they would a stray that stopped showing up at the back door." Dearborne ground the butt of his cigarette into the bottom of the glass. "Do you know what a second is, Doctor Pascoe?"

"One sixtieth of a minute."

"True. But I was referring to dueling."

"Dueling? You mean like, 'ten steps, turn around and fire'?"

"Exactly."

"Wasn't the second the guy who had to step in if the first guy chickened out?"

"A common misconception. The second was more of a representative. He honed or loaded weapons, arranged the duel, things like that. The second hangs around to make the life of the duelist easier. They take no risk, and they reap no glory. They are servants, like my father, and like you. Learn to like being a lapdog, or decide, like I did, to be a contestant."

"Assuming I have information you want, which I don't, how does giving it to you make me any less of a servant?"

"It doesn't. It shows a willingness to cooperate, which goes a long way in this town. Cooperate and be rewarded, or be difficult and go from being a second to being a third, and you wouldn't like that, just ask my first wife."

Pascoe thought about Rasmussen's ramshackle farm with its sloping floor. "We're done here. If you've made your point, get out. If you haven't, get out. Think I'll hang on to that piece of firewood. If I find you around here again, you'll be too busy pulling it out of your ass to talk."

Dearborne pulled out a credit card sized cell phone, punched a button, and raised it to his mouth. "Bring the car." He snapped the phone shut and returned it to his coat pocket. "My driver will be here in a minute, do you mind if I wait inside?"

Pascoe wanted nothing better than to make Dearborne wait in the cold, but the man's arrogance astounded him into allowing him to stay.

"Do you give a shit about anything Dearborne? Do you even know your daughter is missing?"

Dearborne started buttoning his coat. "Not my child, not my concern."

"So you say."

Dearborne shrugged.

"Your latest wife, did she really leave with someone else?"

Dearborne shrugged again. "Why not? It doesn't embarrass me if she did. In any case, she can't show her face around here again, not trustworthy, is she? Loyalty means something in this community. Maybe you'll be a better student." Headlights flashed across the kitchen window. "There's my car. Thanks for your time Doctor Pascoe, think about what I said."

Dearborne reached down to Barclay, who had not left the man's side, and gave him a final rubdown before sliding into the night. Barclay remained stretched out on his side and followed Dearborne's progress out the door. When Dearborne was gone, the dog met Pascoe's eyes, and thumped his tail weakly against the floor.

"Don't even try," Pascoe said.

The latest edition of *The Freedom Monitor* was in stores the next morning, and even at such an early hour there was only one copy left in the stand at the convenience store where Pascoe got his coffee. Devon's murder continued to be main story, but Kutulas' focus had shifted to the handling of the case. "Incompetence in Loudon", read the headline, followed by an expression of shock that no one had yet been arrested while the police wasted time harassing the loving brother of the victim. Pascoe was not mentioned by name, but referred to simply as the brute who assaulted Vaughn at his sister's funeral. *At least there's no picture this time*, thought Pascoe. That should put Harkin in a better mood.

It had not. Harkin's voice rumbled from his desk before Pascoe had fully crossed the threshold. "Hope you plan on putting in a full day."

"That's the idea," Pascoe replied.

"Not lately. You take off without asking, cancel appointments and piss off clients, and decide answering your pager is optional."

Maggie harrumphed in agreement. Pascoe winced. "I was on call last night."

"On call would imply you were available to take a call. You were scheduled to be on call, but I wound up clearing a choke in the middle of the night when the service couldn't reach you."

"Left my pager in the truck. And turned off the phone. I, uh, didn't feel like being bothered last night."

"Poor you. After getting to bed after two this morning I was woken at five by a very irate phone call. Care to take a guess who it was?"

Pascoe shook his head.

"Matthew Dearborne, a most influential man. Feels harassed because he couldn't provide enough information about a horse that died on his farm to satisfy you. Now you're pissing off someone who isn't even a client. This has got to stop. All of it. Today. Don't start taking advantage of me because we've been friends for so long. You're not irreplaceable."

Pascoe's temper flared. "Apparently. But Dearborne is? Bet you'd love to get him as a client. Do you know what he thinks of people like us?"

"Don't care. What I care about is the reputation of this practice, and getting on Dearborne's bad side isn't going to help any."

"So you're going to let the people with all the power dictate everything?"

"You don't understand power Jordie."

"Sure I do. Wealth equals power. My mother certainly understood."

Harkin shook his head sadly. "Your mother was ignorant, as are you. I didn't say Dearborne was powerful, I said he was influential. Wealth equals influence, but not always power. What runs the economy around here?"

"Lots of things," Pascoe said. "Corporations, politics, some old family money I guess."

"Really. I haven't noticed corporate offices looming over Middleburg, or factories spewing smoke in Upperville, and last time I looked, politicians did their business about sixty miles east of here. None of that stuff fuels the local economy, it just provides the money."

"Same thing."

"Your mistake lies in that assumption. Horses run this economy from top to bottom. It starts with the big pool of money from outside. People move out this way, buy a chunk of property, look out their window and see an empty pasture. So they buy a horse, or two, sometimes in Europe, but even then they bring along a local for advice. Then the horse needs training and the owner needs lessons. And don't forget, someone has to shovel the shit, mow those lovely pastures, and nail up fence boards. Gotta have a feed store, and gotta have a vet to take care of the darlings when they get sick. See what I'm getting at?"

"It's what I said. We're the help. Horse mechanics."

Harkin held up a crooked forefinger. "More than that. You forget why most of these folks have horses in the first place."

"And why is that?"

"Because they think they should. Because everybody else they know has one. And by God, if they're going to get a horse, they're going to have a better one than their neighbor. Folks around here haven't gotten lucky; they've risen to the top because they don't consider second place an option. If they buy a mount for half a million dollars and it sits in a pasture, or worse, loses to the pony clubber who bought her horse at the auction, how does that affect the ego? We have the power Jordie, because we know what makes the beast tick."

"That's ridiculous. Seven or eight other vets are a phone call away. You're not irreplaceable."

Harkin chuckled. "Guess I deserved that. But I would say, humbly, this practice has practically cornered the high-dollar horses, and a good deal of the second tier farms as well. Why is that, do you think? Can I poke a horse with a tetanus shot with more dexterity than Randolph? Do I undercut our competitors? Hardly."

"Maybe you've just been around longer."

"True. This area does have affection for tradition. Or it could be I pay a little more attention to what my clients value. I help people best their neighbor, and I don't interfere with their privacy. It's a sacred contract, and everyone knows I won't break it. That doesn't make me useful; it makes me indispensable. Lately though, with the photograph in the *Monitor*, the cancellations, and now Dearborne, well, it all damages the reputation of the practice, and as much as I love you Jordie, it's unacceptable to clients, which makes it unacceptable to me. You need to straighten up, because I'd rather practice alone and take call every night of the week than risk losing what I've built over the last fifty years."

Pascoe sat in his truck and watched the White's Ferry barge carry a load of cars across the Potomac. He was late to his next appointment but didn't care; observing the steady fight of the boat against the crosscurrent slowed his pounding heart. He had cursed Harkin for not supporting him. Maggie looked away in embarassment as he stormed off.

Cooler now, Pascoe was more irritated at himself than the lecture. Harkin had it right. From the beginning, betting had been about more than just money, it was about being a part of the game, owning two-minutes of a horse's life and believing that predicting the outcome made him somehow better than his father. That's what it came down to, needing to feel more powerful than his father and seeing money as a measure of that power. Carlyle and Wallace proved how misguided he had been. He didn't own anything, and at the moment had less freedom to make decisions about his life than his father ever had. Harkin had power all right, and the respect of men who routinely graced the covers of Forbes and Time, by realizing what was precious to them.

Even the tallest ladder has a top rung, so a man surrounded by equals is measured by more subjective criteria. Some own sports teams or cars and send them into battle, often losing millions in an effort to best a peer for the possession of a shining silver cup. In Hunt Country a more genteel way emerged. Combatants are four-legged, and ovals of dirt or rectangles of sand substitute for stadiums. On the surface, it's good-natured competition, but what would someone do for a ribbon of blue silk and how would they reward the person who helped them get it?

Maybe Dad figured out more than I gave him credit for. Pascoe would have to think on it further. For the moment, he had a stable full of horses waiting for him to float their teeth, and if he didn't get moving, he'd be working until late evening.

As it turned out, a horse with a sole abscess kept him working past nine, making a long day even longer. He was happy to find the door tightly shut; he was in no mood for another unexpected visitor.

Many hours past sunset, breath steamed inside the house and Pascoe continued to wear his winter coat long after a fire had been lit. Barclay curled up so tight his eyes barely poked above his tail. The cold sapped the appetite. Instead of fixing dinner, he wrapped a down comforter around his body and switched on the television.

He woke sometime later, sweating inside his makeshift cocoon. The house was warm, and Barclay unwound himself and lay basking in front of the stove. Still in a coat, Pascoe stepped outside and gathered an armful of wood before putting on some water for tea and rummaging through the sparse pantry.

The phone rang halfway through a bowl of Dinty Moore Beef Stew. He was taking the next two nights of Harkin's scheduled emergency duty in trade for forgetting the night before. He looked to the nightstand; the pager had been silent and it was unusual for the service to try the phone first. He was no less surprised to hear Hunter's voice; his several attempts to call and apologize had gone unanswered.

"Jordan, how soon can you get over here?"

"Twenty, thirty minutes tops. Which horse is it? Not Banker?"

"Horse? No, my truck won't start and I need a lift." Hunter took a deep breath and held it before starting over. "It's David. He's been arrested for the murder of Devon Dowry."

CHAPTER ELEVEN

"Goddamn it, let me see my brother or so help me God I'll kick your ass all over this station!" Hunter had not spoken a word on he way over other than to grunt thanks, but found her voice when stopped by the duty officer.

"M'am, your brother is being questioned right now, and it's my understanding he has waived his right to an attorney."

"Waived his rights? Did any of you fucking storm troopers happen to notice my brother's condition? Did anyone think, hey, this dude can barely tie his own shoes, maybe we should find out if he has some sort of guardian?" The officer paled. "Tell you what. The sheriff is just outside, bathing in the adulation of the press. How about I go ask him?"

"Won't be necessary Miss Stuart, come with me." Monroe Ridgeway poked his head through the door leading to the back of the station. "Besides, they probably heard you already."

Monroe's size momentarily unsettled Hunter, and she backed up a step before grabbing Pascoe's hand and dragging him along. The detective opened his mouth to protest, but Hunter's jaw was set. "Doctor Pascoe as well then."

They were led to the same room in which Pascoe had been questioned. There was a tape recorder on the table. David sat on the far side in unmatched plaid flannel pajama tops and bottoms and unlaced Sorrel boots on his feet. He was slouched and glum until he saw Hunter, and then his familiar grin spread across his face. Hunter embraced her brother. She wouldn't stop stroking and kissing the top of his head, which embarrassed David to no end.

"Just to be clear, Miss Stuart, no one has questioned your brother," Monroe said. "This is the first time we've had someone of, uh, special needs, in this circumstance."

Hunter would not acknowledge the big detective. "Are you all right?" She said, examining her brother like she expected bruises to bloom in his skin.

"Yeah. Okay," David said. "Hi Jordan! What ti—"

"Not now." Hunter grabbed David's face in both hands firmly enough to pucker his lips and forced him to look her in the eyes. "Do you know why the police brought you here?" David shook his head as best he could. "They think you hurt somebody. Do you remember little Devon? Stonemason Farm?"

David furrowed his brow, willing frayed synapses to connect. After a few moments he nodded, but Pascoe hadn't seen any spark of recognition and thought David might be nodding to please his sister, or, if nothing else, to get her to let go.

"Say nothing to these policemen," Hunter said. "I need to call for some help. Promise me?"

"Promise," David said, crossing his heart with one finger. "Are you and Jordan here to take me home?"

Hunter looked at Monroe, who shook his head.

"Honey," Hunter said, stroking David's arm. "You may have to spend the rest of the night." David stiffened and pulled back, eyes wide with fear.

"No, no, no, no, no," he said. "This is not home." Tears sprang from David's eyes. The scar on the right side of his face diverted the stream towards the corner of his nose and highlighted his disfigurement to such a degree that Pascoe felt repulsed for an instant.

He looks less than human when he cries. God help him if he does that in front of a jury. Pascoe turned to Monroe. "This is ridiculous. How can you hold him?"

Monroe looked uncomfortable. "Sheriff Ridgeway received an anonymous tip. Without consulting me, a warrant was served on Mr. Stuart's residence this evening and evidence was found linking him to Devon Dowry."

"What evidence?" Pascoe asked.

"A personal item of Miss Dowry's, that's all I can tell you. The DA can provide the Stuarts and their lawyer with details."

"Look at him!" Hunter shouted. "Forget for a moment that my brother would never murder anyone, do you really think he's capable of planning one?"

"My job is to investigate and gather evidence, not judge," Monroe said.

"Well you're doing a piss-poor job," Hunter said. "Sounds like the sheriff's calling the shots."

The detective bristled. Pascoe moved closer to Hunter and David and squatted beside them. He put a reassuring hand on David's leg and leaned in close to whisper to Hunter.

"Have you got a lawyer in mind?" he asked.

"Not exactly. Mr. Donaldson is some kind of lawyer though, he probably knows someone."

Pascoe nodded. "Can they come get you?"

"You're leaving?"

"I know a guy who has a bad habit of opening his mouth too much. Anonymous tips are his style, so I'm going to ask if he gave it."

"Would he tell you if he did?"

"Didn't say I was going to ask nicely."

Bimbo Carlyle lived in a singlewide set back from a dirt road. The road was unlit, but Pascoe had been to Carlyle's enough times to recognize the almost imperceptible break in the brush marking the entrance. He pulled past the drive and parked on the shoulder so the diesel and headlights would go unnoticed, certain Carlyle would slither off if a vehicle approached: this time of night the only visitors were cops and unwelcome guests. Pascoe was certainly one of the latter.

Starlight illuminated the rutted driveway, making a flashlight unnecessary. Contemplating Carlyle's character, Pascoe shoved two rolls of Elastikon tape into his coat pockets before heading in. He was unsure how to get into the trailer. It was overly optimistic to think he would be greeted with open arms, and Carlyle would never be careless enough to leave the door unlocked. As it turned out, Carlyle came to him.

Peacocks were common enough residents on area farms, but Pascoe had not considered one might be shacking up at Carlyle's until he tested the front doorknob and stepped on it. The unearthly yowl and unexpected flapping shocked Pascoe badly and he and fell backward down the short three-step flight of stairs that led to the door. Inside the trailer, lights blazed on, and amidst the noise of pounding feet he heard the telltale ratchet of a shotgun. Pascoe scrambled to the side of the stairs and flattened against the block foundation. The peacock was undaunted. It opened its great fan of a tail, pawed the ground, and fixed onyx eyes on the intruder.

The door to the trailer flew open seconds later, spilling a rectangle of light across the spot Pascoe had been a moment before. Carlyle stood on the top step clad in a pair of black briefs, single-barreled shotgun sweeping side to side, searching.

"Show yourself, you red-haired piece of shit! You ain't getting no more birds of mine!"

Christ almighty, he thinks I'm a fox. Pascoe silently thanked the peacock-eating critter and slid his arm across the threshold behind Carlyle. The cock twisted its head inquisitively.

"Bimbo," Pascoe said.

Carlyle started as if he had pissed on an electric fence. The gun roared, sending shot harmlessly into the night. The bird ran down the stairs, tail folded and dragging. Carlyle looked down and jumped again before dashing back into the trailer. He tripped over Pascoe's arm and sprawled to the carpet. The small set of stairs had no railing, and Pascoe was able to vault onto his back before he could struggle to his knees. It was no contest; Pascoe outweighed the ex-jock by over seventy pounds. For good measure, and more than a little satisfaction, Pascoe slammed his forearm into the nape of Carlyle's neck. Carlyle got the message and stopped struggling.

"Get you a drink Doc?" Carlyle said, voice muffled by the avocado shag carpet.

"In a bit," Pascoe replied.

He shifted position so one knee took the place of his forearm. Carlyle squawked, not unlike his peacock. Pascoe brought the bookie's hands together behind his back and wrapped the wrists with one roll of the tape. Ankles were wrapped withthe other. Angry as he was, Pascoe still winced when he saw the hair on Carlyle's legs. The man was in for a vicious waxing. There was still a couple of feet left on the roll and he used this length to bind ankles to hands. With Carlyle trussed like a rodeo calf, Pascoe tossed the shotgun out the doorway and closed the door before looking for the drink he had been offered.

All he could find was a half-full bottle of Southern Comfort. Every glass in the house was either in the sink or balanced on various pieces of furniture. Pascoe wasn't convinced he could clean any to his standards and pulled directly from the bottle. The warm sweetness of the liquor brought back visions of lying in bed and being spoon-fed cough syrup by his father. *Pretty good memories*, he thought and took another swig. *I guess there is some comfort in this stuff after all.*

Carlyle had not moved or made a sound since his neck had been pinned. Pascoe walked over and toed Carlyle onto his side. Small fragments of carpet and crumbs of food stuck to his face.

"How ya doin Bimbo?" Pascoe said.

Carlyle eyed the bottle possessively. "How 'bout giving me some of that?"

"Sure. Open your mouth. Carlyle twisted his neck until he faced the ceiling and opened wide. Pascoe poured the liquor into his eyes. Carlyle screamed.

"I'm not fucking around Bimbo," Pascoe said, squatting next to Carlyle's face. "Matthew Dearborne showed up at my house. I had the impression you hardly knew the guy, but Dearborne knew a lot more about me than I'm comfortable with, and he got his information from someone. I think it was you."

"C'mon man, I wouldn't give you up. You know—ow!" Pascoe flicked him in the ear. "It was just talk. I didn't know he had a beef with you."

"And then," Pascoe flicked the ear again, "you send the cops after David Stuart. Was that 'just talk'?"

"Stuart? The retar—" Carlyle caught himself as Pascoe cocked a finger. "The, um, mentally, uh, challenged guy?"

"That's the one."

"Don't know that dude. Honest. You're saying I called the cops on him? You gotta believe me Pascoe; I might deal if the price is right, but never to the cops. Never to the cops."

Strangely, Pascoe believed him. "All right then. Tell me about Dearborne?"

"Why don't you just beat he crap out of me and we'll call it even?"

"How about I beat the crap out of you, and you tell me anyway. Here's a thought—do you know what an electro-ejaculator is?"

Carlyle squinted his red, watery eyes and grinned. "Sounds like it might be fun."

"Loads," Pascoe said. "It's used on bulls. They don't train to dummies as well as stallions, so we use this electro-ejaculator. It's a probe, about the size and shape of an ear of corn. Butter it up with lube, shove it the ass, plug it in, and next thing you know, those bulls are humping the air and—presto! —sample collected. Pleasant as it sounds, the bulls don't seem to like it much, and I have a feeling you won't be too keen on it either."

Carlyle snorted. "You don't work on no cows."

Pascoe leaned in until his face was inches from Carlyle's. "Right. But Harkin used to. Back in the day he was the only vet in the county and had to work on all the farm animals. I found one at the clinic. It's an old unit, and rusty, so it might arc a bit, but it should still work."

Pascoe had no idea if Harkin had any cattle equipment, much less an ejaculator, but, if bulging eyes were any indication, Carlyle believed Pascoe had brought one along.

"Look, it's no big deal. Dearborne and I have a little scam running, and when he found out you were talking he got worried and came to me. It doesn't concern you, if you lay off Dearborne, he'll lay off you."

Pascoe's mouth had gone dry. "What scam?" he croaked.

"No way, go ahead and get your 'jaculater thingy. Got to be better than what Dearborne will do." Carlyle set his mouth and closed his eyes like the condemned.

Pascoe was stuck; he hadn't expected a coward like Carlyle to call his bluff. "Suit yourself. I'll just bring the truck around." *Think about it for a couple of minutes Bimbo, let's see how long your bravado holds out.*

He took his time walking back, knowing Carlyle wasn't going anywhere. After sliding to a stop in front of the trailer, Pascoe grabbed the toolbox he kept his hoof equipment in and dumped it out; the clatter was sure to get Carlyle's attention. He threw clippers into the empty toolbox, closed the lid so that a couple inches of cord hung out the side, and jogged back into the trailer. Satisfied Carlyle had noticed the cord, Pascoe slammed the toolbox to the floor, and pushed Carlyle back onto his stomach.

"Bimbo, before I start I just want you to know that I really don't know how the human body will react to this much electricity. So if you don't make it, I'll leave the equipment here. Hell, you might be nominated for a Darwin Award." Pascoe left the clippers in the toolbox and plugged them in. Carlyle bucked at the noise.

"Jesus Doc, I told ya! It's no big deal!" he cried.

"Takes a few minutes to warm up," Pascoe shouted over the racket. "Hey, you got any Vaseline? Ah, screw it, we'll just go dry." Pascoe grabbed the waistband of Carlyle's briefs.

"Doc!"

Pascoe unplugged the clippers. "Sorry, you were saying?"

"It's Montpelier, okay? We fixed the races of his first crop of foals. I spread the money around. For enough cash, a jock might hold back in the stretch, or bump another horse. Stable boys are even easier, because they don't get paid shit. Slip them a little extra and the favorite gets a gash in the leg and has to be scratched. Since the Three Sisters, owning the stud's been like printing money. Dearborne figures he's got another two, maybe three years before the bottom falls out, but in the meantime he's making a fortune. The Japs want to buy him outright for something like a hundred and fifty million. If word gets out, lawyers are going to rape Dearborne for every penny he's got."

"Dearborne trusted you?"

Carlyle pouted. "I know what I'm doing."

"What about Gizmo?"

"Who?"

"Gizmo. Dearborne's ex-wife had a horse named Gizmo that died."

"The first time I met Dearborne it was to talk about this deal and there was no wife, or Gizmo, at the farm."

"You don't know anything about killing horses for insurance money?"

Carlyle twisted his neck to look over his shoulder at Pascoe. "Are you crazy? Dearborne's horses are worth a hell of a lot more alive than dead."

"True," Pascoe said. He went to the kitchen and rummaged around until he found a steak knife. Carlyle saw the knife and struggled frantically. Pascoe kneeled across his back and cut through the tape that connected wrists to ankles.

"There you go Bimbo," Pascoe said, standing. Carlyle rolled to his back. "I can guarantee you two things," Pascoe said, flipping the knife in his fingers. "Dearborne will not hear a whisper of this." Carlyle nodded obediently. Pascoe balanced the blade by its tip on his index finger. "If I find out you've lied to me again, that pesky fox won't need to go after your bird. He'll be eating off your sorry carcass for the rest of winter."

By the time Pascoe arrived home, he could have, at best, managed an hour and a half of sleep. He opted instead for breakfast and a pot of double strength coffee. His hands trembled after the second cup, but exhaustion had passed. He spent a few moments fidgeting in a kitchen chair and drumming his fingers on the table.

He should have slept, or at least tried to. Acutely awake, buzzed from the coffee and the violence, Pascoe's mind returned to the subject he had been trying to suppress, Devon.

There had been a time, not long after Goldrush's arrival, that the big gelding had developed a whopper of a foot abscess. While Pascoe bent over the hoof and pared away sole, Devon hung nonchalantly on the lead, bitching.

"You know what Taylor did? *Grounded* me, or tried to anyway. Said I was talking back too much. Actually, she said 'sassing'. Who talks like that? I mean, what a stupid cow, like she's my Mom or something. As soon as dad found out he un-grounded me."

Pascoe, facing the rear of the horse, could feel her satisfied smirk. Goldrush, free to move his head, pushed Pascoe with his muzzle as a tender spot was probed. "Shorten up on that rope," he said. "Taylor is just trying to get a little respect. It wouldn't kill you to give a little."

Neither piece of advice was heeded; Goldrush continued to use Pascoe's butt as a sounding board and Devon continued to rant. "Come on, she's only thirty or something," she said. "Never had her own kids. The only reason Dad married her is for those big, fake boobs."

Pascoe hit pay-dirt, and pus welled into the divot carved in the hoof. Goldrush responded with a nip. Pascoe dropped the foot, and turned sharply to Devon, holding his left cheek. "You don't know why your father married her, just like you don't know for sure why he married the last one, but he did, and if you disrespect her you disrespect him, and since he's the only parent who's still around, you might want to give him, and her, a break." Pascoe said, his words sharp and short. Devon had opened up an abscess of her own.

Her face crumpled, and Pascoe felt about as dirty as the juice draining from Goldrush's foot. "I'm sorry you got bit," she said. "It was my fault."

"It's not that," Pascoe said, softening. "Let me explain. I don't doubt you appreciate what you have, but there's more to be thankful for than a nice house and a barn full of horses. I grew up with nothing, lived in places smaller than one of these stalls, and showered in the jockey's locker room with a bunch of middle-aged midgets." That drew a giggle. "I'm serious. But I didn't care because I had my parents and nothing else mattered. After my Mom left—" Pascoe acknowledged Devon's surprise. "Yeah, mine too. After she left, my Dad gave up, and even after we moved on to better places, I would have gone back to that rusty, leaky, travel trailer in a heartbeat. Oscar has made mistakes, but he *cares*, about you, about himself, and he's going to keep trying. Maybe Taylor doesn't know how to be a mother, but she's at least trying, so maybe she cares too, and that's better than nothing."

Devon wrapped her arms around Pascoe and squeezed him, pressing her face into his chest. When she pulled away she said, deadly serious, "You should really talk to somebody about all that."

Pascoe laughed into his coffee. He never had taken the little girl's advice. At the time, he had explained away his sudden anger as a response to the bite, but the truth was, Devon was good at breaking through barriers, through the self-protective layers of bullshit adults apply over the years. Pascoe wiped his dripping nose with the back of his hand. "You are such a pussy," he said out loud. He called Hunter.

She sounded weary. She returned to Timberbrook and ran the gantlet of camera crews lining both sides of the street. The sheriff followed, served her with a search warrant in view of the cameras, and was tearing Timberbrook apart. Heavy equipment rumbled in the background.

David was still at the station. Bernie Newcomb, the lawyer recommended by the Donaldsons, argued unsuccessfully for David's immediate release, but had badgered a judge into a bail hearing. A doctor prescribed some tranquilizers, which allowed David to sleep and Hunter to run home. Pascoe promised to be at the hearing.

Harkin was in no mood for it. "You decide where you need to be," he said. "I can cover your calls if I need to. Been doing it a lot lately, people are coming to expect it."

"I'm not canceling anything," Pascoe said. "I only need to be gone a short time. I can shift a few things around."

"If you say so." Harkin went silent, but made a production of gathering things and bustling out the door to be on time for his first appointment. Maggie was content to purse her lips and glare.

David's suit fit tightly on his frame; too much time out of the saddle had thickened his midsection. Newcomb occasionally placed a hand gently on David's shoulder to keep him from gawking at the crowd or smile at Hunter. At first sight she appeared to be sleeping, her eyelids remained shut for four or five seconds each time she blinked. She didn't notice when Pascoe grabbed a seat near at the rear of the courtroom.

Monroe Ridgeway sat within whispering distance of the prosecutor, who was a bent, owlish looking man named Turner. The media was nowhere in sight. Perhaps the judge had banned the press; it would explain the sheriff's absence. Monroe turned and caught Pascoe's eye. Shortly afterward, he leaned forward and said something to Turner. The prosecutor waved him off dismissively. Monroe frowned and left. Pascoe followed as the bailiff called the court to order. The detective waited halfway down the hall, working an ink-stained shirt pocket with his thumb.

"Doctor Pascoe, I had a feeling you might want a word."

"You're actually going through with this."

Monroe shrugged. "I find the evidence, Turner decides what to do with it. The sheriff and Turner have constituents, and by constituents I mean campaign donors. They want this wrapped up. Stuart is their best shot."

"You don't have any evidence."

"We found the girl's cell phone in his apartment, stuffed in a sock drawer. Found it in about two minutes. Had a few drops of blood on it. The lab is running tests to figure out whose."

"Fingerprints?"

"Nada," Monroe said, expressionless.

"You think it's a plant."

"My opinion doesn't matter much. Stuart is *the* guy unless new information changes the direction of the investigation and nobody wants us trying too hard to find any. Any new information is going to have to come from outside the department."

A loud bang came from the courtroom. "Quick," mumbled Monroe. "I'd better get back. Take care, Doctor Pascoe."

The courtroom door opened and the relieved company of Hunter, David, and Newcomb exited. Newcomb gave David a good-natured slap on the back and spoke briefly to Hunter, pointing in Pascoe's direction before leaving for the front entrance. The staccato shutters of cameras could be heard as Newcomb stepped into the cool light of the afternoon. Hunter helped David into his parka and zipped it before heading Pascoe's way, ignoring Monroe as they passed.

"Newcomb looked pleased," Pascoe said.

"The judge reamed Turner for trying to deny bail to someone in David's condition," Hunter said.

"What about the phone?"

Hunter shot a withering look at the courtroom door, which was closing behind Monroe. "It's nothing," she said quickly, "manufactured. Newcomb said it wouldn't even be admitted."

"Great," Pascoe said, watching her fidget with the drawstrings of her jacket. "Sneaking out?"

"Newcomb's telling the press David and I will be giving a statement in a few moments. Should give us time to escape."

"They'll be waiting at the farm."

Hunter sighed. "I know, but at least they have to stay off my property."

Pascoe handed her a key. "Go to my place. I'll grab something for dinner on my way home. You're welcome to stay the night."

Hunter stiffened. "I don't think that's such a good idea."

"It's a one room place, it'll be more like a slumber party. Besides, we should talk. What do you say David? I'll pick up a pizza."

"Pizza! Pizza! Jordan's house!"

"Dirty trick," Hunter said, but took the key. "But don't expect talking, expect scolding."

"Then I'll get some beer too."

Pascoe's pager, set to vibrate, buzzed at his belt the moment he stepped into his truck. Maggie sent a message to call Gail Rasmussen ASAP. Pascoe dialed the number with his thumb as he pulled from the courthouse onto Colonial Avenue. Gail picked up in the middle of the first ring.

"Doctor Pascoe?"

"Yeah. Everything okay with Deadbolt."

"What? Oh, yes, he's been fine since you left. I'm calling about David. Have you seen him? Is he okay?"

"Just left his bail hearing. He had a rough night, but for the moment he seems less stressed than anybody else. You should call, Hunter would like hearing from you."

"I don't think I can, at least not now, it might cause David more trouble. The police left a few minutes ago. The Sheriff said they arrested David for Devon's murder and asked about his history of violence."

"History of violence?"

"His term. Complete nonsense, that's what I told him. David had a run-in with Devon's brother—just being protective of Sam—I'm sure all he wanted to do was put the fear of God into Vaughn. It wasn't serious, he wouldn't have hurt him.

"I think I told you that Sam went to Foxfield. That's where she met Devon, and they became friends. Neither was old enough to drive, so Vaughn used to chauffer them back and forth to visit. David didn't care for Vaughn; he thought it was creepy for a guy his age to willingly drive a pair of young girls to see each other. After Sam's behavior started to change, David got suspicious, and started to make sure he was around when she was dropped off. She would yell at him for spying, but he was worried; she was like a daughter to him. One time he came up on the car and caught them making out—they insisted they were only talking—and flew into a rage. Dragged Vaughn out by his shirt collar and slammed his head against the hood of the car. It had to have been Vaughn who sent the police."

"Did David act that way often?"

"Oh no, like I said, he was just concerned for Sam. After all, she was just a teenager, and Vaughn's what, mid-twenties?"

"The police were only interested in the fight?"

"Asked if David had ever beaten Sam or me and if he had an uncontrollable temper, ridiculous things like that. They were more interested in hearing Sam's side."

"Did she back you up?"

"She's not here, hasn't been since the other night." A tremor entered her voice. "I don't know what to do, she's never been gone this long. The police are saying all these terrible things about David. When I told them about Sam, they started asking questions about David's relationship with her, as if he could have something to do with her being missing. Missing. That's the word they're using, like she's been taken."

"You're sure she ran away."

"She's done it before," Rasmussen said defensively.

"But not for this long."

"No."

"The sheriff questioned you himself?"

"There were two other men with him, but they acted more like bodyguards than anything else. I don't think there was one word spoken between the three of them."

"Help me understand something. This fight—I can understand David's feelings for Sam, but nothing I've ever heard would make me think he'd attack, even someone as nauseating as Vaughn. He must have been provoked."

Static whispered across the connection. "Hello?"

"Nothing provoked it."

"Vaughn knows how to push people's buttons."

"I said nothing provoked it. Just tell Hunter to call me if there's anything I can do to help."

Static intruded again. This time Pascoe was sure she was gone.

CHAPTER TWELVE

Pascoe's last patient, an irascible, congested Appaloosa, sent him home with snot-stiffened hair. He called ahead to Carmela's; a quick beer and soda run timed it so he arrived just as the pizza came out of the oven. Difficult as it was, Pascoe resisted sampling a slice.

Walking into a preheated home was a pleasant change. Hunter had a comfortable fire going and Pascoe was able to remove both coat and sweater immediately, another novelty. Barclay gratefully nuzzled Hunter before rushing to David, who was easily manipulated into a game of tug-of-war.

"Smells good, what's on it?" Hunter asked.

"Sausage and mushrooms. Hope it's okay."

"As long as there's no pineapple, you've got a winner."

"The last person who asked Carmela for pineapple pies lies in an unmarked grave somewhere in Jersey."

"Hope he's right next to the person who came up with the idea in the first place," Hunter said, tearing off a slice and dangling stings of cheese into her mouth. "I straightened up a bit while you were gone, figured it was the least I could do. You're surprisingly neat for a bachelor; I still have nightmares about the stuff I cleaned for David, and that was before the accident."

"Caught me on a good day. Beer?"

"Thanks." Hunter waved the offer of a glass and took the bottle. David came in, drawn by the food, and asked if he could eat in front of the television. It was fine by Pascoe, a majority of his meals were consumed in the same fashion, so Hunter fixed a plate, opened a can of Coke and assisted David back to his seat. Returning to the kitchen, she sat on the edge of the table.

"Here's what I know," she began. "First of all, I like you. A lot. Second, I know there's another woman involved, and you haven't even come close to being honest with me about her. Third, I came across a bunch of files with Virginia Bloodstock letterhead, one of which had Gail Rasmussen's name on it. You saw her picture at my place and acted like you had no idea who she was. Another file had the Dowry's name on it. That's two connections to David. Are going to start being straight with me or should I call Newcomb and see what he makes of all this?"

"It's pretty complicated."

Hunter leaned closer. Both of her eyes seemed to be the same cool shade of gray. "I'm a pretty sharp gal. Try me."

Pascoe explained about the horses and how Wallace had been able to rope him into helping, leaving out the physical distractions. He told her of his fear that Devon's death was linked to the investigation and the guilt that came from it. He finished with a retelling of his last conversation with Rasmussen.

"This Wallace chick needs a good talking to," Hunter said menacingly.

"You might have a tougher time than you think."

Hunter raised a dubious eyebrow. "Poor Gail. She must be sick about all of this: Deadbolt, Sam taking off, and now the police."

"Did you know about David and Vaughn?"

"He never mentioned it."

"But you can imagine it happening."

"I suppose."

"What will Turner will make of it?"

"It doesn't matter. David is a different person. Before the accident, he had as much of a temper as anyone, and like anyone else could get violent if pushed hard enough, but he doesn't have a trace of that old fire anymore. We can go to the mall and some jackass teenager will pull a face and make fun of him, and it's all I can do to keep from ripping the kid's heart out. But David just smiles. Gail stopped visiting, and he didn't get angry, she simply faded from his mind. After the accident, it's like he's been...distilled. That's the only way I can describe it, like all the anger, jealousy—all the flammable parts—evaporated from his personality and left something quiet and clear."

"And predictable," Pascoe said.

"True. We equate predictability with boring, but David is happy. I think Turner will have a tough time portraying him as some kind of explosive animal."

"I'm in the middle of it, and nothing makes any sense," Pascoe said rubbing his eyes with his fists. "Is the scolding over, or should I open another beer?"

Hunter hopped off the table, straddled Pascoe's lap, and kissed him deeply. "No scolding. It's been hard knowing you've been hiding something, but I understand. You're smart Jordan, really smart. You'll figure it out, and when you do, everybody will have to admit David had nothing to do with it." She kissed him again and sat deeper into his lap, a position that was becoming noticeably uncomfortable. Hunter's mismatched eyes were alive again and sparkling.

"What about David?" Pascoe asked.

Hunter tipped her head in the direction of the living room. David was asleep on the couch, a plate with a half-eaten piece of pizza balancing on his stomach.

"The last time he slept was drug-induced, and that wasn't real rest. He'll sleep straight through until morning unless a bomb goes off."

"Still," Pascoe said. "He could wake up."

"Your truck has a heater, doesn't it?"

Pascoe grabbed his keys from the counter without setting her down.

David was disconcerted when he awoke, but the closeness of his sister eased the anxiety and before long he was up and outside throwing a ball for Barclay. Pascoe and Hunter had slept next to each other on the floor in an old sleeping bag and armful of quilts, and aside from some odd kinks in his back courtesy of the truck, Pascoe woke up more refreshed than he had in days. The evening had ended in a slumber party after all.

He left quickly to make it to work on time, inviting Hunter and David to stay as long as they wished, but warned it might be difficult to scrounge ingredients for a decent breakfast. Hunter would head home and brave the press; she couldn't rely on the neighbors to feed and turn out her horses forever. She kissed Pascoe goodbye and made him promise to come to the farm on Saturday.

"I want to get you on horseback and see how you handle yourself in the saddle," she said with a wink. Pascoe rolled his eyes, but agreed to show up sometime in the morning. David crushed him in a bear hug as he opened the door.

Harkin was more civil, pleased to see him at his desk early, pleased to hear he was prepared for an uninterrupted day of work.

"The papers say David is back home," Harkin said. "Can't say the press is too happy with the judge's decision, they've already convicted the boy."

"David's lawyer is sharp, he's not going to let him get railroaded."

King grunted noncommittally. "Hope not, for Hunter's sake. That girl's been through a lot this year. Must be, what do y'all call it? Bad karma."

"I can't imagine Hunter doing anything to bring this on herself," Pascoe said.

Another grunt. "Guess you're right. Make sure she knows they're both in my thoughts."

Pascoe found a message paper-clipped to his daily schedule. It was from Bridges. *Have tissue findings. You owe me flowers.*

Pascoe glanced at the clock—too early for the lab to be open, but Bridges wasn't the type to put in time and pick up a check; she reveled in deciphering the language of cytoplasm. The callback number didn't end in double or triple zeros, so perhaps she had left the number of a back line. He took the chance.

"Histopath." Bridges sounded awake enough to have been at the lab for hours.

"Flowers? I wouldn't have picked you to be the type."

"Oh yeah, I'm a girlie-girl alright. You should see my place, it's enough to make Martha Stewart puke."

"Help me out and FTD will be knocking on your door this afternoon."

"I'll be waiting. The second sample cinched it. It was frustrating at first; the liver and kidney were completely normal. But the heart, crappy preservation and all, showed clear signs of myocardial necrosis. Your horse, my friend, died of carboxylic ionophore poisoning."

"An ionophore. Like Monensin?"

"Exactly."

There was a time when the local feed manufacturer bought grain from local farmers and mixed livestock-specific formulas like Purina did with their Chow line: Horse Chow, Pig Chow, Chicken Chow, and so on. For all Pascoe knew, there was a Cow Chow and thousands of farmers around the country snickering. Many feeds, especially those designed for fowl, contained an ionophore, an antiparasitic drug used to kill a small organism called coccidia. The ionophore stopped diarrhea and costly weight loss, but was highly toxic to horses. Occasionally, a mistake at the plant resulted in Monensin, the most common ionophore, to be added to the horse formula, which resulted in dead horses and lawsuits.

Within the last decade or so horse nutrition became so specialized—and profitable—that manufactures dedicated entire plants solely to the production of horse feeds. Ionophores had no reason to be on site, and deaths from manufacturer mistakes were eliminated. In Pascoe's Toxicology course ionophore poisoning in horses had been mentioned as an afterthought.

"But I sent in feed samples," he said.

"I know. No trace of ionophores, so Tox didn't bother running the test on the stomach contents, it seemed redundant. After I looked at the heart muscle on this other horse, I had them recheck the sample I was holding in the freezer, and guess what they found?"

"Monensin."

"Gobs of it."

"So why didn't you see anything in Goldrush's slides?"

"That's not unusual. Thing is, coccidiostats interfere with metal ion transfer. I'm talking molecular level metabolism here. Chronic poisonings create contractility problems: arrhythmias, incomplete blood ejection, stuff that damages the heart with every beat. Nobody would notice until neurologic signs showed up—not too many horses walk around complaining of chest pain. By then the horse is stumbling around or down and it's too late anyway. A couple of days of a low dose and you would have seen the damage at the post—white streaks in the heart muscle. And if by some miracle you missed it, the cells would have swelled up like balloons and I would have seen it the instant I peeked in the 'scope. But a big, acute overdose shuts down the entire neuro system in a hurry—quick enough that cell damage might not show. After I knew what I was looking for I double-checked the slide from the Goldrush horse and found a small cluster of cells matching the type of necrosis I found on Lexus' heart."

"If the feed samples were clean it makes it pretty unlikely that Goldrush was an accidental poisoning."

"Considering this is the first equine ionophore case since I started here, I'd say both are pretty unlikely, unless either one had access to a big bag of chicken feed."

"Your certain then?"

Bridges was put out. "I wouldn't call otherwise."

"Good enough," Pascoe said. "Is this a carnation or rose diagnosis?"

"Silly wabbit. This calls for orchids."

"Was that about the Dowry horse?" Harkin asked. "Botulism, just like I said, right?"

"Bridges thinks it's Monensin poisoning," Pascoe said.

"No kidding? Lord, the last time I saw one of those was back in the sixties. Old Man Ferguson, he ran the co-op for years, hadn't cleaned out his mixer after making a batch of feed for a chicken farm then mixed up a ration for one of the locals." Harkin scrunched up his face, trying to remember. "The Carlsons, that's who it was. Lost a handful of hunters. The lawsuit cost Fergie the co-op.

"I know you're fond of the Bridges girl Jordie, but don't you think she might be wrong on this one? After all, Dowry feeds his horses well, and Stonemason isn't exactly the type of place to find chickens scratching in the aisle."

"I trust her," Pascoe said. "Besides, they found a hefty dose of Monensin in Goldrush's stomach."

"On purpose? Whatever for?"

Pascoe couldn't give Harkin reasons without explaining the work he had done with Wallace. "Don't know," he said instead, "but at least I have an answer for Dowry. Somebody else can figure out why."

At the end of a long, wet day—snow had fallen mid-afternoon, melting as soon as it touched anything, soaking the cuffs of his pants and flannel shirt—Pascoe found himself taking a precarious way home. The roads were wet, but straight, and the snow had stopped falling, which made for easy driving. But his destination, that was another story.

Maybe it was a subconscious decision, but turning into Wallace's driveway felt more like sadomasochism. Headlights attract attention, once committed there were two options: turn around and give Wallace the satisfaction of seeing him run, or knock on the door and present results he could have telephoned in. When the truck stopped, Barclay lifted his head, saw how miserable the weather was, and decided to stay in the car as he had all day, curled up in a fleece blanket.

Wallace watched Pascoe approach, smirk barely held in check. "Couldn't stay away?"

"I've found out something you need to know."

"It must be important to deliver in person," she said, feigning seriousness. "Come inside and get warm."

She led him to a stool adjacent to a granite-topped island in the middle of the kitchen. "Hungry?"

Wallace's meager offerings would tease his stomach into spasms of protest. He shook his head.

"Wine? I just opened a fabulous Chardonnay."

"Something warm, if you've got it."

"Tea?"

"Sure."

Wallace threw a kettle of water on the stove built into the island. The heat from the burner cleared stiffness from his fingers. Wallace filled her wineglass and sat beside him.

"What have you got?" she asked.

"At least two of the horses in the group, Dowry and Rasmussen, were poisoned."

"Ah, that is news. How did you find out?"

"Luck mostly. Rasmussen gave the okay to analyze tissue samples from her horse. I took them to a lab, and the pathologist found evidence of ionophore toxicity." Wallace stared at him dumbly. "It's a coccidiostat." More staring. "I'll back up. In production medicine, food production, you get paid by the pound. The key to profit is to put as much weight on your product before slaughter. Coccidia are tiny, one-celled parasites that cause diarrhea and weight loss. Ionophores prevent infection, which allows the animal to gain more weight. It's used mostly in the poultry and beef industry, those species tolerate the drug well, but ionophores are highly toxic to horses. Goldrush was given a large amount at one time and it appears Lexus had multiple smaller doses. Good thing for us, if Lexus had been given the kind of dose as Goldrush, it might not have damaged the heart and we still wouldn't know what killed either one."

"So why did Stuart do it?"

"What do you mean?"

"You said whoever killed the horses also killed Devon. Stuart's been pegged for the murder, so I assume he's our man." The teapot whistled. Wallace shut of the burner and grabbed a mug and teabag from a cabinet. "This is great," she said, pouring the steaming water into the mug. "This exonerates our clients. They keep their money because some psycho killed their horse, and Virginia Bloodstock looks good because we came up with some answers. I might even be able to get some cash thrown your way." She dunked the teabag into the water a few times and handed it to Pascoe.

"David didn't kill Devon," Pascoe said. "Or the horses."

Wallace couldn't hide her skepticism. "Sure that's not your dick talking?"

"He barely remembers who he is, and you label him some kind of criminal mastermind?"

"Retarded people are convicted of violent crime all the time. They might not know the difference between right and wrong, but act on impulse.

"How bright do you have to be to throw some poison in a feed tub anyway? Or for that matter, whack a little girl over the head? There's plenty of evidence. They found her phone, right? There was a story today that said Stuart injured one of her horses and was fired by because of it. There are rumors of eyewitnesses who have seen him driving an old farm truck around in the middle of the night. Maybe he's not as damaged as you think."

Pascoe was flustered. "He's learned to drive and that makes him a killer? What about motive? Devon didn't want him fired. He gave Lexus to Rasmussen. What happened to your insurance scam conspiracy? You think guys like Dowry and Dearborne and the Sinclairs all got together and hired the village idiot to pull it off?"

"Maybe it was never about money. Do you know what's going on inside Stuart's head? He was lead dog—top rider in the country; people lining up to take lessons. Probably an Olympics or two from a medal. Boom! Suddenly he's a nobody hauling shit for his sister. Maybe there's a spark of the old David Stuart who remembers what he used to have. What's that do to a guy?"

Pascoe's pager chirped, cutting off his response. He used Wallace's phone to call back and get directions to the emergency. When he was done, Wallace handed him a stainless steel travel mug into which she had transferred his tea.

"You never got a chance to warm up," she said.

"Thanks," said Pascoe, taking the mug. "I know what the papers and the cops are saying, they're wrong. I know David, and he's not capable of this. That's not coming from my dick, it's coming from my heart."

Wallace circled her finger on Pascoe's chest, outlining a heart-shape. "If you find your dick needs to do some thinking, I can find something for it to think about."

Pascoe planted a light kiss on her forehead. "Tempting, believe me. I don't know exactly what Hunter and I have right now, but know I don't want to mess it up."

Wallace backed up and folded her arms tightly under her breasts. "If you're wrong, and the community ties you with Stuart, you'll never work on another horse in this county."

"I'll keep it in mind."

Wallace had given him a lot to think about. Could she be right? Did a part of David rage behind dull eyes and guileless smile? Surely Hunter would know, she scrutinized her brother for any sign of the spark Wallace had talked about, but could she see something she didn't want to?

Such thoughts swirled in Pascoe's mind as he attended the emergency. An older donkey named Pogo, who should have know better, tested a fence and received a deep gash for his trouble.

The Greers, Pogo's owners, must have thought Pascoe rude, because he hardly uttered a word before getting to work. Stitching skin together was more craft than technique, and once a tempo was established—poke, pull, tie, poke, pull, tie—his mind wandered. When the last knot was tight he stood, the crack from his knees reinforcing the silence of the last hour.

"The wound was a little tricky to get together, but should hold just fine," Pascoe said, trying to engage the Greers. "I'll leave you with some antibiotics, but other than that just keep the old guy in a stall so he doesn't tear the stitches out."

"He lives in the pasture," Mr. Greer said, happy the vet turned out to be human after all. "We don't have a space to keep him in."

"You only need a week until the tension is off the skin." Pogo had been brought to the house where there was light to work by, and Pascoe had no idea how the rest of the property was set up. "Is there a place you could rig up for that long?"

"We do have one spot." Pascoe was led behind the main house to a low-ceilinged outbuilding. Netting formed a small half-cylinder enclosing about two hundred square-feet of space to the left of the structure. "It's a bit small, but it's all we've got."

"Have to do," Pascoe said. "Let's check it out."

"Better let me clear George and Martha out first." Curious, Pascoe watched as Mrs. Greer slid open a door on the short side of the structure. He wondered how they planned on getting the donkey into the space and had initially thought the couple might be in for some late night carpentry. A wail of protest erupted from inside the building, followed by the speedy exit of a peacock and his hen, the cock's tail fanned and shaking in anger, the hen screaming.

"Come in," Mrs. Greer called from inside. "Watch out for that pair, I don't believe they're too happy about the eviction."

The birds were too preoccupied with melodrama to take any interest in Pascoe. The coop would need only minor modification to become suitable for the donkey and although he would have to duck coming in, both the ceiling and netting rose just high enough to avoid hitting his head or tangling his long ears. Even so, if Pogo reared the Greers would be calling someone out to close a head wound.

A trashcan in the corner holding feed would also need to be moved. The lid might be secured tightly enough to discourage the birds, but it would take seconds for the donkey to knock over and gorge.

Poultry feed. Pascoe walked over to the can and lifted the lid. Like most people, the Greers had dropped in an entire fifty-pound bag and sliced open the top rather than upend its contents. He ripped off the feed tag and squinted in the weak red light of a heat lamp.

There it was, on the fifth line of the ingredient list: Monensin.

"Everything all right?" Mr. Greer asked.

"You'll need to find another place to store the grain," Pascoe said. "There's stuff in here that could kill Pogo."

"Oh my," Mrs. Greer said. "Does that happen often?"

"More often than you would think."

CHAPTER THIRTEEN

Pascoe didn't care if Bimbo saw him coming; he drove straight to the trailer and hopped out, almost catching Barclay's tail in the door as he slammed it shut. The dog had not had a bathroom break in hours and was desperate to get out.

It wasn't until the front door popped open against his pounding fist that Pascoe noticed the unusuall quiet. The peacock was not on the step to give alarm; in fact, the bird was nowhere to be found. Pascoe slowed and stepped across the threshold.

"Bimbo?" The temperature of the trailer was no warmer than outside. Pascoe felt along the wall until he came to a light switch and flipped it on.

Clothes, food wrappers, and tableware were strewn about the trailer, but it didn't appear in any worse condition than his last visit. The doors to the bedroom and bathroom were both open; if Carlyle was trying to hide, he didn't have much to work with. Pascoe called for Barclay. If anyone was in the trailer, the dog was sure to find them first.

Barclay wove in and out of the rooms of the trailer, tail up and wagging, thrilled to be invited to partake in the scents of the carpet. Pascoe remained in the entry. After a few minutes, Barclay returned, waiting to see what was next on the agenda. He was having a grand time.

Pascoe didn't quite know what to do; he had assumed Carlyle would be here. He sat down in a vinyl recliner spider-webbed with cracks. The heat was off, which indicated Carlyle wasn't returning anytime soon. The question remained whether he had chosen to leave or been forced to. The sprung door reminded Pascoe of the night Dearborne had shown up. Maybe someone had paid a similar visit to Carlyle, though as messy as the place was, who could tell if there had been a struggle?

He started in the bedroom. A twin mattress, the largest size able to fit in the cramped room, sat directly on the floor without a box spring. Stale, unmatched sheets and blankets were piled on top. A small, three-drawer wood dresser was the only other piece of furniture in the room and it stood lonely in one corner, drawers empty and half open. Clothes were in scattered clumps; darks, lights, and whites mingled freely. Pascoe toed one pile tentatively and wondered if they were sorted by stiffness.

The rest of the space was cluttered with food-caked dishes. Current issues of *The Daily Racing Form* and *The Blood Horse* were stacked against one wall with older *Penthouse* and *Hustler* magazines hidden between them as if Carlyle expected his mother to come snooping. Paper cups and tin cans, crusted with food and filled with tobacco spit, traced a curving line across the carpet like paving stones. Empty bottles of Southern Comfort, Jack Daniels, and Jagermeister were heaped in one corner, pint cans of Foster's filled another. Despite the chaos, it appeared Carlyle was a recycler. It smelled like a college dorm.

Pascoe flipped over the mattress and discovered a bed-sized rectangle of carpet two shades lighter than the rest of the room. Behind the dresser he found what he told himself was, at one time, an orange, other possibilities were too disturbing. He didn't touch the porn, unconvinced the magazines would open if he tried, but did flip through the racing publications. Carlyle had scrawled some notes in the margins—some surprisingly insightful—but nothing related to race fixing or the killings. Underneath the stack he found the only cared for object he had come across: a pine box about the size of a dictionary with a thin lid that slid into grooves cut into the sides. Inside, a shiny set of riding silks—a navy and maroon pattern Pascoe couldn't match to a specific stable—were reverently folded. The rest of the room held nothing of interest.

Pascoe moved to the kitchen, which proved easier to search. He cleared the counters by sweeping the filthy dishes into the sink. After that, each cupboard was easy to empty and quick to explore; not much could be hidden among cans of chili and ravioli. The refrigerator was much the same: a shrunken head of lettuce kept beer company in the main compartment. The freezer was stuffed with TV dinners and pizza. Both racks of the oven held warped cookie sheets with a dusting of what appeared to be salt in the corners. Frustrated, he returned to the living room.

It was well past midnight and below freezing in the trailer and both the late hour and the cold were draining. The recliner, tattered as it was, called to him. Fifteen minutes. That's all he needed. Barclay was sure to warn him of any approach. He fell into the chair, pulled the hood of his jacket over his head, levered the footrest up, and was asleep in seconds.

Shaken awake, he feared had drifted off the shoulder of a country road. Pascoe reached for a nonexistent steering wheel and almost tumbled out of the recliner. Groggy and relieved, he sat and regained his bearings. The recliner bucked like a playful colt. Pascoe rocked the chair forward and was startled again when Barclay yelped and shot from underneath the footrest.

"Jesus!" Pascoe yelled, jumping to one side.

Barclay's tail thumped on the floor, and his tongue lolled out of an open, grinning mouth. He trotted back and tried to wriggle his way back underneath. The chair convulsed as the dog dug furiously dug with his front paws. After a few moments of unproductive struggling, he backed out and let out a sharp, impatient yip.

It was a familiar routine. Barclay had shoved more tennis balls into inaccessible places than Pascoe could remember. There would be no peace until he retrieved whatever captured Barclay's attention; such was the obsessive-compulsive nature of his Border Collie heritage. Pasco got on his hands and knees and reached under the chair. His hand brushed against the desired object immediately: the petrified orange from the bedroom. Barclay crouched in the same position as Pascoe, ready for the chase. Pascoe swept his arm to fling the orange from under the chair and banged his knuckles against something hard. The orange dribbled out, stopping before it reached the dog. Barclay snorted in disgust, picked up the orange in his mouth, and trotted off to play by himself.

Pascoe knelt on the floor and sucked a bleeding knuckle. Whatever he hit, it moved, so it wasn't part of the chair. He reached back under, cautiously, and found it again—a metal box slightly smaller than the box in the bedroom. Pascoe pushed it out. It turned out to be a cash box; the same kind Maggie kept at the office.

The box was locked, but easily pried open with a kitchen knife. The inside was carefully organized. The first compartment of the money tray held a stack of cash secured with a rubber band, a thin layer of ones and fives followed by thicker sections of tens, twenties, fifties, and substantial collection of hundreds. It looked to be a couple of grand.

The other tills held their own caches. The first was stuffed with a tightly packed Ziploc bag of pot. The second contained three 35mm film canisters, each packed with a fine, white powder. The third was piled with loose white pills that looked like aspirin.

Pascoe lifted the tray. Underneath, on the floor of the box, lay a spiral bound notebook just small enough to fit in the box. The top of each sheet of paper in the notebook had a different heading; most were initials, but some had nicknames. "Peeps" and "Flash" appeared on more than one page, but a customer with the unappealing moniker "Scab" appeared to be Carlyle's best customer, regularly plunking down five hundred dollars at a time. It seemed that Carlyle had a frequent buyers program, because every now and then Scab was given his fix free of charge. Down the left side, opposite the dollar amount of the transaction, products were written in shorthand combinations of letters and numbers like '1gk' and '3tr'. A hundred dollar bill could get you '1gk', whatever that was.

The box's existence confused the issue of Carlyle's absence. It no shock that he was dealing, honest work seemed anathema to the man, but it was a surprise to find the stash lying around. If he had time to pack and turn off the heat, why leave the drugs and cash? If somebody else came for Carlyle, why wasn't the place torn apart?

Scratching at the front door brought his head around. Barclay growled in his throat and his hackles rose. Pascoe motioned for the dog to be quiet and tiptoed to the door. The scratching stopped. Pascoe steadied himself and ripped the door open. Barclay rushed past, barking furiously. The sounds of a scuffle followed. Pascoe followed as quickly as he could.

Barclay cowered at the bottom of the short flight of stairs leading to the front door. Carlyle's peacock had the dog pinned and pecked and stomped on him unmercifully. Pascoe shoved the bird away with his boot and suffered a sharp pinch to the calf for his trouble. Blood trickled down his leg. Barclay sprinted into the woods.

The bird regarded Pascoe disdainfully, daring him to use the boot again. When nothing happened, the cock turned and strutted to a row of garbage cans lined up against the side of the trailer. He stopped there and yowled.

"Humans are good for one thing at least, aren't they?"

The first two cans were filled with garbage; the third contained feed. Pascoe scattered a handful on the ground to placate the bird before going to his truck and getting a flashlight. With the light he was able to locate the ingredient tag. He ripped it off the bag in triumph like an enemy scalp. It was a short-lived victory. The bag contained COB: corn, oats, and barley. Horse feed, likely swiped from a steeplechase client. Just like Carlyle to feed his bird on someone else's dime. Pascoe slammed the lid back onto the can. The peacock flapped in annoyance before continuing to scratch at the seed in the dirt. Pascoe knew in his heart there would be no Monensin in the bag, but scrutinized the label anyway. After a third time of going over the label line by line it was clear the feed contained nothing harmful.

He had been at Carlyle's too long already and was feeling vulnerable. Time to leave. Returning to the trailer, he grabbed the cashbox, figuring the ledger might prove valuable if he could identify a few clients. Maybe one of them knew where Carlyle was hiding.

As Pascoe approached the truck, Barclay crept out of the forest, taking care to keep the Dodge between him and the bird. When Pascoe opened the door, the dog hopped in quickly and lay on the seat, chin on forepaws, hidden from view.

"Got your ass kicked by a bird," Pascoe said.

Barclay exhaled sharply through the nose, closed his eyes, and ignored him.

CHAPTER FOURTEEN

A low-pressure system moved in overnight, bringing a howling wind that rattled the house and fluttered the curtains. The wood stove failed to push the chill away and Pascoe shivered as he brewed coffee. His head pounded from caffeine withdrawal. Going without the last twelve hours brought on symptoms recognized all too well from previous half-hearted attempts to quit. A pair of aspirin stemmed the pain, but food would need to be added soon if he wanted to preserve his stomach lining.

The greater part of the day was spent catching up with previously cancelled appointments. Clients took advantage, adding extra procedures and horses, knowing the threat of a complaint made their requests impossible to turn down, regardless of the chaos it created. Lunch, taken late in the afternoon, consisted of additional aspirin and a Slim Jim washed down with an energy drink. Calories, caffeine, and clear head combined and suddenly he knew whom to turn to for help.

"Too busy building the gallows or are you still interested in new directions?" Pascoe asked.

"Always willing to listen," Monroe replied.

"Devon Dowry's horse was poisoned. If she confronted someone..."

"I've seen *Law and Order*." Monroe's voice lowered. "We'll need to meet somewhere other than the station, this place has more leaks than Congress."

"Name a place and time."

"How well do you know Harper's Ferry?"

"Been there a couple of times."

"There's an Amtrak station on the Potomac side. Meet me in the parking lot."

"When?"

"The soonest I can get there will be ten."

Pascoe suppressed a groan. He would need more caffeine. "I'll be there."

The wind increased and plunged the temperature into the teens by sunset. The chill had horses on edge, making work difficult and slow. Pascoe eventually finished around eight, which would have left time for a short nap, had he not been feeding his caffeine habit all day.

Instead, he grabbed a bite to eat and perused the entries for the next day's meets at Hollywood Park and Arlington. A couple of races looked promising and these picks were jotted down in his fictional book. If the picks came through, he'd cross the hundred thousand dollar mark in earnings, on paper anyway.

Barclay could not be persuaded to come to the meeting with Monroe, and Pascoe couldn't blame him, opening the front door caused the dog to curl into a tighter ball and skootch closer to the wood stove.

The truck was nearly blown into the guardrail as he crossed over the Shenandoah. At the end of the bridge he took a right into Harper's Ferry and wound around museums and tourist shops until he found the train station. Headlights reflected off a dark sedan at the far end of the parking lot. As Pascoe pulled alongside, Monroe climbed out, stiff-armed in a bulky parka, zippered hood obscuring his face. He rapped on Pascoe's window and motioned for him to roll it down.

"Let's take a walk," he said. The parka muffled his words, but Pascoe got the idea.

"It's freezing. Let's talk in one of the cars."

"Don't be a pussy." Monroe turned and walked toward the train station.

Pascoe wasn't sure what wanting to avoid losing parts of his anatomy to frostbite had to do with being a pussy, but any talk was obviously going to be on the detective's terms. Pascoe pulled a wool cap over his head. His only pair of gloves had the fingertips cut off, but they were better than nothing. Eyes teared as soon as he stepped into the night air. He jogged twisted, back to the wind, hands shoved under his coat, to catch up.

Monroe nodded when he did, but marched on in silence. When they reached the station, the detective angled toward the rail line. Together, they clambered up a short gravel slope to the tracks and walked between the rails southward, toward the junction of the Shenandoah and Potomac. Pascoe spoke first.

"Can I ask a question?"

"Shoot."

"Why do you always call the sheriff 'The Sheriff'? I can understand being professional and all, especially around the office, but every time we've spoken, you refer to him that way. I would expect you to slip and call him 'Dad' at least once in a while."

Monroe stopped and gestured with his arm back towards the town. "You know the history of this place?"

"Sure. Jim Brown. Raided the armory. Big anti-slavery guy."

Monroe nodded, laughing. "Crazy son of a bitch thought he and eighteen men could grab some rifles and start an invasion of the South. They hanged him for that.

"Thing is, in this country, moments like that are some of the *highpoints* of black history. There hasn't been a whole lot to cheer about. Brown was white, but he struck a blow for the brothers. Harper's Ferry was one of many small battles. Some, like Brown's, were lost, but all led to emancipation, civil rights, and the ability for a black man to be elected sheriff, president even. Problem is, the black man who got elected in our county has forgotten the struggle.

"I think he likes being sheriff more than he liked being a cop. So proud he can't see he's become the house nigger for rich white folks. Takes care of business and they make sure he gets reelected. That's not the same man who made me want to be a cop."

"So why help me?" Pascoe asked.

"Because it's what *they* don't want the department to do. A speedy investigation means that nobody digs too deep, and secrets stay covered up. Down the road, if evidence turns up that proves Stuart's innocence, all those rich dudes will leave the sheriff high and dry, and they'll whisper about how the nigger they elected screwed it up, and it will be another two hundred years before another black man is elected to anything. I'm not going to let Dad take a fall like that. If I bring him evidence, he'll listen."

"He seems more intent on controlling the investigation than giving you free rein."

"Then he'll fall by his own hand, but at least it won't be by mine."

"What about Turner?"

"I don't give a rat's ass about Turner. If he wants to get crucified by Newcomb just so his face can be on the front page, that's his business."

They had reached the point where the two rivers merged. In the night, with the wind obscuring noise of the current, the water looked still, like two wide brushstrokes of black paint. The men stood shoulder to shoulder and contemplated the scene like tourists. The wind cut through Pascoe's inadequate clothing and he danced from foot to foot trying to generate heat. Perhaps out of compassion, Monroe abruptly headed back the way they had come.

"What have you got?" he asked.

Pascoe told him about the poisonings, leaving out Wallace's involvement for the time being, and how he had made the connection between the peacock and Carlyle and what he had discovered at the trailer.

Monroe placed a mittened hand against Pascoe's chest. "Hold up. You illegally entered a home, took a couple of grand in cash, and are now in possession of illegal drugs?" Monroe shook his head in disbelief. "Jesus, are you trying to get yourself arrested?"

"Uh, well, I..."

Monroe's Cheshire grin gleamed from deep inside the hood. "Don't worry about it Doc, we're in West Virginia, remember? Not my jurisdiction. But if Carlyle comes back and is stupid enough to file a report, then you might be in deep shit." He continued walking. After a bit he said, "I don't see how any of this is going to help your boy. How difficult is it to get hold of this medication, the poison? Do you need a permit or anything?"

"Anyone who knew what they were looking for could pick it up in the right bag of grain."

"And the sack at the trailer didn't have any. Look, every cop in the county knows Carlyle's a scumbag, but you've got no connection to Dowry."

"No proof, but there's possibly a third, and maybe a fourth horse. One belongs to Matthew Dearborne. Carlyle told me he and Dearborne had a race-fixing scam going on a while back, maybe this is a new scam."

"Insurance?"

Pascoe was relieved the detective came up with the idea on his own. "Why not?"

"And the girl was killed because she found out and was going to talk," Monroe finished. "And her father, a multimillionaire, either agreed to this, killed her himself, or stayed silent after Carlyle took matters into his own hands."

Pascoe chewed on his lower lip, which was cracking from the wind and cold. He couldn't see the detective's face hidden deep within the cowl of his parka, but could imagine his eyes rolling.

"There are rumors that Dowry is in some serious financial trouble," Pascoe said. "If he was about to lose everything, had found a way to stop the bleeding, and someone interfered with his plans, he could get desperate."

"Possibly," said Monroe. "Susan Smith chose a boyfriend over her own children, and people get killed over a month's rent. It wouldn't hurt to find out what kind of shape Dowry's in. What about Rasmussen? Is she part of it?"

"Hard to believe. Without her help I still wouldn't know how either horse died. Carlyle has a training field near her place, maybe her horse was a test case."

"Was hers the first to die?" Monroe asked.

"Nope. But the type of poisoning that killed Lexus could have occurred over a long period. Even I wouldn't know how much Monensin-laced feed to give a horse. Carlyle might have tried more than once before figuring out how much to give."

They reached the station. Monroe left the tracks and headed toward the vehicles. "But you don't have proof Dearborne's horse was poisoned?" he asked.

"No."

"Anyone, other than a local drug pusher, who can corroborate you claim that Dearborne was fixing races?"

"No."

"Let me summarize. Your theory is that a man everyone considers trash hooked up with one of the most respected and influential men in the county, and then conspired to murder the girl who discovered their plan with the knowledge, or at least implied consent, of the girl's father. On the other hand, the prosecution's theory is this: a disturbed young man murdered the girl responsible for having him fired from the first job he was given after recovering from a horrible accident."

"You're forgetting the poisonings," Pascoe said.

"Oh yes, Turner would love to have that." The detective put on a reedy, high-toned, white-man's accent. "Also, ladies and gentlemen of the jury, we have discovered that the accused poisoned the horse owned by the murder victim, a horse he had injured previously with a pitchfork, which, by the way, was the murder weapon. His ex-girlfriend's horse was killed in the same manner, and it's possible *her* ex-husband's horse was poisoned as well." He returned to his normal rumbling baritone. "How much rope do you want to give him?"

"I thought you were on my side," Pascoe said.

"I'm on the side of the truth. I'm not convinced Turner's side is the truth, but I don't believe your cockamamie story either. Something's missing."

They paused at the vehicles. Pascoe looked longingly at his truck, calculating how long it would take to thaw his feet, which had lost all feeling on the walk back. But comfort would have to wait; he still had a favor to ask. He unlocked the truck and took out the cashbox.

"Can you take a look at this?" Pascoe asked.

"Pascoe..."

"We're still in West Virginia. You have no obligation to do anything."

Monroe said nothing. Instead he turned and went to his car and came back wearing thin latex gloves in place of mittens. "Let's make this quick," he said. "These damn gloves suck the warmth right out of you." The detective studied Pascoe's exposed fingertips. "You handle the box with bare hands?"

"I work in the cold all the time. I'm used to it."

Monroe shook his head like he was talking to a second grader. "I'm talking about fingerprints Pascoe. I don't suppose you thought about how it would look if you got stopped, even for running a stop sign, and a cop found this stuff. How were you planning on explaining that it isn't your stash if your prints are all over the damn thing?"

Pascoe almost dropped the box. "Hadn't considered it. I could wipe it down."

"And, being a professional criminal, you know how to do that without missing a spot. Want my advice? Chuck the whole thing off the bridge on your way home." Monroe waggled his fingers. "C'mon, give it here."

Monroe opened the box on the hood of the truck. He whistled when he saw the money. "What are you going to do with this?" he asked, flipping through the stack with his thumb.

Pascoe shifted uncomfortably. "It's not mine. Maybe Bimbo will trade information to get it back."

Monroe looked skeptical. "Uh-huh. Well, no question about this," he said, holding up the marijuana filled baggie. He grabbed one of the aspirin-like tablets next, pulled a small Mag-lite from his parka and examined the pill. "This is a bit more serious." He beckoned Pascoe to lean in for a closer look. "See here on the front? R-O-C-H-E, that's the manufacturer." He turned the tablet over. "On the back they stamped the number two. That's the dosage. What you have here are two-milligram tablets of flunitrazepam. Roche markets it as Rohypnol."

"Ro-hip what?"

"Rohypnol. You know, roofies. Odorless and tasteless. Slip it into a drink and before long the victim is unconscious, and won't remember a thing in the morning. Classic date-rape drug. Psychiatrists used to prescribe it, but it's completely illegal in this country now. Most of it comes in from Mexico nowadays."

"How about the rest?"

Monroe peeled the lid off one of the canisters. "What you have here," Monroe said conspiratorially, "is a white powder."

"No shit," Pascoe said. "Cocaine?"

"Could be baking powder for all I know," Monroe said. "Carlyle looks to be setting himself up as Party Central, cocaine would be my guess. You said something about a notebook?"

"Under the till."

Holding the flashlight in his mouth, Monroe drew the book from under the drawer and flipped through the pages. Several times he returned to a previous page.

"It." Monroe said.

"What?" Pascoe asked.

Monroe pulled the flashlight from between his lips. "I said shit." He laid his hand flat on the open book. "I know who this is." He sounded irritated.

Pascoe leaned over. The book was open to a page with the heading "Scab".

"Yeah?"

"Vaughn Dowry."

"Scab?"

"It's what his friends call him. At least I was told they were his friends by Vaughn's lawyer, who gave me a list of people who would vouch for Vaughn's whereabouts at the time of his sister's death. They all called him Scab. Seemed to think it was funny that his initials were 'VD', started calling him Scabby Dick, and shortened it to Scab."

"Pretty refined sense of humor."

"What do you expect from meth heads? Half of these guys could hardly focus on the questions, but they all swore Scab partied with them all night and didn't leave until late afternoon."

"Vaughn's got himself an expensive habit. What do you make of it?"

"All the purchases listed under his name are for various amounts of 'gk'. I assume the 'g' stands for grams, so I'm betting it's the powder."

"K for cocaine?"

"Does Carlyle strike you as an ace speller?"

"Point taken."

Monroe put the cash box back together. Before closing the lid, he held one of the canisters in his palm and peeled the glove off so that the canister was contained within the body. He spun the glove to twist the cuff and knotted it like the stem of a balloon. His gloved hand closed the lid.

"I'm taking this," Monroe said. "For testing."

"Want the whole thing?"

"Too much to explain. Nobody's going to think twice if I turn in one sample, but if I come in with a whole pharmacy, that's going to raise some eyebrows."

"Carlyle had a pretty good business going," Pascoe said. He let the implication hang.

"And if Devon found out and threatened to turn him in...could be enough of a motive for Bimbo. Or Vaughn. Who stood to lose more?"

"Carlyle would be looking at jail time," Pascoe said. "That is, if he was dumb enough to hang on to the stash after being threatened."

"Seems to me like it would be easier to stop selling to Vaughn and keep the rest of his customers, after all, how would she know?"

"Agreed. Maybe she didn't know about Carlyle. Maybe she found out her brother was using and threatened to tell Dad."

"And then what?" Monroe asked.

"Vaughn doesn't have, has never had, a job. If Oliver cut him off, he'd have no money to party or throw around. What if," Pascoe considered possible scenarios, "What if Goldrush was a warning? Devon threatens and Vaughn responds by killing her horse and implies he'll do the same to her if she doesn't back off."

"You knew the girl, how would she respond? Would she back off?"

Pascoe was around when Devon graduated from pony to horse. The first was a sly chestnut who knew the difference between a trainer and being prodded by the short legs of a twelve year old. After being planted in the arena like a lawn dart for the umpteenth time, Devon changed into a bathing suit, and walked the horse to a pond on the far side of the property. She led the horse into the water, swimming when it got too deep, until the horse had to start swimming as well. Now unable to buck, Devon slid onto his back and steered around the pond until he was so tired both horse and rider were in danger of drowning. Only then did she give him his head and allow him to swim to shore. Rode back to the barn that afternoon and never left his back again without intending to do so.

"She wouldn't back down," Pascoe said. "If anything, she'd give Vaughn a swift kick in the balls."

"Never met the girl, but from what people say I would expect as much. Vaughn's lawyer is never going to let me question him about this. He'll deny Vaughn has ever used drugs or met Bimbo Carlyle, and I've got nothing but a stolen cash box and a ledger with your fingerprints all over both. And if Goldrush was a warning, you'll still have to explain what happened to the other horse."

Stalemate. Dowry and his lawyers could keep the police away from Vaughn indefinitely. There was something though, in the manner in which Monroe Rohypnol came into the U.S. that gave him something to work with.

"Come to think of it," Pascoe said, "Oliver hasn't heard about the poisoning. I should drop by."

Monroe barked a laugh. "I've seen the way you talk to Vaughn. If you think you're going to get a chance at Stonemason, you're crazy."

"Actually, I'm hoping to run into someone else," Pascoe said.

Pascoe followed Monroe's advice and stopped in the middle of the span across the Shenandoah. He idled with flashers on, Carlyle's cashbox in his lap, unable to bring himself to open the door, or even roll down the window, and toss the drugs over the side. Something nibbled at the back of his mind. He recognized the feeling, it was the same as being on the verge of diagnosing a complicated case, or when a trifecta emerged from the confusion of a racing form. A distant part of his mind wanted to make a connection to the drugs, and if he got rid of the cashbox the stimulus would be gone. Pascoe shut off the flashers, put the truck and gear, and finished crossing the black expanse of river into Virginia.

Vets had a habit of running behind; and clients wouldn't call the office unless they had been waiting for over an hour. There was a spot in the schedule where Pascoe could stop at Stonemason, push his next appointment into the latter part of that one-hour window, and neither the client nor Maggie (and by extension, Harkin) would know the difference.

At the barn, midday feeding had just ended. Leaves of clover and stalks of timothy were deposited every twelve feet in front of the stall doors, having fallen from the feed cart as it stopped to distribute its fare. Lumps of clay, dislodged from the convex soles of the horses as they were brought in from pasture, stood like earthen traffic cones in the center of the aisle. A brave mouse darted from stall to stall, gathering kernels of oats.

Emilio was at the far end of the barn, enveloped in a cloud of dust as he pushed debris from the barn with a gas-powered leaf blower. He did well to conceal his shock at seeing the man who had decked Vaughn return to the farm.

"Ey Doctor, I was not told you were coming," he said, pulling a dust mask from his face.

"I was hoping we could talk about Bimbo Carlyle."

Emilio's wide eyes were stark against his dust-covered face. "Who is this you say?" he stammered.

Pascoe reached into a pocket, pulled out a Rohypnol, and bounced it on his palm. "Recognize this?"

"No," Emilio said hoarsely.

"So the next time you come back from Mexico, you won't mind if the DEA pays close attention to your luggage?"

"Please, Jordan."

"Emilio, this isn't about you. But I need answers, and you can either give them to me or the sheriff."

"What do you want me to say? I bring these pills back after visiting my family. Mr. Dowry said I could make some extra money, maybe make it so Maria and Annalisa can come to live here also."

"Oliver asked you to do this?"

"No, Mr. Vaughn. He told me this Bimbo would buy the pills. If I say no, I lose my job. If I go to the police, I lose my job. He would tell all the people I stole from the farm and no one else would hire me. At least this way I make a little money."

"Tell you're story to the cops. Everyone will know what happened and Vaughn won't be able to blackmail you."

Emilio regarded Pascoe with pity. "That's not the way it works. Do you think they'll believe the word of a brown man over a white man? We're the stable hands and gardeners, and we can't pronounce our j's." Even with emphasized precision, it still came out 'yays'. Emilio waved his hand dismissively at Pascoe. "No, I'll take my chances and keep my job. It's a good job."

"But you could go to jail."

Emilio shrugged as if to say, *Jail. Back to Mexico where there are no jobs and no future. What's the difference?*

"It might help find Devon's killer."

Emilio shrugged again, but this time he avoided Pascoe's eyes.

"What are you doing here?"

Emilio looked as if he were going to be sick. Pascoe clenched his fist around the tablet and turned to face the onslaught. Dowry stormed down the aisle, Vaughn pacing obediently alongside, crescent moons of bruised banana peel flesh hanging beneath both eyes. He spotted Pascoe's closed right hand and appeared as nervous as Dowry was furious.

"I realize you don't want me here, Mr. Dowry," Pascoe said as they approached. "But once I found out what killed Goldrush, I felt it was necessary to talk with Emilio. I didn't want the same thing to happen to the other horses, and I hoped I could slip in and out without causing you any distress."

The conciliatory manner flustered Dowry. He sputtered a few inaudible fragments; unsure as to continue screaming or accept the explanation. He found a compromise.

"What are you talking about?" he asked through clenched teeth. "Harkin said it was botulism—a freak accident, maybe poor management." He glared darkly at Emilio.

"That's what we both thought, but the lab concluded that Goldrush was poisoned."

"You can't accuse us of such a thing!" whined Vaughn. His bruises took on a scarlet hue.

Dowry put a hand on his son's shoulder, alarmed Vaughn would do something rash. "Absolutely right," Dowry said. "The insurance company is fully satisfied. They have certified the death as accidental and written us a check. Now, after all this family has been through, you have the nerve to suggest..."

"You'll get to keep the money Mr. Dowry."

"That's not what I meant!"

"You misunderstand. This new information doesn't change anything with Virginia Bloodstock. The substance Goldrush was poisoned by is often an ingredient in other types of feed. The lab didn't detect any in the samples I sent to them, but it's possible Goldrush was given a scoop of grain with a big clump of this stuff in the middle—a freak accident of a different sort. I wanted to make sure Emilio knew so he could take proper precautions."

Dowry calmed down. Now he became fidgety. "What about my pregnant mares? Nobody ever checked the feed in the broodmare barn. I have an entire stable in foal to Montpelier without any live foal guarantee."

It was Pascoe's turn to sputter. "Montpelier?"

Dowry puffed up. Obviously, the young vet was impressed.

"Magnificent isn't he? I don't mind telling you, it cost a pretty penny to breed that many mares, but I should make quite a profit selling at the yearling sales in Kentucky." Anxiety swept away arrogance. "This substance, the one that killed Goldrush, it can't cause abortion, can it?"

"We don't even know if they've been exposed. If you like, I'll tell Harkin you have some concerns and he can come out and draw some blood and collect some feed samples."

"Can't you do it now?"

"Well," Pascoe said, eyes sliding to Vaughn, "I know it's uncomfortable for you to have me on the farm."

"Nonsense." Dowry slapped his son on the back hard enough to make him wince. "We're all men here. Forgive and forget, right? Had a reputation for scrapping when I was your age myself, and I don't hold any grudges. Son?"

Vaughn's crescents deepened to purple. His face was becoming a mood ring. "Right."

"As long as it's okay with you guys," Pascoe said. "I'd hate for Vaughn and I to be at odds, like two guys who fight over the same bimbo. Feelings like that have a way of festering and every time you run into that person it's like picking at a scab." Pascoe offered his hand, and when Vaughn reluctantly shook it after getting a nod of encouragement from his father, Pascoe pressed the

Rohypnol tablet into his flesh and winked.

"That's more like it," Dowry said. "Um, any idea how much the testing is going to cost?"

Pascoe blinked. Dowry never expressed concern over the cost of anything. "For all the mares and the feed? Not more than a few hundred I imagine."

"Not that it matters," Dowry declared. "I was curious, is all. Grab your stuff Doc, my good man Emilio will hold the mares."

Dowry put a hand at the small of Pascoe's back and pushed him towards the broodmare barn, detailing the finer point's of his herd's lineage. Vaughn remained behind, standing dumbly in the aisle and staring into his palm.

CHAPTER FIFTEEN

That night, Pascoe slept a full but fitful twelve hours. A dream nipped at his heels, herding his mind in uncomfortable directions. In it, he frantically worked the *Form,* trying to make sense of a race called the Devon Dowry Stakes, handicapping a murder. It was a small field: David, Dearborne, Carlyle, Vaughn, Oliver, and Emilio were the only entries. The betting window would close in minutes. He scribbled notes and letter-grades next to each stat—motive rather than furlong splits, ties to Devon instead of bloodlines—scratching them out time and time again. With time running out, he ran to lay money down. He had graded on a curve, increasing Dearborne's money motive to an A and inflating the significance of Carlyle's relationship with Vaughn. He had thrown out the lowest score, hoping to improve both Emilio and Dowry's chances, but neither had made a difference. No matter how many times he ran the averages, David Stuart remained the favorite.

The bell sounded, the gate opened and Pascoe woke, flushed and nauseous as if he had truly been at the track. Needing both distraction and nutrition, he dug around in a cabinet and found an ancient box of pancake mix, weevil free, which, as far as he was concerned, made it suitable for consumption. The pancakes turned out poorly mixed and lumpy, and buckets of syrup succeeded in turning them as soft and swollen as wash-worn sponges. However, they settled his stomach and the rush of carbohydrates kicked him awake, as did the single cup of coffee he allowed himself. He was ready within the hour and loading Barclay into the truck when one of the dog's hind feet kicked Carlyle's cashbox off the front seat and onto the big toe of Pascoe's left foot.

Hopping on one foot and swearing loudly—to Barclay's amusement—he realized something had to be done about the drugs. He couldn't convince himself to get rid of them, but couldn't keep them in the truck either because Monroe was right: if he got stopped he would never be able to explain things away. The only good hidey-hole inside the cabin was the wood stove, and that was necessary for survival this time of year. He scouted the perimeter of the house, but every chink in the foundation, every hollow under a bush, shouted LOOK HERE!, so he continued to search.

The second time he passed the woodpile, a solution presented itself. The logs were stacked with smaller pieces on top and large, long burning rounds on the bottom. With a little rearranging, it was easy to form a pocket among the bigger pieces. He placed the cashbox in the hole. Using a hand saw, he cut slices from the ends of the logs he had removed and placed the slices across the opening, forming a false front. When he was finished and stepped away it was hard to tell the fakes from the rest. He turned around after taking a few more steps, removed the cash, and stuffed the wad into his pants pocket before replacing the box. For safekeeping, he told himself.

He drove for Hunter's farm in unseasonably warm weather. Frost melted and dripped from bare trees in an erratic pitter-pat against a leathery pack of leaves. The countryside smelled of loam and livestock and chimney smoke.

Timberbrook smelled of diesel. Bulldozers and backhoes roared and clanked over the grounds, spewing blue smoke as they churned the earth. The phalanx of press vehicles was absent, having either taken the weekend off or gone in pursuit of another story. Two Sheriff's Department cars parked facing the barn. Pascoe pulled his truck in beside them. He held Barclay by the collar as he looked for Hunter, sure the police would be unappreciative of the dog's help.

She was in the barn, grooming Banker. Another bay was cross-tied in the space next to the stallion, and a gray tied in the aisle. She smiled at the wriggling dog and said, "The others are locked in Banker's stall, throw Barclay in with them." Pascoe barely managed to do so without allowing the entire pack to squeeze past. "I was beginning to wonder if you were going to make it," she said.

"Took a while to get presentable."

Hunter made a show of examining Pascoe and sighed. "At least you tried." She gave him a familiar peck on the lips. "David's inside, finishing a sandwich. Still some tuna left, want some?"

"No thanks," Pascoe said, picking a curry comb out of a grooming box, "had a late breakfast. Who should I start with?"

"Marcus. The one next to Banker. He'll be your mount, so you might as well get to know each other."

The big bay leaned into the comb as hunks of dirt were knocked off his long winter coat. "I thought the police were finished."

"You and me both." Hunter scowled as she lifted a saddle onto Banker's back. "Newcomb thinks they're playing mind games, scare us into making a deal. If it continues, he's going to complain to the judge."

Pascoe finished currying and switched to a soft horsehair brush. "How is David taking it?"

"This?" Hunter yanked up on the girth. Banker grunted disapprovingly, turned his head, and would have nipped had the ties not prevented it. She stroked an apology against his neck and backed off two holes. "It's a great big show. We'll have to pry him away from the power equipment."

She wasn't kidding. It took a lot of cajoling to get David onto his mount, and more to keep his eyes on the path. He kept turning in the saddle to look at the rumbling orange machines tearing up the farm. It wasn't until they maneuvered onto a forest trail and lost sight of the destruction that David shifted focus.

Pascoe never had the opportunity to observe David in the saddle, and it was unnerving to see how little the accident had affected this aspect of his life. Reins held correctly. Position balanced and leg in steady contact with Cooper, his mount. Cooper responded immediately to subtle aids, weaving through a strand of sugar maples and shortening his frame to hop over a narrow ditch. Hunter nudged Banker closer to Marcus.

"Hard to believe it's the same person, isn't it?" she whispered, as if speaking aloud would break the spell. "It's like his muscles are hard wired. I'm not even sure he realizes what he's doing."

"How much can he do?"

"I don't know," she said. "I've let him trot, but am too scared to let him canter. You've heard of riding therapy?" Pascoe nodded, he did the vet work for Healing Horses, one of a half dozen therapeutic riding centers in the area, and had seen first hand the dramatic change in the lives of physically and mentally handicapped kids. "If things are still connected in his body, maybe riding can help improve some of the connections up here," she said, tapping her forehead.

They rode on, squelching leaves the only evidence of their presence. A confident buck with a wide, arching rack spent a moment surveying the party before springing away when a goldfinch landed nearby. Full-cheeked squirrels chattered disapproval at the trespass. Further into the ride, a fox darted across their path, full-bloomed winter coat shining like a new penny in the dappled sunlight.

Pascoe lost himself in Marcus's easy, rolling gait and had no idea how long they had been riding, but as they rounded a bend in the trail, the horse leaned into the bit. Banker and Preston also picked up the pace and had their ears forward, a sure sign they were close. Strangely, there was no sound of machinery.

The dozers and backhoes had indeed stopped, but there was still plenty of commotion. Hunter picked up a posting trot and pulled ahead. Pascoe and David followed. An additional squad car was pulled up next to the barn, blocking Pascoe's truck. Behind both vehicles sat a black van with the words CRIME SCENE stenciled on the side in white. The back doors were flung open and someone was arranging clear plastic bags on the floor while another held a clipboard. Yellow tape blocked off a small area adjacent to the manure pile. Steam carrying the scent of compost wafted into the air. Monroe Ridgeway's bulky form stood on the outside of the barrier.

"David," Hunter said, caution in her voice. "Take the horses to the barn. Untack them and throw on some coolers." David looked wistfully at the driverless bulldozer, but obeyed.

Hunter headed directly for Monroe, who was the only familiar face on the farm. "Hey," she said tapping the big detective on the shoulder, "what now? Don't have enough people destroying my farm? Now you block my driveway and spread shit all over the place? You assholes are definitely going to hear from my lawyer."

Monroe turned. "I'll look forward to hearing from Mr. Newcomb then." All of the patience shown the night of David's arrest had disappeared. "As for the vehicles, they'll be gone as soon as the evidence is collected and documented."

"What evidence?"

Monroe cleared his throat. "We uncovered some articles of clothing."

"What, the phone wasn't enough so you had to come back and plant Devon's clothes here as well? You guys need to get it through your head, my brother did not kill Devon Dowry."

"This particular clothing pertains to a different investigation."

"What are you talking about?"

"A runaway. A girl named Samantha Rasmussen went missing about a week ago. Her mother gave a description of what she was wearing the night she disappeared and the clothing we found here matches that description."

Hunter glanced worriedly at the manure pile. "Sam?" she asked with a tremor in her voice. "You didn't find, I mean, there's no way…"

"We didn't find a body if that's what you're asking," Monroe said. "But that's a big pile, and it's going to take a while to sift through it."

David sauntered out of the barn and came over to join his sister. He peered over the tape and said, "You made a mess of my pile."

"You're pile, David?" Monroe asked.

David bobbed his head. "Yup, that's my job. Nobody touches my pile."

"David, that's enough." Hunter said.

"Let me ask you something," Monroe said. The detective walked to the van and removed one of the plastic bags from the back. It held a gray sweatshirt with he word 'Foxfield' applied across the front in Old English lettering. He held it in front of David. "Recognize this?"

"Don't answer him, honey," Hunter said.

David scrunched up his face and his upper body bounced back and forth as he stared at the bag. Suddenly he stopped, and grinned widely. "It's Sammy's," he said. "From her school." He seemed especially pleased to have remembered that tidbit.

"When was the last time you saw Sammy?" Monroe asked gently.

"We're done detective." Hunter grabbed her brother forcefully by the elbow and spun him away. "I'm calling Newcomb. If you have questions, you can do it with his lawyer present." She marched David back to the barn.

"This is nuts Monroe," Pascoe said after the two were gone. "A couple of days ago, you guys were done with Timberbrook. Suddenly you start digging again?"

"All I know is the sheriff wanted us to expand the radius of the search. That expansion included the manure pile."

"How sure are you about the clothing?"

"Being the girl's? Pretty sure. We'll get the mother in for an ID, and forensics will check for hair and blood to match samples from her home, but my instincts tell me they are hers."

"What do your instincts tell you about how they got here?" Pascoe asked.

Monroe pursed his lips. "Don't like it. Seems too obvious, but we're not talking about a guy playing with a full deck, are we? Maybe it didn't occur to him to get rid of Dowry's cell phone, and maybe stuffing some clothes under a foot of shavings and shit seemed like a great hiding spot."

"You sound like the sheriff."

"The sheriff was a good cop back in the day. He taught me to listen to your gut, but if the evidence is talks louder, you gotta listen to it first. There's a lot of evidence piling up."

"Planted evidence."

"Could be. What we need is to do is find Sam Rasmussen, but God help David Stuart if she's in this pile."

Hunter and David emerged from the barn, Hunter bringing her brother to heel with the grip she had on his elbow. She ignored Monroe and came straight to Pascoe.

"Newcomb is meeting us at the station to straighten this out. Could you take care of the horses? Banker, Marcus, and Cooper are dry and need to have their winter blankets put on. The whole barn needs dinner in about an hour. Stall cards will tell you what each gets, and everything in the feed room is labelled."

"Take care of David," Pascoe said. Hunter kissed him on the cheek and turned to Monroe, extending her arms and presenting her wrists to the detective.

"Are you going to cuff me as well, or do you reserve such special treatment for the feeble?"

Monroe bit his tongue. "Neither of you is under arrest Miss Stuart. If you want to come to the station so I can ask David some questions, you're welcome to take your own car."

David had his mouth closed so tightly his lips were white and his brow was furrowed the same way it had when he was shown the sweatshirt. There was no way he was going to say a word without Hunter's permission. When they left, he didn't return Pascoe's wave.

Horses blanketed and returned to their respective stalls, Pascoe let himself into Hunter's apartment, ignoring the complaints of the dogs, who were restless in their stall. A brief exploration of the refrigerator led to the discovery of the leftover tuna, which was enough for the makings of a decent meal.

As he ate, Pascoe was drawn again to Hunter's collection of photographs. He walked slowly through the gallery, scooping tuna into his mouth with a spoon. As he rounded a corner, his thigh bumped roughly into the end of a sideboard, jostling the assorted silver plates and glass trophies displayed upon it. As Pascoe steadied a tall crystal vase with his spoon-hand, he noticed the bent ends of more photographs spilling over the edge of the drawer that ran the length of the sideboard.

He pulled it open, and found more snapshots of David. Pascoe realized all of the hanging pictures were of pre-accident David, while the drawer contained nothing but snapshots taken since he had been hurt. They showed David thin, almost skeletal, his scar raw against a head half-shaved from surgery. Gail was in many, her arm draped protectively around David. Pascoe jumped when he came across a photo of Sam, initially mistaking her for Devon and worrying how the police would interpret it. After today, finding Sam in a picture would be just as bad. As David's hair grew and the scar faded, Gail and Sam faded as well, and the remaining pictures featured only David and his simple, toothy grin.

A loud bang came from the barn. One of the horses was knocking a hoof against a stall door, a not-so-subtle reminder that dinner was late in coming. It only took moments to replace the photos, but by the time he stepped into the barn, every horse had joined in the prompting. Two people could not have held a conversation without yelling.

Pascoe scurried up the ladder to the loft and dropped hay into the stalls. That, at least, had them too busy to make much of a racket, though Banker gave the wall an occasional kick to make sure Pascoe knew his job was not finished.

Most of the horses were in similar enough work that their diets varied only in the amount of grain they were fed. These amounts were listed on the stall cards in whole or fractions of scoops and each feed was placed in individual metal trashcans. The contents of each can were identified in red permanent marker on their sides: oats, bran, and senior feed. The senior diet looked more like dog kibble than grain and was fed to a couple of old timers, horses over twenty whose teeth had worn and had difficulty grinding hard kernels.

Only a small handful of pellets remained in the bag. Pascoe yanked it out and found a fresh fifty-pound sack to take its place. He was about to drop it into the trashcan when he realized there was still something in the bottom. It was difficult to identify in the poor light of the feed room; Pascoe upended the can for a better look.

Another bag of feed, about a third full, top rolled tight like a near-empty tube of toothpaste, plopped to the ground. Pascoe opened the bag and reached in; the contents were much finer than the pellets of the senior diet and sifted through his fingers like sand. Pascoe sniffed and his mind filled with images of feathers and nesting boxes. He brought the bag directly under the light. Written against the plain brown sack were faded red block letters that said, simply, POULTRY FEED; under the generic headline was a line-drawing of an equally generic chicken. The bag had no tag, but it was unnecessary: ingredients were listed in small type under the drawing of the chicken. Near the end, immediately following B vitamins, was Monensin.

CHAPTER SIXTEEN

Pascoe had a problem with faith. He learned about faith from his mother, who dragged him to church because his father prepared to race on Sundays. The church preached to have faith in an invisible God, a God who never responded in person. Still, he believed his mother implicitly, as children do, was respectful in church, and prayed anyway. When his mother left he felt like a sucker, and faith in God evaporated along with faith in Vivian Pascoe. Over the years, this cynicism transformed into a catechism founded on belief in data that can be defined, measured, or categorized.

He sat heavily on the lid of the trashcan marked 'oats' and wondered how to have faith in David's innocence. The appearance of the clothing and feed made him the heavy odds-on favorite in last night's nightmare stakes. He sat until the old timers started kicking the walls.

Hunter slid open the barn door as the last horse was being fed. David had been allowed to come home.

"Didn't expect to see you," Hunter said, hugging Pascoe. "David honey, you must be tired. Why don't you go in and watch television and I'll muck the stalls."

"Is Jordan staying for dinner?" David asked.

"If he wants to." Hunter let the dogs out of confinement and was immediately surrounded in a flurry of wagging tails and snorting noses. After a rambunctious show of gratitude, the entire pack sped to investigate the changes made during their absence.

"I helped myself to the tuna," Pascoe said, "I'm not really hungry."

Hunter stopped brushing large clumps of hair from her pants. "You can stay for the company."

"Can we get pizza?" David asked.

"I really should get home," Pascoe said.

David pouted. "Can we still get pizza?"

"Yes honey, now go inside." David's hips swiveled in a pizza victory dance as he made his way into the apartment. Pascoe could hear him chanting, "pee-za, pee-za" under his breath.

"What's going on?" she asked when David had shut the door.

"Nothing," Pascoe said. "I'm not hungry and have paperwork at the office."

"You're good at a lot of things Jordan, but lying to me is not one of them. Something's changed."

Pascoe pretended to stamp his feet against the cold. Hunter was not going to let it slide. "Are the cops still here?" he asked, buying a moment.

"Passed them on their way out. What's going on?"

"First of all, I'm not taking sides. I found something. Something the police could use in their case against David."

"What could be worse than what they've already found?"

"Remember the cases Wallace and I were working?" Hunter nodded. "And how I felt there might be a connection between the horses and Devon?"

Hunter eyed Pascoe warily. "Sure."

"Goldrush was poisoned by an overdose of an anti-parasitic."

"So?"

Pascoe led her into the feed room and pointed to the bag of feed lying in the middle of the floor. "It's added to some kinds of feed. It's in that bag."

She knelt down and examined the bag, tracing a finger along the drawing of the chicken. "The cops don't know about the horses. Wallace wouldn't let you tell."

"I told Monroe Ridgeway. I thought he might help."

Hunter continued tracing. "You just found this."

"Well sure, he doesn't know about that, but—"

"Then it's not a problem. Take this and dump it somewhere."

"I don't know if that's such a good idea. I mean, at some point you have to face facts."

The tracing stopped. "Face facts?" she shouted. "I'll give you a couple of facts. It's a fact that David cries if I smack a horse with a crop for misbehaving. It's a fact that he thinks the top of the refrigerator is a good place to hide Christmas presents. If you don't believe me, go ahead and look, there's a jar of bath beads there right now, you can tell because there's a gap in the wrapping paper where he forgot tape. Does that tell you what kind of man David is? It tells me the man on the other side of that door, whose biggest thrill of the day is ordering out for pizza for God's sake, is as capable of violence and deception as a child.

"How's this fact? The police tore this place apart. They dumped the contents of every one of those cans onto the floor. There was no mother fucking bag of chicken feed here two days ago just like there was no mother fucking sweatshirt in the manure pile until somebody planted it there. Not taking sides? Right. You're doing something worse: you chose a side and are afraid you've chosen the wrong one. Well, you sure as hell didn't care about objectivity when you wanted to get in my pants."

"That's not fair," Pascoe said. "I'm not abandoning David. Or you."
"Then take the bag."
Hunter's piebald stare demanded a decision.
"I'll take the bag," Pascoe said.

He drove home with the chicken feed on the passenger seat, wondering if he had made a mistake. Hunter rushed him off the farm once he had agreed to take the bag; angry his support of David had wavered.

A sense of déjà vu swept over Pascoe as he turned into his driveway. Three Sheriff's Department vehicles parked facing his front door, lights pulsing blue and red. Spotlights followed the truck until it stopped, then focused on the cab, blinding him. Barclay, unwilling to be locked away again, wriggled out of his grip and escaped. He sprinted to the front door and guarded the entrance, hackles raised, barking furiously at the men in uniform.

"Glad you arrived Pascoe. Save us the trouble of busting in the door."

Pascoe shaded his eyes. Sheriff Ridgeway, wrapped in a wool overcoat, walked over.

"Excuse me Sheriff," Pascoe said, "if you could explain what this—"

"Detective!" Ridgeway bellowed.

Monroe came forward, big frame blocking the spotlight. He handed over a piece of paper embossed with the seal of the Commonwealth of Virginia.

"It's a warrant to search your residence for illicit drugs," Monroe said. "You have to let us in." The detective scratched his chin and surreptitiously tapped a forefinger against his lips. *Don't say anything.*

Pascoe unlocked the front door. Barclay took up a position inside and continued to bark. Two officers, barely out of high school and sporting wispy mustaches, barreled into the house and immediately emptied cabinets and dumped drawers. Barclay scolded them mercilessly.

"No need to trash the place boys," Monroe rumbled. The officers glanced past Monroe to the sheriff, who strolled in behind the detective. A plain-clothed man with him stared nervously at Barclay.

"Just do your job," Ridgeway said, glaring at his son. "Could somebody take care of this goddamn dog?"

"Barclay. Quiet." Pascoe said in an even voice. The dog obeyed, but shot him a withering look, annoyed at being told how to do his job. The civilian jotted notes on a pad. "Campaign manager?" Pascoe asked.

"Press. Fortunate enough to be at hand when we received our tip," Ridgeway said. "You're supplementing your income selling drugs to the citizens of this county, and it is my duty to protect those citizens." Ridgeway nodded to the reporter, who meticulously captured every word. "Stressful duty certainly, but fulfilling, especially when we win a battle in the War On Drugs."

"Tip? Don't suppose you're going to tell me who it came from?"

"Anonymous. I imagine the person was afraid of retaliation."

"Of course," Pascoe said. "I have a DEA license which allows me to have

Barn Politics

controlled drugs in my possession."

"Oh, we're well aware of that, Doctor Pascoe," Ridgeway said, smirking.

The Sheriff's mood darkened as his deputies failed to turn up evidence. The wood stove was searched twice, but Ridgeway ordered it done again and got soot on his coat when he pushed one of the officers out of the way to check it himself. Pascoe offered to start a fire and warm the place up. At one point, Ridgeway methodically circled the room, slamming his heel against the floor, checking for a loose board. Monroe stood expressionless.

Ridgeway ordered the search outside, causing a momentary scare when flashlights bobbed around the woodpile. Pascoe nervously fingered the roll of cash in his pocket. They started on his truck.

"Coffee?" Pascoe asked the room.

The reporter raised his head hopefully. He wore a thin nylon jacket and stood with hands buried in his armpits. The sheriff growled and he went back to studying the floor. It was another twenty minutes before the uniformed teenagers returned.

"Well?" Ridgeway asked.

"Everything in the truck was on the list," said one of the men. "Nothing he's not legally allowed to have."

"We did find this," said the other cop, holding up the chicken feed.

Monroe raised an eyebrow.

"Congratulations, you've uncovered the makings of an underground poultry farm," Ridgeway said.

"It seemed out of place," said the cop.

"You're out of place, you goddamn cracker," Ridgeway said. "Probably needed help finding your momma's tit. I'll talk to you both outside." The sheriff wiped a well-manicured hand across his face and recomposed himself, smiling like Pascoe was his biggest campaign donor. "Sorry we bothered you Doctor Pascoe, I guess my informant was, well, misinformed."

The sheriff tossed his car keys to the reporter, who scurried to one of the patrol cars, started it up and began rubbing his hands in front of the heater vent.

Hope you lose a finger to frostbite, asshole.

The sheriff wore a thoughtful expression as he left. Monroe followed closely and almost tripped over his father when the elder Ridgeway spun around and struck a pose against the woodpile. "One more thing, Doctor Pascoe."

Pascoe would have laughed if the movement hadn't jarred the woodpile and caused one of the false rounds to fall flat on the frozen ground with a click. An exposed corner of the cashbox glinted in the porch light. The sheriff, too preoccupied with his performance, was, for the moment, ignorant of the discovery.

"One more thing?" Pascoe asked. "Been watching too many 'Columbo' episodes? What is it you want to tell me? Don't leave town?"

Ridgeway fumed. "Come on Detective," he said, "we're done for tonight."

"Drive safe," Pascoe said, waving at their backs.

After Monroe's admonishment, the deputies stopped pouring things directly onto the floor and stacked the contents of drawers and cupboards on the countertop and the kitchen table. Clothes were piled neatly next to the drawer they had been taken from. Even so, cleanup would last late into the evening. A phone call interrupted a victorious discovery, a misplaced ravioli can that widened his menu options to three, after tomato soup and fish sticks.

"Hey, Doc."

"Takes a lot of nerve to call after throwing me under the bus," Pascoe said.

"Wasn't me," Monroe said. "If I wanted to throw you under the bus, I could have told the sheriff to take a peek at his shoes. When I learned we were serving a warrant at your place, I was sure they would find nothing. I told you to throw the box in the river."

"How did he know to come looking?"

"My guess is he was tipped off by the lab after the results on the powder came in. You're pissing off a lot of folks Pascoe, there's nothing more the sheriff would like than to throw you in irons."

"But why me? Couldn't you send him after Carlyle or Dowry?"

"I've turned over every rock I can think of, no Carlyle. I could catch Dowry dealing to second graders at Middleburg Christian, it wouldn't matter. The sheriff wants to bust the source."

"Suddenly I control the county coke pipeline?"

"Not coke, Pascoe, ketamine."

"Holy shit."

Pascoe heard the stories, got the DEA advisories. Junkies breaking into vet clinics all over the country to steal ketamine. A few vets had been convicted of selling the stuff. Ketamine is a powerful disassociative. At high doses it knocks a patient unconscious and blocks—disassociates—pain signals from the body to the brain, making it the perfect drug for short surgeries in a pasture.

At smaller doses it's a powerful hallucinogen, similar to PCP, putting it in high demand with the rave crowd, along with Ecstasy. Initially available only as a liquid, it had been unpopular, as most casual users were needle averse. Then some genius discovered that liquid ketamine crystallized it into a user-friendly, snortable powder when baked. Vets had been under siege ever since.

"Do not go outside," Monroe said.

"Huh?" Pascoe said. "Sorry, I was thinking about the quickest way to the river."

"Those two numbnuts the sheriff brought are paying for coming away empty handed. They're by the road, freezing their butts off with a spotting scope and a radio. Grab that box and they'll be dragging you off to County before you get down the driveway."

"Jesus. What do I do?"

"My advice: get some wood and start a fire, it would seem too odd on a night like this not to. The sheriff won't keep them there forever. I'll let you know when they take off."

"Thanks Monroe, I owe you one."

"Damn straight. Why don't you tell me where you got that feed? It was the Stuart's place, wasn't it?"

"Monroe...."

"Listen up Doc. Gail Rasmussen positively identified the clothes. The only reason David Stuart is walking around right now is nobody knows where Sam Rasmussen is or whether she's alive or not, but even so, Turner is going to try to get Stuart locked up before trial.

"My job is to find out who killed Devon Dowry. I think that's what you want too. I'm not sold on Stuart, but that doesn't mean he gets a pass. Interfere again and I won't hesitate to bring you up on charges of obstruction."

A dial tone told Pascoe there was to be no discussion. He returned the phone to its charger and went back to repairing the mess the police had made of the kitchen. Monroe was right: all the evidence pointed to David Stuart and everybody who might know differently had gone to ground— Carlyle disappeared, Dowry hid behind a wall of lawyers, and Dearborne was protected by his position in the community.

Pascoe learned a great deal watching Jack Russell Terriers hunt rats. More often than not, the quarry made it's way to the safety of a burrow. However, this didn't stop the tenacious dogs. They could smell and hear the presence of the enemy, even if they couldn't see it, and found a way to solve the problem. It wasn't pretty, and wasn't subtle, in keeping with their nature. They ripped and tore at the earth until they could squirm in, grab hold, and pull their prey, kicking and screaming, into the light. Pascoe needed a similar solution.

CHAPTER SEVENTEEN

He came upon one by accident. Cleaning forced him to admit how meager his supplies had become. In the local supermarket, a few remaining issues of *The Freedom Monitor* occupied the middle shelf of a modular unit, surrounded by stacks of real estate and used car publications.

This last issue had been hard on the police and uncharacteristically soft on David Stuart—apparently Kutulas was wary of coming down too hard on a sympathetic local legend. Once information about Sam Rasmussen's clothing was released, it was unlikely such restraint would continue.

The paper was an irritant; no doubt the reporter with Ridgeway was in Kutulas' employ and would redirect the paper's venom Pascoe's way. But, while the *Monitor* was ridiculed as a rag, it made it into everyone's hands. If Kutulas was handed an exclusive story, it might heat things up enough to force Carlyle out of hiding. Too much heat, and the whole thing would boil over. Pascoe reached for his cell phone.

"You want to meet with who?"

"You were chatting up Kutulas at the funeral, Ruth," Pascoe said. "I've tried and gotten nowhere, I could probably get an audience with the pope sooner."

"Why?" Wallace asked warily.

"Nothing to do with Virginia Bloodstock," Pascoe promised. He told her about the sheriff's visit. "Somebody wants me out of the way. I need to set the record straight."

"You must to be the only person on Stuart's side."

"Let's just say it's a leap of faith."

Wallace grunted. "Well, my faith in you has paid off. Give me time to flatter him into a favor. But be careful, Kutulas can't be trusted. He seems eccentric, but has more money now than when his father died, and you don't get rich being stupid. Give him the opportunity to screw you over and he will."

"I'm a big boy Ruth."

"So you say, but never give me the chance to find out. Stay close to the phone, I'll call when I have something."

His phone rang fifteen minutes later. Kutulas was not only willing, but eager to meet. Wallace sounded jealous as she rattled off directions to the publisher's home. She had cultivated a relationship with Kutulas, of a sort she was unwilling to discuss, but one thing was clear: Pascoe was being granted access to a place she had never been invited.

Kutulas used his seemingly endless funds to carve a compound from the rocky soil near Waterford, close to the Maryland border. Waterford was a patchwork of dainty and finely made homes. History trumped square footage and residents adhered to strict building covenants that permitted only period paint shades and restricted the height and style of mailboxes. Building an addition onto a cramped cottage was as unthinkable as submitting plans with a stucco exterior. Kutulas paid as much in payoffs as construction costs.

A decidedly non-period brick wall, higher than the truck's cab, encircled the property like the ramparts of a colonial castle. The gate opened automatically and Pascoe continued along a serpentine driveway that wove around nonexistent obstacles, as if a predetermined length had been forced to squeeze into the available space. An uninterrupted sea of tightly cropped grass spanned from wall to house; not one tree, bush, or artistically placed rock marring its surface.

The house continued the brick motif; someone had a Big Bad Wolf complex. Devoid of aesthetic value, the house was a simple, two-tier rectangle with four-over-four windows placed in the second story. The only opening in the first floor was the entrance, which was protected with an outer door of iron bars.

"Doctor Pascoe, come in, come in." Kutulas rifled through a key ring at his belt and unlocked the door. Once his guest was in, Kutulas locked it behind him.

He wore a violet satin sweat suit, the jacket of which was open to the sternum. Whether necessitated by an amazing volume of coarse, black hair or simply questionable fashion sense was unclear. Bare feet displayed long, yellow nails. Head hair, coarse and black like that of his chest, receded severely and made the top of his skull look as if it had been shaved with a letter 'M' stencil. He gestured and Pascoe followed behind slapping feet and *whiz!* of satin clad thighs.

The interior was as ornate as the exterior was Spartan. A hallway was hung with oils and watercolors, an original Wyeth among them, and lined with tables heavy with Chinese porcelain. Rooms contained detailed woodwork and collections of darkly stained, delicate baroque furniture. No cushions were out of place, and no empty glasses or open books cluttered the tables. Nothing more than life-sized dioramas staged to impress.

They made their way to the back right corner of the building and an electronic keypad. Conspicuously obscuring Pascoe's view, Kutulas tapped in a short sequence. There was a deep clang and shudder in the doorframe. Kutulas had Pascoe enter first.

Once in, the door shut and clanged again like a cellblock in lockdown. None of the museum-feel of the rest of the house in here. A blonde-stained, mission style desk with a computer occupied one wall. The others were lined with bookcases supporting black boxes of unidentifiable electronic equipment. Close to the desk, four small television sets switched between scenes of both the exterior and interior of the house, some of which they had traveled through, though Pascoe hadn't noticed any cameras. Kutulas sat in a chair with a built-in massage feature, offering Pascoe a more utilitarian seat. The publisher hovered a few inches above him, and Pascoe was tempted to peek under the desk and see just how far his host's feet dangled above the floor.

"You have some information for me." Kutulas said, rubbing his hands together. "Pray tell."

"No one can know this came from me," Pascoe said. Kutulas motioned for him to get on with it. "David Stuart is being framed for the murder of Devon Dowry."

Kutulas sat stone-faced. His lower lip developed a twitch. Before long he was doubled over with laughter, tears running down flushed cheeks. Pascoe stared, unsure whether or not he was witnessing a nervous breakdown and doubtful he could find a way out of the office.

"Of...course...set...up," Kutulas managed between fits. Blinking the last tears from his eyes, he put his hands flat on the desk and inhaled deeply through his nose, which controlled the laughter, but did nothing for his tomato-red complexion. "Is this your big revelation? Poor David Stuart is being set up by the cops," he mocked. "Tell me something new kid, or get out."

"If you know, why are you in bed with them?"

"Am I?" Kutulas asked. "Put my coverage side-by-side with the other papers and see whose giving Stuart a fairer shake. Tell me, what do you think of my little paper?" Pascoe didn't answer. "No, really, I mean it. What is your opinion of the *Monitor*?"

"I think it's a rag," Pascoe said.

"Then why come to me? Why not run to the *Times-Mirror*?"

"Your standards are lower, but people pick up your paper and read every word. They should know there are others who might have wanted Devon dead, maybe that will give David a chance with a jury."

Kutulas chuckled. "My standards are low. All I do is create a forum for the truth. Newspapers and journalists at the major papers have become slaves to political correctness and business; human-interest stories shoved in where they haven't been able to sell advertisements. Hell, the LA Times keeps quotas on leads that feature minorities, and the DC papers are no better. This area is so white, editors feel a blow has been struck for social justice when a non-Anglo surname appears more than once in a story. Like their metropolitan cousins, what they really care about is not stepping on the sensitive toes of advertisers. How is truth going to get through that bullshit?"

Kutulas ticked off examples on his fingers. "Your buddy Dowry buys two full pages in the *Times-Mirror* on weekdays and an insert on the weekend. Three of the largest car dealers in the metro area have homes in Middleburg and have an entire section in the Sunday edition. You know that store, Deana's? There's one in every mall, right across from the Macy's. The founder named the store after his daughter, who trains dressage horses at a barn paid for by Daddy. Ben Anderson developed Tyson's Corner for God's sake; think he'd put up with an article that might embarrass a leaseholder?"

Kutulas ran out of fingers. He shook it to erase the tally. "I'm not counting small businessmen who rely on the locals. As individuals, they might not have the power of someone like Anderson, but see how fast they leave if a paper habitually prints unflattering stories about their best clients.

"Here's the situation we're stuck in without me: a community with no checks on their behavior."

"So the *Monitor* performs a service."

Kutulas, ignorant of the sarcasm, bobbed his head. "We ask the questions others are afraid to."

"How noble," Pascoe said. "Makes a good slogan. I suppose insinuating I had something to do with Devon's murder was responsible journalism."

"It was. You were close to that kid. Some speculated you were too close."

Some. Pascoe still had a bruise made by a tooth on the knuckle of his index finger to remind him where the speculation came from.

"Nobody else was going to say it," Kutulas continued. "Harkin is too cagey and has too many friends to let a story like that see the light of day. But I don't care. People aren't going to stop coming to me for charitable contributions because I tarnish the halo of Saint Harkin. I put the theory out there, let the people mull it over and come to their own conclusion. Democracy in its purest form."

Pascoe ran fingers through his hair. He wasn't about to argue ethics. "I would guess then," he said, "you're willing to listen to other theories?"

"Ah, the reason for your visit. Something to do with the drugs Sheriff Ridgeway was unable to find?"

"That *was* your reporter."

"The sheriff wanted someone to witness his great blow against society's underbelly. Good press always kicks those campaign donations up a notch. When it didn't quite work out he tried to confiscate my reporter's notebook."

"Did he?"

"For a short time. I reminded the sheriff that my lawyers could run through his entire fiscal budget over the issue of a free press, and it was promptly returned." Kutulas leaned back and laced his fingers behind his head. "Not that there was anything juicy in the story anyway. Cops show up on a tip, find nothing. Wow. I couldn't fill two inches next to the horoscope with that one. But Ridgeway wouldn't have taken the trouble to get a warrant, and he sure as hell wouldn't have dragged my guy along, if he wasn't cock-sure something was there. Tell me about the drugs."

"Do you know who Ridgeway's informant is?"

"Haven't a clue."

"If I tell you what I know, how do I know you won't burn me?"

"You have my word. You'll be 'a source close to the investigation', which, when you think about it, is true."

Pascoe had always been a risk-taker. Risk was what made sliding cash across a betting window or handing it to Carlyle infinitely more exciting than writing bets down in his imaginary book. The case against David was strong, while his own investigation had stalled. If a lightning strike was the only option for a jump, well, so be it.

"You might want to take notes," he said.

Two days later, Pascoe woke to find the most recent edition of *The Freedom Monitor* on his doorstep. He frowned at Barclay, who sniffed the paper as if he had no idea how someone could have possibly approached during the night without his knowledge. The article was printed large type and left no room for anything else on the front page.

VICTIM OF CONSPIRACY
An Editorial by Martin Kutulas, Publisher

Miss Devon Dowry has been victimized once again: this time by a police department ignoring evidence that suggests she was murdered to prevent exposure of county-wide drug dealing and fraud. It's no secret Sheriff Ridgeway has myopically pursued David Stuart for the murder, though common sense argues this individual, this fallen angel of local equestrians, does not possess the acumen to design, carry out, or conceal such viciousness. The sheriff, facts be damned, discards reason for expediency. Fortunately, a concerned citizen has brought forward information lightly discarded by the police.

Shortly before her own death, one of Miss Dowry's beloved mounts perished under circumstances both gruesome and suspicious. This horse was intentionally poisoned. Furthermore, an entire string of horses may have likewise been killed. Why? To this reporter and local insurance companies the answer is obvious: money.

Some readers will scoff at this theory, protesting that Oliver Dowry has no need of money—after all, his Marketplace monarchy provides a kingly income. Or does it? No less a publication than The Wall Street

Journal is ripe with stories of Marketplace closures—apparently an expansion into the hinterlands has been too quick, and overpaying for designer foodstuffs doesn't play in Peoria. In addition, Dowry's path to success is littered with women who command a monthly tithe and are unsympathetic to the vagaries of the business cycle.

With less coming in and obligations unchanged, how does a modern millionaire make ends meet? Difficult as it is, I'll try to imagine myself in such a situation. Maybe I'd fill the bellies of my mares with the spawn of a Trojan Horse and go to bed with delusions of million dollar foals cavorting in pastures the color of money. An influx of cash would stem the tide of creditors, and how hard could it be to liquidate an asset and return more than this poor-performing stock would garner on the open market? How close could a little girl get to a horse anyway? And if she discovered my deed, surely a daughter's loyalty would buy her forgiveness, and her silence?

Of course, I'm a cynical man; there could be another explanation. A child of mine, inheritance shrinking, might, through no fault of his own, become a pawn of the local drug industry. In a county with an uninspired police force such a trade could reap high profit with little risk. If discovered, my lower-class compatriots (for surely no one of breeding could commit such an act) might feel compelled to eliminate any threat of exposure. What's a good father to do, faced with the loss of one child, a second at risk, and a future in flux? Find a patsy and continue on, business as usual, is what I'd do.

But that's me, and as I said, I'm a cynical man. I'm sure there is a reasonable explanation, aside from fraud and obstruction, which simplifies everything. And if another concerned citizen comes forth, I will, as always, bring such information to light.

The Sheriff will say I'm a crackpot; the police have their man and they have evidence proving beyond a reasonable doubt that they do. He will say the department is doing everything they can to stop the influx of drugs into the county. He will say insurance fraud and Ponzi schemes are the dominion of civil courts. Perhaps he's right. Or perhaps there is unwillingness on his part to turn over rocks in his Secret Garden and unearth the slippery creatures living there.

Pascoe reread the article three times. He didn't know much about libel law, but it seemed there was a fine line being walked. Maybe printing the article as an editorial absolved him of any responsibility. One thing was certain: Dowry would be making a lot of noise. Wallace's fears about the meeting proved to be unfounded; there was nothing in the piece to mark him as the source.

At least that was how he felt walking into the office, so he was surprised to find Harkin pacing the room with a rolled up copy of the *Monitor* clenched tightly in one fist. Maggie cowered behind her desk, stray wisps of hair escaped from the strict confines of her coiffure. It made him wonder if Harkin had been doing more than pace.

"Haven't I warned you about sticking your nose in where it doesn't belong?" Harkin said, wheeling toward Pascoe. When he was close enough, he whacked Pascoe on the head with the paper like a puppy who had just messed on the floor.

"Easy," Pascoe said. Maggie gave him a warning look from her sanctuary. "Kutulas is the one digging into everyone's affairs."

The newspaper rapped against his head again. "I don't give a shit about that." Harkin unrolled the newspaper. It was turned to page two, where a headline read: "Local Vet Investigated In Drug Ring".

Motherfucker. The story detailed the events of the other night, identifying Pascoe as a veterinarian who was initially interviewed by the police about his close ties to Devon Dowry. The reporter made it clear, several times, that the inability of the police to find drugs on the premises did not mean Pascoe was in the clear. Apparently, Ridgeway's informant had given detailed descriptions of what to find, and they had reason to suspect Pascoe of being involved because the police had been told to to search specifically for the powdered form of a veterinary drug called ketamine, known on the street as 'cat'.

"Do you know what this means?" Harkin sank into his chair, one hand bridging his temples. "Anybody who's had a horse laid down knows about ketamine; they know we have it, they've seen their horses stoned and stiff-legged, and now there's a story saying you're pushing the same stuff on their kids. They'll put this story together with the one on the front page and you'll become the 'lower-class compatriot' in their minds. Hell, even if they don't believe you're dealing, people are going to suspect you have something to do with the story. And then there's the Feds. They catch wind of this and they'll be making our lives miserable. We'll be expected to account for every tenth of a cc we've used in the past four years, and God knows, the way my eyes are, I've misread a syringe or two."

Pascoe cringed. His record keeping was less than stellar; his inventory was probably off more than Harkin's. The old man had sparked something though.

"What was it you said?" Pascoe asked. "About the horses."

Harkin sputtered, his rant derailed. "What I meant was, people are going to think of their horses, all splayed out and helpless, not blinking, eyes moving around like crazy, and their going to picture their kids like that, and they are going to be mad as hell at whoever they think is supplying them."

Splayed out and helpless. Damn it, why didn't I make the connection before? Black plastic in the stomach. Deadbolt ate Sam's stash.

"The point is," Harkin continued, "people are going to avoid you like the plague. I know you're no drug dealer, but someone's sure as hell trying to make it look that way, and I'll bet it's because of all the snooping.

"For the last time, back off and let the police do their job. If someone wants to frame David, it's going to happen. A shame, but honestly, I doubt he'll even be aware of what happened. Keep messing around and you'll go down too, and stew in a cell for twenty years, knowing you could be breathing fresh air if you had just minded your own business."

Pascoe looked at the little man with the crooked frame and set chin who had practically adopted him more than a decade ago and wondered if he knew him at all.

The Kutulas Effect could be measured by the activity of his cell phone. Voice mail took every call; if something urgent came up, Maggie could page him. At the end of the day, afraid of returning home to find a contingent of reporters camped on his doorstep, he retreated to the lot of a little used community park that afforded two things he needed most: privacy and strong cellular reception. Only then did he retrieve messages.

The first was from Wallace: "What were you thinking? Poisoning, fraud, and local insurance companies in the same story, practically in the same sentence. Phones are ringing off the hook. Clients fishing for a bit of gossip. Clients accusing us of accusing them, even though the story had nothing to do with them. Screaming about breaches of privacy, asking if this is the way we do business, selling customers to the press. The managers are hunting for someone to throw to the dogs, and if any of these idiots can put two and two together, then darlin', this girl ain't going down alone. Call me."

The next message came up automatically. It was Monroe, laughing. "I didn't think I'd ever see the Sheriff madder than when he left your place, but you topped yourself Pascoe. Believe it or not, Mr. GQ missed a spot shaving this morning, and when someone pointed it out, he used a dry razor to touch it up. He's walking around with a wad of tissue the size of a gumball shoved into that pretty cleft chin of his." It sounded like Monroe, in a fit, was pounding on his desk. "He's too busy putting out fires to be concerned with you. Your shadows have been recalled, so it's safe to make that trip to the river. But you still better watch your back."

Monroe was followed by a string of invective laden messages. Obviously, more than a few people were convinced of his involvement in the drug trade. He had no idea how these people got his number, he only gave it to select clients. On the other hand, some of the voices did sound familiar.

Pascoe was rapidly erasing meassages when an unmistakable voice popped up: Dearborne, teeth grinding. "Stupid bastard. You don't realize what you've done. Maybe I made a mistake. I pushed a little too hard; you pushed back. Fine, I respect that. But your little stunt might cost me more than half of Montpelier's book this coming season. Get your ass over here as soon as you get this message and we can discuss how much it will cost to get Kutulas to clear up this Trojan Horse innuendo."

Hunter, who sounded vibrant, followed Dearborne. "Newcomb wants to kiss you, but I've got dibs. He's been riding the cops all day, asking for evidence—"

The phone rang over the remainder of Hunter's message. Pascoe ended the message and connected to the incoming call.

"Pass-cow." The insult came out 'path-cowl', significantly lessening the effect of the taunt. Pascoe could practically smell the alcohol through the connection.

"I'm broke and on the streets, and Carlyle says I've got you to blame."

Vaughn's words were as difficult to translate as those of his toothless, backwoods, good-ol'-boy clients, but Pascoe was getting the gist of the slurs and mush.

"You've seen Bimbo? Is he there?"

"Runnin' scared. Got the hell out of Dodge. Called me. Still got my cell, at least till the end of the month. Wouldn't say where he was, but he said it musta been you who talked. Dad kicked my ass out as soon as he saw the paper. Said I'm a liability."

"Because of the drugs."

"What's it to you anyway? I had a good thing going."

"A good thing. Threaten Emilio into smuggling roofies in from Mexico so you can get a discount. Don't you have some kind of trust fund or something? I mean, why don't you just pay retail?"

"Man, you don't know what you're talking about," Vaughn grumbled.

"Did it make you feel like a big man? Did it impress Sam Rasmussen?"

"What?"

"Sam got her drugs from someone, and I'm betting it was you. What happened, too many rejections from sober, adult women? Figured a stoned teenager might be easy pickings?"

"Shut the fuck up! I like to get high, so what? I didn't have to talk Sam into anything; she came to me asking for shit. I'm no pervert man. Jesus, she's my—"

"Come on Vaughn, what were you going to say? Is she your soulmate? I guess in your mind, it makes everything okay."

"No, no. You don't understand." Vaughn's voice dropped to a whisper. "Sam is my sister."

CHAPTER EIGHTEEN

"Sam is Matthew Dearborne's daughter."

"That's the line, 'Dearborne paid off a lab.' It's an urban myth. Truth is Dad was screwing Gail while Mom was pregnant with Devon. Gail got pregnant, Mom found out, but wasn't the type to put up with that shit. Popped Devon out, got on a plane to France, and left Dad to deal with kids and lawyers."

"I've seen where Rasmussen lives. If Oscar is Sam's father, why isn't she screaming bloody murder to get support?"

"They worked out a deal. Dad had enough bad press with Mom leaving without a bastard daughter adding to his shame. And Gail, she's not too confident in battling Dad's money, knows Dearborne had his case bought and paid for even without the lab. Was sure the paternity test was a bluff, sure he didn't know about the affair."

"He must have known something. Why challenge at all if he didn't have some kind of inkling she wasn't his?"

"Maybe he was throwing everything at the case and got lucky. Maybe a wife came up pregnant he hadn't stuck it to in a while. Jesus, I don't know everything."

"How did you find out?"

"Gail told me after a fight with David. I guess he knew too. I'll admit, things were getting close, but Sam was a tease, you know? Always dressing real sluttish, hugging me, shit like that. Anyway, Gail took me aside and spilled the beans. Ugh, I still get the willies thinking about it."

She was thirteen. Should have had the willies even if she wasn't your sister, Pascoe thought, but didn't say. Don't want to aggravate him.

"There was a deal with Oliver?"

"An account for Sam. Monthly deposits, just like child support, and he pays for her education. Thing is, the account is in both their names: Dad and Sam's that is. She can't touch it until she's eighteen and if Dad even hears a rumor about him being the father, he'll close the account."

"You haven't told anybody?"

"Hell no. Figured if Gail could get money out of Dad then so could I."

"Oliver must be a real son of a bitch."

"Don't I know it."

"Did it work?"

"No. He asked me how I found out, and I lied and said Devon and Sam looked so much alike I got curious and called Mom. He laughed and said if I wanted to write myself out of the will, talking would be the best way to do it. Seems better to wait for the old man's heart to give out."

"If there's anything left by then. Your old man is hard up for cash."

"I haven't looked over his shoulder when he's balancing the checkbook, but the part about the store closures is true, and he's bitching about alimony payments. Cut me off the day I turned eighteen. 'Make it on your own son, it builds character', that sort of bullshit. Made like he was Mother Theresa for letting me stay at the house. Meanwhile, Devon gets whatever she wants as long as she makes Daddy proud. If he's got enough for her, there's money somewhere."

"He's bound to let you back in once everything dies down."

"Fat chance," Vaughn said.

"Maybe I can talk to him," Pascoe said. Vaughn was, and always would be, a pathetic weasel. But there was something genuine in his voice that reminded Pascoe of Devon and he spoke without thinking.

Vaughn laughed, high and hopeless. "Good luck. You'd be lucky to get within ten miles of Stonemason. Got off his shit list, the paper comes out, and the information about the poisoning is spilled all over the front page with Kutulas telling the world Dad did it. Turns the page and finds out his new buddy is the worthless son of a bitch feeding his son's habit. Trust me, the welcome mat has been pulled off the front porch."

"Did Oliver kill Goldrush?"

Vaughn was silent; traffic rushed by in the background. When he spoke, his voice trembled.

"Like you said, Dad is a son of a bitch." Pascoe felt like a priest, the telephone a confessional wall. "But, if anyone's given him a reason to be that way, it's me. Not exactly a model son." Vaughn sniffled. "Devon was Daddy's girl. From the moment she was born, if she started to cry, Dad would give her things until she finally stopped. When you think about it, it's amazing she turned out as normal as she did. Dad knew it too, and admired her. Point is, I can't imagine him doing anything he knew would hurt Devon, even a little."

"What about the insurance? Half a million can change everything."

"You don't get it. Dad was searching for a replacement even before he got the cash. Kept telling Devon not to worry, he would find a horse even better, no matter what it cost, and I believed him. Would have sold his precious broodmares to put a smile back on her face."

"She was murdered before he had a chance to make good, so we'll never know, will we?"

"He hardly sleeps and barely eats now, and when he does get something down, more often than not it comes right back up. When you decked me he didn't care a lick about the punch—might have given you a medal any other day—but it distracted from the celebration of his daughter's life."

Vaughn gurgled. Soon he sobbed uncontrollably. Pascoe was beginning to understand why a psychedelic had been his drug of choice. Pascoe promised to find a temporary place to stay. It wasn't going to be easy to find someone who would put up a personality-impaired addict, but Pascoe had an idea. He wrote down the number he could reach Vaughn at and told him to stay by the phone.

Robin Fellows was a client who ran a halfway house for drug offenders. Everybody was guaranteed employment. Fellows ran a small working farm that catered to local organic markets. He kept a robust vegetable garden, small herds of dairy and beef cattle, coops of laying hens, and a stable of bombproof horses available for city dwellers to rent by the half day. The state paid room and board, and Fellows used the money to pay his tenants well. This produced the lowest rate of recidivism of any halfway house in the state, assured by the purifying power of sweat, and the inmates' fear of being sent back to scrubbing water buckets and milking cranky heifers at four in the morning.

Fellows agreed to hold a bed for Vaughn. "He won't be given a free ride. I'll pay him the same as my other boys, but he'll work just as hard." Pascoe thanked him and relayed Vaughn's number.

Pascoe became painfully aware of numb fingers and muddy, blue-tinged fingernails and realized that the heat leaching from his body was the only thing keeping the cab a degree above the outside temperature. It made no sense to continue suffering in the truck; time to make a house call.

Gail Rasmussen's red plaid flannel nightgown fell to the tops of fleece-lined slippers. Dark circles under her eyes spoke of insomnia. She had a light grip on Deadbolt, who was more interested in greeting than eating. Rasmussen thumped the dog affectionately on his immense neck.

"He knows you helped him. Didn't even bark."

"Oliver Dowry is Sam's father."

Rasmussen's face fell. "Oh. Was it David? Do the police know?"

"Vaughn, and the police don't know. May I come in?"

Rasmussen led him into the living room, where a crackling fire was lit. Pascoe sat in a broken-down love seat close to the heat. "Why would you think David told me about Oliver?"

"The police said David identified Sam's sweatshirt. He barely recognized her after the accident. I thought maybe his memory was improving."

"They're convinced he's responsible for Sam's disappearance."

"I *told* them she ran away."

"How do you explain the clothing?"

"Somebody put it there, that's what I told the police. I'll say the same if they call me to the witness stand."

"You're convinced of his innocence."

"I love him."

"Did you love Oliver?"

"I met Oliver at the track. Friends with the owner of a horse Matthew trained. Matthew was always so busy, and Oliver would come by the farm, acting like he was ready to buy a horse, but really came to talk with me. I felt special, but it wasn't love, it was an escape, a fairy tale. For him it was a conquest. Oliver was as big a mistake as Matthew. Bigger. It left Sam without a father."

"Does she know?"

Rasmussen shook her head. "I can't tell her. It's why we have the distance between us. What are the chances of a teenager keeping a secret that big? If she told anyone it would jeopardize her future. David disagreed, said he would take care of us. If I had listened, where would we be now? He could never provide a better life the way he is." Rasmussen nodded, reasserting her decision.

Pascoe was dumbfounded. "At the cost of the relationship with your daughter."

"Year after year I've dealt with the tears, the pleading, but once I'm able to tell her what she's gained, she'll understand."

"Hasn't she tried to find out herself?"

"Of course. But only Oliver, David, and I know the truth. And Vaughn of course, but I had to tell him to avoid disaster. Oliver was so angry when Devon and Sam became friends, accused me of engineering the whole thing. Am I supposed to forbid her from making friends with the one girl who didn't look down on her?"

"Why didn't you let her go to the funeral?"

"Oliver wouldn't hear of it. He said Vaughn had already made the connection, and didn't need Sam walking around giving other people the same idea."

"Can't be the only guy in town who's knocked up a mistress."

"And won't be the last. Remember, when I got pregnant Oliver was a newcomer, and worse, he was *nouveau riche*. For months he tried to convince Brent Millwood to sell the Stonemason property. If it got out he had knocked up a trainer's wife who didn't have the good sense of their blue-blooded whores to get an abortion he would have been blackballed, and nobody would have sold him enough land to sink a fencepost in, for any price."

"So he got a farm in the right zip-code and convinced himself he had made it. Why hold onto the secret after that?"

"I don't know how these people work. Embarrassment? Concealment might work against him more than the act, no more invitations or inside information. Trust me, the most important thing to Oliver Dowry is perception. You know the expression 'perception is reality'? That's Oliver in reverse. He can't see what he is: a man who busted his ass all of his life and created his empire from scratch. Reality is that he is an amazing man. But before he'll accept it he needs everyone to believe he's as rich, as influential, as good as they are."

"Tough way to go through life."

"There are tougher," she said.

CHAPTER NINETEEN

Reporters were nowhere in evidence at the cabin. Either the cutting cold had forced their departure or Pascoe overestimated his own significance. Most likely the latter.

He gathered wood and made sure the cashbox was secure in its hidden compartment, fed the dog and lit a fire. Kindling was ignighting the larger logs when the phone rang.

"Taking a night off from making trouble?" Mornoe's voice was full of mirth.

"Thinking of retirement. Leave while I'm on top."

"Never top today. You got my message?"

"One of many. Not everybody is as tickled as you are." Pascoe related the conversation with Vaughn and visit with Rasmussen.

Monroe whistled. "On second thought, you may not want to retire just yet. You say you sent Vaughn to Fellows?"

"Thinking of heading over?"

"Damn straight. Might be able to get him in a room without a bunch of lawyers and get some straight answers. Know what has bugged me the most about Stuart? Motive. He just doesn't have one. What reason did he have to kill Devon? He lost a job, big deal. Either he's too damaged to care, or he still has enough marbles rattling around to realize he'll get another—got to be one or the other. Now they tie him to the Rasmussen kid. He may have recognized some clothing, but if you ask me, most of his memories of her leaked out of the hole punched into his skull."

"Vaughn has a stronger motive?"

"Think about it. What's a more powerful motive than love, or the desire for it? Vaughn walks through life in a haze of self-pity. Told to stand on his own two feet while his father lavishes expensive horses on his baby sister. Finds out he has an illegitimate sister siphoning away more money. Might piss him off. If both sisters disappear, who's left to compete for the cash? Or the love?"

"And the horses?"

"Maybe he struck out at them in frustration, but couldn't completely release his anger. We know he has a dislike for Stuart. Who better to take the blame?"

"I'm convinced there are more than two horses involved. There's a pattern here, like the symptoms of a disease. Vaughn is too weak to be the root cause."

"Give me a less benign name than Vaughn Dowry."

"Oliver."

"Looking at him."

"Carlyle."

"Looking *for* him."

"Dearborne."

"Zero motive, even less than Stuart. If Oliver Dowry showed up with a bullet in his head a decade ago, Dearborne would be at the top of my list. But the girls? He could care less about Sam, and it's doubtful he ever met Devon."

Unwilling to submit to logic, Pascoe gave the detective a synopsis of his handicapping formula; gambler's paranoia prevented any discussion of specifics. When finished he said, "Dearborne comes out at even odds with the others."

"Whoop-dee-fucking-doo," Monroe said. "Tell you what, I'll run this by Turner, I'm sure he'd like nothing more than to serve a warrant based on statistics."

"Dearborne had no problem fixing races when it benefited him. Who's to say he wouldn't knock off a couple of girls if they got in his way?"

"Word is, you've had a more than a passing interest in the outcome of a race," Monroe said. "What would you do if a couple of girls got in your way?"

"Completely different," he mumbled.

"Take a look in the mirror, Doc. Maybe you're gunning for Dearborne because he got away with the same thing you got nailed for."

"It's more than the races, not a bruised ego. Goldrush was poisoned, and Devon is killed. Rasmussen's horse was poisoned and Sam disappears. I think Dearborne's horse was poisoned as well, and guess what? His wife, Linda, disappears. He fed me some story about her running off, but the situation is too similar to be coincidence. Instead of knocking yourself out trying to find Sam's corpse, try looking for Linda Dearborne's. I'd like to see Turner try to charge David with that one."

"Nobody needs to look. Unlike Sam Rasmussen, I know where that body is—Gainesville. Problem is, it still has a pulse."

"She's alive?"

"Linda Dearborne, goes by her maiden name, Wilshire, and runs an animal rescue center. The department coordinates with Animal Control in abuse cases: we bust the people and they round up the critters. Those critters are evidence, the people who shelter them testify about their condition. Linda used to attend fundraisers for the sheriff with her husband. I recognized her when I made a trip to her place about a year ago."

"Dearborne lied."

"Seems so."

"Why would he do that?"

"Good question, one I wouldn't mind putting to Dearborne, if I thought I'd get a straight answer. "

"Maybe Wilshire would be more forthcoming."

"In my experience, few are forthcoming when it's a cop asking questions. Ever come across a neglect case?"

"Every now and then."

"Then I better give you her address, in case you need it."

"You don't sound sick," Maggie said.

Pascoe coughed for her benefit. "Can't make it in today Mags, can you just pass the message along?"

"King is going to explode. You better have one foot in the grave and the other stepping in."

"Heading to the doctor as soon as I hang up." This would excuse his absence if Harkin called or stopped by.

"Hope you sound more sick by then."

Noah's Ark Animal Rescue was a far cry from similar organizations. Most operated on shoestring budgets, volunteer work forces, and empathetic hearts; the latter in great supply, the others unpredictable at best. Wilshire's operation was flush with all three.

Four tall and tidy whitewashed barns sided in the Amish style—planks nailed vertically for better air circulation—stood in a row, wide-shouldered Gambrel roofs like defensive linemen. A split rail fence sprung from each end of the flanking barns, and faded from view toward the rear of the property. The fence ran the perimeter, enclosing thirty or forty acres of pasture.

The drive split near the barns into two parking lots: one marked VOLUNTEERS, which was full, and the other VISITORS, which had a few scattered vacancies. Pascoe squeezed the truck into an empty space and followed signs to the office, which was located in the furthest barn to the left. He introduced himself to an elderly woman behind a desk and asked for Linda. The woman, grandmotherly name of Millie embroidered on a pair of sky blue coveralls, picked a walkie-talkie marked with a wide strip of purple tape from a rack on the wall.

"Linda, there's a vet here asking for you." The volume on the handset was turned up high enough for the reply to be heard through the walls.

"I'm in Rehab, have him come to me."

Barn Politics

Millie explained that Rehab was two buildings down. Pascoe thanked her and walked over. Groups of people wearing the same coveralls as Millie wandered around the barns. It was as if Smurfs had taken over Green Acres.

Linda Wilshire bent over a sheep that was skeletal beneath its unshorn, matted coat and, by the smell of things, had a nasty case of foot rot. The ewe bleated with displeasure, but stood remarkably still while rotten hoof was trimmed away and copper sulfate splashed into the lesion.

"Josh," Wilshire said to a Helper Smurf, "set up a footbath at the gate to the sheep pasture. I want everyone going in and out to step through it, otherwise Lobelia is going to spread this gunk to the others." She rubbed the ewe's head playfully as Josh led her out of the barn. She stood, bracing both hands against the small of her back.

Wilshire was almost as tall as Pascoe and might have outweighed him. She had a broad back that fell straight to the hips through a nonexistent waist; coveralls fit her shape as if they had been tailored. Wilshire appraised Pascoe with eyes matched to the color of her outfit, though they lacked the cotton's warmth. Short blond hair was gelled into a forest of tiny spikes, the tips of which had been dyed vivid magenta.

Ah, Millie, Pascoe thought, *does the tape help you remember which handset to use, or are you having a little fun at the boss' expense?*

Wilshire's short mouth was drawn down into a tight line above a severely receding chin. The combination conjured unflattering comparisons to trout.

"You the vet?" she asked, extending her hand. "We're short on space right now. Only taking critical cases of abuse and neglect until we can place some of our resident animals, so if you've got a pot-bellied pig dumped because it's outgrown its cuteness you'll have to go somewhere else."

"I don't have an animal I want to send."

Wilshire blew out her nose impatiently. "Look, if you want to volunteer, great. Millie can help you with that, I'm too busy to handle every little—"

"I'm here to talk about Gizmo."

Wilshire turned away. "We have three Gizmo's, and at least a dozen others have been adopted. You'll have to be more specific." The words came in a rush. If she was going to put up a wall, he was ready to knock it down.

"The Gizmo who carried you on the jumper circuit. The Gizmo who was poisoned. After his death, you left your husband, ostensibly for another man, but I think you couldn't stand to be around him anymore."

Wilshire hissed through her teeth and glanced over her shoulder to make sure Josh was out of hearing range. "Go back to Matthew and tell him to leave me the hell alone; I've kept my end of the bargain and I expect him to keep his."

"I don't work for Dearborne," Pascoe said. "In fact, I'm real high on his shit list right now. He'd blow an aneurysm if he knew we were talking."

"Then maybe I should call and let him know. Do myself a favor." Wilshire played with a hair spike above her right ear. "Regardless, I've got nothing to say to you. You found your way in, find your way out." She walked away from him to another pen and fumbled with the snap latched to the gate. It rattled in her shaking hands.

Pascoe followed. Inside the pen was a sow whose left ear was a stunted, wrinkled mess. The eye on the same side was gone and strips of puckered skin ran the length of her back. She grunted with pleasure at the sight of Wilshire and hobbled to the front of the pen. One of the toes of her right front foot had been amputated.

"Jesus Christ," Pascoe said. "What happened?"

For a moment, he thought she was going to ask him to leave again, but shaking her head as if she felt she was being suckered into answering, did.

"Firecrackers. The kids who did this got all of sixteen hours, one weekend, of community service. Petunia—I know, predictable, but we stick to flower-themes for the girls—amazes me. With all she's suffered, she'll run up to teenage boys for a scratch the same as she did for me. I'd be in a corner wetting myself."

"You're doing a good thing here," he said. "I'm asking you to do another." Wilshire itched the underside of Petunia's chin. He hoped she was listening. "At least two other horses died the same way as Gizmo. Now a young girl is dead, and another is missing, probably because they knew something about the poisonings. I'm trying to stop it from happening again, trying to prevent an innocent man from being blamed, but I need help and I'm running out of time and ideas.

The scratching stopped. "Follow me," she said. "I'll give you the tour."

They started with the barn Millie's office was in, what Wilshire called the Admitting Barn. She didn't explain the other cases like she had with Petunia, and she didn't need to. Most were victims of neglect: wasp-waisted horses patchy with ringworm; cattle so gaunt backbones protruded like mountain ranges; and alongside them sheep, goats, pigs and a handful of llamas, all weak and starved near to death. Some animals cowered at the back of their stalls—victims of some cruelty of another, many with at least one bad leg and some with blood-soaked bandages. Every species stared with the vacant eyes of the defeated.

The second barn was labeled Treatment and displayed proof that even the most damaged animal could undergo remarkable transformation. He hadn't realized how silent Admitting had been, like a church, or a tomb, until they entered Treatment and were greeted with the whinnies, grunts, bleats, and lows of its inhabitants. These animals had a spark back in their eyes and hope renewed in their souls. Even those with clinging black scabs or bristling suture lines came to the front of their enclosures for a pat on the muzzle or a scratch of an ear.

Rehab, where Wilshire had been tending to Lobelia, was for animals with minor problems, or like Petunia, with problems too severe for adoption. Petunia would live out the rest of her life limping around Noah's Ark, reveling in her position as farm mascot.

The last barn, Adoption, was the happy ending of the tour and where visitors gathered in droves; it was his first encounter with un-coveralled humans. Where the other barns were close and stale and smelled of discharge and disinfectant, here it smelled of fresh straw and earth. Glossy, well-fed (an agricultural euphemism for fat) animals ready for a new home scarfed treats from the hands of giggling children.

Wilshire put on a smile and made small talk, encouraging the visitors to get to know the animals and consider adoption, and if they couldn't do that, to make a donation at one of the many boxes set up around the property. If these folks were finishing up the same tour it was hard to imagine anyone not doing one or the other.

He pursued Wilshire out of Adoption to a stretch of fence where she leaned heavily on the top rail, supported by her hands and armpits. More animals grazed and played in the paddocks—among them two bison and an ostrich mingled in a herd of assorted cattle. Pascoe duplicated her pose at the rail.

"The tour was unnecessary you know," Pascoe said. "I sympathize with what you're trying to do, though I have to say, Noah's Ark takes on cases most rescue groups would put down. I'm not questioning your devotion."

"I'm not asking you to gauge my sincerity," Wilshire said, her nose and ears crimson in the cold. "I want you to see what I'm risking. I want you to be absolutely sure you need my help."

"I'm sure."

"Pretty fast answer."

"My friend was murdered."

"Sorry to hear it."

"You two have a lot in common. She also rode jumpers. One of the horses that died was her mount. She was kind, as you are, and generous. She was cute, and whip-smart, and funny. I see a lot of death in my job, and it hardens a person against that kind of thing. Whether a body walks on two legs or four, we all wind up a hunk of meat in the end. But not this one. Not Devon." Wilshire ducked her head at the girl's name like she was avoiding a blow. "Give me what I need, Linda. Please."

"Ask."

"You knew Gizmo was poisoned."

"Not at first. But when the insurance check came in, Matthew refused to spend it replacing Gizmo. Said he had plans for it." Tears filled her eyes. "Plans. I asked him how he could have plans for money he had no way of knowing was coming. An inspiration, he said, one that could change tragedy into something positive. Inflate Montpelier's value, and I could buy any horse I wanted. As I listened to him talk, I realized the horses had stopped being living, noble creatures and become commodities. He knew I would have never entertained the idea of selling Giz.

"A few weeks later I overheard him on the phone, saying something about a friend in a similar pickle. Hung up as soon as he noticed me. I asked point blank if he had killed Gizmo."

"He denied everything," Pascoe said.

"Told me exactly what happened: he hired someone to kill Gizmo to collect the insurance. Matthew is genuinely surprised when others are presented with the same facts and don't reach his conclusion. Thought I would jump right on board once the initial shock was over. Called it smart business."

"He didn't do it himself."

Wilshire silenced the follow up question with her hand. "I have no idea who he paid, he stopped explaining when I started packing."

"What about the friend in the pickle?"

"Could be anyone. To Matthew, a friend is anyone who can do him a favor, and he likes to have a surplus of friends who owe him one. That's how things work at the top. Money is too crass, that's what they pay the help with. They do favors for one another instead: bank loans, stock tips. They barter influence."

"Does Oliver Dowry fall into that category?"

"You're kidding, right? You picked the one name that will *never* fall into that category. Matthew's hatred for Dowry borders on pathological. He would fly into a rage if we were at a party and someone mentioned his name."

"Would it surprise you to know Dowry bred a barn full of broodmares to Montpelier?"

"It would, but it's been a while since I left. Maybe the two of them made up, or maybe Matthew decided Dowry's money was just as green as anybody else's."

"Maybe he wanted Dowry to throw his money away on Montpelier."

"That would be more like Matthew."

"When you left, you had an opportunity for a bit of revenge. Why didn't you turn him in?"

Wilshire watched a dust devil turn leaves and scraps of hay in the air. "I was going to. He tracked me down at a hotel and made a proposal. What was done was done, nothing was going to bring Gizmo back and it would be stupid to shoot ourselves in the foot when we could both benefit from his 'mistake'."

"He offered you money."

"Keeping a mouth shut is not considered crass, it's considered a smart use of resources."

"Montpelier is as popular as ever, so you must have taken the offer."

Wilshire shrugged. "He was right about not being able to bring Giz back."

"Is your new mount everything you could hope for?"

She shot Pascoe a dirty look. "I can't even bring myself to sit on another horse, it would be an insult to Giz. I haven't spent a dime of Matthew's money on myself, every penny has gone to build this place."

"Why risk it all, talking to me?"

"I don't know, guilt maybe."

"You didn't kill Gizmo."

"Didn't I? I didn't say anything when Matthew doubled his coverage. I knew he was a risk-taker when I married him, and I knew how he treated his first wife. Don't tell me what I am or am not responsible for.

"What if you're right, and other horses have been killed, or God forbid, another person is killed, and an innocent goes to prison? What if Matthew is part of it all, how culpable am I then? I've adopted out over a hundred and fifty animals, and my conscience is still muddied, and I feel like a coward. I'm tired of being a coward. Let him cut me off, we'll make do with donations."

Pascoe placed a hand over Wilshire's. "I know the kind of pressure Dearborne can apply when he feels threatened. You're no coward."

He left her at the fence. As he wandered back to his truck, he passed a donation box nailed to one of the barn doors. He emptied his wallet into it, a wrinkled twenty and a pair of dog-eared singles. Winter was a lean time and figured to get leaner for Noah's Ark.

"I hear you're sick," Hunter said.

"To paraphrase Twain: the rumors of my illness have been greatly exaggerated." Pascoe called Hunter from the road after retrieving, and ignoring, another angry message from Dearborne. "How are things at your end?"

"Newcomb has lost some of his earlier confidence. The police grudgingly gave up everything they had, and it looks like they did everything by the book."

"He's still going to argue the phone and Sam's clothes were planted."

"Of course, but Devon's blood is on the phone. Newcomb says the prosecution will argue it was taken from the murder site."

"What's the game plan?"

"He's coming over for dinner tomorrow night to talk with David and discuss strategy. He's hinting at the possibility of a plea."

"What do you think?"

"Allowing David to admit to something he didn't do is unfathomable. But if he's going to jail no matter what Newcomb does, isn't it my responsibility to make sure they don't give him the needle?"

"Think he'd be better off in a cage?"

"He's not some dog you put down just because life gets tough."

"That's not what I meant."

"I know. Sorry. So what are you up to, besides playing hooky?"

"Errands. Trying to find something Newcomb might be able to use."

"Any luck?"

"Maybe. Not much time to process it yet."

"Process for a while and come over later. I still have a few horses to ride, so dinner is going to be late."

"As long as you don't tell Maggie. If she finds out I'm doing anything other than breathe with the help of a respirator there's going to be hell to pay."

"Cross my heart. But that kind of secrecy doesn't come cheap, you're going to have to be extra nice."

"What do you have in mind?"

"Give me time to process, I'll come up with something."

Morning frost stubbornly refused to melt under the weak winter sun, making the road to Timberbrook slick and dangerous in the evening. It was worse in the stretches that remained in shadow during the day, and Pascoe nearly ditched the truck into a strand of pine on the east side of the road. Concentration was pleasant distraction from the circular thinking that plagued him all afternoon.

Dearborne had hired someone to kill Gizmo, had he done the same with Goldrush? What about Dowry, had he and Dearborne come to some kind of truce? Could he be part of the Montpelier scam, ready to cash in on his foal crop? Did Carlyle have a role beyond propping up the stallion? Pascoe desperately wanted an hour with the *Form*; changing furlong splits into letter grades might be the only thing that could dispel the headache.

Barclay spun in frantic circles as they turned into the farm, releasing a blizzard of hair into the jet stream of the defroster. Out of the car the dog bounded off, nose pressed to the ground, in hot pursuit of some varmint or another. Pascoe wiped hair from Chapstick-coated lips with the back of his hand and headed into the barn.

There was no light aside from the thin band that shone from beneath the apartment door. Silhouetted heads jutted from near stalls, attention focused farther down the aisle.

"Hello?" Pascoe fumbled for the light switch.

"Hello?" he repeated.

Lights flickered on, and it became clear that the horses' attention converged on Banker's door. Pascoe trotted over and was relieved to see the stallion standing at the rear of the stall. The big bay's eyes bulged and his nostrils flared. Someone, most likely David, had neglected to remove his saddle and the horse was confused and anxious. The oversight would merit a scathing lecture from Hunter, regardless of her brother's excuse. He decided to remove the tack and shield David from the worst of it, though a patch of saddle-shaped sweat was enough to earn a reprimand. He slid open the door.

David's body lay crumpled beneath the water buckets. His jaw was unhinged and twisted to such a degree that his upper incisors bit into his right cheek. The same impact unzipped his scar from end to end, painting his face and neck crimson and pillowing his head in clotted bedding. Another strike had broken both the radius and ulna of his right arm, bending it back ninety degrees mid forearm. His clothing hid further ruin; dampness seeped through multiple spots over his ribcage and one at the hip; denim and flannel stuck to these spots like leeches. His bladder had released either from fear or let go at the same instant as his life, soaking the front of his jeans. Pascoe had seen enough dilated, unresponsive gazes to be sure there was no life in the body. Still, he felt at David's neck for a pulse. Nothing.

He left the stall and latched the door. Banker squealed, scolding. "Give me a minute," he said speaking aloud to calm himself as well as the horse.

The apartment was filled with a cloud of acrid smoke. Pascoe discovered a roast chicken, or to be more specific, a shriveled, charcoal briquette with drumsticks, languishing in the oven. He flicked on the vent fan, put on a pair of oven mitts, carried the pan to the wash stall and doused it with cold water. Confident the apartment was not about to burn to the ground, he sprinted back. He found Hunter's body in the loft.

CHAPTER TWENTY

Paramedics and police arrived together, followed shortly by the coroner. Pascoe stayed until Hunter was carted away, still unconscious. The police, unwilling to handle the agitated stallion, allowed Pascoe to move Banker. The horse was flighty and shied from quick movement and flitting shadow. A syringe of acepromazine calmed the horse and allowed removal of the saddle. Once Banker was agreeable, dried sweat was scraped from back and flank, and he was loosed into the arena with a large flake of hay and bucket of water.

The sheriff arrived as the coroner bagged David's body. "Doctor Pascoe," Ridgeway said smugly. "From what I've heard, the Commonwealth owes one of the nags a bag of carrots."

"What the hell are you talking about?"

"Stuart would have cost the taxpayers tens of millions of dollars. Next to that, a couple of hours of overtime are nothing."

If he struck quickly enough, Pascoe could knock three, maybe four, teeth from Ridgeway's gloating mouth. One for each month in jail. He unclenched his fists. The sheriff looked disappointed.

"Awfully damn sure of yourself," Pascoe said. "You might be celebrating the death of an innocent man."

"Oh, I don't think so," Ridgeway said. "I have evidence, motive, and opportunity." he jerked his thumb at the gurney wheeling David out of the barn. "I have Stuart, and he won't be able to tug at a jury's heartstrings with his simpleton act."

"It's refreshing to hear of your faith in the system."

"I serve people, not a system, and the people have faith in me."

"No doubt you make every effort to keep *your* people safe. I have a friend in the hospital. Her brother is dead. She'll be happy to learn your budget is in line."

A dramatic exit was hampered by Barclay's absence. A single whistle typically fetched the dog back to the truck, but he had already whistled three times and called his name, and there was still no sign. All the commotion, not to mention the burnt chicken carcass, should have been irresistible. None of Timberbrook's pack had made an appearance either.

He turned to an officer who watched with curious amusement and said, "Have you guys seen a dog running around? Black and white, about this big?" Pascoe held his hand at the level of his kneecap.

The cop shook his head and went back to packing up his vehicle. A thin crescent moon lit the farm, strong enough to illuminate an occasional fencepost and a few trees at the edge of the forest. Beyond that was shadow. Pascoe needed to get to the hospital. He waited a bit longer after starting the truck, hoping the roaring diesel would spur Barclay's return. When it didn't, Pascoe left, checking his rearview mirror until the road demanded his complete attention.

Hunter remained unconscious and was hooked to an IV. Pascoe pretended to be her fiancé and was ushered into her room and the confidence of her doctor. She asked if Hunter had been depressed lately. Under a lot of stress, he said, but not depressed. Drug problem? No. The doctor copied his responses onto a chart. They had pumped Hunter's stomach and not found anything, but were running tests on her blood. There was no telling when she might wake. It was a waiting game.

An hour passed, and Pascoe didn't care much for the game. He was reluctant to leave, but knew he would go crazy watching the IV drip. The nurse's patience was wearing thin; visiting hours had ended thirty minutes ago, if he paced by their station again they would enforce them. That settled it. Better to be gone a few minutes than be thrown out for the entire night.

A market a block and a half from the hospital carried *The Daily Racing Form*. The paper could distract him for a few hours. It would also keep him out of sight of the nurses. He threw a handful of change at the counter and hustled back to the hospital.

Hunter had not stirred. Still on her back, mouth open slightly, steady pulse throbbing at the hollow of her throat. He brushed hair back from her face and whispered her name, but she might have been as dead as her brother. Pascoe opened the paper and sat down alongside the bed in a chair that felt like it had been upholstered in burlap.

As he scanned for an appealing race, a horse caught his eye. Her name was Sister Sue, a two-year old maiden running in the fourth at Arlington. Her sire was Montpelier. He handicapped the race twice: once with no bias and a second where the filly was downgraded for her dubious sire. The lower score placed her near the bottom, only one horse ranked lower and it was a broken down mare that hadn't placed in thirteen starts. At three-to-two, the Montpelier daughter was the heavy favorite. They were giving too much credit to her bloodlines, a common practice with both odds-makers and gamblers. A mistake he could take advantage of.

Anointing Sister Sue caused another horse to be overlooked. Her name was Prospect of War and though she didn't have the most impressive sire or dam, her family tree had deep roots. She was capable of great speed at times, but had difficulty maintaining it for an entire race. She was with a new trainer, and he had procured the up and coming jock Pascoe had read about in *The Blood Horse*. Carlyle's cash was close. He took it out of his pocket and turned it in his fingers. He broke down and counted it—thirty three hundred twenty six dollars. If the line held, she would go off at six-to-one, not exactly a long shot, but if enough money were put down....

"Those ponies are just event horses in training." Hunter smiled weakly from the bed.

"Harder to make a profit betting on three-days," he said, shoving the money back into his pants. "The riders keep falling off."

She punched him soundly in the shoulder and winced, surprised to discover a needle in the back of her hand. She followed the tube to the slowly dripping bag of Lactated Ringers.

"How are you feeling?" Pascoe asked.

"My head is killing me," she said, massaging her temples. "What happened? Last thing I remember is going upstairs to change. Next thing, I wake up and you're grinning like you got hooked up to free cable. I must have got hypoglycemic and passed out. I was too busy riding to eat, all I had was a Diet Pepsi." Hunter scanned the room. "Where's David?"

Pascoe stomach curdled. "Hunter—"

"Where's David?" she repeated.

There was no way to say it gently. "Dead. I found him in Banker's stall. He must have gotten double-barreled while trying to take the tack off."

Hunter's face clenched like a fist. "Impossible. I rode Banker before noon and saw David untack him myself."

"Maybe he tried to go off on his own."

"He knows not to ride without me, knows not to tack up a horse in its stall, especially a stallion." The tears came, along with acceptance. "Knew. He knew those things."

Hunter's sobs brought the nurses running. They backed out respectfully when Pascoe waved them off. He held her tightly and let her mourn. If today she was too busy to eat, the last two years she had been too busy to feel much of anything. Tears fell for her brother's life, the trial of his rehabilitation, for the man before the accident. After a time, the tears and the sobbing stopped. The shaking took longer.

The doctor, alerted by the nurses, arrived to check Hunter's vitals. The questions began as she felt Hunter's pulse and checked reflexes. How old are you? What day is it? What are your parent's names? Slowly, the questions veered in a more personal direction: Do you have any vaginal soreness? Anal? Hunter cut her off.

"You're talking around something. Spit it out already. Can't make my day any worse."

The doctor pointedly ignored Pascoe. "There are confidentiality issues."

"Tell me now, or discharge me. I'm pretty sure my HMO wants me out of here as soon as possible."

The doctor sighed. Pascoe sympathized; she had no idea what she was up against. "We found a drug called flunitrazepam in your bloodstream."

"Rohypnol," Pascoe blurted out. The doctor eyed him warily.

"Yes," she said. "Roofies." She let the word hang in the air.

Hunter flushed. "Oh. Well, no, everything...down there...is fine. How could this happen?"

The doctor, confident she had Hunter's attention and cooperation, continued. "Have you borrowed any medication? The tablets are pretty generic looking and users will hide them in over-the-counter pills, like aspirin. Did you accept a drink from anyone, or could anyone have access to something you were drinking?"

"No," Hunter said. "I was at my farm all day. I finished riding and my brother brought me a soda, but that's all I had the entire day."

"I see," the doctor said. Everybody was familiar with the accusations surrounding David Stuart.

Hunter's feral gaze dared the doctor to continue. Better judgment prevailed. "Well then, I leave it to you to figure out the mystery. By the time you get dressed I'll have your discharge papers ready."

Hunter struggled with the implications on the ride back to Timberbrook. In the barn, she saw the roasting pan and its charred contents on the floor of the wash stall.

"Not my best effort," she joked flatly. "Are the dogs inside?"

"Couldn't find them."

"Barclay?"

"Took off when I got here, didn't show before I left. I expected the whole crew to be begging for dinner when we pulled up."

"I'll get a flashlight. They're probably rummaging in a nasty deer carcass. Last thing I need is to be up all night nursing a pack of puking dogs."

"I'll take the flashlight and round them up," said Pascoe. "Get something to eat before you *do* get hypoglycemic."

"You're right, I'm not thinking straight. I've got to call Mom and Dad. And Newcomb. I need to find a funeral home, that's what you do, right? Do I call the coroner, or do the funeral guys do that? I should get started on an obituary..."

Hunter drifted; Pascoe gently shook her by the shoulders. "Eat first. Sit and rest and don't think about anything. There's time for all that. I'll find the dogs, and we'll work on it together. Okay?" Pascoe led her into the apartment and wouldn't leave until she made a bowl of soup and eaten half.

The moon set behind the Appalachians, plunging the countryside into darkness, making field, fence, and forest indistinguishable from one another. The flashlight illuminated about a hundred square feet at a time. Timberbrook was twenty acres, nearly nine hundred thousand square feet. Fingers were already numb, and it was only going to get colder as night wore on.

The dog had run off to the northeast, so that was where he began, cupping hands to his mouth every fifty feet or so and bellowing "Bar-clay" or "Puh-pees", hoping his fading cry would be replaced with the sounds of scrambling paws. The air was clear and hollow; a door closed on the other side of the valley and it could have happened right next to him, but there was no sign of the pack.

He searched the pastures quickly, knowing the flashlight beam would reflect off the eyes of a dog in the same way a poacher would spotlight a deer. Seeing nothing, he headed for the treeline.

In the darkness, the riding trail looked no different from a deer path or storm gully, and it was easiest to proceed along the shortest stretch of open ground between two points. Even so, roots and rocks hindered feet and blackberry thickets snagged clothing.

Pascoe worked his way around the root-ball of a fallen maple, stepped into nothingness and slid down a slick, leaf-littered hillside. The flashlight fell from his grip, and something glinted in the beam as it rolled to a stop. Pascoe clambered to his feet and swung the light back and forth, but saw nothing but more leaves. He called for the dogs. Nothing.

Probably an old beer can. Still, *something* had caught the light. He made his way across the ravine, clinging to roots that poked from the hillside. There was a depression at the far end, possibly a sinkhole or the remains of an old well. Pascoe waved the light into the hole. Three pairs of eyes shined back.

Hunter's dogs were in a jumbled pile at the bottom of the depression, throats slashed, half submerged in their own fluids. Chinook, the aloof husky, faced south, one empty eye fixed toward Pascoe. It was pure luck the light had hit upon anything; sunken as it was, the location would have been difficult to find in daylight. If a strong wind pushed leaves into the grave it would have been impossible.

No David, No.

There had to be another explanation. A confrontation with a bear? The idea was discarded, a bear would never place the bodies like this. These dogs were a pack, a domesticated one surely, but a pack all the same, with David as their leader. Pascoe and Barclay were tolerated as friendly visitors, but at least one of the dogs always had an eye on them. Aggression toward one of the pack, especially its leader, would be met with bared teeth and relentless attack. Pascoe doubted he could survive one-on-one against Chinook, let alone the whole group. But David, Alpha, could line them up and dispose of one after another with hardly a whimper, as Andrea Yates had done, drowning her children in a bathtub.

A low whine startled him. He spun and slipped, jamming the small of his back against a rock. Barclay, camouflaged in blood and dirt, lay on the other side of the pit with his chin resting on his forelegs. He rolled his eyes and whimpered again.

"Hey boy," Pascoe said softly. "How you doing?"

Barclay didn't move. Pascoe crawled to the dog on all fours, making reassuring noises as he went. Barclay's eyes flitted back and forth from the bodies to Pascoe.

Pascoe palpated the dog gingerly, half expecting to pull back a hand slick with blood, but the gore on his coat was not his own. Pascoe felt his femoral pulse, which was strong and regular. Barclay turned his head away when Pascoe shined light in his eyes, but the pupils constricted normally. The reason for the dog's inertia was not physical, but emotional.

In some circles, bestowing the capability of emotion, grief in particular, to animals is considered gross anthropomorphism. Pascoe believed animals understood the concept of death and were capable of grief. Too often, owners would remove a dog or horse from its companions and take it to the vet office or knacker for euthanasia. Humans shed tears while the animals at home were aware only that a member of their group had left and not returned. This led to days of frantic running of the fence calling for pasturemates or following scent trails in the house. Tranquilizers were given, but only treated the anxiety that grew from ignorance of their companion's fate. It did nothing for the grief.

The best solution involved the survivors, allowed them to be present when the other was put down. Often, one of a pair of horses—so herdbound separation caused them to run into a lather—needed to be put down unexpectedly. Pascoe's recommendation was simple, if hard to stomach for the owner: let the companion watch. Watch its fellow fall to the ground. Watch the rhythm of the ribcage slow and stop. Let the body be touched and smelled so the conclusion can be reached: death has come. Then they understand. Then they grieve. All creatures can deal with finality; few can handle uncertainty. Pascoe stroked Barclay's head and gave him time.

It could have been fifteen minutes, an hour, or two. In the dark, there was no way of knowing. However long it was, eventually Barclay stood and shook as if he had come in from the rain, tongue lolling out one side of his mouth, tail curled over his back. He trotted forward with confidence, which persuaded Pascoe the dog knew the best route home. A short time later, following a path miraculously clear of obstacles, they entered the pasture through a gap in the brush directly opposite the barn.

The eastern sky waxed lavender. Snow, too light to penetrate the forest canopy, dusted the fields and melted under Pascoe's boots. In the barn, Barclay went directly to Banker's stall and snuffled under the door. He cocked his head.

"Tough night for everybody," Pascoe explained. Barclay broke away from the stall and headed for the apartment. Boots and paws were plastered in grime. "Wait out here," he said, pulling the boots off. Barclay grumbled, but rolled into a tight ball on the welcome mat. Pascoe took a deep breath and turned the knob, unprepared to deliver ill news for the second time in one night.

Hunter collapsed onto the couch. "What is going on around here?"

"It looks like someone snapped out there." He instantly regretted his choice of words.

"Meaning what? My psychopathic brother went on a rampage and decided to go for a leisurely trail ride in the dark?"

"I need some coffee." He searched for beans in the cabinets.

Hunter pushed him out of the way. "Sit down, you don't know where anything is. I'll make it. Hungry?"

"I suppose so."

"Eggs?"

Pascoe nodded. He watched as she loaded the coffee maker and started on the eggs. She tossed three into a stainless steel bowl and whisked furiously. The whisking continued like she planned to scramble them at the atomic level. She grabbed the bowl's rim with both hands, and slammed it to the counter. Obliterated egg sloshed over the lip.

"Damn it Jordan, he slipped me a fucking Mickey!"

"Looks that way."

"He brought the Pepsi to me." Hunter grabbed her upper arms as if chilled by a sudden draft. "Why?"

"I don't know."

"Maybe he needed Banker to carry me to the woods."

"It's a possibility."

"Don't patronize me Jordan."

"What do you want me to say? I've had my doubts about David, but done my best to convince myself and everyone else that he had no part in the killings. I'm not about to tell you what to think. You've known him your whole life and I haven't been around long enough to know where the coffee is."

Hunter wrangled a pan from a lower cabinet, tossed in a pat of butter and set it onto a burner. The eggs followed when the butter foamed.

"What if David set my soda can down, and somebody else dropped the pill in? It would have only taken a second. He could have been drugged too, and thrown into the stall afterward."

"Nobody could come onto Timberbrook without the dogs going nuts."

"I don't remember seeing the dogs after breakfast. They could have been lured away."

The delusion lightened her mood. She scraped at the eggs with a turner.

"The autopsy report will tell," Pascoe said. She didn't want to be patronized.

Hunter fumed. Steam from the pan amplified the expression. "Well, what do *you* think?"

Sarcasm was the last straw. He had busted his ass and pissed off half the county, put aside suspicion and common sense for the comfort and good graces of this woman.

"Now you want to know what I think?" he asked hotly. "What I really think? The coroner is not going to find anything abnormal in David. He drugged you. You were blindsided, how far of a stretch is it to consider the other possibilities? That he killed the dogs. That he poisoned Goldrush and Lexus." Implication filled the room. *That he killed Devon Dowry.*

Hunter kept her back to Pascoe. Her shoulders slumped. The eggs were sticking. Noticing, she shoveled those that could separate from the pan onto a plate and handed it, along with a hastily filled cup of coffee, to Pascoe. She returned and filled the sink with soapy water.

Pascoe cleared his throat. "I can bury the dogs if you like."

Hunter dropped the sizzling pan in water. "No. That's something I need to see. After you eat, it would be better if you left."

Hunter scrubbed the pan with a Brillo pad as vigorously as she had beaten the eggs. Pascoe ate a few mouthfuls of his breakfast. "Mind if I hose off Barclay before I go?"

"Be my guest."

Pascoe finished the eggs quickly and had a sip of the coffee. Not wanting to wait in uncomfortable silence while it cooled, he pushed from the table and left. Hunter never turned from the sink.

Barclay reluctantly followed Pascoe to the wash stall. The water warmed quickly and Pascoe was glad; it allowed him to rinse the dog and escape the sound of weeping and breaking glass. As he slid the barn door closed Hunter railed at her brother's memory, a keening wail that echoed back from the charnel pit in the woods, "WHAT DID YOU DO?"

CHAPTER TWENTY-ONE

A wet dog in the passenger seat made driving nearly impossible. Pascoe fought fogged windows with the sleeve of his jacket for a couple of miles before yielding at a coffee shop. He left the truck running and defroster blasting in the parking lot. Fresh stacks of newspapers stood by the register and Pascoe took copies along with a large black coffee. He grabbed a seat at a table near the door and read while the dog dried.

The death of David Stuart was the *Times-Mirror*'s feature story. "Fortunate Accident Claims Killer's Life" it pronounced, incorporating a quote from Sheriff Ridgeway in the headline. In the body of the story, Ridgeway made it clear that Providence had a hand in keeping the case from the whims of a jury. Undoubtedly, piety polled well with voters. As the article continued, it laid out the evidence, portraying David as a kind of Frankenstein's monster whose damaged brain spurred unholy actions. A headshot of David illustrated the point, scar digitally enhanced and vivid.

If the *Times-Mirror* reported the story with restrained relief, *The Freedom Monitor*, in a four page 'Special Edition', grudgingly acknowledged the work of the police, and expressed hope that Oliver Dowry might find solace in the case's conclusion. There was no retraction of the previous allegations. Nothing short of a gun to Kutulas' head would accomplish that, but this story would have the same effect. Within a few days, conspiratorial whispers would have as much credibility as Kutulas himself. Pascoe's future was less certain. His indiscretion with the publisher would make him as fashionable as Bermuda shorts at a black-tie affair. Once Barclay could be seen clearly through the windshield, Pascoe headed for home.

A note from Dearborne was tacked to the front door: *Disregard my last message. Here's a new one: Fuck You. Know the expression 'day late and a dollar short'? An extra day has cost you a lot more than a dollar. My problems have floated away on angel's wings. Should be enough mares in Montpelier's book this spring to pay for a boat. Hope you find a new job near the water so I can wave.*

The words buzzed in his head like the horn at the end of a basketball game, one in which his last second shot bounced off the rim. He crumpled the note in his fist. Barclay traced figure eights with his nose by the door, tail high in the air and wagging madly. Near him lay the discs that covered the space in the woodpile. The cashbox was gone.

Pascoe pressed his forehead against the frozen ground. When it started to hurt, he sat up. He was completely screwed. It didn't matter who had taken the box. The logs could have shifted and Dearborne could have found it when he dropped off the note. Carlyle could have come looking to get his property back, or Vaughn could have come looking for a fix. Regardless, none of them wished him well and the box had his prints all over it. He took some comfort in knowing Ridgeway couldn't have found the box; he'd have a new home in a cell if that were the case.

Damn you and your worthless stud anyway, he thought, throwing the note to the ground. *Worthless stud.* Pascoe looked at his watch. With the hour time difference to Oklahoma, he had plenty of time to run to the bank, get cash, and drive to an off-track parlor in Charles Town.

Big, wet flakes of snow spattered on the windshield of the Dodge. The parking lot of Farmers and Merchants Bank was empty and Pascoe stared at his lap and the stack of bills totaling over seven thousand dollars lying there—he had added his entire savings to Carlyle's earnings. Pascoe snickered. Lucky seven.

He had bet on one thing or another nearly every day since graduation until the time of his disciplinary hearing. After that, he would cautiously drop five bills with Carlyle about every other month and spend the remainder of the time playing with the *Form*, charting his results on paper. That exercise was like giving rock candy to a crack addict .

He needed real action, and the need chipped away at his resolve bit by bit. He had been ready to topple for a while, propped up only by the fear of losing his license and disappointing Harkin, but the last few weeks had been an unbalancing gust of wind.

He contemplated re-depositing the cash. He could put Carlyle's money in the account, for safekeeping. That would be the right thing to do, what his father would have done. And look where it got him. A horn honked. Mary Fischer, a regular client and notorious gossip. She wore a concerned expression, and who could blame her? Unshaven, jittering from caffeine, spattered with forest goo, and grinning at his lap like a madman, he looked the part of the junkie. He flashed what he hoped looked like a well-adjusted smile and pulled away to route 9 and Charles Town.

A scant hour later he drove back, seven thousand dollars poorer. Pascoe had rejected his system and put everything on Prospect of War. The filly led the race from the starting gate and showed no signs of fatigue as she rounded the last turn and sprinted for home. Her odds had climbed to nine-to-one prior to the start of the race and he was looking at over sixty thousand dollars running the stretch with her nearest competitor four lengths behind and the favorite, Sister Sue, still negotiating the turn. Then she stopped. Not slowed, stopped. As the other horses flew by the jockey hopped off the filly's back and held up her left foreleg. The telecast later reported that she had dislocated a fetlock and was being transported for surgery.

Pascoe had never suffered such a loss; his system prevented it. Now he had nothing but thirty odd dollars in a checking account and nearly two weeks until his next paycheck. Hunter wouldn't speak to him. He had forgotten to call Maggie and tell her he would be missing another day of work. Undoubtedly, Monroe was wrapping up the details on Devon's case; cursing Pascoe and the time wasted with him.

The Potomac Valley Complex jutted above the trees to the north, solemn and dark in the falling snow. There might be one person in the county still willing to give him the time of day, and she worked in that building.

This time, no one guarded the front desk; the entire office gathered under crepe paper streamers near the back of the cubicles. He found Wallace at the center, sipping champagne out of a plastic cup. She fiddled with the tie of an expensively attired older man, who, judging by the twitch of his mustache, enjoyed the attention. All eyes swiveled as Pascoe approached. Wallace rescued him from any awkwardness.

"Everyone, this is Jordan Pascoe. He's the veterinarian who ferreted out the cause of death in the Dowry case." She threw an arm around his waist and gave a pinch when he started to open his mouth. "Looks like it's been a tough day out there in the trenches," she said, laughing and brushing at his coat.

"He helped me realize we might have similar cases in our files. In a way, his hard work is responsible for this party."

The rest of the crowd, some with an unsteady hand, raised their glasses. The man Wallace had been cozying up to offered his hand.

"Preston Boatwright," he said. "We are in your debt, son."

"I don't understand." Pascoe looked to Wallace for help. She smiled over her lipstick-stained cup and squeezed him tighter.

"By not settling for anything less than the truth, you provoked Ruth, Miss Wallace that is, into digging deeper. On her own time, I might add." Boatwright beamed like a proud father.

"I have to admit," he continued, "at first the partnership was angry. It made the business look unprofessional. But with the story coming out about that sicko—what was his name?"

"David Stuart," Pascoe offered through clenched teeth. Wallace pinched him again.

"That's it. Now we know someone was killing those horses, and Virginia Bloodstock looks to make a lot of money."

"I don't get it," Pascoe said. "You paid those claims. Is the company trying to recover the settlements?"

Boatwright choked on his champagne. "Heavens no! It would be suicide. The money is insignificant. For those two horses, we paid out—"

"Two? You mean—ow!"

Wallace ground a spiked heel into Pascoe's big toe. "Five hundred for Dowry. One for Rasmussen."

"A little more than half a million," Boatwright said. "But Virginia Bloodstock is now seen as proactive. We won't sit idly by while horses are harmed. The publicity should increase our business twenty to thirty percent, and that, Doctor Pascoe, will pay for those claims tenfold."

"Now you're the good guys," Pascoe said.

"Insurance companies, like lawyers, have always been considered a necessary evil," Boatwright said. "It goes a bit far to say we'll be looked at as 'good guys', but any improvement in image, especially if it separates us from our competition, is a plus. Five of the biggest privately owned barns in the state called about switching coverage, and when the show season starts back up and folks are talking to each other we expect another bump. Ruth's initiative might just put her in line for an office with a view."

Wallace blushed. Pascoe was wondering how much practice *that* took when she stumbled and spilled champagne onto his jacket.

"I'm afraid I've overindulged this afternoon," she giggled. "Doctor Pascoe, would you mind giving me a lift home? Really, I shouldn't be driving."

Pascoe hesitated. Boatwright looked horrified he might consider refusing. "I'd be happy to."

Away from the building and stuck in commuter hell, Wallace sobered up rather quickly. "Hey, cheer up," she said. "We did it. Nobody knows you're involved, and I get all the credit."

"David was a friend."

"If I were you, I wouldn't mention the friendship thing too much, won't do a whole lot for business." She leaned the seat back, kicked off her shoes, and put stockinged feet on the dash. Pascoe turned up the radio and drove.

"Come in for a drink," Wallace said.

Pascoe ran through his options: continue to drive aimlessly or go home and rattle around the house aimlessly. Wallace smiled when he reached for the door handle.

Before they went in, he rounded up the horses and put them in their stalls while she dispensed hay and grain. Barclay romped in the accumulating snow with the greyhound. Afterward, they went into the kitchen where she poured him a glass of Syrah and left to change out of work clothes.

He expected her to return in a pair of sweats like she had been wearing the last time he visited. Instead, she entered the kitchen wearing emerald satin pajama pants that clung where they needed and a small cotton tee shirt cut to expose a hint of belly. She would, no doubt, claim the outfit was practical and comfortable. If he found it sexy, well, that was his problem.

It *was* his problem. Wallace smirked as she poured herself a glass of wine. She put an arm over Pascoe's shoulders and clinked her glass against his.

"To endings," she said, sipping from the glass, "and beginnings." Leaning forward she kissed him with a mouth tasting of cherries and cloves. Pascoe, eager to feel anything but loss and rejection, returned the kiss without reservation. Wallace pulled her mouth from his, sniffed, and whispered in his ear, "Doctor Pascoe, you need a bath."

Pascoe downed the rest of his wine in a single gulp. "I imagine you have a tub around here somewhere."

He woke in the unfamiliar bed with a start. The clock said it was five in the morning. Wallace had proved to be a tireless lover; they had collapsed into sleep only two hours ago. He slid out of bed carefully to avoid disturbing her and hunted for clothes. It was like playing a game of Concentration, replaying last night in his head and matching locations to articles of clothing.

"Walk of Shame?" Wallace sprawled across the duvet, watching him.

"Need to stop home before work, I can't show up in these clothes."

"After work?"

"Will you accept a maybe?"

"Come over here." When he obeyed, she pulled him on top of her and bit playfully at the tip of his nose. "No."

Maggie ignored him. Harkin sat on the edge of his desk, waiting. It was becoming a familiar scene.

"Jordie."

"I know, I forgot to call in yesterday. I was the one who found David, so I've been pretty busy."

"Thought you were sick."

"I was." Cough. "Still not completely over it."

"Hunter said you went home yesterday morning. Plenty of time to recover. And call in to let us know what was happening."

"You know how it is when your sinuses are all plugged up and you're loaded up on Sudafed, you can't think straight."

Harkin crossed his arms. "I tried to telephone, and got worried when you didn't pick up, so I went by. You weren't there."

"Ran out of cough syrup. Stepped out to—"

Harkin held up a hand. "No more bullshit Jordie, please. I'm not your father. This is not about missing a day or two of work, it's about your behavior, and the way it's affecting my business.

"Oliver Dowry called. Said you've been coming onto his property unannounced. Said you set the police on Vaughn. Dowry is a valuable client of mine."

"Let me straighten it out."

"It's not just Dowry. I got another call from Dearborne. I've known Matthew since he rode along with his dad to shoe horses, and now he's threatening to sue the clinic over damages to his stallion's reputation."

"It's a bluff. He won't risk the truth coming out in court."

"That's not the point!" Harkin slammed his hand to the desk, making Maggie jump. "This is the problem, right here. You're the trouble Jordie. You. It doesn't matter whether or not you're right. People want privacy. They want to do business with those who will keep their eyes closed and mouths shut. You can't, or won't, do that, and it's turned into a liability."

"What are you saying, King?"

"I'm letting you go. Two weeks, that's the most I can afford, then I expect you out of here. You've turned yourself into a leper and I can't let you infect the practice." King pulled on his battered hat and stepped out of the office without another word.

Pascoe didn't hear Maggie's expressions of sympathy. *Fired?* He sleepwalked through the day and made excuses about not being completely over the flu. *Fired?* After the incident with the Board, he had always thought that if he went down, he'd go swinging, with Harkin right by his side. Having the old man say the words was a blow to the kidneys. *Fired.*

CHAPTER TWENTY-TWO

Pascoe spent the night with Wallace, hoping it would help him forget, at least for a while, but it didn't, and while she slept with a possessive leg across his thigh, he stared at the ceiling and wondered what the hell he was going to do. In the morning she asked if he was coming over after work, and when he made an excuse about paperwork told him it was fine and to call her when he felt like it but she wouldn't wait around for him to get his head screwed on straight.

David's obituary ran in the *Times-Mirror*. It was published with a pre-accident picture, and said that the funeral was going to be held at Saint Mark's the following day. Pascoe tore it out and stuck it to his refrigerator with a promotional magnet shaped like a syringe.

Pascoe opened the church door with trepidation. There had been no need to rearrange his schedule to attend the service, which spoke volumes about his popularity. It would be discomforting to be the subject of more conversation than the deceased. His worries turned out to be unwarranted.

Hunter sat in the front pew next to an older couple. They were the only people in the church. Whenever Pascoe thought of Hunter, which was often of late, he was reminded one of those little animals that poofs up in mock bravado. Today she was deflated and inanimate, and seemed more compressed by the weight of David's passing than even her frail and shrunken mother.

Few flower arrangements surrounded the casket. Pascoe had expected more respect for the horseman David Stuart had been, regardless of what he had become.

Hunter turned as the church door squeaked closed. She patted her father on the knee and met Pascoe halfway down the aisle. "Have a seat," she said bitterly. "Plenty of room at the front."

"How are you holding up?"

"Better."

Pascoe didn't know how to ask. "Am I early?"

"You're it. Plenty of people called to say how sorry they were about not being able to come. Gail has had a change of heart; she said she hoped he burned in hell. Wasn't expecting that." Her voice faltered. "I thought, I thought...."

"Me too," Pascoe said, squeezing her hand.

Hunter wiped her eyes. "Come see," she said, drawing him to the casket. "You won't believe it."

She was right. Whatever filler, wire, and makeup the mortician employed worked magic. The scar had been smoothed and blended into the rest of the face. David looked as whole as Pascoe had ever seen him, serious rather than simple. He was dressed in a white shirt and stock tie, white britches, black jacket and dress boots; anything less would have been as inappropriate as an evening gown. The illusion was marred only by a bit of bruise that extended beyond the shirt cuff onto the hand of the arm that had been broken. The kick had imprinted detail from Banker's shoe into the skin; nail heads left tiny purple rectangles slightly darker than the shoe's curving trailer. Even the farrier's mark was visible: an overlapping B and C that had been stamped into the iron while the forged steel had been hot and soft.

Hunter waited for his reaction. Pascoe said, "I'm sure he's looking down and nodding with approval."

"Not looking up?"

"The God I was taught about would judge him on the man he was, not what an accident created."

Hunter tucked a loose strand of hair back behind her brother's ear. "I'd like to believe that as well."

A priest entered and waved Hunter and Pascoe back to their seats. When the service was finished, Pascoe followed the hearse and Hunter's truck to the cemetery. With the priest, two men from the funeral home, and the gravedigger present, David was buried by equal numbers of strangers and friends as rain played taps on his coffin.

Pascoe drove Hunter back to the farm after the burial. Her parents had wanted nothing more than to go back to their hotel room and rest, and Hunter had given them her truck. "I have enough food for fifty people," Hunter had said as they turned from the grave. "If you don't help me I'll be eating vegetable plates and cold-cuts for a month."

"Hear you're looking for a job," Hunter said.

"I have a knack for pissing people off."

Hunter, unsure how to respond, pushed a sandwich made with miniature bread slices around her plate like a toy boat. "This is the sorriest wake I've ever been at. Want a drink?"

"Sure."

She went to the refrigerator and held up a pair of beers. "Okay?" Pascoe nodded. Her hands trembled. He wondered when she had last eaten. She popped the tops and handed one to Pascoe, then chugged half her own. "I guess now we're supposed to talk about all these great memories, but you know what? All I can think about is changing bed pans, cleaning the scabs from his head, and helping my older brother button his shirt." She took another long pull from the beer.

"Then talk about that," Pascoe said.

Hunter started to tip the bottle again, but reconsidered. "Right after the accident all I did was stay by his bed and pray he would wake. And then he did, and from that instant I knew something was wrong. He called my name, sounding the same as ever and I thought, thank God, everything is going to be all right. But his eyes, they had this far away look. Unfocused. Ever been with someone who talked in their sleep?"

"Creepy," Pascoe said, nodding. "They're right next to you, but not really there."

"Exactly. That's how it was. Not creepy, but when he spoke you had to listen carefully to know for sure if he was talking to you or having a conversation with himself. I never cared; I had my brother back. Even with everything that has happened, I'm glad he came back and wouldn't change it for anything." Hunter lowered her eyes to the table. "Guess that makes me a cold-hearted bitch."

"It makes you his sister," Pascoe said. "You were a cold-hearted bitch long before the accident."

Hunter playfully boxed his ears. Pascoe talked about how David had made him think of the brooms from the Mickey Mouse cartoon, which made her giggle uncontrollably. They opened more beer and eventually she told stories about David before his injury. How he won Rolex one year with a hangover so bad he threw up after his dressage test. How he forced her to mount up immediately after her first scary fall. How he pushed her and coached her and admitted she had surpassed him as a rider.

"Now I don't know what's going to happen," she said. "I haven't been on a horse in four days. Can't remember how many years it's been since I could say that. I should call Tony to come out and pull Banker's shoes, he might as well go barefoot."

"Hold off," Pascoe said. "Give yourself a little time. You might change your—who did you say you were going to call?"

"Tony," she replied, puzzled by Pascoe's expression. "Hennings. He does all my work. What's the matter?"

Hunter caught up at Banker's stall. Pascoe was inside, examining the sole of the stallion's hind hoof. Banker, curious, craned his neck to look. "There's no mark on the shoe," he said.

"Of course not. Tony doesn't forge from bar stock. Not many do these days."

"David's arm was bruised by a horseshoe with the initials 'CB' stamped into it."

"It must have just looked that way. He had bruises everywhere, and I didn't notice a mark. There's not even a shoer in the area with those initials."

"David wasn't killed by Banker. It's another set up. If he's dead, there's no trial. No trial, no questions, case closed."

Hunter stiffened. "Don't do this. He's guilty, he's not guilty. I'm sorry you lost your job, but chasing some phantom mark is not going to convince King to give you another chance. It's not going to bring David or Devon back. David did these terrible things. There, I said it. Happy? Let it go."

She marched back to the apartment and slammed the door. Pascoe didn't know which was worse: being convinced David was not a murderer or seeing Hunter convinced that he was.

"CB?" Harkin asked. "Doesn't ring a bell. Why?"

"Came across a stamped shoe tacked to an auction horse. New owner wants to follow any lead that might shed light on the mare's history. Thought you might know who still made their own around here."

"Can't help you there. Have you tried the Farrier's Association?"

"The only CB on record is a Christian Baker, he lives in New Mexico."

"Might want to call anyway. Could be someone bought a lemon in Albuquerque and unloaded it. A lame horse can make its way across the country going from auction to auction."

Pascoe agreed, not wanting to compound the lie. Harkin was being civil, congenial even, and mentioning David's death and conspiracy in the same breath might prod him into shortening the two-weeks notice to twenty-four hours, and Pascoe needed that final paycheck.

He thanked Harkin and left for his lone appointment. Word traveled quickly about the firing, and nobody wanted horses treated by a lame duck veterinarian. Except for Old Mrs. Simmons. Kit's leg was still not right and she insisted Pascoe have a look.

Mrs. Simmons was pleased with the way the skin was closing, but, concerned with a little swelling in the lower leg, brought out a favorite family remedy: a mercury blister that hadn't been manufactured in over thirty years. The bottle was thick with dust, but the solution had lost none of its potency. Though the wound looked great, the old stallion had open sores where the blister had eaten away the hide. Mrs. Simmons *tsked* and disparaged Kit for being 'thin skinned' while the wrap was removed. Pascoe slathered the sores with antibiotic cream, rewrapped the leg, and ordered her to ignore it for the next week. The bandage was sure to be wet and heavy with drainage by that point, but it would give the skin a fighting chance before she dragged something else from the medicine chest.

Afterward, she invited him inside for a cup of hot cider. Pascoe's schedule was wide open and the sky threatened to add to the snow already on the ground, so he accepted.

Mrs. Simmons had a quaint, old-lady kitchen. It smelled of potpourri and had walls hung with plates from the Franklin Mint, including the entire Wizard of Oz collection and a handful of Young Elvises. Pascoe sat at a peculiar five-legged mahogany table. A napkin holder sat in the center, deftly made from bent and welded horseshoes. On one end of every shoe were the overlapping letters 'CB'.

Pascoe could barely speak. "This is interesting. Can you tell me where it came from?"

"Sounds like you're coming down with something," Mrs. Simmons said, placing a steaming mug on the table. "Cider should do the trick." She turned the piece in the faint light. "I was given this years ago by the man who shod my horses. Pretty in its way, isn't it?"

"Yes m'am. I don't recognize the mark, is he still in the area?"

"Clyde? He died, must be ten, fifteen years ago. Such a loss, a true craftsman. So unexpected. He shot himself," Mrs. Simmons whispered, as if a neighbor might overhear.

Pascoe sipped nonchalantly, though the cider burnt his tongue. "More surprising then, that I wouldn't remember hearing tales of a Clyde B."

"Well dear, that's because you're reading it wrong." She placed an age-spotted finger at the stamp. "Not B, D. See, the bottom of the C cuts right across the middle of the D."

Pointed out, it was clear. "Dearborne," he said.

Mrs. Simmons smiled at Pascoe like a pet student. "See there, you have heard of him. Now, where is my checkbook?"

Pascoe raised his mug. "Don't bother m'am, the cider is plenty."

"Well, aren't you a dear?"

CHAPTER TWENTY-THREE

Monroe Ridgeway would hear none of it. Pascoe held the phone from his ear as the detective let it be known what he thought of the suggestion to reexamine David Stuart's death. Pascoe couldn't get a word in edgewise before Ridgeway slammed the receiver home. The entire one-sided conversation lasted all of thirty seconds. Moving up the chain of command would be futile, Sheriff Ridgeway wouldn't give him one-tenth the time. Pascoe needed an advocate, someone to plead his case and grease the wheels of justice.

"He's up at the house, resting," Maggie said, eyeing Pascoe the way she would a sales rep promising he only needed a moment. "Doesn't need you bothering him."

"Understood," Pascoe said, flying out the door to his truck, which he had left running. It fishtailed up the sloping driveway.

Curtains were drawn in every window. A stolen glance through the door's peephole hinted at light leaking from somewhere deeper in the house. With an ear to the door he thought he heard Harkin's muffled voice, but it could have easily been a television, or his imagination. He jiggled the handle and, finding it unlocked, let himself in.

"King?"

"In the kitchen."

A set of steps to the left of the darkened foyer led upstairs. A short hallway straight ahead ended at a door and Harkin's voice. On the other side of the swinging door Harkin spread a thick layer of peanut butter across a slice of white bread. A jelly-covered mate lay next to it on the counter.

"Maggie rang and said you were on your way up," he said, mashing the two halves of the sandwich together and taking a bite. He moved a wad of bread from the roof of his mouth with his tongue. "Said you looked like a man on a mission."

"I know who killed David."

Harkin sighed. "Son, don't you think it's about time you stopped all this?"

"I have proof, all I need is someone to help me get the police to listen."

He told Harkin everything, from how it started with Goldrush's death, to Dearborne's manipulations, and finally the discovery of the bruise on David's hand and who that mark belonged to.

"Clyde Dearborne's been dead for more than a decade," Harkin said, tugging on an ear. "You must be mistaken."

"I saw it," Pascoe said earnestly.

"What are you asking? You want to dig the boy up? He's just been put in the ground."

"Right now I need someone who can make the cops hear me out. That's all I'm asking."

Harkin gnawed on his lower lip. "How sure are you about this?"

"I'd bet my life on it."

Harkin's pale gaze bored into Pascoe. "I believe you would. All right, Jordie. The sheriff has his backers, and I've raised a glass with those gentlemen on more than one occasion. They'll pressure Ridgeway into giving you a fair shake if I ask."

"I knew I could count on you. Want me to drive?"

"You'd better, it's getting to that time of day where my eyes don't work so good, and with snow on the road we'd stand a better chance of staying in one piece without me behind the wheel. Let me find my hat."

Pascoe left to start the car. He was back in the foyer when a soft shuffling noise coming from above his head caught his attention. Sam Rasmussen stood at the top of the stairs and clung unsteadily to the balustrade; hair dyed a fiery red. Pascoe stared, dumbstruck.

Pain exploded in his right shoulder and the arm dropped numb and useless to his side. The stairway doubled and pinpricks of light danced like fireflies as he collapsed. Searing pain raced to his fingertips and clawed into his back. His scream ended abruptly as he vomited onto the hardwood.

He was spitting bile when something hard pried under his good shoulder and flipped him onto his back. His stomach convulsed again.

"You brought this upon yourself." Harkin stood above him, sadness, or pity, on his face. In one hand he gripped an axe handle; a horseshoe nailed to the end that normally held a blade. Pascoe knew the tail of that shoe would bear Dearborne's stamp. The business end of the weapon pointed accusingly at Pascoe.

"Jesus boy, I tried to get you to leave it at botulism, the insurance company would have been satisfied and we wouldn't be here right now."

Pascoe panted. He struggled against the pain to slow his breathing enough to talk. "And Sam? Would she be here?"

"My Sammy will always be with me." Harkin motioned to the girl and she plodded slowly down the steps. She skirted past Pascoe at the landing, embraced Harkin in a lover's kiss, and stood obediently at his side. "Sammy needs me Jordie. She's grown up without a man to look up to. I could see that at the pony club meetings, her sitting way in the back, alone most times, dressed like a whore just to get some attention. Well, I saw past that and gave her the attention she deserved, gave her the guidance and structure her mother was unable to give, and she loves me for it."

"She's a child."

Harkin scowled. "Sam is more woman than the bitches out there who have forgotten who I am. Remember what I told you about power? This is power, Jordie." Harkin ran his fingers through Sam's fine hair. "The ability to desire something and take it, mold it, *perfect* it. It's the creation of Eve really. A part of me has gone into her making."

"You're not God."

"No?" Harkin's eyes crinkled at the corners. "Perhaps not. My mother used to take me to the graves of my brothers and sisters and tell me they were so special God had taken them up to heaven. Me, He leaves. Mother said it made me extra special, but I don't think she really believed it. I got straight A's, lettered in football and basketball, and she kept crying over those fucking slabs of granite. She missed my graduation because it was one of the little ghost's birthdays. Can you believe that? A goddamn graveside birthday party for a fucking miscarriage!"

Harkin swung the axe handle wildly in front of him. "My clients though, they could see. I used to be the only veterinarian round these parts and it was like being a god, wrestling with great beasts and curing their ills with poorly understood medicine. I got blown when I saved a favorite mount from colic and fathers or husbands looked the other way because it was cheaper than shelling out money for a new horse. If I had a bowed tendon ready for race day and the horse paid off on long odds it was like I had raised the dead, but better, because the resurrected don't pay sixty-to-one. Times like that, parties were thrown in my honor, tribute laid at my door.

"Some of the locals have forgotten what I've done. Magazines are taking the mystery out of medicine, telling people how to fix their own horses and encouraging them—encouraging them! —to question their vet and order medicine online or from a catalogue. Oh, they pay their respects and invite me to their parties, but I hear the whispers about how I'm losing my touch. Women who used to straighten my tie with an invitation into their bed push away my advances and laugh like I'm a lecherous clown. And you, who could have followed in my footsteps and had it all—the respect, the women, the *power*—I could have watched you take over with pride and only a little regret, but you won't seize the opportunity of your station. Instead, you settle for being no more than a hired hand."

Pascoe clenched his teeth and pushed up onto the elbow of his good arm. "You sound like Dearborne."

Harkin kicked the elbow away, returning Pascoe to his back, writhing.

"Dearborne sounds like me. You should follow his example. I watched him grow up, same as you, burning with a desire to be something. After his father died, he came to me for advice. He didn't fall short when it came time to act."

"You're talking about Gizmo."

"I never even knew the horse's name. Dearborne asked me if there was a way to get rid of it without raising suspicion. I told him to start using Randolph as his vet for a few months and then I would take care of it. Vets nowadays don't even consider Monensin overdose because they've never seen it before, and Randolph is too drunk most of the time to care. Then Dearborne had to go bragging to the Sinclairs. Their horse had fractured its knee in its last race and they were looking at a six-figure pasture ornament. Once Dearborne offered to solve their problem I had to kill their horse while Randolph was out of town, let it bloat up for a day, and fabricate a story about a dead rat in the hay."

"I hope you got paid well, for going through all the trouble."

Harkin spat, nearly hitting him. "Didn't take a goddamn cent. Never would, for that. People around here know who they can count on for a favor if they're in a tight spot."

"Is that what you're doing for Rasmussen, helping her out of a jam by taking her daughter and Lexus off her hands?"

Sam's bottom lip began to tremble. Harkin rubbed the small of her back. "Lexus demanded too much of Sammy's time, she sees that now. First time I tried to get close, that goddamn dog chased me off. Last time I made that mistake. I made her do it, but she disobeyed me and only fed a little of the dose I gave her." Harkin looked disapprovingly at Sam, who stared at the floor and shuffled her feet.

"When the horse wasn't dead in a week, I took matters back into my own hands. Of course, I had to punish the girl, but they have to learn somehow. A few days without a fix and she was willing to do anything I asked. As for Gail, she won't want to stay in that house forever. If it doesn't fall down around her ears first, sooner or later the memories will push her out. If not, well, the loss of a child has been known to drive one to suicide."

"Questions are going to be asked if Sam Rasmussen shows up after her mother kills herself."

"Have you learned *nothing*, Jordie? People don't ask questions because they don't want questions. Besides, who was Sam Rasmussen anyway? A loner. A runaway from a poor family. Who's even going to remember her in a year or two?"

"Devon was her friend, she would remember."

"Yes she would have."

"Is that why you killed her?"

"I tried warning her away. Little girls were easier to control a generation ago. If I said a secret needed to be kept or their horse could get sick and die, secrets were kept. The problem was, the girl had more faith in you than fear of me and got belligerent. Was sure you'd find out what killed her horse and when she had proof, she was going to tell everyone what I had done and what was going on with Sammy." Harkin gritted his teeth. "She threatened me."

Pascoe trembled with fury and shock. He was feeling lightheaded and the only thing keeping him conscious was the electrifying pain. The door creaked open and Maggie swept into the house, dusted in fresh snow.

"Run Maggie," Pascoe croaked. "Get help."

Maggie contemplated him for a moment before booting him squarely in the midsection. Pascoe vomited again.

"No need for that Maggie," Harkin said.

"He's ruining you."

"No darling, I'm taking care of everything, don't you worry. Go upstairs to the bedroom, there's a metal box on my nightstand. Bring it to me."

Maggie trotted upstairs and was down moments later holding the cashbox from Carlyle's trailer.

"Good girl," Harkin said, taking the box. He opened it and removed one of the black film canisters. "Pour this in his mouth."

Pascoe clamped his jaw shut. Maggie looked to Harkin for help. Harkin dug the end of the axe-handle into Pascoe's shoulder; fragmented bone crunched like gravel. When he screamed, Maggie dumped the powder into his open mouth. The bitterness forced him to swallow or drown in his own saliva. Harkin let off the pressure and supported his weight on the axe handle like a cane.

"What about her?" Maggie asked, glaring at Sam, who stood next to Harkin with as much awareness as a potted plant.

"It's under control," Harkin said.

"You don't need that little slut, you have me."

"You were the same age when you came to me, Maggie, and had your own problems. Sammy could never replace you. You can be a tutor to Sam, teach her the rules, what I like, what I don't. It's a very special honor, one I couldn't do without."

Maggie's eyes shone. "You mean it?"

"Absolutely."

Harkin shifted his weight against the axe handle and threw an arm over Maggie's shoulder. She nuzzled the nape of his neck and sighed. Quicker than Pascoe would have thought possible, Harkin swung the handle and caught the free end with the hand that had been resting on Maggie. Slipping behind her, he jerked back, crushing her neck between the span of ash and his chest. Her trachea crumpled with the sound of someone stomping on a soda can. Gasping, eyes bulging, Maggie fell to the floor beside Pascoe. After a long minute, her drumming feet and the asthmatic whistle of her breath ceased.

Harkin returned to using the axe handle for support. "Going to be hard to pin that one on David," Pascoe said.

"Feel anything yet Jordie?" Harkin asked.

He was. The weak light from the kitchen had become a beacon; Pascoe squinted to shut it out. The bicep of his useless arm developed a tic and small, involuntary twitches permeated the rest of his body. He hoped the ketamine would render him unconscious before it progressed, the thought of his broken limb flopping against the floor made his stomach curdle.

"You have an addictive personality Jordie. Will anybody be surprised to find out you had a drug problem as well as a gambling problem? Maggie confronted you as you were stealing ketamine from the clinic and you had to kill her. That should satisfy the Feds when they come asking about my missing inventory."

Pascoe laughed. Vibrant trails of green and blue followed Harkin's movements. Next to him, Sam had started to blink. The shoulder pain receded like an ebb tide. "Then what? I'm found in a stall, trampled like David? Even Ridgeway might find that suspicious."

"Probably would. But if they find your truck in a ditch with this stash in your position," Harkin tapped the cashbox, "I doubt they'll ask too many questions about how the arm broke. It will also explain how David got hold of the drugs he gave to his sister."

"You drugged her."

"Technically, no. David did. It was easy to convince him to put it in her drink, I told him it would make her sleep and we could go on a trail ride together, just us big boys." Harkin's face was a mass of swirling color with a disembodied voice emanating from the vortex. "That boy turned out to be more useful than I imagined. Before, he had too much influence over Sammy. She was starting to doubt our relationship because of his concern. She may have even loved him more than me." Harkin swung the axe handle in the air. "Had to rectify that situation.

"If Hunter hadn't come home he would have been dead two years ago. Instead I had to pretend to be saving his life, and then visit him in the hospital. I was sweating bullets when I walked into his room, but he smiled at me through his bandages like I was his best friend. In a way, I was. I visited David from time to time to see if the barriers were breaking and he would realize his pal was fucking his surrogate daughter. And you know, he was making progress. When I vetted Banker he shied away like a dog that's been kicked too many times." Harkin's chuckle buzzed in Pascoe's head.

"Why wait so long to finish the job?" The question was clear in Pascoe's head, but must have come out mushy, because Harkin looked confused.

"What? Ah, *finish*. Well, getting close to David with Hunter hovering around was impossible. All I could do was hope his neurons didn't reconnect." Harkin paced, as if he were lecturing a class. "I tried to get her out of the way. Gave David special 'vitamins' to feed to Bathsheba before an event, just enough Monensin to screw with the heart and nervous system. I reckoned there was a good chance the mare would wreck and relieve me of Hunter. After that, I could play the Samaritan and take David under my wing, just as I had with Dearborne and you. It was a long shot, but as you know, when long shots pay off, they pay off big.

"David's survival turned out to be a blessing: I had a scapegoat. All I had to do was eliminate the dogs so I could meet David without Hunter's knowledge. Left some drugged meat in the forest, then came along later and slit them up, knowing they would be found and David would be blamed. What better way to convince everyone of his guilt?"

Pascoe's pain shrank to a pinpoint beneath his collarbone. He was aware of it, but only vaguely, it existed separately from his body. His eyes zipped back and forth, painting Jackson Pollack colors in the room. His body arched in spasm until only his feet and head contacted the floor and then released, sending him crashing to the floor. The corners of his mouth pulled back in a rictus. He strained to hold on; if he lost consciousness now, it was over. He forced words from a mouth he could not make move.

"Surprised...Sam...let you...kill sister."

"What did he say?" Sam asked timidly from behind him.

"Nothing sugar," Harkin said. "Go upstairs."

"Devon. Sister. Oliver father."

Pascoe heard movement and his head stopped thrashing. Sam knelt on the floor and trapped his head between her hands. She stared into his face. "Oliver is my daddy?" Pascoe nodded as best he could.

"Stop it!" King roared, dropping the axe handle and pulling Sam away. He spun her to face him and shook her violently. "Listen to me! Remember what I told you. You don't need a father, I'll take care of you."

Sam pounded on Harkin's chest with her fists. King encircled her in a bear hug. "No!" she screeched, pushing him away.

Harkin, unprepared, stumbled and tripped over Maggie's legs, tumbling him to the floor. Harkin was close and vulnerable; vestigial instinct prodded Pascoe to act, but his muscles were in continuous contraction, and his body was stiff and unbending. Harkin scrambled on the floor, battle-scarred limbs unable to gain purchase.

"You'll pay for that girl," he growled, every syllable dripping consequence.

Arms pinned to his side by ketamine, Pascoe rolled over, and, like a seal humping along the beach, flopped across Harkin's chest and wriggled until the depression beneath his sternum lay over the old man's mouth and nose.

Harkin twisted beneath him to no avail. When struggling was unsuccessful, he tried shoving his thumb between Pascoe's ribs and tugging at his shattered shoulder. Pascoe, drifting in a ketamine sea, felt none of it. Gradually, he became aware of a pulling sensation and a vague sense of wetness at his abdomen. *My God, he's trying to chew his way out.* It was his last thought before slipping into darkness.

CHAPTER TWENTY-FOUR

Vision returned first. Didn't help much, facing the floor, Harkin's unmoving body beneath him, soft weeping near by. Before long, embers of pain glowed in his shoulder and a pocket of fire at his belly. He desperately hoped he wouldn't have to watch intestines spill from a ragged whole.

Minutes later, Pascoe felt more connected. The pain was excruciating, but the need to move greater. He drew his knees up and sat back on his heels, clutching his stomach with his good arm. He explored the wound tentatively through a shirt torn and wet with blood. Skin and muscle were ripped in several places, but the abdominal cavity was intact.

The room swam, and Pascoe almost tipped over before the vertigo subsided. Fingers on the injured arm hung almost half a foot lower than the other and rested flat and useless against the hardwood. Pain flared again in the shoulder, but subsided enough for him to consider standing.

Sam curled on the floor next to Harkin. "I'm sorry," she said again and again, stroking his body and whimpering.

Pascoe, rethinking his ability to stand, shuffled on his knees to the kitchen and dialed 911.

Monroe was the first to visit. "How's it going?" he asked, sinking heavily into a chair.

"Considering I had five hours of surgery, my arm will be strapped to my side for more than a month, I've had two blood transfusions and sixty-five stitches that itch like I crawled through poison oak? Not bad."

"At least you're not complaining."

"Here to read me my rights?"

"The sheriff would like nothing better, but he's got enough egg on his face as it is."

Pascoe scowled at the big detective.

"Okay," Monroe said. "Me too. You were right about Stuart."

"How's Sam?"

"Going to have a tough time getting off the drugs, she's been using for a couple of years. Mother took her to Burning Oaks, the rehab clinic outside DC where all the senator's wives and kids wind up. Private rooms, nurses, psychiatrists, that kind of thing. Gonna cost a fortune."

"Sam's got relatives with money."

"Yeah, I guess she does. Found your buddy Carlyle."

"Where?"

"Shacking up in barn that belongs to one of his steeplechase guys. Soon as he found out we were looking into a drug charge, he decided Carlyle was more trouble than he was worth and gave him up."

"You're charging him? You can't use the stuff I took from his place."

"True," Monroe nodded. "But I got a warrant anyway. Turns out, Carlyle isn't the best housekeeper in the world. He was cooking ketamine on cookie sheets and leaving them in the oven. We found over a gram of crystals stuck in the corners."

"Where did he get it?"

"Harkin. Started supplying Carlyle once Sam Rasmussen caught his eye. Carlyle was told to get her started with freebies, cut her off, and send her Harkin's way. Once hooked, there was only one guy she could get a fix from. Harkin repaid the favor by keeping Carlyle flush with ketamine."

A black and white blur dashed past Monroe and onto the bed. Barclay's entire body wriggled, shaking the bed and eliciting a wince from Pascoe. He hugged the dog with his free arm and tolerated the face-licking frenzy. Hunter entered, smiling broadly at the scene.

"Hey," Pascoe said, mussing the dog's head, "how did you manage to get him in here?"

"Didn't take much," Hunter said. "You've made quite an impression on the nurses." She put a hand to her face and stage-whispered to Monroe, "I think it's the sponge baths."

The detective ducked his head and coughed. "On that note, I guess I'll leave." As he stood up, he rested a giant hand on Pascoe's leg and squeezed. "Take care, Doc." He nodded a "Miss Stuart" to Hunter before leaving. She took his seat.

"How did you end up with Barclay?" Pascoe asked. "I sort of remember begging the paramedics to do something about my dog, but they thought I was hallucinating."

"The detective called me. Barclay was going crazy if anyone came close to the truck and they didn't know what else to do." The dog rolled to his back, exposing his belly for Hunter, who obliged him with a vigorous rubbing. Barclay's leg thumped uncontrollably on the bed. "Big bluffer," she said.

Pascoe grabbed her wrist. "How much did they tell you?"

"They said you were hurt, King and Maggie were dead, and they were sorting everything out. They were wrong about David. Just like that. 'Oops, sorry we wanted to send your brother to the gas chamber.' So what happened?"

Pascoe told her what he could. If it was hard for her to imagine her brother a murderer, it was no easier to replace him with Harkin. She was trying to make sense of it all when a nurse carried a huge bouquet of red and white roses into the room and set it down on a table next to the bed. "Lot's of well-wishers today," she said.

Pascoe smiled politely and reached for the card. *Sorry I couldn't come in person, but Preston is the jealous type. Told you not to wait too long. Love, Ruth.* Above the fold Wallace had stamped her pursed lips in a shade of pink he knew she wouldn't be caught dead in. Hunter attempted to peek at the card.

"Client," Pascoe explained, crumpling it into a ball.

EPILOGUE

The surgeons wouldn't allow him to leave for a week, convinced their repair would fail if he left any sooner. Would have kept him longer if Hunter hadn't promised to confine him to a bed at Timberbrook.

They had, of course, missed Harkin's funeral. It was well attended. According to the *Monitor*, there was debate as to whether Harkin was truly responsible for it all, citing his sterling reputation and insinuating Pascoe, recently connected to drug dealing, had gained a great deal from the death of the revered veterinarian.

Harkin had left him everything. Pascoe found himself in possession of a house, practice, and full bank account, but little hope of a career. Regardless of what people were or were not willing to believe, Pascoe had betrayed their trust. Dearborne sounded the note first, in a well-verbalized guest editorial, and it reverberated throughout the horse community, gathering voices as it went. Pascoe might pick up some business giving meat-horses penicillin at the auction, but was finished in Hunt Country.

For the time being it didn't matter, he could do nothing but wait and see if the resentment passed. It would be months before he could risk having his arm jerked around by an unruly yearling. Hunter indulged him with *The Daily Racing Form*, though she staunchly refused to lay any money down at the parlor. Days were spent handicapping every race he could. Nights were spent with Hunter...carefully.

"You're sure about this?" Hunter asked, arms crossed under her breasts. Barclay sat at her feet and leaned protectively against her legs.

"I can't stick around here, that's obvious enough."

When the shoulder healed, Pascoe attempted to reopen the clinic. There had been only a single call the first month: Morgan Stokes offered to take the house and practice off his hands at fire-sale prices. In the middle of the second month, with the telephones still silent, he made the deal.

"I don't care what anyone thinks," Hunter said. "Stay with me, we'll get by. Banker's won his last two events. He'll compete in four-stars by the end of next season. He's the one Jordan. He'll get me the medal."

Pascoe threw a suitcase into the bed of the truck, empty now of all of his equipment and covered with a fiberglass cap.

"What do you want me to do? Clean stalls? Be your groom?" He was shouting. He didn't want to leave this way. "I can't do that Hunter," he said, lowering his voice. "Not now anyway." He slammed the tailgate shut.

"Can't you see what your doing? You hate your father for letting his addiction ruin his dreams. Hate your mother for leaving. You're making the same mistakes, Jordan. You'll wind up hating yourself."

Being a veterinarian had been everything to him, not the reputation, not the status, but the in-the-trenches, messy work of healing, whether it be Mrs. Simmons' Kit or Dowry's precious mares. If only the realization had come sooner. The pull to leave on his terms was strong, but the pushing threat of failing on someone else's was stronger. If he was going to repeat the mistakes of his family, he was going to do it away from people he cared about.

"Look, Barclay will scam you out of a million treats and get as round as a tick if you let him."

If he didn't leave now, he never would.

Hunter observed him with that maddening, knowing look. A spark of mischievousness, missing since his intentions were announced, was back. She grabbed his face in both hands and gave him a lingering kiss. It felt more like a see-ya-around than a goodbye. They separated, and Pascoe climbed into the truck and drove off. Hunter's arm and Barclay's tail waved in synch with each other.

Outside of Knoxville, the sun touched the horizon as Pascoe merged onto I-40. With occasional catnaps at rest stops and a healthy supply of coffee, two days from now he'd hit the outskirts of Vegas.